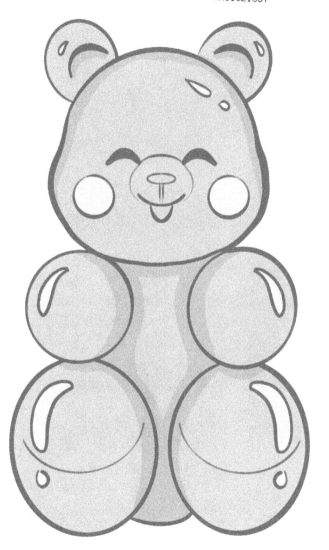

Her Favorite Jack-O-Lantern

REBECCA RENNICK

Copyright © 2023 by Rennick Rennick

ISBN: 979-8-218-21952-9

All rights reserved.

No part of this book may be reproduced or transmitted in any form or by any means, electronic or mechanical, including mechanical photocopying, recording, or by any information storage and retrieval system, without permission in writing.

This book is a work of fiction and any resemblance to persons, living or dead, or places, events or locales is purely coincidental. The characters are productions of the author's imagination and used fictionally.

Cover & Interior Art by Speckled Plum
Formatting by Rebecca Rennick

For those who were labeled the weird kid. You're not weird. Everyone else is just boring.

part of

The Gummy Bear Orgy Series

sweet but naughty rom-com's

To the citizens of Laconia, New Hampshire: Please do not take this as a reflection of your character. I'm sure you're all wonderful people. This story is fictional and not based on real people in your town.

1 – Sally

Hell, I've masterbated to that face for years

My new neighbors moved in last night. New neighbors are common here, since the house next door is a rental. I don't have the best track record with people who rent that house. The last family was religious—not that there's anything wrong with being religious. They were nice people but just didn't care for my particular . . . style. Black was not their favorite color, and it is mine. They avoided me and gave me a wide berth. Kept conversations infrequent and to a minimum. They moved when their one-year lease was up and bought a house on the other side of town.

I don't blame them. It's not their fault. They judge based on their limited, biased opinion of my outward appearance. They're not the first people to dislike my way of life or think I'm something that I'm not because I like black and creepy, weird things and have a lot of pumpkins on my porch . . . year round.

Whoever my neighbors are moved in late last night and don't appear to have much stuff, with only one small U-Haul truck parked on the street. Maybe the rest of it is being shipped in a POD container? The woman two renters ago used one. She only stayed for six months. She was a regional manager for Target and was only here to set up the new one they had just built. It's a sensitive topic in town.

Laconia, New Hampshire, is not a large town. It's, actually, rather small. With less than fifteen thousand people, it's not tiny, but it's no bustling metropolis. Several residents were against the new Target. Others were all for it. Some—like me—didn't care either way, as it was not up to any of us.

So, it's likely the remainder of my neighbor's belongings may be on the way. The small U-Haul used for the necessities.

Either way, when I woke up this morning and realized someone new was living next door, I went right to baking. Best to make a good first impression with delicious, homemade warm and gooey baked goods. I decided on pumpkin spice marshmallow-topped cookies—leaving out any nuts, in case of allergies—since it's finally October, and no one can complain about my choice in flavors now.

Just because I liked pumpkin spice and hazelnut year round doesn't mean there's something wrong with me, Mom.

While the cookies bake, I shower and dress. Since I washed my curls yesterday, they'll be good for a few more days, I only wash my body. My short black ringlets are bouncy and shiny this morning, unlike when they go all Medusa on me. I pick out the friendliest outfit I can manage, which means opaque dark-purple tights paired with a black mid-thigh flared skirt and a matching cropped purple sweater over a white button-up with the cutest Peter Pan color. And because I can't *not* wear something Halloween—it is October, after all—I pin on my jewel-encrusted tarantula brooch and slip on a pair of ruffle-cuffed black socks and my platform Mary Janes with similar spider embroidery. My makeup is simple but still dark, and I don't care what people say. I love my purple lipstick. It stays.

After placing the still-warm cookies on a pumpkin-shaped plate, I sprinkle on powdered sugar before arranging them in the most aesthetically pleasing way possible. Eight cookies laid out, perfectly displayed and stacked, waiting to be eaten. Six would be too few, and twelve is far too many, but I've found eight to be a perfect number of cookies for neighbors. It says I tried but not *too* hard. They don't need to know I baked them from scratch this morning. Most people assume they're from a box mix anyway. Only the truly interested ones ask.

Taking in a deep fortifying breath, I stand at my front door, preparing myself for the inevitable. Wide eyes, friendly but stern refusal of my cookies, and then the questions. *That's your house? Why is it black? Is that a real hearse? How many pumpkins do you have?* Hopefully, these people aren't crazy religious and think I'm a cultist Satan worshipper. Makes for an awkward morning walk to the mailbox when your neighbors are crossing themselves and "discretely" throw holy water on you. Those tenants only stayed three months.

Four years ago, my grandmother moved into an assisted living facility, and in all her amazing awesomeness, she gifted me her old Victorian house. She always supported my weirdness and appreciated my love for interior design.

She figured it would be a good first project, and she was right. I was still in school when she gifted it, but that didn't stop me from refinishing, stripping, refurbishing, updating, and redesigning the entire house. Every single room, top to bottom, got a massive face-lift, keeping the original Victorian uniqueness but with my own dark and slightly creepy twist.

It worked out great as my senior project. I got an A. Because people in design school are way cooler than girls who hit their peak at sixteen and can't seem to realize high school ended. A lot of things needed to be done to the house that weren't just cosmetic. Updating old wiring and plumbing took a long time, and remodeling a three thousand square foot Victorian is not cheap. And I had to do a lot of it by myself. Which was amazing but exhausting.

Now, however, I have my dream home and no mortgage. Much to my family's dismay. They think what I did to my house is hideous. But they don't have to live in it, so they can fuck off. This is my sanctuary, and no one can tell me what to do. But my mother never fails to bring up how I live in this big old house all by myself and how my sister, the married one with a kid, had to purchase her own home with her husband. That's just as big and spacious, mind you. Like I don't deserve this house because I'm single with no children and like creepy things.

My sister, Emily, is married to her high school sweetheart, who also happens to be the town dentist and is good at his job. He makes plenty of money, and they can afford their massive brand-new house. But that doesn't matter. What matters is that I got mine for free and didn't immediately hand it over when Emily got married. Seems like a slap in the face to my grandmother if you ask me.

Steadying myself with one more internal "You can do it!" I step outside onto my porch and nearly trip over a screaming white blur.

"Casper! What are you doing right in front of the door? You nearly made me drop the cookies for our new neighbor."

Completely ignoring my scolding, she just meows and saunters past me into the house, her grey and white tail twitching, her tiny orange bell jingling.

"Well, fine, then. Good morning to you, too. I'm going over to meet our new neighbors. Would you like to join me?"

Casper stops and sits, staring at me, before licking her paw in her way of saying no. No, I do not.

"Okay, then. Wish me luck." I give her a head scratch before righting myself and shutting my front door.

I don't bother locking it because one, I will only be a few minutes, and two, no one comes near my house, for fear of being cursed. By what, I'm not sure. Maybe because my house looks like it belongs to a witch?

Stepping out into the autumn air a cool breeze nips at my neck and legs, not enough to make me shiver but just enough to be refreshing and make you want to burrow into a cozy sweater, which I'm already wearing. I pull the cuffs of my sleeves over my hands to keep them warm under the heat of the cookie plate as I make my way down the porch and onto my front yard.

Passing a dozen pumpkins, carved and not carved, giant skeleton spiders, cats, bats, fake spider webs, and a full-scale walking pumpkin king—what can I say? I like Halloween—I sidestep a tombstone and round my house to the neighbors. It's also a Victorian, but instead of pure black, like mine, it's robin's-egg blue with a sweet creamy white trim.

It's cute and classic. The standard house for New Hampshire. There are no Halloween decorations—yet—or porch furniture or any personal items to hint at who they are.

Pulling out my phone, I check the time to make sure it's not too early for an unscheduled drop in. Nine thirty. Should be late enough to not seem like a nosey neighbor. I slip the phone back into my pocket and fortify myself for what's to come.

The wooden steps creak under my shoes as I ascend the porch. My heart is a terrified bat trapped in the cage of my ribs as I stop in front of the pretty blue door. With one last deep breath, I knock three times. Any more would seem pushy.

Silence.

Hmm, maybe they're not home. I try the doorbell in case they are upstairs.

More silence.

Maybe they work early and are already gone? Turning around, I check the driveway along the opposite side of the house. There's a pickup truck parked there, dark green and rugged-looking. Not like rust-under-the-wheel-well-dropped-a-few-bodies-in-a-lak rugged, but well-used-and-loved rugged.

The creek of cold hinges alerts me someone has, indeed, heard me. Whipping my attention back around to face the door, I am met with a large broad, *naked, male* chest. Wow, that's a lot of muscle. Wet, dripping muscles. My new

HER FAVORITE JACK-O-LANTERN

neighbor . . . is a hunk. I'd check for a wedding ring, but considering he's only wearing a towel, I doubt he'd have his jewelry on, too. Except for the long silver chain with two dog tags dangling between his lovely, sculpted pecs and all that tan, golden skin.

Shit. I should probably look at his face. Yeah, that's the neighborly thing to do. Right? Yes. Face. Eye contact. Right. okay. Here we go.

"Hi, I'm . . ."

The words die in my throat with a high-pitched squeak, as I get a good look at his face.

I know his face. I dreamed about it throughout high school. Hell, I've masturbated to that face *for years*.

Strong jaw, slightly crooked nose, plump bottom lip, dreamy blue eyes, and dirty-blonde hair that is now short and clean cut but used to be long enough to brush across his brow. My secret high school crush, Jack Campbell.

Jack. The guy who first made my lady parts tingle. The hottie who played on the football team and partied on the weekends with all the cool kids. Who could make me swoon with one look. The guy everyone loved. The all-American boy next door who everyone's mother would love their daughter to bring home for dinner.

You know that sound old computers made when they tried to connect to dial-up internet? Yeah, that's what my brain is doing right now. Frozen, trying to connect to reality. There's no way Jack Campbell, Laconia High's golden boy quarterback and homecoming king, is living next door to me. And he's naked . . . in a towel. Right in front of me.

"Hi. Is there something I can help you with?" my high school crush and new neighbor Jack asks.

"Uh... umm... I..."

Words are a foreign concept, and my brain is still static in my ears. His mouth is moving, but I can't hear anything. Not while staring at him all grown up and muscular. Eight years away in the army has been good to him.

Of course I know what he's been doing since graduating high school. I'm a stalker. I'm lame like that. I live in a small town, where the most exciting thing is the election for the new head of the PTA.

He furrows his brow, that telltale look of apprehension on his beautifully perfect face. Cobalt-blue eyes look down at me, confused, yet still kind and patient. Then those eyes shift down to the cookies and back up to my gaping face.

The mush in my head still isn't working, and when it finally sparks a thought, that thought is *Run. Turn around and leave.* And I do. I spin around to flee but barely make it to the stairs when the heat from the cooling cookie plate reminds me that I'm still holding them. In my panic, I bank a hard one-eighty, thrust the plate of cookies into his hands, and I think I mumble something about "welcome to the neighborhood," but I can't be sure.

Keeping my eyes diverted from his, and his oh-so-tantalizing body, I make my escape across the lawns and into my house. My knees shake so hard I have to lean against the back of the door to keep from falling.

That did not just happen. Did it? I must be dreaming because there's no way in hell my dream guy is living next door, playing out my all-time favorite fantasy.

2 – Jack
Me and wood do not work well together

Moving back to my hometown was not what I had planned to do, then again, I don't really plan anything these days. After eight years in the army, I am used to others telling me what to do. Making my own schedule and deciding when to eat and what I'm going to do for the day is . . . unsettling. I still have my old routine I stick to in the morning. Wake up at six, go for a five-mile run, work out, eat a full breakfast, then shower and dress. After that . . . I'm clueless. I don't know what to do with myself.

There are still boxes to unpack. My furniture hasn't been delivered yet, which is what I thought the knock on my door was this morning. I was pleasantly mistaken. Instead, in front of me stood this short, cute, curly-haired woman with an ample chest, a nipped-in waist and that flouncy little skirt of hers. Like a miniature hourglass I want to set on the shelf I don't have and stare at all day until the sand runs out. Her flustering only made her that much more adorable. With her spider brooch and pumpkin plate of cookies.

I figured opening the front door in my towel wasn't the "proper" thing to do. And I know how the people of Laconia love their propriety but figured it would be okay if it was some truck driver dropping off the furniture I ordered. With the woman's stunned reaction, I could tell she appreciated the view but wasn't sure what to do about it with her wide violet eyes and stunned silence. I probably scared the poor girl.

That idea vanished as soon as I saw which house she ran back to. There's no way I could have scared a girl who lives in an all-black house covered in dark, creepy Halloween décor. So, it was probably more appreciation for my nudity, and I don't mind that. Sexual attraction is healthy. Public nudity isn't as scandalous as the Goody Two-shoes of this town would like to believe.

I would have stood there, pondering the anxious petite cutie from next door had I not been naked and the wind nearly freezing my balls off. I tried to catch a glimpse of her through the windows. Managed a couple of flashes of her pacing and flicking her hands wildly as she passed by the open curtains flitting about her house. It looked like she was talking to someone, but I never saw another person. I did, however, see a white cat perched on the windowsill, watching her studiously as if it were following her conversation. Or was she talking *to* the cat?

I give up my watch to answer the door for the second time this morning—this time, fully clothed—which turns out to be the delivery man. Directing the men with my couch, I point to where I'd like it to be placed. Along with a kitchen table and chairs, a recliner, a few end tables, and that shelf I wish to put my hourglass neighbor on. Not nearly enough to furnish the whole house. Jusy the basics. Enough to make it functional and livable. I brought my bedroom set with me, so I, thankfully, had something to sleep on last night when I arrived.

I don't need this much space for just one man, but there was nothing else in town available to rent, and I was not going to stay with my parents or one of my sisters. Thanks to years of barracks and close quarters when deployed, having my own quiet space is a blessing. I suppose I'll have to find a purpose for the extra rooms. Maybe a home gym? An office? I have no use for an office, but it seems like what's expected. Maybe it'll come in useful once I find a job.

A job. Fucking hell. I haven't even begun to think about job hunting. What am I supposed to do in this town? Become a bus boy at the local diner? A janitor at my old high school? A cashier at the corner market? None of those sound appealing. There's always Autumn, my sister. I could ask to work in her flower shop until I figure my life out. I'm already getting a headache thinking about it.

The delivery men finish setting everything up as Dax, my oldest friend, walks through the open front door.

"Jack. Looks like you're settling in all right. Nice couch." Dax circles the living room, inspecting the couch and recliner. Plopping down on the plush gray cushions, he hums in approval. "Comfy."

"Glad you approve. I just picked it out from the online catalog. Looked nice enough."

After closing the front door and thanking the men, I

join him on the couch, and he's right. It is comfy. I didn't pay much attention to all the specifics. It was a good price, fit the space, came with delivery and setup, so I chose a calming, neutral color and bought it. Same with the rest of the furniture. Simple, wooden, four-legged dining table for six with matching gray upholstered chairs. None of the furniture has much personality. Just functionality. That's what I know. Functionality. Lack of clutter or unnecessary items. What is necessary is a large TV so I can watch the games in peace.

"So, what's your plan now that you're home?"

"I have no fucking idea."

Dax scrubs his stubbled jaw, scratching it with a thoughtful expression. He's a good-looking guy—maybe a little rough around the edges, but that's why I like him. Unlike me, he didn't leave right after high school. He wasn't running away. He stayed, learned a trade, and got a job working at Wood Works, a locally owned company that specializes in anything and everything made of wood. Handcrafted beautiful pieces that last a lifetime or longer. Chairs, tables, wardrobes, bed frames, cabinets, desks. Clean, simple functional pieces and others that make a statement.

His disapproving, inquisitive eye dissects my new furniture. It's nowhere near the caliber of his work. I don't blame him. But if I'm going to invest in a thousand-dollar dining set, it better be worth it. To be something in my style that I'll appreciate for years. Right now? It's not worth it. I don't have a style.

"Maybe you could come work at the shop with me? I could teach you a few things. We're always in need of a good sander," he says thoughtfully.

HER FAVORITE JACK-O-LANTERN

Thinking maybe if I work there, I'll get rid of my basic furniture, which sounds great, but he forgot one tiny important fact.

"Do you remember wood shop class in high school? When we made bird houses and jewelry boxes?" Leaning forward, I rest my elbows on my knees and raise a brow at him.

Furrowing his brow, he visibly searches his memory for that day in class. The moment he remembers, his eyebrows shoot up, and a knowing smirk appears on his lips.

"Oh, yeah. I remember now. You decided to make a jewelry box for your sister, and none of the angles matched up. The lid wouldn't even shut more than halfway. And if I recall correctly, you even had a smear of blood on the bottom?"

"That would be correct. I nicked myself while *sanding* the wood. Scraped my hand like a rug burn. Left a streak across the surface."

I would have sanded it off or made a new piece had I not been so irritated by my inability to do something so simple.

Dax laughs at the memory, no doubt picturing my pissed-the-fuck-off face when I threw the damn thing across the room and shattered it against a brick wall.

"Oh, right. Why were you so bad at wood shop again?"

"I don't know. But me and wood do not work well together."

"That's unfortunate for the ladies. Don't tell anyone in town, or you'll never have sex again."

We both know I have no problem pleasing the ladies. I had plenty of female "friends" in high school who were more than happy to kiss and tell. These days, though, I prefer to keep my sexual conquests to myself. I'm not a horny teen anymore, and I have more respect for the women I sleep with.

"Okay, fine. Maybe not Wood Works. We'll find something else for you. Don't worry."

Speaking of ladies... Dax might know something about my intriguing new neighbor. I feel like I should know who she is. Something about her is familiar, but I can't put my finger on it. And it's going to bug me until I figure it out.

"Hey, Dax, what's the story with my neighbor?"

"Which one?"

"The cute one with short black curly hair and violet eyes. She lives in that black house."

I try to keep the interest out of my tone. The last thing I need is for him to gossip with his wife about my interest in a woman on my first day back.

"You mean Silly Sally? The Halloween freak?" He guffaws and lets out a barking laugh.

The immature name bristles at my nerves and seems rather cruel for a woman who was nice enough to bring me welcome-to-the-neighborhood cookies, which were fucking delicious, by the way. I ate four already.

"You know this town hosts a huge pumpkin festival every year."

"Yeah, in October. Not year round. Half of those decorations at her house. They don't come down. She leaves them up *all year*." He says rolling his eyes.

"Even at Christmas?"

I can just picture it now, Santa hats on the skeletons and twinkle lights twisted around pumpkins. Actually, sounds kinda fun.

"Yup."

"I guess, to each their own."

"Sally's a nice girl and all, but the whole creepy Halloween obsession is a bit much."

Dax doesn't seem to have animosity toward the girl herself but rather her taste in décor.

"So . . . Sally?"

"Yeah. Smithson. She was two years behind us in school. Started that Halloween Appreciation Club. Wore a lot of black." He twirls his hand around as he so eloquently explains.

"Oh, yeah, I remember her. Her hair was longer then, frizzier."

And she didn't have the nice rack back then, either. She filled out in the past eight years. No longer that scrawny little teenager I vaguely remember.

"Yeah, she's basically been the town's weirdo ever since high school," he continues, lost in his own thoughts and recollection, as if I've not said a word, like I didn't go to the same high school and know the same people.

"Well, she's cute and nice. Brought me cookies this morning. Not very talkative, though," I say, not entirely convinced he's listening.

"Oh, yeah. She brings cookies to all the new tenants, or so I hear. To try and soften them up to having her as a neighbor and break it to them gently that the hearse parked in front of her house isn't a prop."

"Wait. She actually drives that?"

I thought she was just invested in the décor. I turn in my seat on the couch, as if I can see through the wall to her driveway next door, to check if the hearse is there.

"Nope. That is a functioning hearse that she drives all over town. Creepy as fuck if you ask me."

I keep my mouth shut and nod, turning back to face him. Don't argue. Don't stir the pot. Follow orders and keep quiet. That's what the army taught me. So that's what I do.

I haven't lived here in eight years, and I have no idea what things are like anymore. I know who these people are, but I don't *know* them anymore. This could just be his opinion, not the opinion of the whole town.

Dax stands and does another lap around my practically empty rental house. "So, is this it? Do you have any boxes you need unpacked or something? I'm here to help."

For the next two hours, we unpack the two dozen boxes containing all my worldly possessions. Minimal kitchen utensils, small appliances, a few plates, and cups. Bathroom towels, sheets, blankets, rugs, and toiletries. My workout equipment and clothing are last.

Breaking down the boxes, we fold them into the recycling bin and then stand on my lawn, observing the houses on the street.

The houses are large with spacious yards. A few houses have low fences but most have none at all, each lawn impeccably maintained with precisely cut grass and symmetrical piles of leaves. Driveways are clean, and gutters are clear. Really, it's the all-American dream town. The images you see on postcards and posters.

An uneasy feeling of being out of place sinks in my gut.

"Come on. I'll take you to lunch. Reintroduce you to the town. It's the least I can do while we brainstorm jobs for you." Dax pats me on the shoulder and steers me toward his truck.

Maybe going into town and reacquainting myself with Ma's milkshakes can make me focus on starting my life up again, rather than wondering what my neighbor Sally is doing and when I might see her again.

"Sure. Sounds great."

3 – Sally

Fuck carb counting, I love carbs

"Shut up! Shut up! No, he is not."

"Yes, he is."

"Jack 'The Hunka-Hunka Dreamboat' Campbell is your new neighbor?"

Peyton, my best friend since elementary school, sits across from me, her jaw practically hitting the floor. While Chloe, my other best friend since grade school, is silent on speaker phone.

As soon as I calmed my raging anxiety this morning—and stopped pacing and talking to my cats—I group texted Peyton and Chloe.

<u>Me:</u> *You guys are never going to believe who just moved in next door.*

HER FAVORITE JACK-O-LANTERN

Peyton: Into the rental house?
Chloe: Of course the rental house.
Peyton: You never know maybe the other neighbors moved out.
Chloe: Highly unlikely, they've lived there since the dawn of time.
Me: LADIES focus please. Mr. & Mrs. Klientstien haven't moved. Someone moved into the rental, and I'm freaking out.
Chloe: Why?
Peyton: Was it a priest? I can see how that can be problematic.
Me: No, it's not a priest.
Chloe: Nudists? Is it nudists?
Me: No why would nudists move to New Hampshire in October?
Chloe: They're from Alaska?
Me: Again focus ladies, we have a defcon 1 situation here.
Peyton: Yeah Chloe focus, stop rambling.
Chloe: okay fine we're focused. Who is this person who moved in that warrants defcon 1 status?
Me: It's too much to put in text. Can we meet?
Chloe: I work till 4, we're short staffed today.

Chloe is a vet tech and works at the local animal shelter. I would never interfere with her work. She has single-handedly made sure dozens of strays have gotten adopted.

Peyton: I have a few clients this morning, but I can meet for lunch.
Me: okay. How about Ma's? I need deep fried everything.
Peyton: I'll be there. Say 11:30?
Me: Sounds good.
Chloe: What about me? I wanna know who's got you all worked

up.
__Me:__ *Can you take a break and call us when we're at Ma's?*
__Chloe:__ *Yes. Don't you dare talk about it before I call.*
__Me:__ *Oh now you're interested.*
__Chloe:__ *I was always interested. I just didn't know it was so major.*
__Me:__ *Oh it's major.*

Now here we sit. Peyton is staring dumbfounded, while Chloe is trying to form a coherent response. I need someone to coach me through this. I don't know how I'll survive living only two walls away from my fantasy man. I've already proven I'm incapable of speaking to him and that my crush on him is as raging now as it was in high school. This is going to be impossible.

Stuffing my face with Ma's famous milkshakes and onion rings is helping. Fuck carb counting, I love carbs. In every form of potato, pasta, and bread.

My insensitive uncle always said I should be the size of a blimp with how much I eat. No matter his crass words I still eat what I like, the majority of my weight settling in my boobs and ass. Which my mother reminds me on every possible occasion to cover up. Because "good girls don't show cleavage or ass crack."

Peeling apart my third giant beer-battered onion ring, I remove the inner strip of gooey onion, add it to the pile on the side of my plate, dip the golden fried breading in a hearty helping of ranch, then shove it into my mouth with a small whimper. I'm going to stress eat, I just know it.

"What am I going to do?"

"Well, first, we're going to make sure your vibrator is fully charged because you're going to need it. Then we're going to install infrared cameras outside your house to record him walking by the window, naked and dripping wet, just out of the shower." Peyton bites her lip and smiles.

"Seconded. Just don't tell Sam," Chloe adds in a conspiratory whisper.

Oh boy, they're going to lose it when I tell them the next part.

"I kinda sorta already saw him naked and wet fresh out of the shower."

"Wait, what?"

Peyton's voice is so high I'm pretty sure the dogs at the animal shelter three blocks away heard her. Her gorgeous hazel eyes twinkle with mirth and perv-girl lust.

Peyton is a hottie, a pervy hottie. Silky, straight red hair that barely brushes her shoulders and perfectly pouty lips. All long legs and toned abs, thanks to her love of yoga, which she teaches at the local gym. Guys and girls all love her, and she loves them. She's all free love and open sexuality.

Wish I could be as confident as her. Instead, I live vicariously through her and her dating life, which is full and fun. Mine is nonexistent.

The last guy I dated dumped me two months before our wedding. That's right. I'm that girl. The one too blind to see her fiancé didn't love her for her but for what he thought he could make her.

Since then, I've had this stigma on me, and I've embraced it. I am the town weirdo, and I'll probably live alone with my cats until I die of old age in my creepy black house. And now that will include pining over my hottie neighbor, who will more than likely have an active sex life. I mean, there's no way the single women of Laconia won't be all over him when the gossip mill spreads the good news of his return.

Peyton is practically foaming at the mouth for details. I don't blame her. I would do the same.

"You sure move fast. It took me a month to get Sam naked and dripping wet in front of me. How did you manage that in less than twenty-four hours?"

It's nice of Chloe to think I had anything to do with getting him into his naked wet state, but we know I didn't.

"When I went over to bring him my customary welcome-to-the-neighborhood cookies, he answered the door in a towel, still dripping wet."

The words come out breathy and wanting.

"Holy shit. I wish I'd been there to see it."

"I took a picture."

"Of him naked?"

"No, perv—I took it through the window while he was directing the delivery men who dropped off his furniture."

"Good call." Peyton grabs my phone and opens the photo app without hesitation.

There aren't very many boundaries between us. We are all comfortable airing our dirty laundry to each other. Any photos she might stumble upon on my phone isn't anything she hasn't seen before.

Shoving one more clump of ranch-drenched breading in my mouth, I wait for her to find the most recent photo. I zoomed in as far as possible without losing picture quality on Jack standing on his porch directing the deliverers. He still looks perfect in his stretched tight T-shirt over his broad shoulders and loose-fit jeans that do nothing to hide the strong legs beneath. If I thought the man was sexy before, high-school Jack has nothing on Army-soldier Jack. He's all concealed power and barely restrained strength.

Peyton pinches and zooms in even closer, her face inches from the screen as she devours his image.

"Wow. He sure did grow up well, didn't he? I've had my hands all over the people of this town, and I cannot wait for the day he goes searching for a massage therapist to work out the kinks in those muscles. I'll give him a rub down he'll never forget."

"Hey."

"Only if we haven't convinced him to fall madly in love with you first, of course." She unglues her lusty gaze from my phone.

"Send me the pic. I want to see," Chloe pouts from the speaker.

"Don't even think about it," I scold, grabbing the phone from Peyton before she can do just that.

The last thing I need is for that photo to get passed around and someone to discover I was taking pictures out my window like a creeper.

I'm totally cool with them ogling him, as long as there's no evidence. They know my deep-seated crush is not only on his physique but the person inside it.

Peyton has no problem getting whomever she wants, and Chloe has the best fiancé in the world, but Jack has always been off limits. I called dibs freshman year of high school, and as any loyal friend would, they abided by the rules of dibs. Look but do not touch. Sadly, I also have not touched. At least not in person, but in my dreams, we've touched *a lot*.

I groan again at the thought, dropping my forehead to the table with a thunk that rattles the silverware. This is going to be so hard.

"There, there, my poor sex-deprived best friend," my unsympathetic best friend mocks as she pats my head. "Maybe him living next door will be a good thing. He'll get to know you and see how amazing you are and want to bang you on every day ending in Y."

Highly unlikely, but I like her optimism. I bang my head a few more times on the table for good measure. Maybe I can knock some sense into my thick skull. It doesn't work, and I return to eating my comfort onion rings, still thinking about what sex would be like with Jack. Naked, sweaty, hard muscles flexing, him thrusting against me, inside me.

"What is that noise? Is everything okay over there?" Chloe asks.

"Yeah, Sally's just having a meltdown."

"Oh, so just a normal Monday."

"Basically."

My two best friends talk about me as if I can't hear them, and I don't really. I'm too busy having my meltdown, which feels like it's literally happening inside me. *Is it hot in here?* I'm really hot. I fan myself with my hand, but that does nothing. I'm still melting from the inside out.

"Does Ma have the heater turned to max or something? I'm roasting."

"I'm fine. Doesn't feel hot to me."

"That's because you're barely wearing any clothes." I gesture to her cropped sports top that's barely more than a sports bra, matching leggings, and a lightweight zip-up hoodie exposing her drool-worthy body. Damn her and her love of regular exercise.

Peyton shrugs, unaffected. I, on the other hand, am still sweating bullets. Pulling at the collar of my sweater, I'm still not getting enough air. This sweater has to go. Pulling at the hem, I strip it off over my head, ungraceful as always. It catches on my spider brooch, which I didn't realize I had pinned through the sweater *and* shirt. I'm stuck with my arms halfway over my head, panicking and flailing, sweater wrapped around my face.

"A little help, please."

"Got it." Peyton snakes her dexterous fingers through the mess of sweater and shirt and remove the brooch, pulling it out like Houdini escaping a straitjacket.

Meanwhile, I clumsily remove the purple monster trying to eat my face. I love this sweater, but right now, I hate it.

Flopping it down on the sparkly vinyl bench next to me, I let out an un-lady-like groan of relief.

"Better?"

One precisely arched brow twitches as Peyton surveys my muddled state.

"Better."

"Here's your spider." She hands me back my brooch, and I reattach it.

"Thanks." Instead of dropping my head back on the table—because I'm pretty sure there are crumbs and salt stuck to my forehead now—I lean back and drop it against the back of the booth. "What am I really going to do, guys?"

They're both quiet before Peyton answers in a sincere tone. "Why don't we go get your favorite pumpkin spice cake and latte from The Roasted Bean next door and go back to your house to figure it out, while secretly spying on your hot neighbor?"

Her tone remains calm and level, probably trying not to spook me into another freak out.

"Good idea, Peyton. I'll catch up with you two later. I want to see that picture and hear all about it, okay?"

"Yeah, okay. That sounds good. We'll see you later, Chloe."

HER FAVORITE JACK-O-LANTERN

I finally have my pumpkin spice latte and cake in hand, and my anxiety has subsided, and maybe things will be okay. Maybe I will be able to live next door to Jack and not be a complete and total wreck.

"I'm going to use the bathroom real fast. I'll meet you outside."

"Okay. No problem."

Peyton makes her way toward the back, while I head to the front door, latte in one hand and cake in the other, purse on my shoulder and sweater draped on my arm.

Reaching the door, I realize my hands are full and spin to press my back against the bar to open it just as someone on the outside pulls it open. I stumble backward, now having leaned my weight onto nothing, and my precious pumpkin latte splashes out of the lid and lands right on my white shirt. *Motherfucker.* I nearly fall on the sidewalk. Luckily, someone with better reflexes than me reaches out a steadying hand and catches my elbows before I land on my ass.

"Satan's balls. This is why I don't wear white."

Mumbling to myself, I try to wipe away the spilled liquid but am unsuccessful, as my hands are full and flicking at it with my fingertips is doing absolutely nothing. I'll just have to clean it as soon as I get home so it doesn't stain.

"Are you okay?" asks a deep, sturdy voice that tickles my nerves all the way to my toes.

Looking up into the eyes of my savior, I come face-to-face once again—with Jack.

This time, his eyes and lips are smiling, looking down at me with humor and warmth, crystal-blue specs of sea glass sparkling at me in the autumn afternoon. No man should have eyes so beautiful. It's just not fair to the rest of us on the receiving end.

"Yeah . . . fine . . . hot," I stumble so eloquently, pointing to the brown spot on my shirt.

"Oh, crap. Was that my fault? I'm so sorry. I should have warned you I was opening the door. I thought you saw me."

You'd think I would have, too. I need to start paying closer attention to my surroundings, especially if running into Jack is going to be a common occurrence.

"It's Sally, right? We weren't properly introduced this morning. I'm Jack."

Oh my god. He knows my name.

"I know." I blurt out, nearly barking it at him. Clearing my throat, I try again at a more acceptable level. "I mean, I know. We went to high school together."

"Right. We did." He smiles again. Big and broad, and I'm gawking like a looney tune. Warm fingers linger on my arms as I realize he's still holding me.

If he lets go, will I fall? It's a high probability.

"I'm sorry if I was inappropriate this morning. I thought you were the furniture delivery guy, and I didn't want to miss him."

He doesn't look at all sorry for being inappropriate. Jack was the epitome of inappropriate in high school. I doubt answering the door in a towel even makes the top ten on his list of inappropriate.

"It's no problem at all. You can be inappropriate whenever you like."

What the actual fuck just came out of my mouth? My brain has short-circuited again and disconnected from reality.

Jack chuckles and keeps grinning at me, his eyes angling down to my lips, lingering there in a way that tangles my insides. He's not in the least bit perturbed by my blunder. He does, unfortunately, remove his hands from my arms, and the breeze chills the spot where the warmth had just been. I stutter, trying to compose myself, when a group of people exit the coffee shop, pushing me out the door and onto the chilly sidewalk. It's much colder now that I'm not wearing my sweater, even with the hot latte on my chest. Which I barely notice, with all my attention intently focused on Jack now.

"So, I guess we're neighbors."

His attempt at a segue is awkward and cute. Wait, does this mean he's trying to converse with me? *Okay, don't panic, breathe. You can do this!*

"Uh, yeah. I guess we are." Smooth, Sally, real smooth. An awkward pause lingers as neither of us seem to know what to say until I bark out, "Did you like the cookies?"

His smirk is far too sexy for the middle of a workday on the sidewalk outside The Roasted Bean.

"Yeah, they were great. I, uh . . . already ate four of them," he admits sheepishly, a slight pink tinting his cheeks.

"Well, it doesn't look like you ate any of them."

Chuckling, I think I'm pretty funny, waving at his impressive, flat, muscular stomach. He does, too, if his twitching lips are any indication. This time, he contains his smile, though. But I see the mirth in his eyes.

He thinks I'm funny.

"Hey, Jack, thought we were going to Ma's? Oh, hi, Sally." Dax, Jack's best friend from high school, walks up behind him and smiles politely.

Shouldn't be a surprise they're together. From what I heard, they kept in touch through the years. Dax is a nice enough guy, I guess. We don't hang in the same circle, but we know each other's . . . family.

"Hi, Dax. You guys hanging out today?"

"Yeah, just showing him around town, reintroducing him to the old haunts." He slaps Jack on the shoulder and grins like he has plans.

Plans that don't involve me. Got it.

"Cool, well, you guys have fun with that."

Before I can die of mortification, the sweet, saving voice of Peyton cuts through the tension.

"Sally!" Finally emerging after an eternity from the coffee shop, she jogs to meet me and the two men openly staring at her. "Oh, hey, boys. Jack. Heard you were back in town. Nice to see you again."

Jack watches her carefully, likely trying to figure out who the hell she is. It was surprising he knew my name. It would be less surprising for him to remember hers. She was far more popular in school than I was.

"It's good to be seen." He squints and cocks his head. "Peyton. Right? You were on the dance team, performed at the football games."

"Yeah. They were mandatory," Peyton comments offhandedly, not even blinking or shifting tone as she does. In a move of best friend support, she circles the men and links arms with me, facing off like we're preparing for the most intense game of red rover on the playground.

"I heard you and Sally had a little run-in this morning. Something about a towel and—"

I elbow Peyton in the ribs before she can start talking about any part of Jack.

Knowing her, she'd go straight for the dick pic, just like a serial Tinder dater. I was far too shocked this morning to even consider looking down to check out that particular piece of his anatomy.

"Yeah. She brought me cookies, and I was extremely rude answering the door in a towel."

"Oh, I doubt she thought it was rude." Peyton pinches her lips between her teeth desperately trying to hold in her laughter.

"Well, I'm glad I didn't offend her delicate sensibilities. I don't know if I could live with myself if I had offended my new neighbor on the first day."

Jack is joking with her, being friendly and relaxed as if they were longtime friends.

Peyton retorts with something I'm sure is witty and

smart and slightly inappropriate, but I don't hear it. I'm too busy trying to control my breathing to keep from passing out. If this is how it'll be at every interaction with Jack, I won't make it a week.

Dax interrupts Jack and Peyton's friendly tête-à-tête. "Well, we should really get going, Jack."

"And where are you two headed off to? Making mischief already?"

I don't know how Peyton intrudes on people's personal business without sounding rude and nosy. Yet, she always gets her answers.

"Just lunch at Ma's. We've been unpacking all morning and worked up an appetite. Does she still make the best milkshakes in town?" Jack looks at me.

Why is he looking at me? Is he asking me?

Peyton's not-so-subtle elbow to my side tells me that yes, yes, he is asking me. And I should answer.

"Yes. She does. My favorite is the bubblegum-marshmallow. Sometimes, she even puts gummy bears in it if she has any."

Dax wrinkles his nose, but Jack smirks at me with one corner of his mouth. "Mine is mint-vanilla. Most people like mint-chocolate, but I prefer vanilla." He winks at me like we share an inside joke, and I about swoon right here on the sidewalk.

Should I wink back?

No. Definitely not.

With my luck, I'd look like I'm having a stroke, he'd call

nine-one-one—because he's a gentleman—then I'd have to explain to the EMT that I was trying to wink and *not* having a stroke, thus forever fermenting me in the hall of shame and embarrassment. I'd never be able to leave my house again. I don't know how I'll continue my interior design business. I guess there's always Facetime.

"Although I haven't ever had gummy bears in my milkshake, I'll have to try it sometime. How do you get them through the straw? Seems like they'd get stuck."

He's talking to me again, like I should talk back to him. I should probably say something, but nothing comes out. I'm frozen in my disbelief, and after a moment silence from me, Jack's features settle into a nondescript look.

"Okay, well . . . I guess I'll see you at home later." He turns to leave, then turns back to me. "Because I live next door. I won't be hiding in your house. Promise." He holds up his hand in a boy scout pledge with a sheepish grin on his face.

Bummer. I would be totally cool with him breaking into my house, stripping naked, and waiting for me in a steaming bubble bath surrounded by candles. I have the perfect bathtub for it now that I've remodeled my master bathroom.

"Right. Good one." I finger-gun point at him like a massive weirdo, especially since I'm still holding my coffee cup and cake.

If I could, I would whack myself in the head, but that would only result in me wearing all of my latte instead of only a small splash of it.

Daring not to move, Peyton and I stand, unabashedly staring as Jack and Dax walk next door to Ma's, until they open the door and enter, finally relieving me of the heart palpitations that always appear when Jack looks at me.

A whoosh of breath vacates my lungs once he's out of sight, and I slump into Peyton. "Can we please go home and wash this latte out of my shirt before it stains? And maybe google how not to shit your pants in front of a hot guy you like?"

"Sure thing, hun. Come on, I'll get you all cleaned up and train you how to speak on command, like a dog. That way, you don't freeze up in front of Jack again. I'm not going to be there to rescue you every time, you know."

"Yeah, I know."

4 – Sally
What's wrong with my aura?

We make it back to my place, where I change into a new black long-sleeved shirt and remove the drying coffee stain from my white shirt. I am a master stain remover, after all—I have to be, with my ability to attract any and all sauces, liquids, and foods whenever I wear white. Which is why I've discovered how to remove red wine, tomato sauce, bacon grease—and even blood—out of my clothing. Which is why my favorite color is black.

The best thing I've found to remove stains? Foaming hand soap. I have no idea why it works so well, but it does. Just because I know how to remove stains doesn't mean I enjoy having to do it or having to worry about spilling on myself because I'm wearing white. I don't know how people wear white pants. I would be too afraid to sit down. Because

I know the moment I did, I would have a stain on my ass that would make me look like I shit myself.

So, I usually stay away from white, especially if food is involved. Today was a fluke. I hadn't intended to remove my sweater, since the weather is getting colder, but I also hadn't intended on running into my high school crush and getting hot flashes.

"It's simple, really. Just open your mouth and speak. You do it to me all the time. God knows you do it to your mother. Just focus that energy at Jack."

Peyton and I have made ourselves comfortable on my couch, which is soft and plush and a beautiful burnt orange to complement the emerald-green walls.

I wanted this room to be rich and cozy. Warm and inviting but still elegant, with rich, deep jewel tones, dark accents, and gold hardware. The theme is a mixture of Studio Ghibli and gothic ghost, with dark florals and gothic interpretations of Ghibli characters: a zombie Catbus, a Kohaku ghost dragon, and plenty of No-Face.

Everyone thinks it's all about Halloween to me, but that's only because it's the only holiday that embodies my personality. I like other things that aren't specifically Halloween, like cozy sweaters on cold nights and Egyptian mythology. People just don't care to get to know me well enough to learn that.

"You want me to talk to Jack like he's my mother?"

Peyton chuckles.

I don't think being sarcastic and snarky to Jack will win

me any points. Me and my mother tolerate one another. We just don't see eye to eye on . . . well, a lot of things. She has good intentions. I think. Everything just comes off like criticism and disapproval.

"No, maybe not like he is your mom, but the confidence you have when you talk to her. You're not afraid to speak your mind to her, so don't be afraid to speak to Jack."

The "confidence" Peyton's referring to isn't confidence. It's avoidance and learned self-preservation. The reason conversations with my mother no longer turn into full-blown arguments is because I learned when I was a teenager that it doesn't matter. It doesn't matter what I say; she will always believe she is right and I'm wrong. That I can't make good decisions for myself and that my life is in ruins until I "stop playing around and become an adult."

I am an adult, dammit. That's why I get to choose how to dress, what color to paint the walls of *my* house, what kind of car I want to drive, and what type of career I have. Those are my choices, and I have to live with them and any consequences from them.

But since she will always disapprove and consider me an immature failure, I just tune her out, nod and let her talk to herself. As long as I don't engage, she eventually runs out of steam and moves on. Then I do whatever the hell I please. Sometimes, I just can't stand it and blurt out something sassy, which rarely helps.

"Ooh"—Peyton bounces in her seat next to me, eyes lighting up—"you need to do those mediation stretches I showed you. They'll calm and center you. Help you center your chi."

I've tried her mediation yoga pose thingies before, and although I felt nice and limber and tired after, it didn't do much for my inner peace.

"I don't think they work for me." Pulling my legs up under me on the couch, I sink farther into the cushions, allowing the warm, squishy comfort to calm me.

"Nonsense. You just have to open yourself to the possibilities. Allow it in. Trust me, your aura will thank me."

"What's wrong with my aura?"

Peyton claims she can see people's auras, and I'm not sure I believe in that kind of thing, but I'm not taking any chances.

"It's all chaotic," she says, waving around my head as if something were physically pulsing off me. "Staticky, like a live wire. You desperately need some calm." Quirking one side of her lips, she looks at me from under her eyelashes. "You know what's really good for calming one's aura?"

"Let me guess. Sex?"

"Sex."

"And who, pray tell, am I supposed to have sex with?" I ask haughtily.

I know who I want to have sex with, but the likelihood of that happening is about as much as me flying to the moon on a cloud of farts.

"I can think of at least one man for the job." She winks.

"Yeah, let me get right on that. I'll just go next door with another plate of cookies. Only, this time, I'll be the one in the towel. He won't be able to resist me," I say sarcastically.

If only I had the courage to do such a thing.

"Well, it's a little dramatic for my taste, but it'll get the job done."

I roll my eyes at my best friend because it's totally something she would do. Before I'm able to tell her as much, my phone rings on the coffee table. The Halloween movie theme song blares. I pick it up and see Mr. Hanson's name on the screen. Holding up a finger to Peyton, I swipe to answer.

"Hello. Sally speaking," I say as chipper as possible.

I've known Mr. Hanson since I was a kid, but since I know this is most likely not a social call, I figure I'll be somewhat professional.

"Oh, hello, Sally. Mr. Hanson here from Hanson Hardware. Just wanted to call and confirm that you'll be here later this week."

The Hanson family has owned Hanson Hardware for three generations. Mr. William Hanson, or Bill, is in his early fifties and is a super sweet man, friendly and accepting of me without judgment. He just thinks I'm quirky, which is a large step up from freak.

"Yes, Mr. Hanson. I'll be there on Thursday." I assure him.

"Good. And you're bringing one of those skeleton head pumpkins you grow for the display window, right?" he asks, as if I could forget. He's been asking since last year, when I discovered the technique to make them.

"Absolutely, Mr. Hanson. I saved the best one just for you."

"Wonderful. And it will be the same charge as last year?"

I had thought about charging him more since I only charge him two hundred dollars, but I just can't bring myself to take more money from him. They're a well-standing business and family in town and, from what I can tell, are doing just fine. They're such nice people, always giving back to the community. It's the least I can do to decorate his windows and front register counters for the holidays without raising my fee every year.

It's a little something I do on the side to make more income. My interior design business is growing—slowly. I've done jobs here in town and in neighboring cities but nothing to push me into the realm of a known designer people refer to their friends. It can't always sustain me in the slower months, when there aren't as many jobs. Luckily, since I don't have a mortgage or car payment, my bills are manageable.

Some, like Mr. Hanson, only hire me for the larger holidays, like Halloween and Christmas, when I put up more intricate displays and decorations that'll be up for multiple weeks. Others have me do the major holidays and smaller ones, like Easter and Fourth of July.

The Fourth of July is a rather large holiday celebration in this town. The people may not decorate or celebrate it for multiple weeks, but let me tell you, from July first to the

HER FAVORITE JACK-O-LANTERN

fifth, it is all red, white, and blue and fireworks.

"Yes, Mr. Hanson, same as last year."

"Alrighty, then. We'll see you Thursday."

"See you Thursday."

Hanging up, I place the phone on the cushion next to me and drop the fake smile I donned to force joviality in my tone.

"So, I guess you'll be pretty busy this week, huh?"

"Yeah. You know this is my favorite holiday to decorate."

Thinking about decorating display windows and store fronts on Main Street has me smiling for real now. I love this holiday and all its creepy crawlies. The best part are the jack-o-lanterns. Those are my favorite and my specialty. No one in town can carve a pumpkin like I can.

"I know." Checking the time on her phone, Peyton sighs wistfully. "Well, I have two more appointments this afternoon, so I gotta get going. I'll talk to you later." Standing, she grabs her purse and sweater and heads for the door. "Oh, and if you see your neighbor in a towel again, make sure to get him completely naked next time. Okay?" she says with a wink.

"I'll make sure to do that."

"And then you call me after. I want all the juicy details."

"You got it, boss."

With a quick hug goodbye, Peyton skips out the door to her car. Before she drives away, she calls out her window one last time, "And don't forget the meditation poses. They're best to do after a nice hot bath and in as few clothes as possible. Clothing restricts your movement and smothers your aura."

With one last wave as she drives away, I stand on my porch watching her leave, shaking my head and trying not to laugh, then subtly look at Jack's house. His truck isn't in his driveway, so he must still be out with Dax "revisiting old haunts"—whatever the hell that means.

At least I can do some work without wondering what he's doing next door.

5 – Jack
Apparently, I like to watch

I've been sitting across from Dax in Ma's Diner, enjoying her homemade deep-fried everything and gulping down my mint-vanilla shake, while trying to brainstorm job ideas for almost an hour. So far, we've come up with: waiter, professional male prostitute, cashier at the new Target, and town mayor. Needless to say, I don't plan on applying for any of these positions.

Dax so helpfully suggests the wanted section of the local newspaper. It's not a completely shit idea, and I make a mental note to pick one up on my way home. I don't need a job right away. I have plenty of money saved up. While I was in the army, I didn't have many expenses. The military paid for my barracks on base. I bought a used truck, and I didn't need to buy much beyond food and some basic necessities.

Without a family to take care of or any real bills to speak of, I was able to squirrel away most of my money into savings. Now that I'm out, I suppose I can look into buying a house. But I'm not sure I want to live here permanently. I hadn't even intended on leaving the army, but when my reenlistment came up, my sisters convinced me not to.

The army wasn't my dream—hell, it wasn't even on my list of possibilities. After high school, I was supposed to go to college, get a degree in something and then make a career out of it, whatever that may have been.

Plans changed after the accident. After Jordan died. The army was his dream, not mine. But after what happened, knowing it was all my fault, the least I could do was live my life for something more. For him. Fulfill his dream, since I didn't have one.

And I did. I enlisted right out of high school and haven't been back since, not even during leave. Family would come to me, or we would meet somewhere on a family vacation. It was too hard to see all the places and people who reminded me of high school and my epic fuck-up. I'm only now able to return because of the incessant badgering of my family. I couldn't stay gone forever.

I've lived in Germany, South Korea, England, and Japan while deployed for the army, and they were all amazing places to live and learn, but none of it was really for me. I learned a lot, grew as a person, but I'm still as clueless about my future now as I was when I was eighteen.

There's always the option to return to college, using the funds from the government's GI bill. But what would I study? Where would I attend? It's a whole new set of questions and unknowns similar to the situation I'm currently in. Until I know what job I want to have for the rest of my life, there's no point in registering in school. I'm not looking forward to being a twenty-six-year-old college freshman.

I can see Dax is about to offer another gem of an idea when his phone rings in his pocket.

"Hi, honey," he says as he answers the phone.

I only hear his side of the conversation, so I can only guess what is being said on the other end.

"You are? Right now? Can it wait? Okay, okay, I'm on my way." He hangs up and returns his phone to his pocket. "Sorry about that. It was the missus. I'm going to have to take a rain check."

"Is everything okay?" I ask, concerned for his wife Julia. I've only ever spoken to her briefly on the Facetime chats I've had with Dax, but she seems like a nice person.

"Oh, everything is fantastic. We're trying for baby number two, and its ovulation week."

"I have no idea what that means."

He chuckles and grins like a mad man. "It means I get to have a lot of sex every day of the week and have to be available at the drop of a hat for her."

"That doesn't sound too bad."

"It's not bad at all." After pulling out his wallet, he sets a few bills on the table to cover his meal.

Guess I'll have to relearn town another day.

"I'll catch you later."

With that, he's gone out the door in long strides. I would be, too, if I had a wife I adored, calling me for middle-of-the-afternoon sex.

After I finish my shake and pay the waitress, I make my way back home after driving a few circles around town. Most of what I remember is still here, with a few additions and subtractions. Later, I'll reacquaint myself with everything else, perhaps with the help of one of my sisters, since Dax is busy.

It's near to four o'clock when I pull into my driveway, noticing Sally's black hearse parked next door. I wasn't intentionally looking to see if she was home. My gaze just happened to drift over her house as I was pulling in. Really. Okay, maybe it was partially intentional. It is a Monday, after all, and I'm curious what kind of job she has that she can be out at lunch with her friend and back home before four.

I make my way into my barely furnished rental house, paper in hand, intent on scouring the "Help Wanted" section. It yields very little. At least very little of what I want to do. There's a few maybes if I'm desperate, but until then, I'll keep looking.

My house is quiet, so freaking quiet. No boisterous roommates or middle-of-the-night sirens for drills, no pounding on doors. There's no one demanding anything. And without a TV to fill the silence, it's like the house has taken on a life all its own. This is the first time since I left the army that I can sit and listen with nothing to do and no one to answer to.

To fill the time, I decide to get up and clean. The house is good-sized, with three bedrooms and two-and-a-half baths, and a spacious living and dining room. There's even a legitimate den with built-in bookshelves lining three of the four walls. I have no idea how I'll ever fill them all.

Being of older design, the rooms are partially separated with half walls and archways but open enough you don't feel confined. All are lined with hardwood flooring—which reminds me: I'll have to buy some area rugs, not only to protect my feet from the cold in winter but to cut down on the echo. It doesn't help with the feeling of emptiness this all-too-big house brings me.

I dig out cleaning supplies from a box under the sink and spray down the counters before Swiffering the hardwood floors, wiping down the bathrooms, and collecting trash I have accumulated during the move. Filling my time with idle work to keep my mind from spiraling down the seemingly endless hole of realization that I don't know what the fuck I'm doing with my life.

Mid-mental chastising, my phone rings, and I set down the rag I was using to clean the baseboards to answer it. Sitting back on my heels, I pull the phone from my pocket. On the screen is a picture my sister Sophie sent me of her and all four of her children on the last Fourth of July, smiling and holding sparklers.

It was part of her persuasion tactics to get me to

move back home. Come home so I can see my nieces and nephews grow up, be part of their lives. Come to Fourth of July parades and cookouts and family dinners every Sunday, which, in the end, obviously worked, since I'm cleaning my rental house no more than five miles from the house I grew up in.

I missed a lot when I was gone. Hannah, Sophie's eight-year-old, was born right before I enlisted, and I missed the birth of the twins, Melanie and Mason, who are already five and shooting up like bean stocks. I've barely gotten to know any of them.

Cooper, Sophie's oldest at eleven, will be a teenager soon and will need his Uncle Jack around to teach him what he can and can't get away with. Mom's getting older. Dad's close to retiring. Autumn, my second-oldest sister, is still single and thriving but on my case nonetheless to be home. We're a close family, always have been, and I know it's been hard for them with me away.

They know why I did it and supported my decision, but I guess they couldn't allow me to live someone else's dream forever. They want me to be happy, and I love them for it. I just wish I knew what made me happy.

"Hey, Sophie," I say casually as I answer her call, trying to make it sound like I'm doing more than dusting my base boards.

"Hey, Jack. How are you settling in?"

There's so much optimism and joy in her voice it's hard not to smile.

"Fine, just doing some cleaning."

"How is the house? Have you met any of the neighbors yet? I'm pretty sure Mom said one of her book club friends lives in that area."

I chuckle because I'm sure, someday soon, said friend will show up on my doorstep with a casserole and a granddaughter in tow who just so happens to be single and my age.

Ever since my mother discovered I was returning home from the army, she's been not-so-subtly hinting at me finding a nice local girl to marry and settle down with, no doubt giving her half a dozen more grandchildren.

I think about the one neighbor I have met, and her adorably flustered face comes to mind, from this morning with the cookies and this afternoon with the coffee. *I wonder if she's single.* I didn't see a ring on her finger, and so far, she's the only one I've seen at her house.

"Yeah, I met one neighbor."

I don't elaborate, and, apparently, that's not enough for Sophie.

"Which one?"

"Sally. She lives next door. She brought me cookies."

Seeing this conversation won't be a quick one, I plant my ass on the floor and lean against the wall, propping my free arm on my bent knee.

"Did she, now? That's awfully nice of her to do on your first day."

So much insinuation is laced in her tone I can almost see

the sardonic nodding of her head and pursing of her lips.

"Mmhmm."

"Sally . . . why does that name sound familiar?"

Please do not tell me my sugary-sweet but mouthy sister is an imbecile who has drunk the Kool-Aid and believe the nonsense Dax was saying about Sally. I still don't believe she's as crazy as he makes her out to be.

"Oh, is she the one with the black house? She always has the best Halloween decorations."

"Uh, yeah . . . Apparently, we went to high school together, but she was a few years behind me," I admit tentatively, wondering what else Sophie knows about Sally.

She has after all lived here full time. She would know more about the people in this town than me. Sophie is seven years older than me, though. Would she really know much about Sally, who's a decade younger than her?

If the gossip in town is any indication, then, yes, she would.

"Yes, that's it! She's the short girl with the curly hair that always drives the hearse and dresses like Wednesday Addams."

"She's a lot nicer than Wednesday Addams, Soph. She's actually really sweet. I ran into her at the coffee shop by Ma's this afternoon."

"Ooh, she's sweet, huh? Is she cute, too?"

"Soph . . ."

"I haven't actually met her before, so I'll have to believe whatever you tell me about her."

That's her subtle way of saying she's not judging.

Running my hand down my face, I sigh. "Okay, fine. Yes, she's cute. Ya happy now, Soph?"

She laughs. "Don't tell Mom you think a girl's cute. She'll be measuring you for a wedding suit while you sleep."

We both laugh now.

My marital bliss is of the utmost important to our mother. Yet, Autumn has been living in town this whole time, being single with not even the hint of a fiancé, and she doesn't even get the third degree. Is it because I'm the baby of the three of us?

"Is that the only reason you called? To hound me about finding my neighbor cute?"

"No, that was just accidental luck. I was calling to check in on you and make sure you're going to be at dinner on Sunday. If Mom knows you'll be there, she'll be less likely to show up at your house every day this week."

She has a point.

"Of course I'll be there. I wouldn't miss it for the world. And I know Mom wouldn't let me, even if I wanted to."

"Good. I'll let her know so she'll let you settle in—in peace. And we will see you Sunday. Maybe you could bring your nice, cute neighbor."

"Don't push it, Soph. When and if I start dating anyone, I'll let you know. Until then, just don't tell Mom I said anything about Sally."

She huffs and groans. "Fine. Ruin all my fun." Through the phone, a high-pitched scream rings out, then giddy laughter, loud thudding and then Sophie scolding the rambunctious children. Kids are great, but I am definitely not ready to be a dad. "I gotta go, Jack. I'll talk to you later, and I will want to know more about your cute neighbor."

I don't get to tell her there's nothing to tell—other than she bakes one hell of a cookie—before she hangs up to the sound every child knows. The ever-dreaded countdown from three. Sophie is almost as short as Sally, but she's tough and doesn't put up with anyone's bullshit. I wouldn't want to see what happens when she gets to one either.

Hanging up, I remain seated on the floor for a minute, turning the plastic and glass repeatedly in my palm. Again, the quiet of the house washes over me, and I feel the need to move, the urge causing me to twitch and fidget with my phone even more. Unable to sit still any longer, I return to dusting the base boards.

Eventually, there's nothing left to clean as dinner time rolls around. I order a pizza—with a side salad so at least I eat something healthy today—because, of course, I have absolutely nothing in my fridge and pantry and didn't go to the grocery store. When I realize this, I make a list on my phone of what I'll need to get tomorrow. Which is basically everything.

With nothing left to do after eating half of my everything pizza and cleaning every surface of my house, I make my way up to my bedroom. I fold and hang my clothes that I didn't get to this morning and make my queen-size bed with clean new sheets and a quilt my grandmother gave me before I left for the army. It's thick and heavy, enough to keep me warm on cold nights in New Hampshire.

While putting away my personal items, I find a few books and decide to read to help me relax. Making myself comfortable in plaid pajama pants and a gray thermal—the nights are getting colder as we roll into October—I prop up pillows on the bed, flick on the small table lamp on my nightstand, and open a book to settle in.

The primary bedroom is at the back right corner on the second floor of the house, with windows facing the backyard and tree line of the woods, which also face Sally's black house. I hadn't paid much attention to the views until I sat in my bed, which faces the large window and Sally's house. I have curtains, but I haven't drawn them, allowing in the light until darkness washed it away.

With the sunlight gone, I can see into her windows. There are a few lights on, and a warm beam emanates from within. Even with soft black curtains drawn, I can see through them like a gauzy film, the light from inside illuminating the window like a glow box. I don't think Sally realizes they're see through because she doesn't seem to notice my small light on in the window from what appears to be her bedroom.

Enthralled by learning more about my cute little neighbor, I watch her move around the room, her dark ringlet curls bouncing, as she prepares herself for something. She's wearing a dark robe, and in the two minutes I've been watching her like a creeper, it never occurred to me that maybe I shouldn't. And when she unties and drops the robe, exposing milky-white skin clad in nothing more than black panties and a black lace bralette—yes, I know what a bralette is. I'm a man, not an idiot—I realized I should have closed my curtains. Stopped watching. Done something else other than close my book and turn the light off so I can watch her without being caught.

When she crawls onto the floor and twists herself into strange and oddly sensual positions, I shouldn't get up and walk over to the window to get a closer look. Or stand in the shadow of my curtain, concealing myself. And I most certainly should not reposition myself to the opposite side of the window to get a better angle of her ass as she thrusts it skyward and presses her head to the floor.

And just like that, my cute little neighbor becomes my sex kitten neighbor. All the blood rushes to my dick. I haven't seen a naked woman in a long time, and I'm pretty sure the army laces our water with some anti-horny drug. Most of the time, I wouldn't even wake up with morning wood. Now that I'm out, my boners are back with a vengeance, and there's no stopping them from pitching a tent in my sweats.

And now I'm a Peeping Tom. Fuck. Turning abruptly from my window and all that skin, I pull the curtains shut.

I should inform her that her curtains are see through. Even though it will obstruct my view, it's the proper, neighborly thing to do. She would want to know. Or maybe she wouldn't. I don't want to embarrass her.

HER FAVORITE JACK-O-LANTERN

I'll definitely tell her in a few days . . . maybe a week. Perhaps a couple weeks. We'll play it by ear, and if it comes up in conversation, I'll mention it.

6 – Sally

Now I'm getting aquainted with his backside

I hate to admit it, but Peyton was right. Going through the routine of poses and stretches she taught me actually helped. I may not be as cool as a cucumber or sexually satisfied, but I'm calmer, more centered. So, this morning, when I wake up before my alarm, I'm pleasantly refreshed and alert. Feeling like I could take on the world.

Some days, I wake up and question everything, feeling like the failure my mother thinks I am. Second-guessing my decisions, regretting my impulsive choices that have led to be the weirdo everyone in town whispers about behind my back, the one left at the altar—so to speak—alone and unwanted, with nothing more than my cats and pumpkins. Sure, I have friends, like Peyton and Chloe, but no man in town will date me. The few dates I have gone on in recent years were forced upon unsuspecting men who had no idea who they were going out with.

Thankfully, today is not one of those days. My confidence is high, and my positivity is in full force as I roll out of bed and stretch, reaching out with my fingers and trying to make myself taller, as if that'll work. If it did, I would be a giant and not the pip-squeak I am at barely five foot three.

Going about my morning routine, I feel good about the day, brushing my teeth, gently combing my curls back into submission, picking out a much more festive outfit than yesterday. Choosing a black-and-white-striped dress, the collar and cuffs adorned with embroidered spiderwebs paired with my jack-o-lantern purse and skeleton hand hair berets. Much more on par with my normal October attire. Not that I wouldn't wear this any other time of the year, but now, at least, no one can complain about it.

Laying my dress and tights out—black netted spider webs—I turn on my heels and dance to the music playing in my head. During one rather impressive spin, I pass by my window and spot my new neighbor in his backyard, doing push-ups . . . *shirtless*. I halt as my eyes catch his tight muscles.

Before, I got an up-close-and-personal introduction to his chest, and now I'm getting acquainted with his backside. As he presses up and down, his shoulders flex and extend. Biceps bulge, and I can even see his ass clenching under the loose shorts he's wearing. Mike Meyer's damn him for being so physically fit. If he were in a horror film, he would definitely *not* die. Hell, he'd probably be the hero and kill the psychopathic murderer on the loose. I'd be the first girl killed, thanks to my lack of athletic ability and short legs.

Jack does a rather impressive maneuver and jumps up to his feet. He's sweaty and glistening in the early-morning light, which highlights see every ridge across his strong shoulders and back, and when he turns—those abs. A pitiful whimper escapes my lips as I watch him shift from push-ups to pull-ups. Now his chest and abs come into view as he uses a strip of railing on his back porch to lift his body.

With his knees bent, ankles crossed, and the coiling of his body, not to mention the clingy shorts, I am also getting an eyeful of his generous package. Lucifer help me not ravage this man in his sleep—although, I suppose Lucifer would be all for little ravaging. And I can't blame him. This man is worth a felony charge.

As I stand here, watching him move and bulge and flex, my lady bits get all worked up. My nipples harden and stand at attention beneath my nightgown, aching for someone to touch them, secure their lips around them. Ease the growing pressure within me, a feeling I haven't experienced in years, not since Myles. The sensation is not new or unexpected from watching the man I was so infatuated with as a teen girl and am probably still infatuated with. What is surprising is the powerful grip it has on me. The increasing demand for relief.

For a moment, I contemplate getting my vibrator out while watching him to ease the tension between my thighs. But that would be weird, right? Masturbating at my window, watching Jack outside. It would be creepy and wrong. Yet, as the growing need intensifies, I really, *really* want to.

On its own accord, my hand slides up my stomach, and I cup my breast, squeezing gentle but firm while rubbing my thumb over my peaked nipple. The corresponding electric current racing straight to my core has me squeezing my thighs together in response. It doesn't assuage the need but makes it worse.

Satan's balls. Living next door to Jack will not be easy. Peyton was right. I need to make sure my vibrator is charged. If this is what I have to look forward to waking up to every morning, I may need to buy a backup.

The urge to reach for my beside drawer and pull it out is almost undeniable. With great effort and self-restraint, I resist the urge to shove my hand down my panties. But I don't walk away from the wonderful view just yet. There's nothing weird about enjoying a leisurely gander out my own window.

Jack drops down from the porch overhang and reaches for a towel to wipe his face and neck. It's hypnotizing until he looks up toward my house, and I squeal as I drop to hide under the windowsill. *Did he see me? Was he even looking at my window?*

No. He wasn't looking at me. He was glancing around. There's no way I would be the object of his attention. Just in case, I lie on the floor before crawling to my bed to stand. Because if he were watching, I don't want him to see me popping up from under my window, making it obvious that

I was hiding.

I go about my morning, pretending as if nothing happened. *I wasn't watching Jack out the window like a stalker, and I did not grope myself while fantasizing about him putting those muscles to work . . . on me. Nope not at all.* And eventually, my lies sink in, and I'm able to run my errands guiltlessly.

After buying the supplies and decorating items I'll need for the display windows, I return home, ready to carve the final pumpkins I'll need. This is my favorite part of the holiday. I love pumpkins and carving them so much that I have my own pumpkin patch in my backyard. Along the back tree line, I installed a chest-high wooden fence running from one property line to the other in a rectangular shape. I couldn't leave it all boring and brown, so I painted the fence in a black stain to match my house. And on the gate, a large jack-o-lantern smiles back at my house.

At first, I only grew a few pumpkins for my own use, taking my time, learning to carve properly. I even learned how to carve the exterior without puncturing the interior, giving it shades and depth, creating pictures and scenes rather than just faces. I keep a toolbox of carving knives and tools just for that purpose. When I started offering holiday decorating services, my little patch grew to a large one. Instead of six to twelve pumpkins, I now grow upwards of thirty, ensuring proper shape and color, treating them like growing children, with timed watering systems and canopy covers to protect from burning and spoiling.

Last year, I discovered this technique that if you place a

small baby pumpkin in a mold made in a specific shape, the pumpkin will take on the shape of the mold. I tried a few, but my favorites were the skull, a heart, and even a classic jack-o-lantern shape. Mickey heads are popular online but not in nearly as high demand as the others here. These pumpkins take great care to grow, and once people learned I could grow them in shapes, they began preordering them for their Halloween displays.

To my great regret, I decorate the main street windows of Daphne's Delights, a clothing boutique run by my high school nemesis, Daphne Brighton, the quintessential mean girl. Except she can, unfortunately, appear sweet and polite, convincing all the parents and teachers she was the perfect angel. This ability translated into her adult life. Most of the town still believes her to be perfect. However, those on the receiving end of her dislike know better. She's sly and conniving, making everything appear to be as she wishes, with her as the victim and me as the bad seed.

Her tricky bullying ways may have been what led to people considering me a freak. At least they know now that I'm not a bad person. They've moved on from thinking me bad to just weird.

Although I loathe Daphne with a passion, she pays the most for my decorating services. That may have been intentional . . . it was completely intentional. I denied her dozens of times until she said the right thing in front of the right people, and it was agree or become more socially outcast. I chose the route that kept me from committing murder. That didn't mean I couldn't charge her triple my normal rate. I told her she had to pay my fee, or I wouldn't do it.

She pays, and I deliver the "best window display on Main Street," per her demands, which include three large skull-shaped pumpkins. She also requires a few small heart-shaped ones to place around her register.

Growing them takes precision and timing to ensure they are fully grown and shaped by October. Which is now. Which also means it's time to pick pumpkins. The rest of my day will be filled with gutting and carving the last few jack-o-lanterns, eating fresh-baked pumpkin spice cupcakes I also picked up in town, and low mien noodles from The Golden Dragon, the best Chinese food in town.

Grabbing my stem-cutting knife, I make my way outside to my patch with a smile and a skip in my step.

7 - Jack

So you're what? A professional jack-o-lanterner?

Small-town life is extremely boring and filled with far too many people sticking their noses in my business. All I wanted to do was go to the grocery store and buy my food and come home. The citizens of Laconia decided otherwise. Every aisle I walked down a new person stopped me to either comment on how big I've gotten since they last saw me when I was knee-high to a pig's eye or reintroduce themselves with some story of how we met in high school or how our parents were the best of friends. More than one woman stopped to flirt with me and inquire on my future plans and not-so-subtly ask about my relationship status.

Next time, I may have to have my groceries delivered so I can avoid all the gossip and chatter at the store.

Parking in my driveway, I am happy to be back home in

the peace and quiet that only yesterday seemed unbearable. Thankfully, I also picked up a new TV while I was out, which means no more reading in bed and staring out my window at Sally.

Unloading all the food items first, then the TV, I bring everything inside and fill my pantry and fridge. I stocked up on everything so I wouldn't have to return to the grocery store anytime soon.

Installing the TV takes only a few minutes. Still no cable, but who really has that these days? Everything is streaming through online services. Once I get my internet up and running, I'll be set—which should be Friday, according to my appointment.

I stand at my kitchen sink, rinsing off some potatoes for dinner, when I hear the cutest high-pitched yelp come from outside my window.

Looking up, I see a petite body clad in black-and-white stripes moving around in Sally's backyard. Crouching behind a dark black fence, she has blobs of orange and white in her arms.

She stumbles and drops one, cursing loud enough I can hear her all the way inside. Again, she tries to load up her arms with what I can now tell are pumpkins. She's far too small to be carrying all those at once. She manages a few steps before they wobble again, nearly toppling over. I can tell she won't make it all the way back to her house like that.

Dropping the potato in the strainer in the sink, I stride out of my back door and jog across the yard. I make it to her right before she can drop all her precious cargo.

"No, no, no, no, no," she cries as her Jenga'd pumpkins tilt. She spins and tries to rebalance herself, turning her back to me.

I don't have time to round her to catch her pumpkins before they fall, and I have to reach around her back and hug the pumpkins and her to my chest.

"Whoa there, steady now. I gotcha."

"Oh my goodness. Thank you."

Sally is warm and small in my arms, allowing me to wrap them easily around her and her pumpkins, which appear to be from her very own pumpkin patch I hadn't noticed before. I've never known anyone with their own pumpkin patch. It's cute, and from what I've learned, so very much her.

In our arms are nearly five pumpkins of various sizes. I've looped one arm around the bottom largest one and the other around her arm at the middle, bracing my palm flat against her hand, which is soft and silky. Our fingers instinctually intertwine as we hold the orange squash.

Sally looks down at our arms and then twists her head around to look up at me, and I can feel her body tense when she realizes I'm the one holding her.

"Oh, Jack. Hi."

"Hi, yourself." I can't help but smile at the flustered shock on her face.

For a moment, we're silent, staring at one another. She may be frozen in my arms, but she's still soft and curvy, and

I find I like the feel of her pressed against me. I haven't been this attracted to a woman in a long time, and this itching desire to pull her closer, even when I barely know anything about her, is unexpected.

With her cute stuttering and wide eyes, and even with Dax's unfavorable opinion about her hobbies, I'd still like to know more about her. She intrigues me with her skeleton hair clips, bright violet eyes, and black lipstick on lips that snag my attention, like they did yesterday at the coffee shop.

"I, um . . . was just trying to take my pumpkins inside," she finally whispers, relaxing and softening beneath me, gaining confidence with each word spoken. All the while keeping eye contact with me.

"I can see that. If I hadn't had caught you when I did, they may not have made it."

"You're probably right. I was a little ambitious trying to carry them all at once."

A sweet and timid smile crosses her lips, and my grip on her hand tightens at the sight. She's cute when she's not smiling, but when she is smiling . . . she's beautiful. A radiant glow of pure light. How could anyone think of her as a freak with a smile like that?

"Why don't you let me carry these for you," I offer, not really wanting to let her out of my arms but knowing I can't stand here all day. That would be weird, no matter how far back we've known each other.

"Yes. Okay, thank you. Um . . ." She tries to shift, trying to free herself from our embrace but failing. "How should we . . . ?"

Reluctantly, I attempt to assist her. It's not working. "Place your right hand down where mine is on the bottom pumpkin." She does, and I resist the urge to slide my hand over hers. "Okay, now lean back a little so the pumpkins rest against your chest." Again, she complies and follows my directions, leaning toward my chest and gently resting her head against my shoulder.

God, she feels good against me. And that's my cue to stop touching her before I pop an uncontrollable boner against her ass.

Slowly, I release my hands, ensuring she is balanced. In two fluid steps, I stand in front of her and pluck the pumpkins out of her hands, nestling them neatly in my arms, leaving her to carry only two of the smaller pumpkins.

"What are all these for?" I ask, nodding, not only at the pumpkins in our arms but the rest still in the fenced-in patch behind her. It's cute but also strange, and there has to be a reason other than decorating her already-covered front and back porches.

"Oh, um . . ." she pauses, worrying her bottom lip between her teeth, making her even cuter. *How does she not get black lipstick all over her teeth?* "Well, I carve them for some of the businesses in town."

Just adorable. Especially with the cute pink splotches that appear on her cheeks. There's no way she is anything like the gossip around town. I've been here two days, and it's astonishing the amount of talk I've overheard. It's amazing she's lasted this long in this town and can still smile so openly.

"So, you're, what, a professional jack-o-lanterner? Is that even a thing?" I give her a smile and hope she doesn't find me too corny.

Most women weren't interested in me for my goofy sense of humor and didn't get it when I joked around. Probably why none of them lasted long.

"If it were, I would definitely be one but no. I am not." She sighs wistfully, caressing the pumpkin in her arm lovingly. "It's just a hobby."

She really does have a think for pumpkins.

"So, what do you do, then? For work, I mean."

Sally turns and walks toward her house, and I follow. I have to admit I am very curious about the inside of her house. With a black exterior and hearse parked in the driveway, the inside must be as astonishing.

"I'm an interior designer."

That was not what I expected, not that I had an expectation. It kind of makes sense, though. She definitely has a style of her own.

"Wow. That must be a fun job."

"I like it well enough. I wish I had more clients, but it takes time for small businesses to grow."

"I'm sure it does. I wouldn't know anything about it. I can't even figure out what kind of job I want now that I'm out of the army," I admit, surprising even myself.

"What do you mean?" Sally steps onto her back porch

and opens the back door, gesturing for me to enter.

That won't do.

Stepping up behind her, I hook the edge of the door with my elbow without releasing the pumpkins. "After you."

"Well, at least someone in this town is still chivalrous," she mumbles, blushing.

Following Sally, I forget what we were talking about the moment we step foot into her home. We've entered into an open-concept kitchen and informal dining area. Black cabinets are paired with dark wooden butcher-block counter tops and white subway tile backsplash that create a warm, inviting space with a dark twist.

On one wall is a large apothecary cabinet filled with dried herbs and spices, hand-labeled in glass bottles and drawers. Old recipe posters are framed on the walls along with a hanging rack of mugs. Her dining table is black with dark plum tufted chairs that look rather inviting, matching the floral print wallpaper on the two walls of the dining area.

Her home is far more personal than my own. Nothing hangs on my walls, and I don't even know the style of the dining set I purchased. Sally knows who she is and isn't afraid to show it. I on the other hand don't know who I am anymore. All I have is what I learned in the army, and now that I'm a civilian again, even that has no place anymore.

"You can put the pumpkins on the counter."

"What?" I was so entranced by her house that I forgot I was even holding the pumpkins. "Oh . . . right."

I set them down on the island stretching through the

center of the kitchen. She's placed large strips of what appear to be butcher paper across it and has a small toolbox sitting at one end and a trash can ready for the scraps.

Sally takes the pumpkins and lines them up with the others, taking great care with them. They look perfect, no blemishes or flat sides. They look solid and fresh. These aren't the result of random unattended vines. These were cared for properly, like the kind you see in home and garden magazines, and on HGTV.

"Your home is beautiful. You have a real talent."

"Thank you," she whispers softly, almost too afraid to accept the compliment, until I give her a toothy grin that seems to put her at ease. "If you think this is nice, you should see the rest of the house."

I know it was probably meant as an offhand comment, but I would very much like to see the rest of her house.

"I'd like that. Maybe you could give me a tour sometime."

"Oh," she starts, eyebrows raising in surprise. She wasn't expecting that. "Sure, I think that can be arranged."

Slowly, Sally returns to organizing her pumpkin-carving station when I notice all the other pumpkins in the kitchen. Some plain, others carved in varying designs from smiling traditional jack-o-lantern to full graveyard scenes with zombies. Holy shit, she's talented.

"Wow. You did all these?" I ask as I move closer to the pumpkins.

"Yeah. The zombie one is for Ma's Diner. She requested a zombie theme this year. The werewolf and skeleton cat are for the animal shelter. They're some of my favorites."

With every minute I spend with Sally, she appears to visibly relax and grow more comfortable around me—better than yesterday, when she couldn't utter a word. Although that could have been in part to the nudity.

"So, you just carve pumpkins for all the businesses in town out of the goodness of your heart? I hope you don't mind me saying, but I don't think this town deserves it."

A bark of laughter echoes through the kitchen as Sally tries to stifle it with a hand over her mouth. The sound is warm and welcoming, and I wouldn't mind hearing it again.

Clearing her throat, she tries to hide the smile but can't quite smother it completely. "No, I suppose they don't, but I don't do it for free. Well, I do for the animal shelter. The rest, I charge a small fee for my time, and they pay the cost of supplies and decorations."

"Decorations? You decorate, too?"

She nods. "Yeah, for a few of the major holidays. It's kind of my side hustle. It helps bring in extra money until I'm able to support myself with my design business."

"So, if I wanted to, I could hire you to decorate my house for Halloween? Or just decorate it in general? It's pretty pathetic over there. I have absolutely no style."

It could definitely use a little personalization. It's depressing to have a home so bare. Barracks are supposed to be bare, not your home.

"Well, I'm a little booked up this week. But maybe I can squeeze you in next week. No promises."

I like this more relaxed and open Sally. Conversing with her is far more fun than just watching her stare at me, all flustered. Although that's fun, too.

"Well, then, maybe you could just teach me how to carve a pumpkin."

Again, she worries her lip, glancing at her pumpkins on the counter then back at me. Considering my request. I take the moment to take a closer look at her. Her outfit is far more extravagant than the one she wore yesterday. Striped and ruffled, with spider embroidery and far more themed accessories. Is today a special day, or was yesterday? Is this how she normally dresses? According to the whispers I overheard, she dresses like every day is Halloween. What I saw yesterday didn't appear to fulfill that description. This, however, does.

She grabs a black-and-orange polka-dotted apron from a hook and loops it over her head and ties it around her waist. The apron is not a standard store-bought one. This one has a ruffle of black-and-orange stripes around the bottom and is made to cinch at the waist and flare out easily over her full skirt.

"All right, then, fine. You can carve one pumpkin," she says firmly, holding up a finger at me, for further clarity. "And if I approve of your abilities, you can help me do the rest."

"And if you don't approve?"

"Then, you'll be assigned to seed-cleaning duty."

"I suppose that's fair." I chuckle.

HER FAVORITE JACK-O-LANTERN

She's a demanding little thing when she gets going, isn't she?

Nodding at the door, she gestures toward the backyard. "Go pick a pumpkin from the patch. I've already gotten all that I need, so you can have your pick of what's left."

8 – Sally

What in the ever-loving nightmare on Elm Street?

Jack Campbell is in my house. He's in my house, wanting me to teach him how to carve a pumpkin! Okay, no big deal, just another Tuesday. *Just be cool.* Right, like I've ever been cool in my life. This is going to be a disaster I know it. I'm going to cut off my finger while showing him how to carve a pumpkin—or worse, cut off his.

No. Do not be a freak about this, Sally. He's just a regular guy. Yeah, a regular guy with massive muscles, a nice ass, a sweet, friendly smile, and just saved my pumpkins from utter obliteration.

Jack is only gone for a few minutes before he returns, striding in with a generously sized pumpkin in his arms. There was no way I could have ever imagined this day turning out like this. With Jack in my house, helping me carve pumpkins. Peyton would be proud that I only froze for a few seconds before gaining enough composure to speak. She'll be telling me "I told you so" for weeks, knowing her meditation stretches worked.

Now to just put myself back in Zen mode so I can continue my newfound calm. There will be no cutting off of fingers and no more squeaking. I am a grown-ass woman, and I can spend an evening with a man, carving pumpkins without having a panic attack.

At least I hope I can.

"So, do I get a pumpkin-carving apron, too? I'm dying to know how I look in one," Jack asks, smiling broadly.

I am still a little taken aback by his interest in spending time with me and doing something most people consider childish.

Turns out Jack is more of a big kid than I thought, with his easy smile and joking manner. I can't help but wonder about him. I thought I knew what kind of person he was in high school, the cool jock with a heart of gold and boy-next-door appeal. I thought it had more to do with being the most popular guy in school. Perhaps I was wrong. It seems his easygoing personality made it easy for him to befriend anyone.

"Absolutely." Squinting at him, I cock my head to the side, sizing him up and trying not to ogle him. It's hard, but I manage. He looks good in the dark-wash jeans that hug his thighs and fitted sage green Henley that does the same curtesy to his arms. "I think you're a purple-apron kinda guy."

He just grins, rolls up his sleeves, and becomes the sexy guy in every romance novel ever written right in front of me. *Thank you to whomever made him buy that shirt.* His forearms flex, and his biceps strain at the resistance of his sleeves.

Clapping his hands, he rubs them together eagerly. "Bring on the purple."

The apron I hand him is similar to mine but purple, with a silhouette trim along the bottom of a graveyard and creepy old houses. It's frilly and fun and far too small for his large frame. He looks like a dad playing dress up in his daughter's clothes. It doesn't matter to him one bit. He ties the ribbons with a bow and twirls, posing in the most ridiculous attempt at mimicking a supermodel., doing something with his face that reminds me of *Zoolander*. I burst out laughing at him. Who knew Jack was so funny?

"How do I look?" he manages through pursed duck lips.

I smother my giggle. "Fabulous, darling. I think you could make the cover of GQ."

We cut the top of the pumpkins, clean out the insides, and place all the seeds in a massive bowl that sits in the islands center. Jack works on his pumpkin, standing on the opposite side of the island across from me. His hands are large and strong, and he's able to scoop out the guts of his pumpkin in three graceful handfuls. I, on the other hand, am still working through mine at five scoops. Damn my tiny hands.

HER FAVORITE JACK-O-LANTERN

Eventually, we get them all cleaned out. The pumpkin I'm carving will be for the local gym, Power Fitness. They requested demonic, mutant jack-o-lanterns, the classic triangle-eyed style but possessed by demonic spirits, creating mutinous pumpkins with lots of teeth. It will have a venom-style mouth that will stretch around half the circumference. Utilizing the layers of the pumpkin's shell, I'll be able to create depth and perspective.

"What would you like to learn to carve into your pumpkin?" I ask Jack once we're both ready to begin carving.

Jack thinks for a minute, looking at his pumpkin and the ones I have lined up on the side counter. Scratching his jaw, he purses his lips in an alluring display that makes me want to suck on them. Then he looks down at the frilly apron around his waist.

"How about a cemetery scene?"

"Are you sure? That's going to require some delicate knife handling. Do you think that's something you can manage?"

He quirks a brow at me with a matching pull at the corner of his lips. "Sweetheart, I was in the army for eight years. I know how to handle a blade."

The endearment—I know is not intended to be personal—sends a flutter through my chest. No one ever calls me sweetheart. I get the occasional "honey" in the southern "Oh, honey, bless your heart" way. It's rarely meant to be endearing or friendly.

"Sweetheart, huh? I didn't know we were on such casual

terms. Does that mean I can call you buddy or hot stuff?" Catching sight of his dog tag chain tucked inside his shirt, I offer another alternative. "Or maybe sir is better suited?"

"I kind of like sir. Makes me feel . . . in charge," he jests. His eyes glaze over as they roam across my face, searching for something. "Perhaps sweetheart isn't appropriate for you. Maybe"—he looks down at the pumpkin in my hands—"pumpkin or pumpkin pie is better."

"Well, I do like pumpkins."

"Obviously."

Jack wasn't kidding when he said he knows how to handle a blade. His carving skills are above par, and he catches on quickly. But he's not as good as me. We're quiet once he gets the hang of it, only asking which tool to use to get his desired effect. It's nice to sit in comfortable silence with another person. It's been a long time since I had that with anyone.

I'm finalizing the teeth on my monster pumpkin when I nearly slice clean through it at the sound of Jack's startled yelp.

"What in the ever-loving Nightmare on Elm Street?" I turn to find Jack staring at Binx, who has sat on the counter directly between him and his pumpkin, meowing insistently.

I stare at Jack. Did he really get scared by a cat?

"Are you afraid of cats?"

"No," he states firmly, furrowing his brow. "He just surprised me is all. I wasn't expecting him to jump up like that." Reaching out a tentative hand Jack rubs Binx's head,

HER FAVORITE JACK-O-LANTERN

and he graciously accepts, pressing into his hand demanding more. Jack obliges, scratching behind his ears and then down his back.

"He's a friendly little guy, ain't he?"

"That's Binx. He is extremely friendly. He'll let you pet him all day long if you're willing." Reaching over I give him a brief scratch of my own, but he's so involved with Jack he barely notices me.

"Binx? Like from Hocus Pocus?"

"Exactly like Hocus Pocus. After Thackery Binx—in cat form, of course. He was a rescue from the shelter, as was my other cat, Casper, who is not as friendly as her name suggests. She is very ornery and persnickety. She's under the assumption that we are here to serve her. So, don't be offended if she ignores you."

"You mean Zachery."

Looking up, I lock eyes with a serious-looking Jack. His baby blues are bright and glittering. I'm so focused on them I almost forget to speak.

"Excuse me?"

"Zachery Binx, from Hocus Pocus."

"No, I meant what I said. Thackery Binx."

Jack scowls adorably.

"Thackery isn't a real name."

"Yes, it is. Have you even seen Hocus Pocus?"

If he's seen Hocus Pocus, he would know it's Thackery. Maybe he hasn't and has only heard people talk about it and that's why he thinks he's right.

"Of course I have. My sisters made me watch it when we were kids."

"Well, then, you know you're wrong."

"Am not."

"Oh, you want me to prove it to you?"

"Yes."

I pull my cell phone out of my pocket, bring up my IMDB app, and type in Hocus Pocus, ignoring Hocus Pocus 2—because it's nowhere near what we deserved for a sequel, especially after thirty years of waiting. So, I just pretend it never happened.

Holding the screen out in front of his face, I show him the cast where it clearly states the characters name, Thackery Binx and the actor who played him, Sean Murray.

His brow furrows even further in disbelief.

"Ha. Told you."

I may be a little smug in my victory, but I don't care. His humble look of defeat is well worth it.

"I guess you were right."

A lighthearted grin crosses his lips as he accepts his defeat without argument. One more characteristic that makes him the perfect man. There's nothing more irritating than a man who argues about being right, even when he's not.

"Never question me about Halloween movie trivia. I will always win."

"Duly noted." He mock-salutes, and it's rather endearing to have an ex-soldier salute me. I think I like it. "So, how many businesses do you decorate for Halloween?"

"Let me see"—I tap my chin and screw up my face, counting in my head—"maybe a dozen. I only have a few left. Ma's Diner, Hanson Hardware, Daphne's Delights and Power Fitness. The rest of them, I've already finished. Places like the animal shelter like to decorate earlier in September. All I have to do for them in rotate out their old pumpkins and replace them with fresh ones."

I return to carving my demon pumpkin, making sure the teeth are nice and sharp with varying layers and multiple rows.

"And you do this all yourself?"

Finally, Binx wanders off, leaving Jack to return to his pumpkin carving. He holds his scalpel-like knife poised but watches me, waiting for my answer.

"Yup. Sometimes, Peyton helps if I really need it. Chloe works at the animal shelter, and she helps me decorate there, but that's it." I fiddle with the scraps on the counter before brushing them into the trash can.

Jack stares at me and with those delicious sapphire eyes, watching me. It makes me twitch and I feel the need to readjust everything every two seconds.

"So, what you're saying is, you have to go to all these businesses and decorate them by yourself?"

"Yes?"

His question has me questioning my answer. Didn't I just tell him that's exactly what I planned to do?

"And if you had help, it would make it easier?"

"Yes . . ."

I have no idea what he's getting at.

"Okay, I'll make you a deal." He sets his blade down and places both hands firmly on the countertop, leaning in, looking me square in the eyes.

That is a lot of eye contact.

"Deal? I didn't know I needed to make a deal."

"I'll help you decorate whatever businesses you have left to do if you show me around town and help me look for a job."

I literally have no words. I was not expecting that and am not sure if I should accept. *Is there a downside to this?* I feel like this is some sort of trap to get me in a vulnerable position. It wouldn't be the first time someone I thought I could trust lied to put me in a position to be mocked and laughed at.

Jack is so far out of my league it's like we're not even playing the same game. He's playing football, and I'm playing ping pong. The two don't mix. *Us*, even as friends, is unfathomable. Not to mention all the gossip it'll start if we're seen around town together. Maybe I should do it just to stir shit up and make all the housewives squirm in their designer leggings.

"Why do you need me to show you around town? You lived here before. Not much has changed."

"Maybe not, but it's enough that I don't feel like I know anything or anyone anymore. You can help refresh my memory and show me anything new in town."

He doesn't even flinch as he says this. He's serious.

Tapping my nails against the counter, I try to rationalize saying yes without sounding eager. "Why can't Dax take you? I thought that's what he was doing yesterday?"

I would much rather show him around than Dax, but I also don't want to step on any toes.

"Apparently, his wife is ovulating, and he has to be available . . ."

One shoulder lifts in a shrug, a small furrow in his brow. I guess that was a little TMI for Jack. I try not to chuckle but fail. It smooths out the wrinkle between his eyes, and he relaxes.

"So, you'll help me, then? In exchange for manual labor, of course. I wouldn't dream of not repaying the favor."

I think for a minute, really wanting to say yes immediately, but my self-preservation is telling me it's a bad idea. But it sounds like such a good one.

Watching him stand there, solid and still waiting for me, looking as if my answer will solve all his problems, I feel like maybe I can trust him. He hasn't lived in this town for almost a decade and isn't like those who can't accept someone different like me. He hasn't once said anything about what I'm wearing or my makeup. He even complimented my house. Not even my mother does that.

"You know I drive a hearse, right?" He nods. "And you know you'll have to be seen with me in public, right?" He nods again. "And that, most likely, two minutes after we go out in public together, people will start gossiping about us."

He shrugs like it's no big deal. "And you're okay with all of this?"

"Why wouldn't I be?"

He has been gone far too long and doesn't seem to remember how it is to live in a small town and be the outsider. Then again, I guess he never was the outsider. He always fit in, accepted by all. Why wouldn't he be now?

"Because being the subject matter of all the gossip in town is not as fun as it sounds."

He ponders that for a moment, glancing around my kitchen, before returning his gaze to me. He still doesn't look concerned.

"I think I can handle that."

But can I?

"Fine, it's your funeral. I accept your deal."

When I reach my hand out, he firmly grasps it and shakes, holding on for a beat too long and running the pad of his thumb across the back of my hand before releasing it. Shivers radiate from the spot long after.

"Deal. What time should I be here tomorrow, and do I get to ride in your hearse?"

"You actually *want* to ride in my hearse?"

Jack grins widely and stands straight. "Abso-fucking-lutely. The only other chance I'll get to, I'll be dead. Won't really be able to enjoy that now, will I?"

His lightheartedness is tangible and infectious, spreading from his relaxed manners and washing over my nerves, setting me at ease around him. Something that rarely happens around other people who aren't Peyton or Chloe.

"I suppose not. Be here by ten. I have to wash my hair tomorrow morning, and managing my curls into submission takes a little extra time."

At the mention of my curly hair, he tilts his head to the side inspecting said curls, like he's taking them in for the first time and doesn't hate them.

Having Jack examine me so closely makes heat rush to my cheeks and crawl down my neck the longer he stares at me. On instinct, my gaze drops along with my chin. I'm a small person and making myself smaller, near invisible, is a talent of mine. It helped a lot in high school, when I wanted to fly under the radar. To disappear into a crowd to avoid people and being seen. I suppose if I really wanted to be invisible, I wouldn't dress how I do and live in a black house. Oh well.

"I think your curls look wonderful."

His voice is soft but low and husky. That can't be right. No one has ever spoken to me with a tone that sultry. My curls must remind him of someone else.

Clearing my throat, I reach up and push a curl behind my ear. "Thank you."

My tone is not as breathy as would be expected after such a compliment. Instead, I sound dejected, as if the compliment was an insult.

I can't see Jack's face, but I can feel the confusion in the silence that follows, which I break before it gets too awkward. People staring at me for prolonged periods of time makes my skin itch.

"Would you like to stay for dinner? I was going to order Chinese food." Taking a tentative peek up from under my lashes, I catch him watching me. I avert my gaze back to the pumpkin in my hand, hoping like hell he doesn't say no but dreading the possibility that he will.

"I would like that very much."

9 – Jack

Who knew bats could be sexy?

My alarm goes off at six o'clock, but I'm already up and lacing my running shoes. Today will be the first step back into life as a civilian, to figure out how I'm going to spend the rest of my life. Ever since returning to my hometown, I've felt adrift, floating around with no purpose or meaning. I need to find a purpose. I won't last long like this, putzing through life like a lost puppy.

Which is why I woke up this morning more alert and optimistic than I have been in weeks. I don't expect to find my perfect ideal career first thing, but at least I'm taking action, doing *something*. And being helpful and productive by assisting Sally. The fact that she's cute has nothing to do with it. That's just an added bonus. I would have been just as optimistic if it were Dax taking me around—maybe not as excited about it but still hopeful.

Striding out my front door, I set my pace faster than normal, barely noticing the early-morning chill against my exposed skin. In a matter of minutes, I won't feel it. My natural body heat keeping me insulated.

When I return home after my five-mile circuit, I go straight to my backyard, strip off my shirt, and settle into my workout routine. Pushing harder than I have in weeks, it feels good to sweat and burn and feel.

I almost double my reps in my eagerness to start the day. My energy and adrenaline spikes as I finish my squats, grab my T-shirt, and use it to wipe the sweat from my face and neck. Glancing up at Sally's house, I'm instantly drawn to her bedroom window, the one I haven't allowed myself to look at since the other night. Blinking, I trying to clear the sweat from my eyes. I swear I just saw movement. The long dark curtains sway in a breeze not created by an open window.

Taking that as my sign to get my ass in gear, I make my way inside to shower and make breakfast. By the time I'm cracking eggs and turning bacon, it's eight thirty, and again I catch myself looking out my kitchen window toward Sally's house.

I wonder if she's up yet. If she's eaten breakfast. Maybe I should bring some over as a thank-you for making me cookies and for letting me tag along with her.

Yes, I think I shall.

I toast some all-grain bread and add freshly cut

strawberries to the plates with scrambled eggs and bacon, arranging it to look presentable.

Before I leave the kitchen, I grab her pumpkin plate and tuck it under my arm to return to her. I'm not sure if she intended for me to keep it, since she didn't say much that first morning, but I washed it all the same. Figured I would be a good neighbor and return it.

Using the front door this time, I make my way across our lawns, passing her decorations and getting a better look at them. They're well made and placed with precision. A giant fake spider web and spider fill the space between two posts, with skeletons everywhere. Crawling out from under the porch, bursting from the ground, and even hanging from the rafters. Her front porch is lined with pumpkins, both carved and not. One is in the shape of a skull, as in the pumpkin *is* a skull, not carved into one. I have no idea how she did that, but it's cool.

I knock on her door, loud but polite. She lives in a big house, and if she's in her bedroom, I want to make sure she hears. Just to be sure, I also ring the doorbell. It makes a gong-like noise inside, none of that high-pitched tinkling like the one at my house.

Within a minute, the black door opens, and Sally stands before me, tightly tucked into an oversized bathrobe, her hair damp around her shoulders. The curls are slick in tight ringlets framing her face. Her face is free of makeup and freshly washed. She looks shocked at my appearance on her front porch. I suppose I am early.

Her mouth opens and shuts unsure what to say. Then she spots the plates, and her brow furrows in adorable confusion. I put her pretty little mind at ease.

"I thought I would bring you breakfast to thank you for the cookies." I hold out the two plates in front of her. She pinches her mouth to one side, hungrily eyeing the food.

"Oh, that was really nice of you. I'm not quite ready yet."

When she looks up at me from under her dark lashes, those uniquely violet eyes of hers glow in the morning light. The dark strands of her hair offsets the pale creaminess of her skin. A soft pink tongue licks out at her lips, drawing my attention to her mouth, with a pert Cupid's bow that is obvious without the makeup. Yesterday, those lips were covered in black lipstick, but now they're bare . . . just like the rest of her.

"That's all right. I don't mind waiting. But the food's going to get cold." I gently wave the plates in front of her face, tempting her with the undeniable scent of bacon.

No one can say no to bacon.

She releases her death grip from her robe collar and accepts the plate. "Okay, fine. I'll eat, and you can wait for me to finish getting ready. I'm not going to rush, though. I said ten, and I have till then to be ready," she scolds.

As if I wouldn't wait for her.

"Of course. I would never dream of rushing your process."

We step inside, and since I entered and exited through

the kitchen back door last night, I didn't get to see the rest of her house.

The entryway is spacious, accentuated by a twisting wooden staircase rounding the back corner. There's a narrow table along one wall holding candles, trinkets, and what appear to be skulls and, of course, more pumpkins.

The walls are painted black, and the floor is a patterned tile of matte black hexagons that fade off into the hardwood flooring of the rooms beyond. A golden mirror hangs on the wall above the side table, the frame large and swirling with bats and bony fingers curling around the edges from behind. It's unnerving and beautiful all in one.

The chandelier is black and gold, dripping with black crystals. I've never seen anything like it, and I'm speechless as I follow her through an archway to our left, passing a living room of emerald-green walls and an orange couch. I get barely a glance of it before we enter the kitchen.

Sally places her plate on the table, and I follow suit sitting in the plush but firm purple chair. I forgot to bring silverware with me, but Sally is already walking back with two forks in hand and a butter dish for the toast.

Her robe has fallen open at the neckline, and when she bends to sit, I get a flash of pale skin and marvelous cleavage. It was easy to tell before she was well endowed but knowing firsthand there is no padding involved in those curves has me swallowing hard. That slip of flesh is quickly hidden again when she sits and tightens her sash.

The eggs and bacon are still warm, and the toast still

crunchy. I watch in curious fascination as Sally picks up a slice of bacon and shoves half of it in her mouth. Closing her eyes, she moans quietly as she chews.

Note to self, Sally loves bacon.

"Good?"

Nodding, she shoves the other half of the bacon into her mouth and chews eagerly. My laugh is muffled by my own mouthful of bacon.

"So, where are we going today?"

Sally chews and swallows. I like a girl with an appetite, and she's eaten almost every scrap of food on her plate.

"I need to make stops at the animal shelter and The Sweet Exchange to make drop offs, then we'll be decorating Ma's Diner today."

"So, it's going to take a couple days to get all the ones you have left, done?"

How intricate are these decorations? Not that I have any other plans for the foreseeable future, but I thought it would be only one day, maybe two. I'm more than pleased to spend more time with her, though.

"At least till Friday."

It's Wednesday. I suppose I could be doing something worse . . . and far less interesting.

"Alrighty, then. I'm down for that. I don't have anywhere else to be." I give her my best warm smile, and the apples of her cheeks redden.

So adorable.

My tongue swipes out across my bottom lip, dragging

Sally's eyes down to focus on them. To mess with her, I suck my bottom lip into my mouth just ever so slightly. It has the desired effect. Sally sucks in a breath and quickly looks away.

Just so fucking adorable.

How did I never notice her in high school? Oh, right. I was a self-centered party boy who didn't pay attention to anything that wasn't booze or boobs. I was a fucking douche.

"I need to get dressed," she announces much louder than necessary. To make her escape, she stands without cleaning up her plate. "I'll be back. You can wait here."

"Can do."

While she's busy upstairs, covering up that cute, luscious body of hers, I clean up the plates and stack them to take back to my house. Then, like any good guest, I snoop. Well, not really, I just take a long leisurely look around her living room I didn't get to see before. Taking in every knickknack and art print, I peruse the inviting green walls and surprisingly cozy orange couch that looks straight out of an old Victorian mansion. I suppose that was the intention, since this is an old Victorian house.

Her house holds so much personality and individualism. Something I feel like I used to have but lost. I focused on being all that I could be while enlisted, putting all my energy and focus into succeeding at every task. Fighting my way to the top of my squad and even my platoon. Never resting or losing sight of my target or stopping till I hit dead center.

Having nothing to direct my energy at, having nothing to strive to achieve . . . gives me pause. Will I ever find myself again?

Running my fingers along an end table, over the tops of fringe lined floor lamps, and rounding a low stool shaped like a mushroom, I think Sally could help me. She knows who she is. Embraces and nurtures it. Perhaps some of that will rub off on me.

Forty-five minutes later, footsteps echo down the wooden stairs, and I stand from where I was comfortably reclining in her "pumpkin couch," as I've dubbed it. With brisk, peppy steps, Sally descends like an orange-clad Barbie, but with curly black hair and half the height.

Her glorious chest is snug in a fitted orange T-shirt with little black bats all over it. Her curves proudly on display, thanks to black suspenders that frame her breasts like a picture, with her shirt tucked inside a short pleated black skirt—the kind schoolgirls wear but far less appropriate. Her thighs are covered in sparkly orange tights, a black bat on each quad, its wings wrapped around her shapely petite leg like a garter.

Goddamn. Who knew bats could be sexy? Not me, not until right now.

"I like your tights," I blurt out. *Shit.* Now she knows I was checking out her legs. *Nice one, Jack. Real mature.* Because I'm already digging, I might as well go all in. "I liked the ones you wore yesterday, too. The fish net spider webs. Very on par for the season."

HER FAVORITE JACK-O-LANTERN

Goddammit. I'm an idiot. That doesn't seem to translate to Sally because she's smiling shyly and twirling a strand of shiny curls around her finger.

"Thanks. I have a whole collection. They're kind of a staple in my wardrobe." She shifts from twirling her hair to fiddling with the hem of her skirt as we meet in the foyer.

Now that we're closer, I can see she's wearing a head band with black bat ears on them. I didn't think it was possible, but she just got cuter.

Why don't people like her again? I can't seem to figure that one out. She's been nothing but welcoming and friendly since I got here. Is that just because we went to the same high school? Doesn't seem like it to me. That's just who she is. I can tell.

Reaching up, I flick one of the bat ears like I would a cat's. They aren't hard like I expected but flexible like some sort of vinyl material. Shiny and black.

"I sort of feel a little underdressed now."

My wardrobe is fairly basic these days. Mainly consisting of jeans, sweats, cargo shorts, and plenty of plain, solid-colored T-shirts and a few Henleys. I own exactly one jacket and two hoodies. Plus, all the ACUs I accumulated over the years. Not sure what I'm going to do with those or my dress uniform.

A mischievous twinkle flashes through Sally's eye as she looks over my jeans and black T-shirt that, ironically, reads *Army* across the chest.

"If you're open to it, I might have something for you

to wear. Only if you're interested. You can totally say no. It won't hurt my feelings."

She adds the last part hurriedly, as if I were offended by her offer.

"Sure. Whad'ya got?" I ask, reassuring her with a positive tone.

She bites her lip, runs back up the stairs, then returns moments later with something orange and plaid in her hands, holding it behind her back sheepishly as she shuffles toward me.

"If you don't like it, you don't have to wear it." She eyes me again, tilting her head so her curls shift to one side. A short, rather rambunctious one falls across her brow before righting itself when she tips her head back. "It should fit. Might be a little snug, but I think it'll work."

"Well, what is it? The suspense is killing me."

Pulling her hands from behind her back, she holds up a black-and-orange plaid button-up flannel. The orange matches her shirt and tights almost perfectly. We'd look like a matching pair, but that doesn't make me want to wear it any less.

Gently taking it from her hands, I hold it up to my chest, inspecting the size. She's right. Could be iffy. I'll have to put it on to know for sure. So, I slip my arms in. The flannel is soft and warm but still feels brand new. Surprisingly, it fits with only a slight pull across my shoulders, so I'll wear it unbuttoned to make sure I don't rip through it like the Hulk.

HER FAVORITE JACK-O-LANTERN

Walking over to the entry way mirror, I inspect my new orange flannel clad torso, and I don't hate it. Actually . . . I really like it. It's fun and bright and loud.

"This is awesome. How do I look?" Holding out my arms, I spin to face a smirking Sally.

She knows I'm fishing for a compliment, but she doesn't seem to mind.

"Much more on par with the season," she quips back with my own words, and I like her snarky side.

"Oh, ha, ha." Pulling at the collar, I flex, testing the limits of the material. "Only a little snug in the shoulders but otherwise fits just fine." I do a little twist, checking out the backside in the mirror. Not bad. "Looks brand new. Is this for your boyfriend?"

I know it's a tacky way to ask if she has a boyfriend, but I can't help it. If I asked outright, it would be even more obvious. And if she does, and this belongs to him, I really shouldn't be wearing it. That would be weird.

"Oh, no," she quickly assures me. "I bought it for my ex, but we broke up before I could give it to him."

By the sound of her dejected tone, it seems like there's a hell of a lot more to that story than she's letting on.

"Good. I would feel weird if you had a boyfriend and I was wearing his clothes and gallivanting around town with you."

She smiles, but it doesn't quite reach her eyes. Yeah, definitely more to this ex than she's admitting. I let it slide and don't prod because it seems like a sensitive topic. I'll let her tell me in her own time. Because I will find out about this guy and possibly punch him in the face by the look of the frown on her pretty face.

"No. I am painfully single," she admits. And I can't help but be happy about that fact.

Sally turns, opens a hidden closet like Harry freaking Potter, pulls out a fuzzy orange sweater, and slips it on. A bat brooch already pinned to one side of the neckline glitters as the light hits the stones. I hadn't noticed it at first glance. Seems today's theme is bats.

This woman puts more time and effort into her attire than I ever have. If I'm going to be hanging out with her, I may have to step up my game. Not with bat pins and ear headbands but maybe a patterned shirt or flannel. I like this one. It's so soft. I run my fingers up the sleeve, feeling the soft material and second-guessing if I should wear this. I don't want to ruin it.

"Are you sure you want me to wear this? I don't want to ruin it."

"No, it's fine. You can have it if you like. I don't need it."

A restrained frown crosses her pretty face. What did this ex do to her to make her so hurt over it? I don't even know who he is, and I already know he's an asshole. He must be. What other explanation would there be for a guy leaving someone as thoughtful and adorably cute as Sally?

"If you're sure. It is really nice."

"Absolutely. It's not getting any use hanging in my closet."

"Thanks."

"You're welcome." The uncomfortable look is gone, and her eyes brighten as she looks up to me, determination flashing through them. "Are we ready?"

Holding out one arm toward the front door, I gesture for her. "Lead on."

10 – Sally

He's a humper

Our first stop is The Sweet Exchange Bakery, where I . . . we drop of the washed and dried jars of pumpkin seeds from all the pumpkins I've carved so far this Halloween. I like to donate them to the bakery so they can make roasted pumpkin seeds to go in or on their delicious pastries. I have no need for thousands of pumpkin seeds. Only a few dozen to reseed for next year, and the small jar I keep and roast for myself.

It only takes us ten minutes, and we're in and out of the bakery, grabbing a pumpkin spice cupcake to go. I always get hungry and need a snack while decorating. Ma will most likely feed us, but I just love pumpkin spice cupcakes. You can never have too many.

We got a few strange looks when we entered. There

weren't too many people left in the bakery since most of the early morning rush had long gone. Only a few of the stay-at-home housewives lingered, along with a few teenagers who were most definitely supposed to be in school. They're brave for coming where they'll be seen, and no doubt ratted out within the hour to their parents.

Daisy, who works at the front counter almost every day, looked like she wanted to say something. Ask why we were together. I could see it in her shocked face that she didn't even try to hide. I didn't bother filling her in. It's none of her business. Plus, where would the fun be in that? If we clarify why we're together, then we won't get to hear all the ridiculous speculations. Sometimes, they can come up with some real doozies.

The most ridiculous being I'm a witch and brew potions to curse people with. I wish.

We leave, slide back into my hearse, and buzz over to the animal shelter where Chloe works. I already texted her we would be coming to drop off their new pumpkins.

I could hear the shock in her text when I told her Jack Campbell would be with me. I didn't have time to explain everything, so she got the quick "I'll tell you about it later" explanation. She wasn't happy, but I don't have time to text her the whole long story. She'll just have to wait.

The animal shelter is a decent-sized facility that can hold hundreds of animals. Thankfully, it's a no-kill shelter, so I don't have to worry about crying because the cute puppy I just saw was scheduled to be put down. To kill an animal just because they weren't adopted in a timely manner is barbaric.

We enter, carrying the three replacement pumpkins, and Chloe is already waiting for me behind the front counter. Her jaw unhinges and nearly sweeps the floor when she sees us. She recovers quickly, though, closing her flytrap and shaking away the shock, plastering on her easy smile.

"Hey, Sally . . . and Jack." Her chocolate-brown eyes shift between us, and she mouths *wow* to me when Jack turns to set the box of pumpkins on the counter.

I mouth back, *I know.*

"Jack, this is my best friend, Chloe. She also went to Laconia High with us."

Jack, the polite gentleman he is, reaches his hand out to shake hers. "Ma'am. Nice to meet you. I'm sorry if I don't remember you from high school. I'm starting to realize I didn't really know anyone I went to school with."

His brow pinches with embarrassment as he, apparently, just now realizes we all knew him, but he didn't know any of us.

Chuckling, she reaches out and accepts his hand, shaking it firmly, no doubt. Chloe's got some hidden muscle on her having to wrangle animals all day long.

"I am most certainly not a ma'am. You can just call me Chloe."

Jack relaxes and chuckles. "Sorry, habit. Army and all."

"Not a problem. It's sweet but unnecessary." Jack nods, not in the least bit embarrassed for calling her ma'am, though. It really must be second nature after so many years.

Her Favorite Jack-o-Lantern

"And not knowing everyone we went to high school with sounds like a blessing to me."

"No. I think I missed out not knowing more people."

Jack's eyes shift to me for a second unexpectedly. A fluttering flock of bats stirs in my chest for the second time this week under his scrutiny.

Thankfully, Chloe breaks my awkwardness.

"These pumpkins look amazing, Sally. You've outdone yourself this time."

Chloe turns the pumpkins around inside the boxes to inspect them closer, and I must admit, they are getting good.

"I've been practicing."

It's still difficult for me to fully accept a compliment. I pull the sleeves of my sweater down over my hands and fiddle with the fuzzy fabric, redirecting my attention to it rather than my amazing, supportive friend, who means what she says. Unlike others.

"You're just in time. The other pumpkins were starting to get soft. Come on, I'll help you switch them out."

Chloe eyes all three pumpkins and chooses the werewolf one from the box. We walk down to the end of the counter where the old pumpkin of a zombie beaver is looking more like a Squishmallow.

"We should put this one here," she announces, placing the werewolf pumpkin next to the Squishmallow beaver.

One thing I do with my pumpkins—that I think is rather ingenious—is that I install led string lights inside the pumpkins instead of using real or fake candles. This way, they can have a remote control and change colors if they like. Makes it so much easier and way more fun. It only takes me a few minutes to remove the lights from the old pumpkin and install them in the new one.

Taking the sad zombie beaver, I place it in the empty box we brought. It separates the fresh ones from the old and makes it easier to transport the softened pumpkins. I'll use them to make compost and mulch for the pumpkin patch. The circle of life and all.

Chloe turns the lights on and chooses a red that makes the werewolf glow under a blood moon. "Okay, come on back, and we'll swap out the others." Chloe spins, and her long blonde ponytail whips behind her, straight as a board.

I'm jealous of her straight hair. It's so much easier to maintain than my chaotic curls. She doesn't have to buy special products and learn techniques to keep her hair from turning into a frizzy Chia Pet. Apparently, this jealousy works both ways because she always says she's envious of my natural curls, since her hair won't hold a curl to save its life.

I guess the saying "the grass is always greener on the other side" is true. We always covet what we don't have simply because it isn't ours. Humans are strange.

Another pumpkin is sitting on a desk inside the back hallway I would label a vet tech station. There's a computer and filing cabinets and a phone. Chloe chooses the half skeleton cat for this station, and we swap them out.

The last pumpkin is in the kennel area on the tall desk

HER FAVORITE JACK-O-LANTERN

at the end. We have to pass all the dogs to get to it, and I take the opportunity to scratch behind many ears and boop noses. Most dogs here are friendly, so I'm not too worried about being bit. If there were a problem animal, they wouldn't be in the main kennel, and if they were, Chloe would tell me because she knows I can't keep my hands to myself when I see a cutie floofer.

About halfway down the kennels, I spot familiar black fur already jumping and barking, eagerly awaiting my arrival.

"Sparky. What are you doing back here? I thought you got adopted again?"

"They returned him a few days ago." Chloe answers for him.

"No way. How does he keep getting returned? He's the sweetest boy ever."

My words turn into baby talk as I attempt to pet him through the fencing, only able to feed my fingers through, which he happily licks.

"You know why."

I do know why. Sparky is a bit of a humper. He basically humps everything and everyone, even after being fixed. He can't help it. It's just who he is. Why people feel the need to return him for it is beyond me. It's a natural act that shouldn't be shunned. People are so . . . prudish.

"People are the real animals," I mumble to Sparky.

He barks, probably agreeing with me I decide.

"And why does he keep getting returned? If he's such a great dog?" Jacks curious voice startles me. I'd been so focused on poor Sparky that I'd nearly forgotten Jack was here.

"He's a humper," Chloe states flatly.

"A humper?"

The confusion on Jack's face is comical.

"Yes, a humper—as in, he likes to get his freak on with just about anything." Chloe crosses to the counter and drops off the last new pumpkin.

Jack follows her and sets the old pumpkin in the box then returns to me at Sparky's kennel. "That doesn't seem like a fair reason to return him."

"It's not," I agree.

Chloe opens the kennel and slips a leash on Sparky so he can come out and say hello. We've met often before when I visited Chloe to meet for lunch, decorate, and help with fundraisers.

Sparky has been in and out of here for the past year, going through at least three families. Poor guy. He's the most adorable black lab puppy just under two years old. It shouldn't be that hard to find him a home. People are so uptight, wanting their pets to be boring mouth breathers with no personality.

"Why don't you adopt him, then, if you love him so much?"

Jack's question is warranted with how many puppy kisses I'm getting right now.

"I would, but Casper and Binx don't particularly like dogs. Plus, I go on business trips for multiple days sometimes,

HER FAVORITE JACK-O-LANTERN

and the cats can take care of themselves, whereas this cutie pie can't. I would feel horrible leaving him with a sitter." I give Sparky's face a good squish and a big kiss.

Jack kneels next to me and shows Sparky just as much love. Sparky is loving the scratching and petting, abandoning me for his larger hands. *I don't blame you, buddy, I would leave me for him, too.*

"What about you? Are you interested in adopting a dog? Sparky seems to like you."

Jack pauses, pondering Chloe's question. "Maybe. I've never had a dog of my own. We had one when I was a kid, but my dad mostly took care of him." Jack gives Sparky another hearty scratch behind the ears.

"You should definitely consider it. Dogs are amazing companions and alarms. You'll always know when someone's near your house."

Chloe is really trying to sell it to Jack now. It doesn't matter who walks through those doors. She'll convince you to adopt a pet in no time.

"I'll think about it," he concedes.

Standing, I watch Jack pet Sparky and then glance up at Chloe, who is staring at me, eyes bugged out. Her gaze shifts abruptly between me and Jack then back to me, tilting her head in question. We then fall into a wordless conversation of eye gestures, raised eyebrows, pursed lips, and mimed motions.

Hers saying, *What in the actual fuck? How did this happen?*

Mine responds. *I have no idea. Stop being weird. You know*

how much I had a crush on him. Yes, I know he's hot.

When Chloe doesn't get the full story and answer, she clears her throat and addresses Jack, pulling his attention from the sixty-pound dog who thinks he's a ten pound lap dog.

"How exactly did you end up helping out Sally?" I stifle a grimace.

"Actually, she's helping me out."

"Oh, is she now?" Chloe turns her wide eyes on me suspicious mirth dancing across her face.

"Yeah. We made a deal. I help her with her decorating, and she shows me around town, refamiliarizing me with where everything is, who everyone is. That kind of thing. I didn't really keep tabs on everything over the past years, and I'm afraid I don't really remember much." He stands and brushes off the dog fur covering his flannel.

Watching him put on that flannel was painful but also therapeutic. The reminder of my ex dumping me pinched at my heart. It always will. The bitter taste of rejection always lingers in his wake.

But seeing Jack put it on and smile, so happy wearing it, released something inside that leeched at my heart. Easing the cold sting into a warm tingle that spread, and I relaxed.

I had bought the flannel as something simple but still in the Halloween spirit for Myles to wear. He didn't like to dress as thematically as I do, so I figured the flannel was a good middle ground. I never got to test my theory, since he dumped me and took back his ring.

HER FAVORITE JACK-O-LANTERN

It looks far better on Jack than it would have on Myles, anyway. He's broader, more muscular, and the shirt hugs his form, accenting the shape of his well-maintained body. So much better on Jack.

"And the matching outfits? That was . . . what? A coincidence?"

I don't hide my eyeroll. Chloe is poking and prodding, and she won't be satisfied until I'm thoroughly embarrassed.

"Do you like it? Sally gave it to me." Shifting to my side, Jack slings one arm around my shoulders, pulling me close, not flush but close. The way we fit together is knee weakening. He's so much taller than me, and I fit right under his arm perfectly.

Chloe keeps a close eye on my reaction, and I try to remain calm, but my racing heart is making that difficult.

"I felt underdressed next to her, so she graciously gifted me the coolest piece of clothing I now own."

"Is that so?"

"Yup. The whole matching thing was an unintentional, happy accident. Don't ya think?"

He has no idea how much Chloe is trying not to laugh right now. But I do. I can see it in the strain in her neck as she bites her lip and nods.

"Oh, yeah. It really is."

She's thinking the same thing as I am. If anyone sees us, they'll assume we're together, and Jack's only been in town three days. They'll all assume I seduced him, and he's an undesired participant. Everything will mark me as the predator and him the unsuspecting victim. They might all think I'm a witch, but if I could cast spells and curses, I would have done so long ago on all of their judgmental asses.

I give Chloe a microscopic shrug. Nothing I can do about it. They'll think whatever they want, anyway. I try not to let it interfere with my life. I'm not always successful.

"Well, I'm sure you two have lots left to do." As Chloe leads Sparky back into his kennel, he whimpers at being removed from all the butt scratches and gives us the biggest puppy-dog eyes known to man.

"We're going to Ma's Diner to decorate," Jack announces.

He's so eager to be helpful he doesn't realize what he's doing.

"That should be fun. Make sure to call me later, Sally, to discuss that matter I mentioned earlier."

That's her code for *call me to tell me how the shit hits the fan.* Because it will, no doubt. Sooner or later.

11 – Sally

Your blood splatter looks more like explosive diarrhea

Ma of Ma's Diner is really Dorothy Lewis. No one has called her Dorothy since she and her husband Ed Lewis opened the diner nearly forty years ago. She's been Ma since day one. It's been a staple in town since then. A place where we all come for birthdays, first dates, midnight shakes, and breakup binge eating. Like the bar in the show Cheer's, where everybody knows your name. Ma knows her customers personally.

I've been decorating the diner for the past three years now, and of the dozen people in town I like, Ma ranks highest on my list.

It's just after the lunch rush when we arrive, arms filled with containers, holding all the decorations for Ma's zombie diner.

"Ma! I'm here," I call out as we stack containers on the floor next to the fifties-style counter lining the length of one wall.

Ma's is nestled in the middle of a strip of stores, longer in length than width, stretching all the way to the back to the open window into the kitchen. Ma believes in transparency and simple fresh ingredients and wants her customers to see that. The food may be greasy, but it's quality grease.

"Sally? Is that you, darlin'?" comes Ma's booming voice from somewhere in the back. She appears in the doorway to the back office. "I have been looking forward to this all week." Ma walks briskly from the back in long elegant strides.

Her movement's second nature through her diner—that's more home than her house just a few miles away. I'm pretty sure she spends more time here than there.

For a woman in her early sixties, she's spry and energetic, no doubt from all the years on her feet in this very establishment. She's plump but strong. Her arms probably have more muscle than mine. Her dark gray hair is pulled up in her customary bun, not a strand out of place. Again, I envy those with tamable hair. Dark green eyes glimmer at me, matching her sparkling smile.

It's weird how people of this town either accept or exclude me. Some of the elderly community think I'm a hoot and love my colorful, fun attire, complimenting me on my style and confidence. While the people my age or my parents' age and everything between mostly dislike my oddness. They look down at me and consider me less than because of my life choices, thinking I'll never succeed to their degree of "adulthood." Then there are the teens, who accept me more than the rest. This new generation is open to all the weirdness. Unfortunately, I don't mingle with teenagers. Why couldn't teenagers be this cool when I was one?

Ma lifts the hinged bar top and pulls me into a warm, tight hug.

"You look beautiful today, my dear." Ma always compliments me, believing everyone deserves at least one positive word of affirmation a day. "The ears are a nice touch." She pulls away and gives me once-over.

That's when she notices Jack standing behind me, much closer than one would expect. Her head cocks in question, hands resting on her apron-clad hips. Typical response, even from people like Ma.

"Jack Campbell, all grown up and back home, I see. Your mother told me you were moving back. It's so good to see you." With another grandmotherly embrace, she hugs Jack, who eagerly reciprocates.

"It's good to see you, too, ma'am. I've missed your milkshakes. The army just doesn't know how to make a proper one."

"I would think not. No one can make a shake like mine." She scoffs. Inspecting Jack, she squeezes his arms and pokes his stomach. "You look a little thin. We should get you something to eat."

He chuckles, smiling down at her. Like most people, she's shorter than Jack but taller than me. He is anything but thin, he's thick with muscles and broad shoulders.

"I would like that very much, ma'am, but I'm here to help Sally."

"Is that so?" She eyes him skeptically.

"Why do people keep questioning it like it's so unbelievable?" Jack's smile falters, and he scowls down at Ma—not angrily but obviously displeased with everyone's reaction to us together, even just as friends.

Ma stammers, clearly taken aback by his blunt question. I don't think she realized what she was really saying when she asked. "Oh . . . I . . . well, you just got back, and it's unexpected is all. I can't speak for others, but I don't mean nothin' by it."

Patting his chest, she turns back to me and slips back into jovial conversation, leaving behind the brief awkwardness. "Now what have you got for me this year, Sally? I'm dying to see these decorations."

Opening containers and bags, I quickly run through what I've prepared and plan to do with everything. When listing it all out like this, I'm happy to have a helper. I didn't realize I had created so much work for myself, especially things that require long arms to reach.

"Well, it looks like you two have your work cut out for you. I'll leave you to it, and if you need anything, you just holler. And when you get hungry, you let me know. I'll cook you up somethin' good."

HER FAVORITE JACK-O-LANTERN

"Yes, ma'am."

Hearing Jack say ma'am is oddly sweet. Not many people are that properly polite anymore. It's endearing, and I like it almost as much as him calling me pumpkin or sweetheart, which he hasn't done since that conversation, but his voice still echoes in my ear.

Ma pats Jack's cheek and winks at me before returning behind the counter. Why did she just wink at me? Does she mean something by that? I'm so confused. She's never done that before, and I have no idea what to make of it. I shake it off and get to work, directing Jack and handing him items.

While we're stringing lights under the bar countertop, Jack surprises me with a question I didn't expect.

"So, what's the story with this ex you mentioned earlier?"

He says it nonchalantly, like we talk about this stuff all the time. I've barely had three full conversations with him, and he's already prying for the good stuff.

My body uncontrollably jumps, and I whack my head on the underside of the counter, cursing under my breath and rubbing at the welt no doubt forming on my head.

"Oh, shit. Are you okay? I didn't mean to make you hurt yourself." Jack rubs at the spot on my head, his fingers brushing against my own.

Once again, slowly threading around mine but not holding on, like they did in my backyard holding the pumpkins he saved. The delicate touch made me tingle then, and it makes me tingle now.

It's so unexpected and flustering that I have no idea how

to respond to his subtle attentions. They feel like flirting, but that can't be right. Guys don't flirt with me, especially attractive, sweet guys like Jack.

While his sleeves are rolled up, I've stripped out of my sweater. All the physical work and proximity to Jack has me working up a sweat. Our bodies are almost plastered together under the low bar while I place the lights, and he attaches them with the command hooks. It's been difficult to focus, to say the least and my temperature hasn't cooled in the slightest. Especially with our fingers tangled against my head, his face close to mine, inspecting my possible wound. As usual, my throat has forgotten how to make words, and I stare at him, breathing heavily.

I am such a freak.

"Doesn't look like you're bleeding. I think you'll live," he jokes with a soft, reassuring smile. Unfortunately, his hand returns to the string of lights.

"That's good, I guess. I was worried for a moment I'd become part of the zombie brains decorations."

Why is that what comes out of my mouth when it finally decides to speak words? I am so weird, and he is going to realize it any second now and run screaming from the diner.

Instead of staring at me like a monkey jerking off in the zoo, Jack laughs. *Laughs.* And not at me but with me. The sparkle in his eyes eases my awkward tension enough that I give him a slightly self-deprecating chuckle. But even my self-inflicted injury isn't enough to deter him from finding out about my ex because he reiterates his question.

"So, about this dumbass ex of yours . . . ?"

"What makes you think he's a dumbass?"

He stifles a snort but doesn't seem at all embarrassed about it. Not like I would be. "He must be. I could tell by the way you acted when you mentioned him. He definitely did something wrong, and I'd like to know what."

He wants me to explain the whole sorted history? I glazed over it earlier for a reason. He's possibly the only one in town who doesn't know what happened, and I kind of like it that way. But the way he's looking at me says I won't get away with brushing it off again.

"Um . . . he didn't really do anything. Just the same old story. It didn't work out, and we broke up."

The side-eye he gives me suggests he's not believing that one bit.

"Sure didn't sound like just a normal breakup to me."

"I guess it wasn't completely typical. But it wouldn't be the first time it happened to someone."

There's a pause in our conversation as we shift and move to the next section. Unfortunately, he doesn't drop the subject as I would have hoped he would.

"And what exactly did happen to you?"

I gnaw on my bottom lip. I opted out of lipstick today so I don't have to worry about eating it. I take a few breaths before answering. "We were engaged. He wasn't just my boyfriend. He was my fiancé."

Jack's hands still, and I can feel him searching my face, but I don't turn to look at him. It's hard enough to admit out loud, I don't need to see his beautiful face while doing it. Might as well get it over with. It doesn't seem like he's accepting my vague answer.

"He didn't want to marry someone who 'acted like a child, pretending every day was Halloween,' or so he told me."

"He actually said that to you?"

His voice is low and rough, and I can't quite make out if he's disgusted, surprised, or just curious.

"Yeah. Apparently, he thought my whole creepy Halloween obsession was just a phase that I would grow out of. But when we started planning the wedding and he learned I wanted a dark gothic theme set in a haunted mansion with a cemetery on the grounds and a black wedding dress, I guess he realized it wasn't. He gave me an ultimatum, give up that—which makes me *me*, stop wearing black clothes covered in bats and dress like a normal girl, OR break up." I inhale a long breath through my nose and let it out slowly through my mouth. "I thought I loved him. I thought he loved me. But, in the end, he didn't really love me. He loved the idea of having a wife, someone he could dress like a doll and control like a puppet. That wasn't what I wanted to be. How could I give up everything I loved just to make him happy? It didn't seem right. So, I didn't."

Silence greets my confession. The sounds of the patrons in the diner dull around us, clinking silverware and muffled chatter doesn't fully register in my brain.

All I can hear are the heavy breaths coming from Jack

less than a foot away from me, the shift of clothing as he adjusts his position bent down on one knee. A gentle hand tentatively cups my cheek to turn my face to his. His normally bright sea-blue eyes are stormy and hard. I imagine this is what he looked like in the army. Stoic and filled with firm determination.

He says nothing at first, just bores into me with those storm-cloud eyes and a surprisingly tender grip on my chin, ensuring I can't look away. I want to, but I couldn't even if I tried. No man has ever shown so much of himself to me in one look, exposing the harsh lines of his insides that I just know not many have seen. My skin tingles where his fingers linger on my chin, a rippling awareness of our proximity and intimate embrace. *People could be watching.*

"Whoever this idiot is, he is no man. Because no real man would treat a woman, especially one as astonishing as you, with such disrespect. He didn't deserve you, and you made the right decision."

That's the first time anyone other than Peyton or Chloe has taken my side in the breakup. People assumed my Halloween obsession drove him over the edge and that I pushed him away with my craziness. In a way I had, but he tried to get me to change for him, and people agreed I should have curtailed my "hobby" to appease him. Like it was all my fault, that I brought it on myself and had to deal with the consequences. As if he had no part in lying to me about loving me and accepting me for who I am.

The unexpected praise has my body heating to almost

unbearable, my insides melting to goo. The air in my lungs nearly evaporates inside the oven that is my chest.

I can faintly feel his thumb stroke my face, dangerously near my lips. The urge to suck on it has me snapping my mouth shut and clenching my thighs together against the unexpected ache.

A smile rivaling the sun flashes across his face, morphing it from serious storm clouds to lighthearted delight.

"Come on, Pumpkin, we still have a lot to do."

"Yes, sir."

It takes me at least fifteen minutes to calm myself and speak without stuttering like a fool or whimpering like a lovesick puppy dog for Jack.

"Can I ask you a question? Since you asked me one, I figure you owe me."

"That seems fair. What's your question?"

We move from the bar counter, having finished with the lights, and return to the front of the diner to apply the fake dripping blood down the front windows. Jack drips the washable paint from the top of the window, while I hold the can below.

"Why did you join the army?"

—Jack—

My hand freezes, paintbrush dangling, startled by my own visceral reaction to her simple question. Those closest to me know my reasons, but everyone else was left to make their own assumptions. They probably think I did it out of some altruistic reason of patriotism and duty and honor. That couldn't be farther from the truth.

After a pause, I return to painting the window, reluctantly beginning the tale that led to the last eight years of my life in the army.

"Do you remember Jordan? He was in my class in high school."

"Yeah, I remember him."

Of course she would. Even classes now know who he was. At least the story of him. There's still a memorial statue for him in the quad of Laconia High School, some contemporary sculpture meant to symbolize his youth and personality. I have no idea if it fits him, but his name is engraved on it along with an excerpt from a poem written by William Blake.

> *"To see the world in a grain of sand*
> *And a Heaven in a wildflower*
> *Hold infinity in the palm of your hand*
> *And eternity in an hour"*
> *In Memory of Jordan Welsch*

I think it's supposed to instill in us our mortality, to remind us that life is short and finite. A lesson I learned all too well.

"Before the accident, we were talking about what we wanted to do after high school. I told him about my plan to go to college, although I had no idea what I wanted to major in. Something broad and easy that could be applied to a variety of careers. I assumed Jordan would be going to Yale or Harvard or somewhere just as prestigious and make his brain even brainier. But he surprised me when he said he wanted to join the army. He wanted to give back and do something that mattered. To be someone who mattered. To do more with his life than just make a lot of money and buy expensive things. Going into the army was his dream. After he died, going to college to party, and, in all sense of the word, be a loser, just sounded selfish."

Small delicate fingers tipped in black wrap around my forearm, stilling my movements. For a long heartbeat I stare at her hand resting on my arm, her fingers unable to completely circle my muscles. A contradiction made physical. One I don't dislike. That looks appealing, and I wouldn't mind seeing more of it.

"Did you know the accident was my fault?"

The words slip past my lips faster than I can hold them in. It's for the best. I need to admit it out loud at some point. The military therapist tried to squeeze it out of me on many occasions. She never got the whole story. She didn't need it, didn't deserve it. For some reason I feel Sally does. She makes me feel tranquil in her presence, soothing the prickled, rough edges chafing the inside of my ribs ever since the accident.

"What?" Sally asks, not in anger or pity, just curiosity. "I thought Jordan was driving?"

I clear my throat and take another look at her hand on my arm. It steadies me enough to admit the truth. "He was. But he was only in the car driving because of me."

Sally's brow pinches as I watch her watch me, those entrancing lilac eyes of hers soft but concerned.

"I don't understand."

Well, here goes nothing. She'll either pity me, be disgusted by me, or think I'm a fool. None of which I want to see in those beautiful eyes. And yet I'm still going to tell her because I want nothing hidden between us. Strange, considering I've only known her a few days, and I couldn't even tell my therapist I saw for three years.

"I was drunk at a house party. I don't even remember whose. I was going to drive home, even though I'd been drinking. Jordan stopped me. Usually, he wasn't even at those parties, but since high school was almost over, we had convinced him to come out. He, of course, was sober and took my keys, forcing me into the passenger's seat, so he could drive."

Jordan was the guy everyone could count on, the levelheaded one who always made the right decisions. Unlike me, the one that made decisions based on the level of danger and excitement. The higher chances of intoxication and nudity, the more I wanted to do it. People always saw me as the smiling jock, the friendly guy who would help clean up after a food fight in the cafeteria, the one all the parents liked, but that was only because I made sure never to get caught. Not that I wasn't that nice guy everyone knew, I just wasn't the perfect kid they all thought I was.

I partied, I drank, I fucked. I just did it off school property and away from the prying eyes of teachers and adults. In the end, I suppose it didn't matter. It caught up with me all the same.

"If I'd been more mature and just crashed on the couch or not drank so much, he wouldn't have been in that car. He wouldn't have been trying to get me to stop climbing out the window to howl at the moon. He wouldn't have drifted across the line into oncoming traffic. We wouldn't have crashed into that car."

The words choke in my throat, and it feels like I may never clear the blockage. That is until Sally reaches out and gently rotates me to face her straight on, slipping her hand into my free one. My grip has become a vise, clamping the paintbrush, hindering her ability to hold both my hands. So, her grip remains on my wrist instead.

She gives me her full attention, her focus on me and my words. Not the handful of patrons eating casually around us, unaware of the fracturing of my soul as I admit my deepest regret to a woman I only just met.

Sally may have known who I was in high school, but I

never knew her. And I'm regretting that now, too. I realize my time in the army was not just to assuage my guilt but to make up for my utter tomfoolery as an adolescent.

With her reassuring squeeze, I continue.

"It's a miracle the driver of the other car lived. It's a miracle I lived, but, apparently, that's what happens when you're drunk and in a car accident. Your body goes limp and loose and barely feels the effects. Jordan wasn't so lucky. Anyway, that's why I joined the army. For him. To do what he couldn't."

Sally's thumb rubs small circles on the soft skin on the back of my hand. It's . . . grounding. Securing me here in the present, returning me from the past but not my guilt.

"His death wasn't your fault, Jack. You can't punish yourself for something that can't be changed. You can only look ahead to the future." Her head tilts, and her expression changes as something shifts in her thoughts. "Is that why you need my help looking for a job?"

Thankful for the change in subject, I let out a slow but heavy breath, the edge of my lips quirking. "Yeah. I have no idea what to do with myself now."

"And you think going around town will . . . spark some sort of realization?"

Regrettably, her hands release mine, and a drop of red paint falls to the floor and lands on the canvas Sally insisted on laying out. I see now why.

"I guess I just figured putting myself out there, back into life as a civilian, would at least force me to figure it out."

"Does this mean you're contemplating being a professional window painter? Because I would highly advise against it. Your blood splatter looks more like explosive diarrhea."

A deep, throaty laugh bubbles in my chest, and I can literally feel my muscles unclenching, releasing the tension from our conversation. The taut string inside my gut eases, Sally's smile returning.

I take in my attempt at art on the windows and cringe. "Do you think if we tell Ma it's supposed to be exploded brains, she'll believe us?"

Giving my atrocious painting another once-over, Sally scrunches her cute nose and grimaces. "I don't think so. Why don't you quit while you're ahead and let me finish."

"You know, I think you're right. I fear I may only make it worse."

As I pass her the paintbrush, my fingers brush hers, and the *whoosh* of blood in my ears has me missing the jingle of the doorbell and the subsequent footsteps of whoever entered—until that high-pitched voice I would know even if I went deaf rings out behind Sally.

"Oh my goodness, Jack Campbell. What a surprise."

12 – Jack

I'd probably snub her with the flourish of a circus ringleader

Sally's hand freezes on mine when we both hear a rather loud, feminine voice call out my name. Above Sally's head, I see Daphne Brighton, ex-prom queen, ex-head cheerleader, and my ex-girlfriend. Mahogany-colored hair flows around her stunned face, but I have a feeling she knew exactly where I was.

When we were dating, she would pull the same face, feigned surprise, when she knew exactly what was going on. She was good at that. Faking it. Faking her affection for me, her friendliness toward others, her compliance, her perfect grades, her orgasms. All her grades were bought, and she was as far from well behaved, as I was.

Maybe that's what initially drew me to her. The secret, hidden bad girl. But she wasn't a bad girl. She was a mean girl with a pretty layer of polish to make her shine like a good girl. Eventually, I saw through her façade and ended it. That didn't keep her from trying to crawl back inside my pants, and I regretfully admit I had let her. More than once.

That's most likely why she's hunted me down my first week back in town. Because I know for damn sure she isn't coming to Ma's of her own choice. She always told me Ma's was for "poor, ugly people who couldn't afford better." She's a rich bitch snob if I ever met one.

From the looks of it, she hasn't changed much other than having some work done. Her lips are a little fuller, her breasts a little larger—still not as nice as Sally's—and when she smiles, there are no wrinkles at her temple, which must be due to Botox.

If her family weren't one of the most influential and well connected in the county, I'd probably snub her with the flourish of a circus ringleader. As it is in small towns, though, if I were to outright insult her in public, that would make the rest of my family's lives uncomfortable.

I once witnessed her single-handedly destroy a person's life without even one ounce of suspicion thrown her way. She has a way of manipulating situations to her desired outcome. Telling her no in public with witnesses will only fuel her ire. That is not my intention first thing back home. So, I play the dutiful good army boy and greet her politely. Trying to smile without cringing.

"Daphne. What a surprise."

She brushes past Sally, as if she's not even there, hip-checking her just enough to push her out of the way. Without permission, she presses her hands flat against my chest and invades my personal space. If there wasn't a wall behind me, I would back away.

"I can't believe you've been back in town for days and haven't come to see me," she pouts.

Her dull brown eyes, which remind me of cold, bitter tea, turn up to me, trying to be cute and doe-like but failing miserably.

"I've been busy."

"Well, we're here now. We should catch up." Her claw-like nails scrape across my chest, and a cold shiver climbs up my spine.

Deliberately, I pull her hands from my chest and guide her away from the red painted window I'm dangerously close to jumping through to escape her.

"It's nice to see you Daphne, but I'm busy right now," I say, trying to lace my words with sincerity. It's difficult to execute, and I end up somewhere in the flat, bored tone.

Daphne tries to scrunch up her nose and be adorable like Sally but falls short since the Botox in her face won't let her do more than squint her eyes at me. She's only twenty-six. Why did she need so much work done? Where Sally is soft and natural, Daphne is sharp and plastic.

Outwardly, she looks pristine and perfect, with the proper amount of makeup to look natural but not be natural. Her clothing is, no doubt, designer and without a single wrinkle or stitch out of place. Inwardly, she's a tangled knot of deception and arrogance.

She bites her fingernail, pursing her glossy pink lips, trying to be seductive, making sure I notice her bare ring finger.

Great, she's single. This is going to be a nightmare. Dealing with Daphne hadn't even crossed my mind. I figured she would have ensnared one of the other wealthy family heirs and forced him into marriage by now. She wasn't even a blip on my radar. Now red lights are flashing and blaring alarms are trying to warn me away. But it's too late. The enemy has landed, and I'm left with my pants around my ankles, unarmed and undefended. You'd think I would be better prepared for such an attack, yet all the training in the military couldn't prepare me for Daphne Brighton.

"Doing what?"

She acts all innocent, like she didn't just interrupt me and Sally. Like she didn't see me painting through the window before entering.

Looking around my shoulder, she glares at Sally. Thankfully, she's turned her back to us to organize the fake blood and tools and doesn't see the almost imperceptible narrowed glare. "Doesn't look like you're doing anything to me. What could be more important than catching up with an old friend?"

She's goading me, and she knows it. Sally clearly knows it, too, if the stiffening of her shoulders is any inclination.

"I've already promised Sally I would help her today."

The grin she gives me is menacing, and I don't like it

one bit. Especially when she firmly plants one hand on her cocked hip. Her face shifting to that feigned sweetness with upturned brows, fluttering eyelashes, and downturned pout.

"I'm sure Sally wouldn't mind parting with you. I mean, it has been eight long years since we've seen each other after all. She wouldn't want to infringe on our reunion." Raising one eyebrow, she shifts her gaze again to Sally, and the urge to step in her line of sight to shield her nearly overcomes me. It takes great effort to stand still and not sneer. Relaxing my face, I settle it into indifference. If she catches even a whiff of affection toward Sally, I have no doubt she'll make this ten times worse.

"Do you, Sally? You don't mind if I steal Jack away to reacquaint ourselves with one another?"

It's phrased as a question, but there's no request in her tone. She's telling Sally what she's going to do.

If I weren't so intimately familiar with Daphne and her ways, I would think she's being sweet and considerate, which is exactly what she wants people to think.

From the corner of my eye, I catch the orange twirl of color and can feel Sally's disdain and apprehension radiating from her. Apparently, I'm not the only one acquainted with Daphne's true self.

"Of course not, Daphne. I wouldn't dream of interfering with your reunion. I'm sure Jack would love to catch up with you."

No, I wouldn't, and I'm positive Sally was enjoying spending time with me. She's just afraid of angering Daphne, and I don't blame her. If she's anything like she was in high school, I can only imagine what she's capable of now as an adult.

"I don't think that's a good idea right now, Daphne. Perhaps we can schedule something for later—"

"Don't be silly. Sally understands and doesn't mind. Come. I'll take you to dinner, and we can catch up."

Rounding on me, she laces her arm through mine and holds on like a vise. It would be obvious if I tried to shake her off. I try to put space between our bodies, but she's like Velcro at my side.

"I . . . um . . . but Sally's my ride. We carpooled here." I turn to Sally for support.

She is my ride, and this is my last-ditch effort to brush off Daphne. But she's already returned to her containers of decorations, loudly shuffling things about and not fooling anyone.

"It's okay. I can drop you off. It's no bother at all. I would love to."

"Sally?" I call out, a soft-spoken plea.

She doesn't turn but stops, a roll of black duct tape gripped tightly in one hand. "It's fine, Jack. I'm almost done here anyway. You should go with Daphne. Catch up with your friend."

There's hurt in her tone but ice in her words. She won't fight this. Not many people would stand up to Daphne. The day someone puts her in her place, I can only hope to be present to witness it. But that day is not today. This is not the hill worth dying on.

"Okay, as long as you're fine with it. I made a promise to you, and I don't go back on my word. If you need me, I'll stay."

For a moment, I think she will say yes, to admit she still needs me and give me an escape route from spending a meal listening to Daphne's tinny voice. But she doesn't. She shakes her head and rummages through the boxes. Her eyes never making contact with mine.

"No. No. I'll be fine. You just go."

Resignation settles around us both, and I know there's no way I'm getting out of this now, not without making a scene.

"All right. I'll talk to you later, then."

I say my goodbyes to Ma, then Sally, who doesn't acknowledge me with much more than a wave over her shoulder. I'll apologize for Daphne's behavior later. Maybe I'll bring her one of those pumpkin spice cupcakes she likes so much as a peace offering.

Daphne drives us to the country club—where all the wealthy families in this town are members—in her annoyingly fancy Mercedes. It's connected to a golf range, tennis courts, indoor swimming pools, saunas, ballrooms, a bar, and the restaurant.

I'm forced to endure two hours of tiny food portions of unrecognizable, "edible" things, a one sided conversation from Daphne chronologizing the last eight years, and countless reintroductions to people she thinks are important.

Most people she introduces me to are people from high school that I've all but forgotten, people in positions of influence in the community, and other women of the club. I'm pretty sure she's showing me off like a new piece of jewelry draped around her neck. It's sickening and degrading.

I'm finally able to convince her to leave and drive me home with excuses of unpacking, even though I have nothing left to unpack.

When a preening Daphne drops me off at my house and nearly invites herself in, there's a new pumpkin on my porch next to the cemetery one I carved yesterday. This one is a white skull, it's head bursting with exploding brains made of pumpkin guts.

Even after spending the evening with Daphne and wanting nothing more than to escape her, I pause to get a good look at the pumpkin. I don't dare look to Sally's house. Daphne, no doubt, already knows she's my neighbor. But when I'm safely inside, I take a quick peek out the window to see if I can spot Sally. I can't, but I know she's in there, and she knows I'm in here. My fascination with Sally is only growing, and the more time I spend with her, the more I want to know about her. Like the fact that she donates pumpkin seeds to the local bakery every October and knows rescue dogs by name at the animal shelter. And even though people in town think she's a freak, she still decorates the businesses with a smile. Dressing however she wants, being unapologetically her.

The flannel she gave me hangs on the hook by my front

door, waiting for its next use. It won't have to wait long. I plan on wearing it frequently. *Is that weird?* Should I not wear the same shirt multiple days in a row? I wore the same exact thing every day in the army, and a flannel is more like a jacket or sweater, right? So, when I wear it tomorrow, no one will care.

That's my logic, and I'm sticking to it.

13 – Sally

Minus the sociopathic tendancies and homicidal rage

Yesterday was a fluke. It had to be because no one like Jack would willingly spend time with me and be so friendly—and dare I say *flirty*.

Daphne arriving to whisk him away made it that much clearer. We're from two different worlds. He belongs in that shiny, perfect world of Botox and country clubs with Daphne, while I belong in my dark freak world of skeletons and bats. Alone.

Today starts off a lot less optimistic than yesterday but a lot more realistic. It's an all-black kind of day. Channeling Wednesday Addams, I pick out my all-black dress with white collar and cuffs, black opaque striped tights, platform two-toned Oxfords, and a black wide brimmed fedora. If I tried, I'm sure I could blend in with a shadow.

HER FAVORITE JACK-O-LANTERN

    Today, I'm decorating the hardware store and the gym, but both of those are simple jobs, nothing as detailed as Ma's or Daphne's.

    Ugh. Daphne. I have to see her tomorrow, and I'm sure she'll, no doubt, tell me all about her time with Jack, rubbing it in like salt in a wound and be all too happy to do it.

    Daphne rarely focuses on me, thinking me beneath her manicured status. Not even important enough to gossip about. I like it that way. She ignores me, except for twice a year, when I decorate her window display. I avoid her as much as humanly possible. It's a good system that works well for us.

    It's harder to ignore Jack. Hard to ignore him leaving with her. Hard to ignore him coming home with her. Though, thankfully, she stayed in her car and didn't go inside with him. If she had, I may have died a little inside. Sure, he offered to stay if said I needed him. But there was no way I could say anything against Daphne. He shouldn't be spending time with me, anyways. I'm not his "people." I don't have long perfectly styled hair, daddy's bank account, and a Mercedes. I don't frequent the country club and spend summers in the Hamptons. I don't get mani-pedi's with the girls on a Thursday afternoon while drinking mimosas and scrolling through my Insta feed.

    Venturing downstairs, I ignore the windows, not wanting to see Jack out back working out again. I take my time making breakfast, which consists of a toasted bagel with cream cheese. With my bagel halfway in my mouth, I still at the sound of my doorbell. *No one rings my doorbell.* No one ever comes over to my house. Not even my family. So, who the hell is at my front door?

Dropping my bagel on my plate, I quickly chew the bite in my mouth while making my way to the front door. Peering out through the peephole, I see Jack on my porch. He's holding a white pastry bag and wearing the orange flannel I gave him—this time, with a white shirt and black pants.

A giddy little bubble pops in my stomach, and I can't stop my smile from spreading. Jack looks positively boyish as he nervously shifts his weight from one foot to the other and rubs the back of his short hair with his free hand.

Why is he here?

Opening the door is the only way I'll find out. After flipping the lock, I open the door to Jack, who stands tall and watches me eagerly.

"Jack—"

"Wow. You're a real-life Wednesday Addams, aren't you?" he exclaims.

"Minus the sociopathic tendencies and homicidal rage."

It's not the first time I've gotten the comment. He laughs, I laugh. It feels good to laugh with Jack.

"What are you doing here?"

"I brought you this." The white pastry bag is unceremoniously shoved into my hands, giving me no chance at refusal. "I wanted to apologize for Daphne yesterday. That wasn't polite of her to interfere with our work. But it's . . . hard to tell her no."

I bet it is.

"It's fine. You two are old friends. Isn't she your ex-girlfriend?"

I damn well know she is. I still remember the day they broke up. It was a wonderful day. He even spoke to me. Nothing more than an "Oh, sorry, I didn't see you there," but it still counts.

Damn. I was pathetic in high school. I guess little has changed. I still get excited flutters when Jack talks to me. At least now he knows my name.

"Yeah, we were." He seems to grimace, but I can't get a good look at his face as he turns to look out at the street as a car passes.

Shoving his hand in his back pockets, he rocks back on his heels, far more at ease than he was when I was watching him through the peephole.

"So, are we still on for decorating today?" he asks.

Does he not want to talk about Daphne because they started something up again last night? It's not out of the realm of possibilities. He doesn't seem like her type, the egotistical prick type, but I may be seeing him through sherbet-colored glasses. Maybe he's into that kind of thing. The bright-and-shiny-and-perfectly-polished type. And that, most certainly, is not me.

My surprise is quick but fleeting, replaced with a confused affection.

"You still want to help me?"

"Of course I do. Why wouldn't I?"

He appears slightly offended I would even think such a thing of him. I don't, but I also didn't expect him to show up with—sniffing, I open the bag to see the most beautiful sight in the world: two large frosted pumpkin spice cupcakes. My favorite.

"How did you know these are my favorite?"

"I didn't, but I did notice you had one when I bumped into you at the coffee shop and then you bought one when we went to the bakery. I figured I couldn't go wrong with one. So, I bought two."

"Smart man."

"I like to think so."

Once again, we drive with all the decorations stacked in the back, where caskets usually go. Jack is oddly comfortable riding in my hearse. He even seems to like it. He doesn't even notice when people turn their heads to look at us when we stop at a red light.

First, we go to Hanson's Hardware. Mr. Hanson is ecstatic to see his skull pumpkin and places it right by the register. We decorate his counter and front window, then move on to the Power Fitness.

I had expected Jack to be interested in the gym, since

HER FAVORITE JACK-O-LANTERN

he seems to like working out every morning and is clearly physically fit. I was right. The kid who works the front check-in desk offers Jack a tour, and he eagerly accepts.

I string lights, hang origami bats, and place the jack-o-lanterns while he can't stop talking about signing up for a membership and checking out the classes they offer. It's the first time since he's returned that I've seen him show interest in something.

"You're really into fitness, aren't you?"

His smile is ridiculously dazzling and adorably cute.

"It was what I liked best about the army. The physicality of pushing myself to my limits to be the best version of me. Their motto is 'Be all you can be' for a reason."

Jack takes the origami bat from my hands and hooks it on a string far out of my reach, not even having to ask what to do. If he doesn't find a job in town, maybe I can hire him as an assistant. The arm reach alone would be worth it. I can't pay him much. Maybe he'll take pumpkins and baked goods as payment.

"What else did you like about being in the army?"

Since learning he only enlisted to satiate the guilt he had over Jordan's death, I've been curious to know if there was anything about being in the military that he enjoyed.

He shrugs one shoulder. "It was rewarding knowing I was there to defend my country and family if needed. I met a lot of great people, learned a lot of new things. Shooting big-ass guns was pretty fun, too."

We settle into a comfortable conversation that flows

from one topic to the next, making our time decorating pass quickly. As we're cleaning up, our conversation rolls around to Halloween and the events and parties happening in the next couple of weeks.

"Do they still do that pumpkin festival like they used to? I remember it being a lot of fun."

"Oh, yeah. Still the biggest party in town."

"When is it?"

"A week from Saturday. They block off Main Street and make a whole street fair out of it. There are games, food, live music, a fun house, a couple carnival rides, and, of course, plenty of jack-o-lanterns. They line the street with them. Practically everyone in town brings one, and we vote on which is the best."

Jack picks up the empty container we used to bring in the decorations and leads me out to the parking lot like a gentleman.

"What do you win if you get the most votes?"

"A ribbon and a gift card to whichever business donated to it this year. And, of course, bragging rights for a whole year."

"Of course." He agrees while loading the boxes into the back of my hearse. "Why else would you want to win a jack-o-lantern contest? Have you ever won? I feel like with your skills you should win every year."

"No." I shake my head, my voice growing small. "I don't enter."

Jack pops out from behind the back door, staring at me,

his eyebrows in his hairline. "Well, that makes no sense. You're the pumpkin queen."

A blush creeps up my cheeks, and I let out a girlish giggle. "I don't know about that."

I use getting into my car as a distraction to calm my pulse, ducking behind my door and sliding into my driver seat. He follows suit, circling to the passenger side, and gracefully falling into his seat.

"Seriously, why don't you enter the jack-o-lantern contest?" he asks again, once we're buckled in and idling in the parking lot.

I grip the steering wheel, inhaling through my nose and exhaling a shaky breath before answering. "I did one year. Even though it was by far the best carving of the bunch, everyone knew it was mine and ... voted for someone else."

The admission is small and painful.

He sneers in disgust. "What is with these people? You'd think a town that holds a pumpkin festival every year would be more inclined to appreciate your love of Halloween."

I grunt acknowledgment but say nothing else. There is nothing else to say. It would be a waste of breath.

"Well, I think you should enter. Maybe this year will be different."

"Not likely," I mumble as I pull out of the parking lot and drive us home.

This was a horrible idea. I should have never brought Jack along to decorate Daphne's store. It's Friday, and the only store we have today is hers. Ever since we arrived an hour ago Daphne has not only interrupted to flirt with Jack but so have her customers. We're barely getting anything done with how many times we've had to stop due to intrusions of the "Oh my goodness, Jack" type. It's like every single woman is shopping at Daphne's today. I'm pretty sure every female in his graduating class has walked through that door and feigned surprise at seeing him here.

I wouldn't doubt one of Daphne's minions got the word out. Daphne herself wouldn't have done it because she would want him all for herself. Maybe she already does and the others are hoping to dissuade him. Whatever it may be, they all smile and greet Jack and ignore me, their eyes not even stopping as they scan past to Jack.

Because I'm not a stuck-up Barbie doll, I could tell you each of their names. I would bet every cent I own that none could tell you mine beyond "Halloween freak."

Daphne's Delight is a store made for, well . . . Daphnes, women who like to dress in glittery pastels and tiny floral patterns. It's lined with the latest in trendy fashion and accessories, purses that cost more than a car payment, and brand labels that normally wouldn't be available outside brand stores. Polished crystal chandeliers hang from the ceiling lined with bohemian tapestries and gold filigree-framed mirrors lean against the walls. Unlike most typical stores, Daphne's doesn't carry high quantities. She purposely

HER FAVORITE JACK-O-LANTERN

limits her stock to create demand and prestige. The racks are spaced out, with only half a dozen of any item in limited sizes. Daphne's is most definitely not inclusive in the least.

If she didn't pay me six hundred dollars to decorate her window, I would never set foot in this place.

When Daphne started building it a few years back, I just knew it would be pretentious and insipid. Daphne Brighton was too good for existing buildings and had to purchase empty land at the end of Main Street, erecting what looks like a metal and glass box for her precious store.

The store stands at the newer end of Main Street, where stores have been updated or are new businesses. While, at the opposite end of the street, the classic old trip lies: Ma's Diner, The Coffee Bean, and my favorite antique secondhand store.

People praise the Brightons for helping reinvigorate Main Street, but I don't appreciate unique brick architecture being covered or completely removed. There are other ways to update the old strip stores other than ripping them out.

"Jack," Daphne singsongs as, for the fourth time, she inserts herself, delaying our progress *again*. "Why don't you just let Sally finish everything up, and you and I go grab some brunch at the club? I'm sure mommy and daddy would love to see you again."

Mommy and daddy? Is she four years old? What twenty-six-year-old still calls their parents mommy and daddy? I barely want to call mine mother and father.

Jack steps down from the platform of the large display

window to speak with Daphne. I don't know if he does it to get closer to her, farther from me, or to keep her from me. Either way, I appreciate the distance from Daphne but dislike her closeness to Jack. A skitter of ice prickles up my back, while my stomach hollows out every time I hear her voice.

"I don't think so, Daphne. I made a promise, and I already ran out on Sally the other day, and we still have a lot of work to do."

His tone is flat and uninterested, but she soldiers on.

"It's Sally's job. I pay her to do it, not you."

"Well, she's paying me."

"In what? Pumpkin seeds and animal bones? Besides, she does this alone every year. She doesn't need you." She grins and bats her eyelashes, fingering the buttons on his flannel.

"She may not need me, but I'm only here because of her. We have a deal, and unlike some people, I don't flake on my commitments for brunch at the club."

He doesn't raise his voice or lace anger in his tone, but he doesn't need to. Words are plenty enough.

Daphne guffaws at him, chuffing like a gorilla trying to save face. Pinching her glossy lips together, she tries not to look like she was rejected in the most indifferent way.

"Right, of course not. You're an honorable man who sticks to his word. That's a sexy quality in a guy."

Gag.

"We'll just go another time, then. When you're not busy.

I'm sure Sally doesn't have many stores left to decorate, as she always tends to leave mine for last."

Now she's back to her bitter, nasty self, like the affront of his rejection never happened.

Seriously, can nothing bring her down a notch or twelve? I don't even think explosive diarrhea from food poisoning would affect her. Shame. I'd like to see that. From afar.

To my utmost shock, Jack doesn't appease her or schedule a time to have dinner with her. He stands there, looking down at her silently, then turns back to the display window. Easily climbing up the large ledge with those powerful long legs of his., slipping back into what he was doing before her hissy fit.

Trying not to stare, I keep my eyes trained on what I'm doing while watching her reflection in the glass. First, she's shocked, staring at Jack's back, then she turns her gaze on me. Not so shocked anymore but livid. Fucking great. Where I normally fly under her radar, I now have a giant target on my back.

Like I said before: big mistake bringing him here. But when Jack insists, there seems to be no telling the man no. There also appears to be no way to force him to say yes, either.

14 – Jack

I just didn't mention it was in sexual favors

Outside Daphne's Delights, Sally and I pack up her hearse with empty containers and boxes, and I can tell she is ready to be free of this platinum hellscape. Everything about this morning has been uncomfortable with Daphne. She's far more aggressive now than she was in high school, and that's saying something. I was trying to be professional when I rejected her brunch offer. She didn't seem to grasp the concept well. It's a miracle she can manage a store at all and keep it running.

I Know Sally wants to get as far away from here as possible, but I haven't wandered through Main Street and seen everything that's changed. Plus, I was hoping to spend more time with her, maybe have lunch at Ma's, a far more pleasurable prospect than the club with Daphne. And I won't let Daphne ruin our day.

Before Sally can swan dive into her car and burn rubber out of here, I casually intercept her and lean on her door.

"Got any plans for the rest of the day?"

"Not really. I usually need a good detox after a morning spent with Daphne."

I laugh and then laugh harder when I see her serious face. She is not kidding. That only makes it that much funnier. I need a detox, too.

"Would it be alright if we detox together?"

Her serious face softens, and that sweet deer-in-the-headlights look she gets sometimes flashes briefly before she blinks it away.

"Sure. Why not?"

Extending out my arm, I gesture toward the sidewalk at the front of the shops, indicating I would like to walk. Her eyes shift from me to the street, to her car, and back to me. Gripping her cute coffin purse, she accepts my suggestion and walks toward the street.

We fall into step next to each other, me on the inside and Sally on the street side. I correct our positioning with a gentle tug on her elbow, shifting her to the inside.

It's quiet for a few heartbeats, so I break the tension because I want to hear her soft voice and laugh at her unintentionally funny jokes. "I like your tights today."

They're glittery gold with star constellations. Making her appear to be a celestial goddess. I've fantasized about peeling her tights off her short, shapely legs. Find the pale, creamy skin she keeps hidden underneath. Thoughts of her bare legs have kept me awake at night since I saw them through her gauzy curtains. Ever since then, I've imagined what she looks like beneath all the tights and high-collared dresses. That one brief hazy view was not enough to assuage my unhealthy craving.

Those mocking tights are paired nicely with a velvet royal blue dress that nips in at her petite waist with a wide black leather belt, and hugs tightly to her breasts. Which may or may not have been the reason for my slow progress today, watching her profile bend and stretch was . . . painful. It gave me a hard-on I had to hide by remaining crouched, which then gave me a leg cramp.

"Oh, thank you. I told you I had a lot."

"I'm starting to see that you weren't kidding. Do you always wear dresses? Do you even own a pair of pants?"

She laughs, and the sound is sweet and melodic. I want to hear more of it. "Yes, I have a few pairs of pants if the occasion calls for it."

"And what occasion would call for it?" I ask as we pass by a store lined with fancy dog collars and treats. There's even a doggy stroller in the window. People are so weird.

"Hiking, camping, um . . . yoga when I decide to take one of Peyton's classes. I have a pair of sweatpants for really cold nights. But mostly, I like dresses. When it gets cold, I have these tights that are actually fleece lined leggings but still look like tights. So, I can still wear my dresses."

"Dedication. I like it."

HER FAVORITE JACK-O-LANTERN

We pass another store, this one selling imported olive oils and balsamic vinegar. Then there's the corner store that's been here forever and is literally on a corner. I stop Sally with an extended arm out across her chest—without touching her amazing chest—until it's safe to cross, and we continue to stroll through town.

A few people nod and say hello when passing. It isn't until the fourth person does it that I realize they're only looking at me, and I'm the only one responding. Sally doesn't say a word or acknowledge the passersby. None seem to be anyone I know, no one from our graduating class or friends. Just everyday people walking by politely saying "afternoon" or "hello."

It's when I notice the last couple turn suspicious eyes onto Sally that I can't stand it anymore.

Flustered and annoyed, I blurt out, "Okay, what is with everyone?"

Sally turns to me, startled, because she was staring into the window we're passing. Not even paying attention to the other people on the street.

"I'm sorry? What do you mean?"

"Do people really think you're so weird they can't even say hello in passing on the street?"

Her cheeks turn pink, and her eyes drop, causing her Susie Q ringlets to fall in her face, obstructing her from my view. *Not gonna happen.* Tilting her chin up with one finger, I force her to look at me. At my touch she freezes. Luckily, we're in front of a brick wall to one of the stores rather than a gaping window.

"Don't hide from me, Pumpkin. I'm not afraid of you."

That gets a small quirk of her lips but nothing more.

"People here are just a little old-fashioned, and although they love their holidays, they love them in the traditional, basic sense. Plain, boring triangle-eyed jack-o-lanterns, tacky Halloween scarves, and sheet ghosts in the yard. My idea of Halloween is too creepy and unsettling for them. Skeletons, fake blood, loud, gothic clothing year round, blue lipstick, and dark eyeliner." She gestures to her dress and then her makeup, which, indeed, is dark smoky eyes and edible indigo blue lipstick to match her dress.

The quirk growing on those tempting lips has faded. This will not do. She's too sweet and nice and cute to be brought down by simple-minded people who don't understand or appreciate her personal sense of self.

Stepping in close to her, I eat up her personal space with my body, inhaling her scent for the first time. It's crisp, like apples and warm like autumn leaves with a hint of cinnamon. Inhaling deeper, I pull more of her into me. Her breath tickles my neck as she tilts her head back on her shoulders to look me in the eye.

"Well, they're missing out. Because, from what I've learned, spending time with you this week, you are a generous, thoughtful, loving, talented person. They would be better for knowing you. So, it's their loss that they don't understand you. Not everyone is supposed to be understood, just accepted for who they are. Personally, I'm glad I get to monopolize your time. Just imagine how many men I would have to fight off if everyone liked you." Shaking my head, I smile and over dramatize my words for her benefit, pushing a curl out of her face so both those beautiful lilac eyes are visible.

"Nope, you should count yourself lucky people ignore you. If not, you'd always be bombarded with date proposals and fangirls who would follow you around everywhere. You'd never have a moment's peace. It's much better this way. For both of us."

Finally, she smiles, even though she's trying to fight it, pinching her lips together to hold it in. But she can't, and, eventually, it breaks through and lights up her face.

"Thanks."

We start walking down the street again, this time slightly closer, her arm brushing mine every so often as we walk. Taking our time, Sally points out what's new and what's changed. In a quiet moment between stores, she twists her fingers together, clearly wanting to say something.

"What is it?" I ask, hoping she won't say "nothing," like women always do when, really, it is something.

"Why did you tell Daphne I was paying you?"

"Because you are. I just didn't mention it was in sexual favors." I give her a panty-melting smirk and wink, and the apples of her cheeks redden so deeply you'd think it were below freezing out here. Her face contorts in alarm, then shifts to a hungry desire I do not disapprove of before settling on the horror that I might actually mean it.

"I'm just kidding, Sally. You're paying me in tour guide services and pumpkin-carving lessons. So, just keep telling me what's changed while we walk down to Ma's, where we'll have a late lunch, which I will pay for, and we'll call it even. No sexual favors."

Her shoulders drop along with her eyebrows as she visibly relaxes, and I just can't help myself.

"Unless you want to, of course." I give her another wink, and a tiny bit of pink returns to her cheeks, but her eyes aren't bugging out of her head in disgust but more narrow at me with restrained amusement.

Returning to our stroll, I keep close to Sally, this time purposely brushing my arm against hers. A silent sign of support I hope she understands. It may also be my way of subtly flirting with her. Touching her silky soft hair only has me wanting to touch more of her, all of her.

Sally is quiet for a minute before she sucks in a breath and continues with her tour guide duties.

"Right. Well, a few years back, some kids were pulling a prank at the high school and set fire to the gym. They had to build a whole brand-new one, which is much nicer than that old musty one. Mr. McKenna finally retired at the ripe old age of two hundred—"

"Good for him."

I like this girl's sense of humor. She's witty.

"—and Mrs. Perkins is now the Dean of Students."

A cold chill rolls down the street, stirring the fallen red leaves on the sidewalk, tussling them around our ankles. Sally shivers, and I realize she's only wearing a chunky knit scarf that sits around her neck like a yarn snake, that couldn't possibly be keeping her warm enough in the dropping temperatures.

"Are you cold?"

She shrugs but wraps her arms around herself, rubbing up and down, creating a friction against her biceps.

"Come here." Lifting my arm, I open the side of my flannel, inviting her in. She stares at me, perplexed, with the cutest little scrunch in her button nose. "You're cold, I'm warm." She still is unsure, but it's obvious she wants to accept my offer. "Promise I won't bite. Unless you ask nicely."

That gets a small smile out of her, and her apprehension melts just enough that she gives in after another icy breeze ruffles her skirt.

Sliding her under my arm, I wrap my flannel around her back and tuck her in tight against my side. She feels right against me, a perfect fit. At first, she keeps her arms wrapped around her body, but that only lasts a few awkward steps. She gives in and wraps one small around my back under my flannel. In this position, I'm sure we look like a couple enjoying an afternoon walk through town. The thought is . . . warming.

Sally cuddles in close, and I can feel her body relaxing into mine as we walk. Visions of many afternoons spent like this flash through my mind of her and me strolling through the streets. First just us, then us and our friends, and, finally, us and a few kids running around our legs and laughing wildly. One a rather rambunctious little girl with jet-black curls.

Fuck. Did I just fantasize having children with this woman? Wow, I was not expecting that. I didn't even know I wanted that. Hadn't even given it any thought before. A spouse and children were something my sister had, not me.

"Thanks. I'm kind of always cold. I should have brought a sweater. I guess working at Daphne's threw me off."

Her quiet but soothing voice shakes me from my shocking thoughts, bringing me back to the here and now.

"You're welcome. I'm always warm. You're welcome to use my heat whenever you like," I say through my muddled confusion.

I have to put that away and look deeper into it later.

"Careful, I might take you up on that."

Her eyes are downturned, but I can see the edges of a playful smirk on her lips.

I'm looking forward to the possibility.

We eventually make it to Ma's, where we have a delicious meal and milkshakes. Mine vanilla-mint, hers bubblegum-marshmallow. She makes me laugh and smile more than I have in the last eight years. In the span of one meal, I relax in a way that I'm realizing only happens when I'm with Sally.

Something about her eases me. The way she ignores the snide looks from people and is still herself, even though she knows changing her clothes and painting her house white would make them stop. Still, she doesn't do it. She

HER FAVORITE JACK-O-LANTERN

would rather endure the ridicule and be a social outcast than minimize her personality. And, for that, I like her more.

She's what I aspire to be. Unapologetically herself, no matter the consequences. Doing what makes her happy. I'm discovering what makes me happy. And her name is Sally.

15 – Sally

Is that blood?

Saturdays in my house are lounge-pants-and-oversized-cardigan days. It's the day I spend lounging around, catching up on TV and ignoring everyone in town except my hot neighbor during his morning workout—which is now, apparently, part of my morning routine. Roll out of bed, sneak to the window, watch a shirtless, sweaty Jack, possibly touch myself when unable to resist, die of shame, repeat. Whatever, I've made my peace with it. Even on a Saturday, Jack still runs at six and is back in his backyard by seven, shirtless and sweaty and shiny.

I may have indulged my horny desires this morning. After a week of watching him, it was all I could do not to leap out of my window and ravage him on his lawn.

He was halfway through his push-ups when my hand

slipped up my short nightgown and right down my panties. I was so wet and horny I didn't even need the vibrator. My fingers were more than sufficient. Circling my clit and running through my wet folds. Dipping inside my clenching heat. My other hand pinching my nipple through my nightgown. Watching his flexing body sent me spiraling, sinking my fingers deep, plunging them in and out. When he started wiping off his sweat after doing his pull-ups, all I had to do was circle my clit a few times, and I was coming hard.

It wasn't my proudest moment, but it sure as hell was a pleasurable one, one that makes my panties wet all over again.

To distract myself, I have a snack with my episode of *The Masked Singer*. I scuttle into the kitchen on my socked feet, my oversized black knit cardigan hanging off my shoulders to my knees.

After my early-morning whack-off, I cleaned up and changed into my black lounge pants with cartoon cupcakes topped with jack-o-lanterns and eyeballs. I forgo the bra today too. It's a true relaxing day.

I grab my Hint of Lime Tostitos and salsa, a bowl of mini dill pickles, and a Coke Zero, then head to my couch nest. Pulling the coffee table near flush with the cushion, I hit play and munch away.

Not even five minutes later, I'm about to discover who the Rubber Duck is when, for the second time this week, my doorbell rings.

It's not Peyton because she's spending the day with her sister, and Chloe is with her fiancé at puppy training for their six-month-old golden retriever they adopted last month. It's definitely not my parents. They always make me come to them, and my sister is too busy with cleaning her perfect house and hand-painting signs and making wreaths for her booth at the pumpkin festival next weekend to spare time to come bother me.

If she wasn't a perfect enough housewife and a stay-at-home mom, she also makes cutesy yard signs and holiday wreaths for every holiday imaginable. Even Presidents' Day.

Shoving another salsa-covered chip in my mouth, I crawl out of my nest and make my way to the door. The doorbell rings again. I look out the peephole. I didn't think Jack could surprise me any more than he already has, yet there he stands in sweatpants and a hoodie.

"Don't you have other friends you can bother on a Saturday afternoon?" I ask, from behind my closed door, completely sarcastic.

I would never complain about Jack knocking on my door. He could be here, serving me a petition signed by the whole town to force me to repaint my house—again—and I wouldn't care. I'd still open the door instead of pretending not to be at home, like I did the last time they tried to serve me a petition.

It's not going to happen, Karen. I'm not part of an HOA, and I own my property outright. No one can tell me what color to paint my house.

HER FAVORITE JACK-O-LANTERN

"Yeah, but they're not as pretty as you. Plus, they just want to talk about the *good ol' days*, and I don't particularly want to talk about high school."

Jack thinks I'm pretty.

"I don't blame you." Unlocking the door, I don't even think twice before opening it for him. I lean against the edge and bite my lip, tasting the salt and lime from the chips.

"Is that blood on your shirt?"

"What?—Fuck!" Looking down, I see I've dribbled salsa on my pale orange shirt, the red splotch dripping like blood down my chest. My braless chest. "No, it's salsa."

Turning, I go straight for the kitchen, leaving my front door wide open and Jack standing on my front porch. Once I have the salsa cleaned off, I venture back to find Jack waiting in the foyer, front door closed and hands in the pocket of his hoodie.

"So. You're wearing pants."

"How very astute of you to notice. Today is casual pants Saturday."

Looking down at his own sweatpants, he chuckles. "Well, I guess I'm appropriately dressed, then."

"So, what brings you over? Need another pumpkin-carving lesson? Or was it the sexual favor you were hoping for?"

With every minute I spend with Jack, I get bolder and more confident in my conversational skills. And, apparently, funnier. I don't think I've joked with someone this much who wasn't Peyton or Chloe.

"Given those options . . ." His grin is wicked but playful. "I actually came over because I was bored and sitting alone in my empty house, thinking about you over here alone in your empty house and thought maybe we could hang out together and not be alone in our empty houses."

He looks so cute and boyish standing there, with his hopeful expression. It hadn't even occurred to me to go over and see if he wanted to hang out. It has been a long time since I've had a normal friend, let alone a man like Jack. So funny and thoughtful and attractive. Even in sweats and a hoodie, his body is still strong and bulky beneath the soft fabric. He looks cozy. I want to curl up on him like a cat.

"I'm just watching TV and snacking. But you're more than welcome to join."

"What are you watching?"

"It's called The Masked Singer. Have you seen it before?"

He shakes his head and looks down at his shuffling feet.

"No. I don't really watch much TV beyond football and the news."

"You're going to love it. Celebrities dress up in the most ridiculously awesome costumes and masks and sing in a competition. The judges have to try and figure out who the celebrity is without seeing their face or hearing their voice beyond singing." Grabbing his elbow, I drag him into my living room, explaining the rules of the show and who I think the characters are.

We plop down on my couch, and I toss him a throw blanket as he kicks off his shoes and gets comfortable.

HER FAVORITE JACK-O-LANTERN

"Would you like something to drink? I have water, milk, blueberry lemonade, Coke Zero, I think some tea."

"Blueberry lemonade sounds good."

"Do you like pickles?"

"What?" He chuckles and looks up from the TV, where I have the show paused on the image of the Rubber Duck-costumed celebrity.

"Pickles. Do you like them? I love pickles. They make a great snack."

He smiles at me, warm and open, not at all judging me for being weird and snacking on pickles while wearing Halloween cupcake pants and a salsa-stained T-shirt. He settles into my couch, looking completely at home and right.

I wonder what it would be like to spend every Saturday on the couch with Jack. Watching goofy TV shows and eating whatever the fuck we felt like. Shutting out the world and everyone in it. Cocooning ourselves together in a heap of plush throw blankets and each other. Legs tangled and fingers entwined. Mouths finding one another. A girl can dream.

"Yeah, I like pickles."

We finished watching the episode and are now watching *A Nightmare on Elm Street*, the 2010 remake. Most remakes are crap, but I like this one. It stayed true to the original.

With every shift and readjustment, we do this dance of inching closer to one another. We started not touching each other, sitting a respectful distance apart, me leaning against the couch arm, him sitting in the center of the couch. Now, thanks to our super stealth, our thighs press against each other, and our shoulders brush when we move.

This is surreal. I'm cuddling on the couch with Jack Campbell. High-school me is freaking out, while adult me is smacking high-school me, telling her to shut the fuck up and enjoy it.

Being so close to Jack always makes me hot, and wearing this giant cardigan under thick blankets is only making it worse. I don't want to move, but I have to take off this sweater before I die of heat stroke.

When I'm finally free of the suffocating material, I lean back to find Jack has repositioned himself again, this time with his arm low behind my back. His hand gently curves around my hip, pulling me close to his side in a way that says *I want you near me. I want to touch you and feel you against me.* It's in the most smoothly obvious way possible while leaving me plenty of opportunity to slide away easily if I didn't want to be here.

Of course I want to be here. I've wanted that since I was fourteen years old. I never though it would actually happen. But here it is. Me, curled in close against him, with Jack's arm wrapped around me, his lazy, hooded gaze looking down at me.

"I'd really like to kiss you now, Sally."

I think my heart just stopped.

I swallow hard and clear the frog in my throat. "You do?"

It still comes out croaky and uneven.

"Very much so. I've been thinking about it all week. Every time you wore purple or orange lipstick, I wanted to kiss you to find out if it was flavored. Find out what you taste like."

The fingers around my waist shift eagerly, wrinkling the fabric of my shirt and riding it up, exposing hot skin. His fingers make contact, and my heart sputters and stutters like a dying engine. I lean into him, pressing our chests tight together. Even sitting, he's still taller than me, angling his head down to mine. He stops inches away that feel like miles. God, I want to kiss him.

His other hand caresses my now bare arm, eliciting goosebumps in his wake. Those fathomless blue eyes of his watch my mouth as my tongue involuntarily licks my bottom lip.

"Can I kiss you now, Pumpkin?"

His words are whisper-soft against my mouth, waiting for permission.

My hands slide up his firm shoulders and wrap around his neck. Unsure he's even real, that he's even sitting here on my couch kissing me., I lean in and press my lips to his, soft and tentative. This could all be a vivid hallucination brought on by spending so much time with him. As soon as it starts to get good, I'll wake up alone, having fallen asleep while watching TV on my couch.

But I don't wake up. He doesn't disappear as his lips take control, pressing firm against mine, demanding reciprocation. His hand is now flat on my back under my shirt, burning fingerprints into my skin. His kiss is confident and sure but exploratory. Discovering the best angel to fit against me, the right amount of pressure to make me quiver.

A quiet moan escapes when he licks the seam of my lips. It's warm and slick, finding my tongue and eagerly sliding deeper, tangling with it in a dance I don't know the steps to but somehow follow along.

It's been a while since I've kissed anyone. I was starting to think I'd forgotten how.

Jack doesn't give me a chance to question my skills, shifting his hands on my thigh and dragging me on top of him. Positioning my legs on either side of his hips straddling him.

Freddy, Jason, and Michael. That is his dick. I am sitting on Jack's penis, and it's *hard*. My panties are quickly growing damp under his skillful kissing and the press of his erection against my center. I've forgotten how good it feels to have a man's hard body pressed up against mine. It's intoxicating and dizzying.

My hand runs up the back of his head, searching for hair to grab onto, but it's too short and is soft fuzz on all sides. The only length is an inch or two on top. Even with as short as it is, it's still a sensation I'll burn into my memory forever. My other hand grips the hood of his sweatshirt, holding on for dear life. In one fluid motion, Jack breaks our kiss long enough to lean back and pull the hoodie off over his head, flinging it over the back of the couch, leaving only a white T-shirt between his skin and my hands.

Reaching back around his shoulders I can feel his radiating warmth through the thin material. Our lips finding each other once again. We're all hands and fingers, searching for purchase, something to caress, to touch, to feel. Those delicious muscles I've been drooling over are now under my fingers. Hard and wanting. His fingers grip my hips and drop lower, cupping my ass and squeezing firmly. The action causes me to jerk forward, pressing me harder against his erection, and he groans into my mouth. I can taste his desire.

Breaking our kiss again, Jack presses his forehead to mine. "Pumpkin, there is little I wouldn't do to you right now, but please don't torture me. I want to take my time with you. I don't want to rush this. You're too special for this to be a meaningless hook up."

His words are balm to my soul and kindling to my libido. He wants me, but he doesn't want to rush it. That's fine by me. Kissing him is like winning the lottery. With every experimental taste and press of his lips, I hit the jackpot all over again.

"You think I'm special?" I breathe against his lips.

"Extremely. You are so much more than anyone I've ever met. I've been drawn to you since you brought me those cookies, which, by the way, I dream about. I'm going to need you to make me some more."

Between his words he places soft kisses against my neck and collarbone. The last one is open-mouthed right over my pulse point.

I shake so hard I'm sure he can feel it.

"Mmhmm. okay. Cookies. I can . . . do . . . that."

I can barely get the words out as my breath catches in my throat with each press of his mouth against my body.

His mouth returns to mine, and we make out on my couch like a couple of teenagers. But less awkward and aggressive, more caressing and patient. Without a care in the world and no rush to move beyond the kissing and fondling.

His hands find my bare breasts under my shirt, weighing them in his palms. They spill out over the cups of his fingers, and he seems to like that. His fingers leisurely glide over my nipples, pebbling them into peaks. The sensation of his touch vibrates through my entire body.

My hands seek his contracted abs under the waistband of his sweats. They twitch and tense with every pass of my fingers. So many rippling ridges that contract the longer we fool around.

I could do this forever.

16 – Sally

I was a soldier not a medieval knight

"I'm sorry. What did you just say?" I ask my mother, who randomly invited me over for Sunday dinner.

I had plans to reciprocate Jack's casual appearance at my house yesterday with one of my own to his house. If it led to more fooling around, so be it. My plans were quickly dashed when I received her call asking me to dinner.

She has been rambling on about the most recent gossip around town. Normally—including today—I tune her out. None of it ever matters to me or involves me beyond the usual complaints. So, why bother wasting energy on it? But I'm sure I just heard my name and Jack's in the same sentence—not directly spoken to me because Mom likes to skirt around the subject and regurgitates "what she heard" instead of asking me directly.

Is this why she brought me over tonight under the guise of a family dinner? Not only am I present but so is my sister but not her husband or their daughter—the cutest niece in existence who I don't get to see nearly enough of—which can only mean this was last minute for everyone.

"*I said* Linda told Ida that she saw you and Jack Campbell walking down Main Street and entering Ma's Diner together and that you two looked rather cozy. And I told her that was highly unlikely. You and Jack aren't even friends. Why would you be going to lunch together?"

Ouch. Low blow, Mom. Nothing new, unfortunately.

Mom was a cheerleader, a multiple-club member, and all-around popular girl in high school. Having a daughter who is and always has been the outcast weirdo has been trying on her delicate sensibilities. Her social standing and status damaged thanks to my inability to fit in. Like it's my fault the ladies at the club pity her for having me as a daughter.

Holding in the snide remark I would like to lash out at her, I grit my teeth before speaking.

"Actually, we were together. He's my new neighbor and has been helping me with my Halloween decorating around town."

"Really? Why would he do that?" she asks before taking a delicate bite of peas in that stupid fancy way on the wrong side of her fork, like that's going to make her look any less patronizing.

A blind person listening to our conversation would never think we were mother and daughter. Unfortunately for my mother, anyone with two working eyes, or even one, can see we're related. To her great dismay, a lot of my looks came from her. Dark inky-black hair with big bouncy curls, hers far more subdued than mine. We have the same small button noses, pronounced cupids bow lips, and heart-shaped faces. She's taller and less busty, but my unique lilac eyes are mine, the only thing that separates me from her.

"Because he's a good person?"

The words come out sardonic, and I mean them to. Margaret Smithson may pretend to be all benevolent acceptance, but she is anything but.

"That's undeniable. He's always been a good boy, and his family so well liked in town. But that still doesn't explain how you two came together." Another delicate bite, mashed potatoes this time. "Just because he's your new neighbor doesn't mean he's obligated to help you with anything."

I groan but try to muffle it by taking a big bite of steak, along with an eye roll I'm sure she sees. Maybe if my mouth is full of enough food, this conversation will end, or at least keep me from saying something that will exacerbate the situation.

"True," my perfect sister Emily chimes in. "He's not obligated, but perhaps he offered? I'm sure if someone like Jack saw anyone struggling, he would offer to assist. Isn't that how military guys are?"

"That's possible. But why would he be eating with Sally? I'm sure he has plenty of family and friends to catch up with since he returned. It seems rude to ignore them to eat lunch and wander around town with Sally."

I ignore them and continue eating. It's not important for me to be a part of this conversation. Anything I say won't be heard anyways.

"Perhaps she's paying him," my father, the ever unhelpful, suggests.

"Unless that was his payment. Were you paying him in food?"

Oh, she's talking to me now? How nice to be included in this conversation about me.

"No. I wasn't paying him in food or at all. He was the one who paid for lunch as a thank-you for showing him around town."

And teaching him how to carve pumpkins. I don't mention that part as they think pumpkin carving is a waste of time, as if a person can't have a hobby they enjoy.

"Why would he need to be shown around town? He grew up here," Emily asks between bites almost as delicate as our mothers.

"I don't know, ask him." I shove a massive bite in my mouth and chew . . . loudly. Just to piss them off. It's the least I can do.

"No need to be barbaric, Sally," Mother scolds.

I make my next bite smaller, and I chew with my mouth shut, but I do so with obvious indignation.

"You shouldn't monopolize his time. You two are so different. You don't want to interfere with his life. We don't want a repeat of what happened with Myles, now do we?"

My body tenses, and my fork stops halfway to my mouth. Her low blow just dropped lower. The tender steak and buttery mashed potatoes sours in my stomach.

It's one thing for strangers to say hurtful words about my failed relationship. They hold no weight. They know nothing of the truth. For my mother to say them and my father and sister to agree when they know the truth . . . well, that's a horse of a different color. Puke green like rot and poison.

My family continues eating, as if nothing is amiss, while I slowly die of rot from the inside out.

"Who was that girl he dated in high school? Wasn't she one of the cheerleaders?" my mother asks, continuing the conversation I wish would just end already.

Emily nods. "Daphne Brighton."

"Oh, yes, of course. Such a lovely girl. So pretty and successful with her store. I just saw her parents at the club. What a wonderful family."

Are we thinking of the same Brightons? Because the Daphne I've met is anything but lovely. Her parents might be decent people, but I've don't known them. With the way their daughter turned out, though, I can only imagine that was their doing.

"Perhaps now that he's home, they'll reconnect."

I suppose they already have. Then again, I was the one with my tongue down his throat last night. I was the one sitting astride his strong hips and straining erection. *Not* Daphne. She was the one he publicly told no, that he snubbed to help me.

He may be the jock, and I may be the freak, but he still likes me. At least enough to make out with me and round second base.

I would really like to make it second base again, maybe third base. Driving it home wouldn't be too bad, either. Not with that bat he's packing.

Oh, yuck, and now I'm picturing him and Daphne and using that bat. Dammit. Now I'm really going to be sick. I just have to remind myself it was almost a decade ago and that he kissed me. Not her. It was my house he came to yesterday. My couch we cuddled on and watched TV on, and my breasts he was fondling.

Maybe if I tell myself it enough times, I'll believe it.

"You can do this. It's not that hard. People do it all the time. Just walk up to his door, knock, and ask him over for dinner. Easy peasy lemon squeezy. But what if the other night was a fluke? What if it was a moment of weakness? He could have just been horny. What if I ask, and he says no? What if he says yes? Then I'll have to make him dinner. Do I have something to make for dinner? What if he hates my cooking? No. Stop being negative. He won't say no—

maybe."

The conversation with myself is not going well. I feel like I'm losing no matter what side of the argument I'm on. It's been two days since our make-out session on my couch, and I haven't seen Jack since, other than his morning workouts. I've finally worked up enough courage to invite him to dinner—well, almost. I'd better hurry and settle this disagreement with myself because I'm pulling up to my house.

I'm parking in my driveway.

Now I'm sitting here like a weirdo in my car, staring at his house.

Time to get out, Sally. Like Nike says: just do it. The worst that could happen is he could say no. Your life won't end, and the world will keep spinning.

With a deep breath, I force myself out of the car. My feet falter halfway across my lawn, still not on board with my decision. When I see a shadow cross a window in Jack's house my feet revolt and turn me back toward my front door.

Nope, not going to wimp out. I will do it, I tell myself, and force my feet to pull another one-eighty back toward Jack's house. I only make it three steps before my brain and my feet argue again, and I spin in a circle, muttering to myself.

A gooey splat near my ear stops my pacing.

"Lucifer's big red testicles. Dammit." I groan and eye the white splotch on my shoulder.

"That's an interesting choice of expletives. Is that bird

shit?"

"Aaaah!"

Jack's deep voice scares me to the point of cringy girl screaming. Somehow, I completely missed him walking toward me amidst my brain versus feet battle royale. His smile is disarmingly dazzling, and for a split second, I forget I was freaking out about asking him over for dinner. All while the dripping bird crap on my shoulder slowly absorbs into my cardigan.

"I didn't see you there."

"I know. You were busy arguing with your feet."

"Right."

"So, is that actually bird poop?" He points to the offending white spot.

"Unfortunately." I want to take off my sweater and run inside to clean it, but my nerves have me standing in place only a few feet from Jack, twitching nervously. "I'm a beacon for sauces, stains, liquids and apparently bird crap."

"Were you coming over to my house for something?" he asks in a tone suggesting he wasn't watching me out the window, knowing damn well I was heading to his house, but the look in his eyes says he was.

"Yeah, I was wondering if you wanted to come over for dinner?" I cringe at the pathetic break in my voice, but his smile doesn't falter a centimeter.

"I would love to. Perhaps then you could give me that tour you promised."

"Right. I can do that." I give him a lopsided grin, partially relieved that he said yes and partially nervous about giving him a house tour.

Jack follows me to my house. Stepping up onto my porch, I pull out my keys. When I slide in the key, a shriek and holler stops me before I can turn it.

One human, one animal.

"What the fuck? Go away. Back off, you vampiric beast." Behind me, Jack is swatting wildly at the air, ducking and dodging a black blur of wings and fur.

"No, no, no. Don't hurt him." Grabbing Jack's arms, I still his movements before he's able to swat the creature.

"Don't hurt him?! He attacked me," Jack shrieks, his voice reaching pitches I didn't know he could reach, holding his hands over his head.

"He didn't attack you. He was trying to say hello to me, and you got in the way."

"What?"

The furry black creature settles and hangs upside down from the frame of my front door, stretching and curling his leathery wings around his cute little fur body.

"Batty. There you are, my little cutie patootie." I rub the top of his head and scratch.

Most would probably not consider petting a wild bat, but this isn't just any bat. This is Batty. He's the least vicious thing you'll ever meet.

"Is he your pet?" Jack asks, keeping a healthy distance away from Batty, while I coo at the oh-so-scary creature hanging in my doorframe.

"No. He just likes me. Found him one night hanging from the rafters of my porch. He was weak and hungry. I figured out he's a fruit bat of some kind possibly a black flying fox. They're not common to this area, so I figure he must have gotten lost." Batty yawns and lets out a cute little shriek, his way of saying hello. "I guess he liked me because he stuck around. He never goes very far. I see him nearly every day or every other day. Leaving out bowls of fruit for him. He's probably just hungry." Batty cackles at me, asking for more scratches. I oblige because he's too cute to say no to.

"Are you sure he's not going to bite you? Don't they carry rabies?"

"He would never bite me. He loves me," I say in a baby voice and making kissy faces at Batty. "He was a little wary of me at first, but as soon as I gave him his first piece of apple, he was fully in love with me."

Jack scoffs. It is a little weird that a stray wild bat would domesticate himself so easily, but that's what happened. Guess I'm just lucky like that. Who else can say they're friends with a bat?

"How come you didn't think of a more interesting name for him than Batty? Seems rather on point for you."

"Oh, he is named after someone. Batty from *Ferngully*. It is a rather boring name, but I like the reference. Batty was one of my favorites as a kid."

"Aren't you a little young for *Ferngully*? Were you even born when it came out?" Looking back over my shoulder, I catch Jack with a sardonic look on his face.

His eyes shift between me and Batty, making sure he isn't going to fly at him again.

"No. But I wasn't born when *Star Wars* came out, or *The Shining*, or *Alien*, or *The Little Mermaid*. That doesn't mean I can't know and love them."

"Good point."

I unlock my door, open it, and walk in right under Batty into the foyer. Jack, on the other hand, is almost eye level with Batty and doesn't make a move to enter.

"He's not going to bite you and suck your blood. He's a fruit bat."

"That doesn't mean he won't bite me just for the fun of it. Just because he likes you doesn't mean he'll like me."

His face is a mess of wide eyes and contorted eyebrows, washed in fear and disbelief. The amused teasing dissipated when faced with imminent death by fruit bat. He's so cute when he's afraid of small furry creatures.

"Weren't you in the army?"

His gaze instantly locks with mine, narrowed and perplexed.

"Yes. What does that have to do with anything?"

"Didn't they train you to be a big strong man who fights evil and protects the innocent?"

"I was a soldier, not a medieval knight," he jeers, but the tension in his expression and posture have loosened.

"Same thing. Just duck and go around him. You'll be fine."

Ever so slowly, he does, bending over nearly in half and practically running through the doorway and holding his hands protectively above his head. Jack doesn't stop until he's behind me, a safe distance away from Batty.

"You know you're cute when you're afraid."

"I'm not afraid, just . . . cautious."

"Right. Are you brave enough to watch him while I go get him some fruit?"

Jack looks at me like I said I was planning on sacrificing him to a man-eating llama.

"You want me to watch the wild bat hanging in your doorway while you go get it some fruit?"

His words are slow and controlled, and his eyes shift from me to Batty to make sure he hasn't moved.

"Yes."

"Suuuuure." He doesn't sound too sure, if the pinch in his brow is any indication.

After feeding Batty and making sure he's gotten enough affection, then hand-washing out my cardigan to remove the bird shit, I make dinner for me and Jack.

We eat and talk like old friends, with some obvious flirting involved. The dishes are washed, and the table is cleared when Jack takes a closer look at everything in my living room.

"So, how about that tour? I wasn't kidding when I said I wanted to see the rest of your house."

Most people don't even want to stop on the street in front of my house, so someone asking to see every room in it and compliment me on it is unusual. But, for once, I am more than happy to show off my hard work to someone who appreciates it.

"Of course. Follow me."

I show him the downstairs library and den, then my office before making our way upstairs. The upstairs is a little more personal than the first floor. I have collectibles and framed photos of some of my most memorable moments.

Jack lingers on the photos in the hallway, leaning in close to see beyond the edges of the frames, as if he could poke his head into the scene in the photo.

"Most of these have Peyton and Chloe in them. You three have been friends for a long time, huh?"

"Yeah. They've been there pretty much for every important time in my life. High school graduation, college graduation, breakups, the first day I owned this house, my first paying interior design job, spring break. I was there when Peyton got her massage license and kinesiology degree, when Chloe graduated from veterinary school and met her fiancé. We're kind of like the three amigos."

Reminiscing about my two best friends and everything we've been through together expands and tightens my heart. They're my real family, the ones who accept me for who I am and support me no matter what. The ones who supported me in high school when I almost gave up on my love for all things creepy. They shunned Myles after the breakup and took me out to a place where you get to break TVs with a baseball bat to work out my anger in a healthy, safe environment.

"I don't see many family photos. I thought you had a sister?"

"I do. She's normal. Doesn't like my creepiness any more than my parents do. We don't exactly see eye to eye on many things. They're more pearls and mimosas, if you know what I mean."

It's the nicest way to say I'm a freak, even in my own family and not even they like how I am. Jack says nothing, doesn't push the subject or ask why, and I'm thankful for it. Explaining it is worse than admitting it. He just taps on a picture of me, Peyton, and Chloe on a beach in the Bahamas.

We went on a trip after Chloe graduated, as she was last of us to, having way more classes to take to be a vet than a yoga instructor or interior designer. We're all in bikinis, standing in ankle-deep crystal-clear water with coconut drinks in our hands and smiles on our faces. We may be the best of friends, but we are all different. Even in only swimsuits, it's evident in this photo. Mine is black with mesh panels and a cute little ruffle around the waist of the bottoms, the top plunging, showing plenty of cleavage. Peyton's is pale blue with tiny strings and triangles that leave little to the imagination, and Chloe's a bright purple and the most practical, the top more like a sports bra with wide supportive straps.

Three girls who couldn't be more different somehow found friendship and acceptance in an unconventional bond.

"I like this one. You look happy," Jack comments on the beach photo. He doesn't ogle it like a lecher, as one would expect. No, he's looking at our faces, the pure joy we're all experiencing. "You should smile more. You have a beautiful smile; it lights up your whole face. I like seeing you so happy."

A warm blush grows on my face, and I bite my lip to hide my smile. Nothing in this world is greater than being complimented by Jack.

"I'll keep that in mind. I don't always have a reason to smile, so, sometimes, it's hard."

"Well, anytime you want to smile, knock on my door. I'd be happy to help."

Jack turns from the photo and gives me one of his stunningly easy smiles. My face heats more, and I release the smile I'm trying to conceal. It's not as big and free as the one in the picture but real all the same. One that lights me up in the way he said I should do more.

I turn from the photos and continue my tour, Jack trailing close behind through the open loft, guest bedrooms, guest bathroom, and, finally, my primary bedroom.

17 - Sally

I've dreamed about it for so long I can't tell if I'm still dreaming

My room is spacious and filled with personal items that fit well in my black space. Somehow, I made black comfortable and warm, with textures and breaks of soft gray and deep violet, with accents of gold. I left the hardwood floors intact, just refinished them with a dark stain and laid down fluffy area rugs.

The light from the chandelier above is bright but dimmable so as not to be blinding at night. I set the dimmer to sixty percent, bright enough to see but not enough to feel blinding—"mood lighting," as Peyton would say. It was her idea to add in the dimmer. I'm thankful for it now.

"Wow. Your room is way nicer than mine. All I have is a bed, a nightstand, and a dresser in mine."

Showing Jack my bedroom is so surreal. Him in my

space makes me tingle all over. He's walking around my room, looking at the knickknacks on the dresser, the framed art, and photos on the wall, my collection of brooches laid out neatly in clear, lidded display boxes.

Something in his slow, methodical movement as he makes his way around my most personal space has me watching him closely.

When Myles and I were dating, we didn't live together, even after getting engaged. He had his place, and I had mine, and since mine was often under construction, we stayed at his place mostly.

I've never had a man in this bedroom. Sure, Myles stayed over a few times but never in this room. This room wasn't finished until after we broke up. I've never "christened it." There's never been a man in this bed, on my sheets, running his fingers across the comforter, and pulling off his socks to test the softness of the area rug under his toes.

I stay by the door, pressing my back against the doorjamb, allowing Jack to explore my space without my interference. Waiting for his verdict. Run away screaming or . . .

Jack finishes testing the softness of my rug and turns his attention to me, eyeing me curiously, running his gaze up and down my body.

I fidget, rubbing my tight-clad thighs together. Purple with cartoon eyeballs today, one of my flashier pair. He eyes them but doesn't even flinch before running his gaze back up my body to my face. His eyes volley between mine. Something simmering in them.

"Your bedroom is very you. I like it."

"Really? It's not too—"

"It's not too anything. It's just right. It's just you, and there's nothing wrong with it."

His voice is low and gravelly, and when did he start moving toward me? When did my heart start racing so fiercely?

Jack moves like a panther, practically crawling in slow motion over the floor. Sturdy legs reach toward me and eat up the distance. Stopping only once his body is flush against mine. His hands graze my sides, pausing at my breasts, and the caress of his fingers circle the swell of them until his thumbs press my nipples and stroke tenderly.

The soft press of his lips to the shell of my ear has me shivering all over. His touch is still so unexpected but oh so delicious as he buries his face in my neck, nuzzling and inhaling deeply. Sensual lips move against my skin, peppering me with kisses and licks, tasting me, testing me.

My back is against the wall, and Jack is pressed against me just enough to keep me from moving. He's not demanding or aggressive, but I want him to be. I want his hands all over me, his mouth tasting every inch of me. I don't want him to be unsure of what he can and can't do.

"Jack."

His name is a moaned whimper. I can't think straight with him kissing me like he is.

"Yes, Sally?"

I can feel the words spoken against my collarbone, and I

shiver, a throb pulsing between my legs I know will only get worse with every touch.

Running my hands up his T-shirt-clad biceps I give them a good, tight squeeze, drawing his attention in a way that makes him reciprocate in kind. Sandwiching my body between his and the wall, he releases my breasts. His hands slide down my body, seeking leverage holding my hips against his.

"I..."

My words are cut off with the firm press of his lips, kissing me with an eager hunger. Sucking on my bottom lip, he bites gently, eliciting a moan I can't suppress. Our hips press together, and I feel just how much he wants me. His erection hard and straining, pressing high on my stomach. Our difference in height keeps his cock from being where I want it most.

He notices, threads one hand under my knee, picks me up, and wraps me around him. My dress bunches around my hips, allowing his cock to nestle perfectly between my spread legs. The delectable pressure causing wetness to pool there.

"Better?" he asks into my mouth.

"Better," I agree adamantly, grinding into him unabashedly and pressing his hardness against where I need him most.

Fuck, he feels good. I don't want this to stop. I don't want this all to be a dream. It's too good to be real, but I don't care. If this is a dream, I never want to wake up.

I don't know how long we're locked together, pressed against the wall, humping each other while still clothed. Eventually, it becomes too much. I need more skin and less clothing. I want to touch all of him, feel all of him. So, I reach down, grab at the hem of his shirt, then pull it up his body. It catches on his armpits, I can't remove it while his arms hold me up.

Jack stops kissing me and pulls back enough to look into my eyes, making me focus on him and him alone. There is no one else, nothing else in our bubble. Just us and our heavy breathing. There is no judgment or disgust. Only us and our desire for one another.

"If you don't want this, tell me. If I'm too aggressive, just say so, and I'll back off."

"Don't you dare back off. I want you in any way, every way. I want everything. You're all I've ever wanted. I still can't believe you're really here. It doesn't seem real. I've dreamed about it for so long I can't tell if I'm still dreaming."

Jack presses a soft kiss to my lips before pulling back again. "You're not dreaming. I'm here, I'm real. And there's nowhere I'd rather be than here, in your black bedroom. Holding you. Kissing you. Having you."

His words are gravelly and punctuated with small kisses along my jaw and neck. Making it that much harder to pay attention, but I still hear them. I still feel them.

"You're perfect just as you are, Sally. Don't question my presence. I'm here because I want to be. I'm here for you and only you."

My body and emotions are running on overdrive, and his words are amplifying them to something beyond what I'm capable of holding in. I'm happy and moved and touched to the point of utter destruction.

Squeezing my eyes shut tight, I try to calm myself to focus. But a lone tear strays down my cheek. Jack sees it and stills.

"Why are you crying? Did I hurt you? Did I say something wrong?"

Jack tries to pull back and release me, but I cling to him like a baby koala to its mother.

"No. You did nothing wrong." Pulling away from the wall, he cups my ass and carries me over to my bed before sitting on the edge with me in his lap. "I'm just an emotional baby is all. No one has ever said anything like that to me. It's . . . unexpected."

I let out a long breath and wipe the stray tear from my face, blinking back any others. This is not a time for tears. It's a time for kissing and exploring. To discover uncharted territories with Jack. Discover them together.

Crying should not be a part of that. It won't be. I won't let it. They may be happy tears, but I don't want to make him uncomfortable. I don't want him to think he's done something wrong. He could never do anything wrong.

So, I straighten my spine and focus on Jack, the here and now. Our bodies close together on our fingers and lips. Nothing beyond this room matters. I resume my exploration, again attempting to remove his shirt. This time, I pull it off over his head and touch the chest I've been gawking at out my window all week.

Jack slips his hands under my dress, and his fingers dig in under the band of my tights, while effortlessly rolling us on my bed, pinning me beneath him. His weight on my body is a welcome comfort. One I hadn't known I needed or wanted.

Myles wasn't as big as Jack and was always so gentle with me because of my small stature. I don't want to be handled with kid gloves. I want to be manhandled and taken as the woman I am.

The weight I have decided I want more of lessens as Jack leans on his elbows and crawls down my body, kissing down the center over the top of my purple dress. Plucking open a few buttons with his teeth that line the center front, exposing pale skin, which he flicks his tongue over before continuing south. Settling himself comfortably between my legs.

"I want to peel these tights off you every single time I see you wearing them."

"I wear them every day."

"I know. You also tease me with them every day. Tormenting me with what is hidden beneath. Begging me to peel them down your legs and strip you bare."

His fingers inside the band of the tights slide down, hooking my panties along the way. He doesn't lift my skirt to get access, although it's ridden up plenty in our groping. He pulls down the tights and panties in one fluid motion.

Rolling the thin fabric down my legs, shifting down the mattress to remove them completely. They're discarded somewhere on the floor. I don't care where because I'm bare under my dress for him now. The wetness slick between my thighs.

Like a treasure hunter finding a never-before-seen artifact, Jack unbuttons the remaining buttons on my dress from the bottom up, reverently discovering my body inch by inch. Not stopping until he's revealed the entire length of me, bare, except for my bra covered breasts framed by the pooling fabric of my dress. He brushes aside the material completely to get a better look.

"Perfection."

The word is barely a whisper. I don't have time to process it because he's pulling the dress down my arms and reaching around to unhook my bra in a move that leaves me naked in a matter of seconds. While he is shirtless, he still wears his jeans slung low on his hips. They do nothing to hide the press of his straining cock against his zipper.

"I didn't expect you to be the tattoo kind of girl, although now that I think about it, it does make sense."

The tattoo he's referring to is a sternum tattoo of a fine line bat. Its wings stretch out beneath my large breasts in delicate lace-like designs dangling from its points, gotten as a fuck-you, breakup tattoo.

He leans down and—oh fuck yes. He's licking the wings of the bat tattoo and tracing them with the tip of his tongue. It sends fresh wetness between my legs, and I make a sound of pure ecstasy.

His mouth moves along the edges of my tattoo and up the full mound of my breast before making contact with my nipple. I moan again, writhing beneath him, feeling his touch throughout my entire body. An electric current ignites every nerve ending all at once. I reach down, wanting to grip his cock through his pants, but he's too tall.

I jump when his fingers make contact between my thighs, a soft stroke along my folds that causes me to rock my hips into the movement. It's been far too long since someone other than myself has touched me there. It's too much and not enough all at once. I want more. I need it. Now that we've started, there's no stopping.

"More," I tell him.

He chuckles against my breast, sucking and biting my nipple with just enough force to cause pain and pleasure.

"Greedy little thing, aren't you?"

"Yes. You started this, and now you have to finish it."

"Gladly."

His hand works between my legs, stroking and pressing and circling in a way that has me moaning his name and fisting the blanket at my sides. His mouth moves down my stomach and joins his fingers. Licking up my center and pressing an open-mouthed kiss to the top before sucking on my clit, which makes me scream. I'm going to come if he does that again.

"Do that again," I tell him, egging him on with small thrusts of my hips against his firm grip and mouth.

He slides his hand to my thigh and presses me farther open as he uses his shoulder to do the same to the opposite side, allowing him more access to my needy pussy.

I should be embarrassed by my eagerness and more subtle with my desire. At least that's what Myles expected of me. But I'm not. I don't hide myself or feel shame for my desire and lust for Jack. I want him to know how much I want him. I want him to know what he does to me.

That finger teasing my entrance plunges in deep and twists, while that wicked mouth of his sucks on my clit again.

"Oh my god, oh my god," I chant at the overwhelming sensation.

It feels so damn good.

"You can call me sir," Jack says before circling his tongue against my sensitive bud and thrusting his thick finger deeper.

"Fuck. Yes, sir."

Jack growls into my pussy, and I clamp down. My body convulses as an orgasm rips through me tearing me from stem to stern, breaking everything inside of me down to nothing but a melted hot sponge.

Jack laps up my orgasm with eager licks of his tongue, working me over, elongating my climax until I'm a mess of overstimulated nerves. I have to shove him away to make him stop because the sensations are too much.

He prowls up my body and doesn't give me a moment to catch my breath before he's kissing me, pressing my mouth open and sliding his tongue in. He just made my come, and with the press of his hot skin against mine and the taste of him on my lips, I'm already eager to go again.

18 – Jack

How the hell did you do that?

Sally Smithson is not what I expected. She's sweet, thoughtful, witty, and beautiful in a way that has me questioning the standards of beauty everyone else judges by. How others can't see how stunning she is is beyond me. Not only physically, but in every way. Inside and out.

Especially when she comes. All writhing and moaning and calling me sir. Fuck, that was hotter than I had anticipated. I only said it as a joke, but I can't deny how much I liked it. It twisted my need for dominance and power and my time in the army together in a way that had me getting hard at the sound of it. Humping the mattress while my tongue was deep in Sally's pussy. She tasted like heaven, and now I want more. I want all of her.

I may have to taste her again before I slide my aching dick inside her tight heat. She's so petite and small it took only one finger to get her off. I may have to go down on her again to stretch her out first. Because I am not petite nor small.

Sally surprised me with her tattoo, delicate and bold curving around her glorious tits, cupping them like a prize. They are a prize. Perfectly perky and more than enough to fill my hands. On such a small thing as Sally, they should be too much. But they're not. Even at their size, they fit her perfectly. I wouldn't have her any other way.

Sally's hands reach out searching, unbuttoning my jeans and diving below the waistband inside my boxers to grip my shaft and giving it a torturously wonderful squeeze.

"Fuck, Sally. That feels so goddamn good. Do it again."

My hips thrust forward on their own, fucking her small hand, and it makes my eyes cross.

"Yes, sir," she whispers into my ear, making my balls tighten, sending more blood pumping into my already steel dick.

"Every time you call me sir it makes me harder."

"Is that a bad thing?" she asks, all feigned innocence, nuzzling her nose against my throat.

"Not at all. As a matter of fact, you can call me sir as much as you like."

She squeezes and strokes my dick, circling the head with her thumb, and a shiver runs up my spine.

"As you wish, sir."

HER FAVORITE JACK-O-LANTERN

My sweet little pumpkin has turned full Elvira on me. A minx in disguise, walking around town feigning innocence and purity.

"You're not as sweet as you look, are you? Walking around like a good little girl with your high-collared dresses and covered legs. When you're really a sex kitten underneath all those layers, aren't you?"

She giggles, and a shadow of embarrassment flushes her cheeks. For a moment, I think she will pull back into herself, hiding this glorious sexual deviant I've discovered inside her. But she doesn't. She washes it away with determined resolution, a look I can only call sex eyes settling into place.

"You found me out. What are you going to do about it now . . . sir?"

That voice that, was just moments ago, sweet and screaming out her orgasm, is now low and raspy. A sex kitten indeed.

Shucking off my pants as quickly as I can, I am finally bare against her. Gently brushing her hand away and pressing my dick to her wetness, I'm right where I've been dreaming about. She's slick and warm and so fucking right.

Her legs are wrapped loosely around my hips, not demanding or restraining, just holding me. Letting me direct our movements. I can tell she wants me, too. She wants me to take control, to dominate in a way that we both desire. I can see it in her eyes, feel it in the way she rocks her hips against me, hear it in the tiny whimpers in the back of her throat every time I advance on her. It sets me off, makes my dick throb eagerly. I want to be the dominator, to control and command. To have her languid and willing beneath me.

"Are you going to be a good little kitten and do as I say?"

"Yes, sir," she answers immediately, and the inferno raging in my chest ignites at her easy submission.

"Good Kitten," I purr into her ear. Rocking my hips against her, I slide my cock through her wetness coating myself.

Every time I slide all the way up and press my shaft to her clit and my balls to her ass, she whimpers. So, I do it again just to hear it. It's almost like the purr of a kitten when you scratch it just right.

I want to spear my dick into her, hear her scream as I stretch her in that way I know she'll like. But I can't, even with how much I want to, I can't do that on the first time. Instead, I roll us over, placing her on top, her legs straddling my ribs. She's going to come on my mouth again before I sink myself to the hilt in her sweet pussy.

My dick disagrees and wants desperately to be inside her, but I won't let it make all the decisions. At least not tonight. Maybe next time. Before I position her where I want her, I decide to tell her and see how she reacts. I need to know that she's down for everything I want to do. We are, after all, still getting to know each other. I'm still learning her boundaries and desires regarding sex. No matter how much it seems like she wants me to command her, I need to know exactly where her line is first. This way, she'll also keep a little of the control but allow herself to give in to me at the same time.

"I want you to sit on my face, Kitten, so I can make you come against my tongue again. I need to loosen up that tight little pussy of yours before I fill it with my cock."

I can't tell if her flushed cheeks are embarrassment from my words or heated from pleasure.

She sucks her bottom lip between her teeth and rolls it around a few times, absorbing all that I said. Those usually soft lilac eyes are a vibrant violet, shining back at me, glazed over and filled with satisfaction. Her small hands play with my abs and chest, running over my nipples and creating a sensation I've never experienced before.

In the past, I never cared for women touching my nipples, I also never got into the whole sir thing either, but tonight, both are causing lighting to bounce through my veins ending directly in my cock.

Sally, my sweet little kitten, crawls up my body like the feline she is, nodding her approval and making her way to sit on my face, just as I commanded.

Fuck yes.

"Yes," she whispers against my lips as she presses a soft kiss there.

"Yes, what?" I admonish her, pinching her ass just hard enough to make her flinch.

She likes it, though, the heat in her eyes intensifies, and she bites back a groan.

"Yes, sir," she corrects herself.

"Good Kitten." I give her a pat on the butt, soothing the

small sting from the pinch.

She continues her journey up my body and promptly positions her glistening pussy above my face, looking down at me beneath her. I lend her a little power in our shifting dynamic. But she knows who's boss here when I lick up her center and thrust my tongue inside her.

Her head falls back against her shoulders, mouth open wide and pussy clenching around my tongue. She can't help herself as she tries to move against me, tries to grind down on my mouth. I don't let her. I hold her where I want her. Her body shakes in my arms, and I love it.

"Grab the headboard, Sally," I command in a tone, deep and foreign, created from my increasing craving to have her and command her.

She watches me through heavy-lidded eyes and grabs the black headboard, securing herself in place above me. Resuming my ministration, watching her watching me has me so wound up, I'm humping the air, trying to mimic the movements of my tongue. Reaching down, I grip my cock in one hand and match my thrusts to the two fingers I slip inside her letting her move up and down on. Keeping her sweet little pink clit in my mouth the whole time.

Precum leaks from my tip, and I use it to glide my hand up and down my shaft, imagining how good it will feel when I slide inside the heat bearing down on my fingers and face.

Sally whimpers above me, her movements uneven and shaking. "I want your cock. I want you to fuck me with it, not your fingers."

HER FAVORITE JACK-O-LANTERN

I'm surprised by her words, but I can't argue with her. I want that, too, and am totally on board with moving right along to my dick inside her.

"Condom?" I ask, with her still sitting on my face.

She stills above me, which has me sliding my finger free of her heat and looking up to see her looking down, a small frown on her pink swollen lips.

"Umm . . . I don't have any. I haven't exactly needed them in a long time. Do you have one?"

Shit, do I? When I was younger—and not in the military—I always had one stashed in my wallet. Now I don't even think I own any. Can't even remember the last time I bought a box.

"Fuck. No, I don't." I drop my head to the pillow and release the death grip on my dick.

Sweet sex kitten Sally has turned back into unsure, timid Sally, and I don't like it. It doesn't suit her. I caress her ass and hips, soothing the discomfort in her eyes, and press soft kisses to the inside of her thigh.

Sucking her lip between her teeth, she looks back over her shoulder at my naked body, then down at her position still straddling my ears. And then my kitten returns, a slow Cheshire grin spreading across her face, showing me all her teeth.

"That's okay, sir. I know something else we can do."

I barely have time to register her movements and position until I get a great view of her pert little ass shifting over my head. Her knees still around my ears but reversed.

And then—*holy fucking shit.* Sally's mouth slides over my dick, and she swallows me down.

"Holy motherfucking Jesus," I curse without knowing what the hell I'm saying as my eyeballs roll to the back of my head. Unintentionally, my hips thrust up, sliding my cock even deeper into her hot mouth, and she takes it. No gag, no sputter, nothing.

My hands are fists in her sheets, and I am only able to open my eyes when she slides my dick out of her mouth with a wet pop.

"I'm only going to continue when you do, Jack."

That's when I realize we're sixty-nineing. Her pussy, once again, hovers over my face, waiting for me. She wants me to get her off while she gets me off. Hell yes.

"As you wish, Kitten."

With no further delay, I seal my mouth over her core, and she seals her mouth around my dick. This is something I've only done once before, and it was not nearly as enjoyable as this. My tongue against her slit is uncoordinated and sloppy, lacking direction or finesse. It's hard to focus when my tiny little sex kitten it sucking my dick like a hoover.

Her hands work the base of my shaft while her tongue swirls around the tip, licking up my precum. Fuck, this feels good. If I don't focus, I'll come before she does, and that is not allowed.

I refocus on my task, thrusting my tongue inside her pretty pink pussy before pulling out and suckling on her swollen bud, flicking it with the very tip of my tongue.

She seems to like that. With the lightest of pressure, I flick my tongue over her clit in slow, teasing strokes. Using two fingers, I slick them through her wet folds and slide back over her puckered hole, pressing gently and circling. Playing with her, giving her enough to send a shock through her. Returning my fingers to her entrance, I slide them in, keeping up my soft licks. Even with her mouth around my dick and my balls in her hands, I make sure she comes first.

With a groan around my cock in her mouth and a shudder across her skin, she quakes and throbs around my fingers inside her. Just in time, too, because I was losing the battle to hold back my own orgasm.

With hers still coursing through her, she doubles down on my cock, literally. Sliding her hands to cup my balls, she surprises the shit out of me by deep-throating all eight inches of me. Pressing her lips to the base and then swallowing.

"Fucking hell."

I bite into the meaty part of her backside where her ass meets her thigh. I'm trying not to move. I don't want to choke her. But she's not bothered with my heft inside her. Sliding my dick all the way out and then all the way back, she swallows. When her lips are sealed around the base of my shaft, I see stars.

"Fuck, Sally. I'm gonna come soon if you keep that up."

She pulls off my dick only long enough to say "Yes, sir." She seals her mouth over me again. This time, I thrust.

"I'm gonna fuck your mouth now, Little Kitten. If that's a problem, just tap my thigh."

She does no such thing but lifts her head up enough so I have room to thrust up into her mouth. Shit. Circling my arm around her side, I grab on to the back of her head and grip her dark curls, holding her in place, then I thrust up and deep into the back of her throat. She doesn't gag or choke, just breathes through her nose.

"Fuck, fuck, fuck, fuck."

Each of one of my curses is paired with a thrust up, fast and hard. I've never mouth-fucked a girl like this before, and it's got me all kinds of twisted up inside. My teeth gently scrape her inner thigh as I suck on her sweet and salty skin. Licking up her arousal that slowly drips down her leg.

"I'm gonna come baby, if you don't want it in your mouth let me know now."

She squeezes my balls a little tighter. And after one final thrust, I'm coming hard in her mouth. Her lips seal around me, swallowing down every drop, as I pulse out my release. Twitching in her mouth against her tongue and tonsils. It only makes me come more. My body shakes under the force of my release.

When my dick finally stops pulsing, I untangle my hand from her hair and release her head. Her mouth slides off my cock that falls with a soft wet smack against my stomach.

Sally repositions herself at my side, resting her head on my chest. Quiet and content, sated and warm. I wrap an arm around her, keeping her in place locked against me. I don't want her going anywhere. It takes me a few minutes to compose myself enough to speak.

HER FAVORITE JACK-O-LANTERN

"That was . . . how the hell did you do that?"

"I, um . . . don't have a gag reflex."

"No shit?"

Well, that explains a lot.

"Yeah. It's kind of my secret weapon," she admits quietly.

One of her arms is stretched out across my stomach and one leg is tossed casually over my thigh. I could stay here forever.

"That's one hell of a secret weapon."

"That's why it's a secret."

We don't move or get up, neither of us apparently wanting to burst our post coital bubble, even though we're both dead exhausted from it. We slide under the blankets and fall asleep wrapped around one another. It may be the best sleep I've ever had.

19 – Jack

Be grateful we didn't buy you an inflatable dinosaur suit

No matter how many times I knock on Sally's door and make out on her couch, the events of Monday night have yet to repeat themselves. Even though I came prepared each time, having bought a box of condoms the next day after our first night together, it seems my kitten has retreated somewhat, losing her initial boldness discovered that night. That doesn't mean she wants it any less. It's evident in her heavy petting. But when things advance, she recedes. I can't tell if it's fear, nervousness, or timidity. Perhaps it needs to be more spontaneous, like it was on that night. An all-encompassing surge of lust immediately satiated rather than gradually building through extended periods of kissing.

She seems unfamiliar with the natural progression of

kissing to making out to sex. It's easier for her to give in when it's unexpected and urgent. I'll have to remember that for next time because my balls are as blue as Babe the Blue Ox. She's temptation incarnate, and I can only take so much.

It's not that I want her for just sex. There's so much about her that I want to learn, experience, and discover, like where her obsession with the creepy and dark came from. Why she loves carving pumpkins so much. Why she allows the people of this town to look down at her. Why she doesn't stand up for herself when they make remarks and slide her sidelong looks of derision.

Watching her ignore everyone with tension in her posture that proves she hears them but does nothing bothers me. I don't want to see her like that. I want her to smile and laugh in public. I want people to see how wonderful she is, like I do. But most can't move past their predetermined idea of who they believe her to be to see who she is.

I do. I see her.

Even if she tries to hide herself from me. Even if she suppresses her true desires and her inner kitten.

I'm a patient man. I can wait for her to accept it, accept us. But I also want to help the process along. I've been stagnant and living my life for others for too long. I won't let her do the same. Sure, she may be far more herself than I've been, but she's still stuck, allowing others to dictate her direction in life even if she doesn't realize it. I do. Because I've been doing it for much longer and consciously.

I would love to enact my new plan tonight, but my

sisters called me and demanded I come over to spend time with them and my nieces and nephews. It took very little leg pulling. I want to spend more time with them. I want to get to know the kids and for them to know their Uncle Jack. I'm a cool guy, after all.

I arrive at Sophie's house, and her husband Noah answers the door, then lets me in with a smile and handshake. Noah's a nice guy and a great dad. He and my sister have been together for nearly fifteen years. They met at a high school dance and have been inseparable ever since. The entire family loves Noah. I only had to threaten him once to never hurt my sister, and he never has. Smart man. Especially now that I've been trained to kill. But I know I won't ever have to implement my skill set on him.

We all congregate in the living room where there's cubbies of toys and books, large well-loved couches and armchairs, a fireplace lined with carved jack-o-lanterns and rubber bats, and four rambunctious children, and my sister Sophie. No Autumn.

"Where's Autumn?" I ask Sophie as she rounds the children to give me a hug that could crush iron.

She may be small, but she is fierce.

"She'll join us later. She had an errand to run first." She smiles, and I swear there's something in that smile, but it vanishes when her oldest, Cooper, squeezes in to give me a hug. He's the only one who knows me, since he was born a few years before I enlisted.

There's a lot of catching up and playing with the kids

that is far overdue.

I'm giving a horseback ride to Melanie, one of the five-year-old twins, when Autumn finally arrives.

"The prodigal sister has returned!" she exclaims, as all four of Sophie's kids advance on her, screaming and circling her in a group hug I very much wish to be a part of.

It's times like these that I missed staying away from home, while I was repenting and assuaging my guilt over Jordan's death. I shouldn't have stayed away. I should have come home at least to visit. Stupid decisions made by a stupid kid. Well, I'm not a kid anymore, and I intend to make up for lost time. Which is why I'm here now. It may have taken a little strong-arming from my family, but I'm glad they did it.

"Where have you been? I thought this was supposed to be family time?" I joke, wrapping my sister in a tight embrace.

Autumn is nearly as tall as I am, only a few inches shorter, whereas Sophie is the shortest one in the bunch. So, hugging her is easy to do over the tops of the heads of all the kids who still won't release her.

"Come on, you little monsters, let your aunt go so she can say a proper hello to Uncle Jack," Sophie scolds with a smile on her face.

The kids release Autumn and return to the living room and their toys and TV, while me and my sisters smoosh together for a sibling three-way hug. It's warm and strong and a very much missed part of my life.

When we break apart, Autumn smirks at me, then Sophie and holds up a duffle bag I didn't notice. Quirking a brow at Sophie, they have a silent sister conversation I am not privy to. They would do this a lot when we were kids. They always spoke without speaking, leaving me in the lurch unawares. With plenty of pranks to be played and mischief to be had, my sisters constantly teamed up against me. All in good fun, though. We always laughed together after all was said and done.

"Why do I feel like I just stepped into the center of an ambush I can't escape?"

Both women eye me with identical blue eyes. We all got that genetic trait, though only Autumn and I have the height and blonde hair, where Sophie is almost as short at Sally with toffee colored hair, like our dad.

Autumn threads her free arm through mine and guides me toward the kitchen. "We, my dearest brother mine, are going to a Halloween party tonight."

"We are?"

"We are," agrees Sophie.

Both are practically giddy at the idea.

"And this"—Autumn holds up the bag—"is your costume."

"Costume?" I frown.

I haven't worn a costume since high school. Adults wear them sometimes, but I didn't know they were into that.

"Is it required?"

"Yes," they say in unison.

HER FAVORITE JACK-O-LANTERN

"It better not be something stupid."

"Not at all, little brother. We would never do that to you. Actually, I think you'll be very comfortable in it." Autumn bites down on a laugh.

Apparently, something about that is funny.

Reaching into the duffle, Autumn pulls out a pair of fatigues. *My* fatigues, not the costume store rip-off ones.

"What the hell? How did you get those?"

The last I saw them, they were in my closet at home, which I locked when I left.

"I have my ways."

"I'd really like to know your ways, considering my house was locked."

She hands me the fatigues along with a basic green T-shirt, *Army* written in bold black print on the front. This shirt is the smallest one I own. What is she getting at with this?

I raise an eyebrow at my sisters.

"It was last minute." Autumn shrugs one shoulder.

"Besides, why would we bother buying you a costume when people are always dressing up as army men? You get to wear a costume without feeling like you're wearing a costume. Be grateful we didn't buy you an inflatable dinosaur suit." Sophie leans against the kitchen counter, arms crossed and grinning at me. "Cooper voted for the dinosaur, but, unfortunately, that's not the theme of the party, so this will have to do."

Grabbing the fatigues from Autumn, Sophie thrusts

them at me and, in her best mom voice, orders me to get dressed.

This is *not* a Halloween party, at least not just a Halloween party. My sisters tried to block the sign, but I saw it all the same on the way in.

Halloween Bachelor Auction: Men in Uniform.

Those sneaky little witches. I knew the moment we walked through the door to the new high school gym that they had signed me up to be auctioned like a prize pig. They want nothing more than for me to find a girlfriend to anchor me to town, so I don't leave again.

This is further solidified when they led me to the sign-in table to check me in. I'm the sixth in a line of twelve to be auctioned off this evening. The prize? A date with me to the mayor's Halloween party. The winner gets to choose the costumes and we, as the purchased arm candy, must abide.

Just fucking great.

We're turning away from the table when I catch sight of Daphne. She's hard to miss, since she's wearing her high school cheerleader uniform. Appropriate, considering the location.

Could she be anymore pathetic?

Not wanting to deal with all that, I redirect us in

HER FAVORITE JACK-O-LANTERN

the opposite direction and find a much more pleasant destination.

    Sally and her two best friends are standing with another man who has his arm wrapped around Chloe the vet tech. Must be her fiancé. They're all in simple costumes, nothing too flashy. Peyton is a hippie in hip-hugger bell-bottoms and crop top. Chloe and her fiancé are some fifties greasers, and Sally . . . well, she looks mostly normal.

    She's wearing a black dress with a high neckline that hits mid-thigh and a pair of spiderweb fishnets. I wouldn't consider it a costume, by her standards, except for the pointy witch hat on her bouncy black curls. It looks like she hadn't planned a costume and threw the hat on last minute.

    "Who are you gawking at, Jack?"

    Autumn's voice pulls me out of my apparent gawking. I didn't realize I was staring. It's hard not to when Sally is the focus of my attention.

    "I'm not gawking."

    "Yes, you are," Sophie agrees.

    Both sisters flank me and eye me suspiciously. Autumn is a dressed as a traditional French mime in a striped shirt and beret minus the white face paint. Sophie is someone named Maribel in a colorful ruffled skirt. I have no idea who Maribel is, probably a character from a kid's cartoon. Noah stayed home with the kids, claiming this to be a sibling's night out. I think he just didn't want to witness his wife selling her brother. Coward.

    "So, who is it?" Autumn pushes.

They line up with my line of sight, which is still directly on Sally and her group of friends.

"Which one? The witch, the hippie, or the poodle skirt?"

"The witch. She's my new neighbor."

In unison my sisters, gasp and turn wide eyes on me.

"The cute, sweet one?" Sophie stage whispers, as if she's trying not to be overheard but still being too loud. No doubt due to her years of raising four children.

"There's a cute, sweet neighbor? How have I not heard about her yet?" Autumn scowls at me and then Sophie. "How do you know about her?"

"Because I actually call with talk with our brother. Not just to tell him what to do."

"I talk with him. And if I'd known there was already a girl involved, I wouldn't have suggested the bachelor auction."

My sisters' voices are louder than I appreciate, and since Sally and I haven't solidified anything yet, I don't think she would like our personal business being aired so openly.

"All right, that's enough, you two. Keep it down, would you?" I grip my sisters by their elbows to draw their attention to me.

"Sorry, Jack."

Autumn looks truly apologetic. Giving me a small weak smile.

"It's okay, Autumn. Really. I know you mean well."

My sisters look a little less enthusiastic about their little coup now, but I know they meant no harm by it. They just want to see me happy.

"So, can we meet her?" Sophie inquires, a carefully innocent smile on her face.

"I suppose, but don't say anything weird, okay? She's kind of timid around people. She doesn't have the best relationship with most people in town. So, just be nice."

My scolding is firm but sincere. I don't want them to bombard her with small-town bullshit. They won't judge her as others in town do, but still.

"Promise," Sophie swears.

"Of course, bro. If she's really that important to you, then we'll behave."

I don't correct Autumn about Sally being important. She is, even if we've only known each other for a couple weeks. She's kind of become my obsession.

Giving my sisters a curt nod, I relax the tension in my body that tightened my muscles while my sisters bickered over Sally.

The last thing I want to do is approach Sally and her friends, looking angry and hostile. I want her friends to like me and maybe someday consider me a friend as well. They seem like the only agreeable people in town, outside my own family.

Sally spots me as we approach her face lighting up as we make eye contact. She eyes my sisters, but the lightness doesn't fade.

"Hey, Sally, I didn't know you would be here tonight."

"Neither did I. Peyton dragged me here under protest. But now I'm glad she did."

"Same. I was also dragged here under protest. I was also *lied to* about what kind of party this was." Quirking one brow, I side-eye Autumn who, apparently, was the mastermind of this little deception.

"Did they not mention it was a meat market?" Peyton asks, grinning at my sisters.

I think she actually approves of their plan.

"No, they did not. And, apparently, I'm the prize pig on the chopping block tonight."

Peyton smirks, looking me up and down, perusing my far-too-tight Army shirt and worn-in fatigues. "I know who I'm bidding on tonight."

There's amusement in her tone, and I chuckle at her. So do my sisters and Chloe. Not Sally. Her face falls into a neutral, flat expression laced with the tiniest bit of dejection. She doesn't like the idea any better than I do. Has she not told her friends about us yet? Or does Peyton just not care? From Sally's continued silence, I'm guessing possibly both. Would her best friend really bid on me? Going home with anyone but Sally would be an unwanted outcome.

I decide that, when I get a moment alone with Sally, I'll make sure she knows as much. I don't want her to think I want anyone else to win me at this ridiculous auction.

Although I'm sure everyone already knows who the others are, I still introduce them as I was raised to do, making sure that Sally is introduced to my sisters. We're then introduced to Chloe's fiancé, whose name is Sam. They met at college, and he moved back here to be with Chloe. It's kinda sweet, really.

Sally is a little more relaxed the longer we all chat, and Peyton's comment seems to have been a passing thought because she doesn't mention it again.

When Sally breaks away to go to the bar for a drink, I take that as my opening.

20 – Sally

Rocking the boat will only end in me sinking it

I make my escape from the group, claiming to need something to drink. I'm not thirsty, but I need a minute. I already didn't want to be here tonight. Seeing Jack was promising until he announced he was to be one of the auctioned. Then Peyton had to go and be Peyton, making that comment. It's not so much I mind her saying it, since I know that's just her, and she means nothing by it. It just made it clear others would also bid on him, and they are most likely going to win him. People like Daphne.

There's no way I have the money to bet on anyone, and with Daphne as my competition, I'll never win. Getting involved with Jack was a bad idea. A fun one, but a bad one. There will always be prettier, normal girls ready and waiting, some seeking him out. With so many options, he'll never choose me. No one would.

I slide up to the bar to get the nearest bartender's attention, but he's animatedly talking to a Playboy bunny. Yikes. Some people took the costume suggestion far too seriously.

Seeing I may be here for a minute, I peruse the space. The decorations are typical—balloons, streamers, pumpkins, jack-o-lanterns, purple-and-orange string lights. This is just a charity auction to raise money for the new playground in the park, so they didn't splurge on the décor.

Most attendees have abided by the costume dress code, even if it's as simple as mine. I wasn't given much time to dress and pulled out my witch hat before Peyton shoved me out the door and into her car.

The bartenders wear black skeleton T-shirts and face paint to complete the ensemble, which glows under the black lights lining the back shelf.

"Hey there."

Jack's quiet, deep voice reverberates down my spine as his heat warms my entire back, his mouth near my ear and one arm caging me in against the bar. It's deliciously intimate but also innocent to any onlooker.

"Hey," I offer without turning to face him, still trying to catch the eye of the bartender.

"You know this was my sister's idea, right? I didn't plan on participating. I didn't even know this was happening."

He sounds . . . imploring. Seeking my forgiveness. Why would he need that? I'm not his girlfriend. He can do whatever he wants.

"It's fine. You're an adult single man. You can do whatever you like. I won't stop you."

I try to keep my voice even and uninterested and, mostly, succeed.

Reaching around my waist, he uses his free hand to spin me to face him, pressing my back to the bar. Our bodies are mere inches from each other, reminding me of when we were naked, with no space between us. Our hands and mouths discovering every inch of skin. My breath catches at the soft sincerity in his eyes as he peers down at me, lifting my chin so I can't hide under the brim of my hat.

"What I *want* is to be back at your house, on your pumpkin couch, with you in my lap. Nothing between us." He speaks so close, his fingers on my jaw, brushing against the swell of my bottom lip. "I most definitely do not want to be here, being bought by some randy woman hoping to seduce me into her bed. There is only one bed I want to be in, and it's yours." Pausing, he leans in as if to kiss me but doesn't. "So, don't for one second believe that I'm going to forget you because some other woman has to buy my time."

There is no one and nothing around us. All I see and hear is him. So close, close enough to kiss. But we don't. We're just breathing each other's air and trying to read the thoughts stirring behind our eyes.

Jack leans in and presses his cheek to mine, rubbing his two-day-old stubble against my skin. He's been clean shaven every time I've seen him. I like this new growth on him. His lips press the barest of kisses on my throat before speaking into my ear so only I can hear him.

"Do you understand me, Kitten?"

My toes curl at the unexpected and very personal nickname. It stirs the part of me that earned that pet name.

My body responds in kind, arching into his and brushing my breasts against his chest. He makes a low growling noise in the back of his throat at the contact.

"Not here, Kitten." Pulling back far enough to look in my eyes once again, he forces my focus on him. Like it could be anywhere else. "Do. You. Understand. Kitten?"

Every word is as clear and smooth as honey.

"Yes, sir," I whisper against his fingers.

"Good Kitten. Now, how about we get a drink?" He pulls away from me to take up the space against the bar at my side, and I internally whimper at the loss of his touch.

I shake it off as best I can, looking around us to see if anyone noticed our proximity. No one seems to watch me in abject horror, so we should be good. Except Peyton. Her body is angled away from me, but her eyes are watching. Bright and questioning.

She doesn't know everything that's happened between me and Jack. I told her about the first kiss and subsequent make-out session on my couch but not the rest of it. Either I was too shy to admit it all or unsure it really happened. It's still too unbelievable someone like Jack is attracted to me. Here, he stands, at my side, calling me kitten, whispering against my skin, and I still think it's all in my head.

I join Jack, facing the bar once again. He's already snagged the attention of one of the female bartenders and ordered us two of the specialty drinks. It's called Pumpkin Juice, but I have a feeling the only thing pumpkin about it is the color. The drinks are orange and steaming, with dry ice in mugs shaped like skulls. At first sip, my suspicions are correct. It's orange flavored and sweet with a kick at the end of whatever alcohol is mixed in it.

"I have an idea," Jack begins before sipping his own Pumpkin Juice. "Why don't you just bid on me?"

A bark of laugher explodes from my mouth on its own accord. I smother it by taking another sip before clearing my throat to respond.

"I don't have that kind of money. There's no way I can afford you." Jack opens his mouth to respond, but I cut him off before he can. "And sexual favors are not an option."

He smirks and shrugs. "Worth a try."

High-pitched laughter rings out not twenty feet from us as Daphne giggles atrociously loud, drawing all eyes in the vicinity toward her, which was, no doubt, her intention. She always has to be the center of attention.

"With my luck, Daphne will be the one to win the auction," he grumbles into the rim of his cup, dejected by the prospect. "Wait." He jerks his head up, and a devilish grin spreads across his face, his eyes bright with revelation. "You can bid on me."

"We've just established I don't have money for that, Jack."

HER FAVORITE JACK-O-LANTERN

I go for a scolding tone and a hand on my hip, but his glee only grows.

"You might not, but I do. Whatever you bid, I'll pay. Just make sure Daphne doesn't win." He is all but giddy at his oh-so-brilliant idea.

I must admit it, is a not a terrible idea. A way to bypass the system.

"Are you sure? I have a feeling Daphne's been saving up for this."

"How could she? No one knew I would be entering tonight, not even me. She didn't have time to save up. If she planned on bidding on anyone, I doubt she has more than five hundred bucks to spend. I *do* have more than five hundred bucks to spend."

I'm not so sure I could go up against Daphne in a bidding war—in public, even knowing she will most likely lose. I don't do well with confrontation. Especially public confrontation, in front of almost the entire town. If I lose in a bidding war against Daphne, it'll be more than obvious what we're really competing over.

Not only would she win the date with Jack, but she would cement her position in the eyes of everyone. As more than, smarter than, prettier, greater, and in all ways better than . . . me. All my carefully curated kindness and polite duplicity would be overruled.

"I don't think that's such a great idea," I admit hoarsely.

"Sure, it is. It's a win-win in my book."

"If I win. If I lose . . ."

I stop trying to explain. He wouldn't understand. Someone who's always been liked and accepted can't fathom the magnitude of losing something that seems so trivial in their eyes. To me, it's not trivial. It would be a catalyst, the beginning of the end.

I've carved out a little normality for myself over the years, and I'd like to keep the status quo. Rocking the boat will only end in me sinking it. Overwhelmed and drowning in the watery depths I am not built for.

"Then, don't lose, Sally. Just keep raising your little numbered paddle, and all will be fine."

I've been staring off into the flickering lights and glowing aura of the high school gym, so unlike when I attended. Refocusing my eyes to see the distinct shapes and movement around me once again, I see people enjoying themselves. Laughing, smiling, drinking, and dancing. So at ease in the swarm of bodies, none of them dreading the night ahead, only excited about its possibilities.

Turning, I face Jack. He wears an identical ease to those around us, not realizing what he's suggesting.

"You know, if I win, Daphne will be furious, even if it's fair and square. She won't let it lie."

"It's just a charity auction, Sally. I highly doubt she takes it that seriously."

I laugh at the absurdity that Daphne Brighton wouldn't take something this ridiculous seriously. If it's not supposed to be serious, it's important to her. If it is actually important, she could not care less. It's like she was programmed to be superficial and shallow.

"Have you met her? This is probably the second most important thing to her after her precious window display. If she loses to me, it's going to be apocalyptic."

"It's a good thing I'm a trained soldier, then."

His smile is warm and confident. He intends to battle if she puts up a fight. It's his determined assurance that has my trepidation dwindling away on the warm and fuzzies it creates in its wake. A reluctant smile twitches at the corners of my mouth.

"Fine. I'll bid on you. You happy now?"

"Extremely," he rumbles, and his voice feels like sandpaper against my skin, sending happy goose bumps across my flesh.

Jack and I regroup with my friends and his sisters, who are all getting along and chatting away. Drinks in hand, smiles on faces. It only takes a few minutes for the tension to slip into a warm, comfortable feeling.

Sooner than expected, Jack is dragged away to be paraded on stage and sold like a mail-order bride. The rest of us stand on the gym floor near the stage. Waiting for the auction to begin any minute now.

When we arrived, everyone was given a little paper paddle with a number on it for bidding during the auction. Chloe shoved hers in Sam's back pocket, seeing as she already has the perfect man. Peyton has been holding on to hers like a precious treasure, waiting impatiently for the bidding to begin. I had almost thrown mine away, but Peyton insisted I hold on to it just in case. I'd nearly forgotten I even held it until it came time to use it. Something I didn't think I would be doing this evening.

Up on stage, the high school principal is going over the rules and prizes and where all the money will go toward. Behind him stands a dozen men, all attractive in varying degrees. From classically handsome to the boy next door to panty-dropping hotties. Jack being a firm member of all the categories. A prize for anyone, most definitely.

His muscles flex and strain against his too-tight T-shirt. I send a silent thank-you to his sisters for making him wear it. I've seen him in all states of dress and undress, but even I have to admit, there's nothing like a man in a well-fitted uniform.

There are doctors, police, firemen, sheriffs, one in a flight suit of the air force variety, and Jack in his army fatigues. The lineup is a sight to behold. Whistles and hoots and hollers come from the audience from women and men alike. At least everyone is allowed to bid on the sexy men, whether they're female or not.

I try to keep my focus on the stage. Ignoring all the others in the audience as the bidding begins, Jack flashes a supportive smile and a discrete thumbs-up when he catches me staring at him.

"I saw that little exchange you and Jack had earlier. Are things going well between you two?" Peyton asks, her eyes focused on the stage but flashing to mine briefly for my response, her tone playful and optimistic.

HER FAVORITE JACK-O-LANTERN

She may be a shameless flirt, but she is all team Sally & Jack. My number one cheerleader, more than excited for me to be getting close and personal with the man I've crushed on for a decade.

"You could say that."

A blush I'm sure is still visible in the colorful lighting of the room washes over my cheeks.

"Uh-huh. And are you bidding on Army Boy tonight?"

"Maybe."

"You know you'll have some stiff competition."

"I know," I sigh.

"And you're not concerned?"

Her question makes me pause.

I am concerned about many things but not about winning. I don't have to worry about the money to buy him, just the backlash from winning. Hopefully, there won't be too many bidders so that I don't have to spend too much of Jack's money.

It's now that I take a cursory look over the people in the audience and notice quite a few are eyeing Jack and not bidding on the others. One stands out at the front of the crowd. I can't tell what her face is doing with her back to me, but her body is posed in a way I assume is meant to entice.

"I'm a little concerned. Not because I think I'll lose. Jack has promised to cover the cost of me bidding on him."

Peyton raises an eyebrow at me in question. *Yeah, surprised me, too, hun.* "He didn't want . . . anyone else to win him. He said he would pay for me to bid on him and win."

"Okay, so you now have the cash to win. So, why concerned?"

Nodding in Daphne's direction, I indicate the source of my concern. "Because when she loses, my winning won't be as sweet."

"What? Beating Daphne should be the sweetest victory. Don't let her bitchy cruelty ruin your fun. Jack wants you to win the date. He is giving *you* hundreds, possibly thousands, of dollars to make sure *you* win. And goddammit, I'm going to make sure you enjoy it when you outbid that trashy excuse for a woman."

Peyton circles one arm around my shoulder and squeezes me. The biggest grin on her lips as she shifts us closer to the stage.

"I cannot wait to see the steam pouring out her ears when she loses." Peyton practically cackles with joy.

She has always wanted to stick it to Daphne and takes every opportunity she gets. This is just one more tally in the win column.

"Thanks, Peyton."

"You're welcome. Now, pay attention. Jack is up next."

21 – Sally

Xenomorph on a cracker

J ack walks to center stage, swaggering like the hottie he is. He knows who's going to be winning him tonight, and perhaps that makes him a little more confident in his walk. The principal asks him to do a little spin, like all the others have done, to show off the "goods."

The cocky bastard he is, he flexes and poses when his back is turned to the audience, showing off his sculpted back and arm muscles. He smirks over his shoulder supposedly at the audience, but his eyes find mine instantly, and I see the playful sparkle in them.

He is such a goof. I smile in response. I have no idea how I ended up here or if here is even real, but I'll take the warm buzz in my chest that sparked to life the first time I kissed Jack. Something about it feels so perfect, which is probably why I don't believe it, but I also can't fight it.

The principal turns Jack to the audience again and begins the bidding. I don't bid right away. Why bother? I'll just wait till it's the last people bidding. I know who'll be my main competition anyway.

Paddles raise, and soon enough, the price is pushing five hundred, then six. It slows, and the last bid is, as predicted, Daphne, at six hundred and twenty-five dollars. The auctioneer calls for six fifty, and I almost don't raise my hand, still afraid of the backlash. But a pleading look from Jack has me smirking, disregarding Daphne and her wrath.

Waiting till the auctioneer is almost ready to call it is when I shoot my paddle up into the air.

Daphne spins on her heels to find the person daring to bid against her. When she spots me and my paddle, her smiling face morphs into scowling disbelief.

The auctioneer calls for six seventy-five, and Daphne's paddle raises. We go back and forth a few times and reach eight hundred dollars. Daphne has been gradually growing more and more irate with my continued bidding. Finally fuming from the nostrils and unable to stop herself, she moves close enough to speak to me.

"What are you doing?" She snarls at me.

"Bidding. What's it look like?"

The sneer on her face only makes me smile wider. This is fun. Peyton was right. I should enjoy this.

"You don't have the money for it. Why keep bidding?" she spits out, like she knows my financials.

She's right, but she doesn't know I'm being bankrolled tonight.

We continue to raise our paddles, bidding as we talk. With Peyton and Chloe at my sides and Jack footing the bill, I feel more empowered than I ever have before, standing taller and speaking my mind to Daphne in a way I never would have dared to in the past. Since neither of my best friends are bidding on Jack—even though Peyton joked about it—they have no problem focusing all their attention on Daphne and me.

Whenever I hear the auctioneer call out and Daphne doesn't raise her paddle, I do. I don't even know how much we're up to at this point, but it doesn't matter.

"You don't know how much money I have. Why don't you worry about your own finances? Do *you* have the money to cover your bidding?"

For a moment, Daphne looks offended I would even suggest such a thing. Then her face drops. Concern I may be right makes its way through her haze of determination.

She turns her attention back to the stage and listens for the auctioneer to call out the next amount. We've gotten up to twelve hundred dollars during our little tête-à-tête.

Peyton and Chloe laugh at Daphne's floundering as realization washes over her features. She squares her shoulders, putting on an air of confident indifference.

I make the next bid, twelve fifty.

Back to you, homecoming queen. What are you going to do now?

She fiddles with the numbered paddle, seemingly

contemplating if she should keep bidding or not. Shifty eyes flit between the auctioneer, Jack, me, and my friends, then back again. She turns to the stage, giving us her back, as she slowly raises her paddle, upping the bid to thirteen hundred.

"You sure you want to do that?" Chloe asks Daphne. "Maybe you should consult with Daddy first?"

Daphne stiffens but doesn't respond or turn around. She wouldn't give us the satisfaction of seeing her humiliation firsthand. She does *not* want to pay that much. It's obvious she's hit her limit.

But I've created a high for myself, bidding against her and putting her in her place. I want to see her squirm. So, I don't bid right away. I'm sure Jack is panicking on stage almost as much as Daphne is in front of me. No doubt he was excited about my winning and then dreading I changed my mind.

Don't worry, Sergeant, I'll be winning this battle. Or is it lieutenant? Actually, I don't know his rank. I'll have to ask him that later. Either way, that doesn't mean I can't play a little warfare mind games in the meantime.

Daphne looks from the stage over her shoulder to me, looking worried she might have to fork out thirteen hundred dollars before the night is over. Her family may be wealthy, and she may have a store in town, but if the whispered gossip I hear is true, she is horrible with money and in a lot of debt. This would not help her situation.

The auctioneer is calling for last bids—going once . . .

going twice . . .

I raise my paddle. "Fifteen hundred."

Beat that, Daphne.

She doesn't. Her face is a mixture of anger and resentment at not just losing but losing to *me*. It clashes with her cheerleading uniform. I, on the other hand, am feeling something new. Elation and smugness.

Is this what winning feels like? Is this what people like Jack and Daphne feel daily? No wonder they're always so perky and happy. I would be, too, if this were how I felt all the time.

People cheer, mostly from my two best friends, as the auctioneer bangs his gavel, yelling, "SOLD to number one sixteen for one thousand five hundred dollars. Congratulations, and thank you for your generous donation."

Even after spending so much of his money, Jack looks pleased as punch, shaking his head in silent humor at me for making him sweat a little at the end.

The rest of the men are auctioned off. Peyton wins a doctor for five hundred and fifty dollars and is pleased with herself, chattering about playing nurse to his doctor.

When all are done and the bidding over, Daphne is nowhere to be seen, and Jack rejoins our group.

"Cutting it close at the end there," he says, a teasing look in his baby blues.

When he was on stage, they shone under the spotlights like sapphire jewels, and they still retain that bright vibrancy.

I shrug, playing it as cool as I'm able, which isn't very

much. "I had to make sure you were worth the money. Didn't want to make a bad investment."

"Oh, Pumpkin, I'm never a bad investment. I only appreciate with time. My stocks never go down."

We're both laughing when Jack's sister, Autumn, circles around to us.

"Thanks for bidding on my brother," she says, slinging one arm around her brother's shoulders. "None of us wanted him to have to suffer with Daphne."

"You're not a fan of hers, then?" I thought everyone in town had drunken that Kool-Aid.

"Not in the least. Didn't like her when Jack dated her in high school and don't like her now. She's so . . . fake."

We all laugh at Daphne's expense, and it feels good to know others aren't blinded by her false persona.

"Well, you're welcome, but thanks really should go to Jack."

Autumn's eyebrows pull together as she cocks her head at me. "And why is that? He was the one being sacrificed to the masses."

"He is the one paying that hefty sum I just bid."

She turns her confused expression on her brother asking with a look what the hell I'm talking about.

"I told her I would pay whatever she bid as long as she made sure Daphne didn't win."

Understanding loosens her pinched brow, and she nods.

"Good thinking, bro. Looks like you learned something after all in the army."

"I learned more than that, you know."

We talk about Jack's career in the army, and I discover he is a sergeant after all. We also talk about how it is being back in town and all the plans his family has for him.

I wish my family were like his, wanting to spend time with me—not because of ulterior motives or to look good in the public eye but because they love me and nothing more.

"You're coming to the Pumpkin Festival tomorrow, right?" Autumn asks me, hopeful, as if we're friends planning to hang out.

It's nice.

"Oh, um, probably. I usually go for a bit. It is, after all, celebrating Halloween, and I love Halloween."

"Perfect. You should go with Jack."

"Autumn," her brother chides.

"What? She should go with you. Show you around, enjoy the festivities. Maybe even have some fun." She elbows her brother, smiling and wiggling her eyebrows with absolutely no subtlety.

"I can ask her to the festival myself, Autumn."

"Well, then"—she waves in my direction, toward my dumbfounded face—"ask away."

Jack glares at his sister, squinting, communicating something that makes her smile bigger. Her hand is still extended in my direction as she waits patiently, not at all uncomfortable with her forthrightness.

Jack clears his throat and turns away from his sister with

a bashful head tilt as he doesn't quite meet my eyes. How fucking adorable. Jack Campbell is shy about asking me to the festival in front of his sister.

Wait.

Jack Campbell is going to ask me to the festival in front of his sister. Xenomorph on a cracker.

"Sally, would you like to go to the Pumpkin Festival with me tomorrow?"

I'm speechless. I've lost all control over my vocal cords. Sure, we've been spending time together but not in public. When we were out together, we had a reason, an excuse, something to tell people when they questioned us. If we were to go to the festival together, there is no reason other than we wanted to. Because he asked me.

Will people stare? Will they say things behind our backs? I don't want to make Jack a pariah in the community, but...

He's looking at me, so hopeful. There's no fear of being out in public with me or concern for what it will mean. He's not looking over his shoulder to see if people are watching us now. He never has. He doesn't care what others think, and for a moment, neither do I.

"Sure. I mean, yes, I'd love that."

"Wonderful." Jack turns to his sister, who is watching our interaction with big doe eyes and an expression I don't really know. Encouraging? Delighted? She wants us to go together, too? Strange.

"See, Autumn, I'm a big boy and can do things myself."

"Good, because if you didn't, I would have had to take

matters into my own hands." She smirks and gives me a conspiratorial wink.

I think I like Autumn.

After thoroughly enjoying myself at a town function for the first time in years, the night slowly ends, and we're all asked to pay our bids.

Chloe and Sam say their goodbyes, Chloe squeezing me tight in a hug reserved only for best friends before doing the same to Peyton and heading home.

Autumn and Sophie also head home, since they drove separately from Jack, who has gone to the bathroom, leaving Peyton and me to make our way to the table to settle our bids.

I, of course, can't pay mine until Jack returns. There's only a few other people in line ahead of us when Daphne appears out of nowhere with one of her floozy friends at her side, drink in hand and a suspicious smile on her face.

"I suppose congratulations are in order. You did win that bid fair and square." She raises her glass toward me, as if we were about to cheer to my victory over her.

Since I have no glass, I just watch her, silently waiting for her to say whatever it is she came to say.

"Thanks?" I grumble when it seems she's waiting for a reply.

"Of course. We're all adults here. We can be civil and friendly about a little charity auction. It's all fun and games anyway. It doesn't matter that you had to buy a date with Jack. We all know his tastes lie . . . elsewhere."

I'm pretty sure he likes the taste of me, but that doesn't stop the splinter of doubt that worms its way under my skin. It's no secret who he dated in high school and what girls he was into back then.

I'd like to think different of him now, but who am I to know? I've had a crush on him for years—a decade, even—but I've never known him till now. And that has only been for a couple weeks. Can you get to know someone on a deeper level in that amount of time?

Am I fooling myself, thinking there's something between us?

I can feel Peyton winding up to let something rip right out of her mouth, aimed for Daphne's smug smile, but I stop her with a light hand to the elbow. A silent warning to keep quiet. I don't know if Daphne is right, but arguing with her will solve nothing.

Peyton snaps her mouth shut with a grunt of disapproval. She's always advocated for me to be more confrontational and proactive when it comes to putting Daphne in her place. It's just how she is, but it's not how I am.

Daphne takes our silence as an invitation to keep talking, even though I wished she would have taken it as a hint to shut the fuck up and leave.

"Jack and I are meant for each other. We always have been. This little game he's playing with you is just an amusement. Once he's had his fill, he'll come right back to me. Just like he did in high school. So, go ahead, have your little date. Come Christmas, it's my bed he'll be warming up on the long cold nights. And you'll be right back where you should be." She takes slow, menacing steps toward me until she's only a short arm's reach away, but I don't back up. I may remain silent, but I will not cower. "In the shadows, far away from us *normal* people."

I want to say something so badly but can't. Fear and experience have conditioned me to stay silent. To be quiet and small, stay out of the way, don't antagonize. In the end, I'm always the one on the short end of the stick. I will be, no matter how I got there. As such, I'm resigned to be there. If I shut up and take it, she'll get over it faster and move on.

My shoulders drop in the defeat she was looking for, and I expect her to turn and leave with her friend flanking her. She doesn't. She gets closer, leaning in to stage whisper in my ear.

"Back off, you Elvira wannabe. He doesn't want you. No one does. Or was that not obvious when that poor guy you duped into marrying you called things off when he realized what you really are? A loser and freak. Just leave us be and crawl back into the black hole you came from."

Hard thumping beats at my rib cage, trying to rip through and break free to run away. Crawl into a dark hole and hide, just like she said I should. A burning starts behind my eyes, and I fight hard to control my breathing and blink back the tears threatening to fall. It's a Pavlovian response to Daphne's taunts. I've heard them so many times in my life it's just automatic to cry. She didn't have to bring Myles and our failed relationship into this, but of course she would.

Anything she can use against me she will. She has no limits or morals.

I'm sure Peyton is seconds away from speaking the words I forced her to swallow before. She doesn't get the chance, as Daphne's cup tilts and the contents spill down the front of my dress.

"Oops. Sorry. It slipped."

Yeah fucking right.

My dress is black, and the drink won't stain—thank goodness—but that wasn't the intention. It wasn't to ruin my clothing or stain my dress. It was to embarrass me however she can. Make me feel insufficient and inconsequential.

It's working.

Peyton's gasp at my side is all righteous indignation, and I'm barely able to grab for her arm again, squeezing tightly to keep her from lunging at Daphne. I don't need to bail her out of jail for aggravated assault again. It's not enough to silence her mouth, however.

"You're a real piece of work, you know that, Daphne? And I don't mean the pretty kind, but the kind made of garbage glued together and called art. The kind that pretends it's more than it is, even though it's made of broken bicycle parts and leftover food wrappers."

Daphne looks slightly offended, but her victory has her schooling her shock quickly and laughing off Peyton's rather accurate description of her.

"Whatever. You're both freaks."

And then she's gone, leaving me sticky and dripping and

HER FAVORITE JACK-O-LANTERN

Peyton breathing fire out her nostrils.

"Why didn't you let me at her? You know I could have taken her out easily."

That, she could have. Peyton may look unintimidating, but she's got a lot of hidden muscle and controlled rage under all the spandex and smiles.

"I know, but it wouldn't have changed anything."

"It might have. You never know till you try. And I would very much enjoy trying."

But I have tried, and I have learned. It doesn't make a difference. It only makes it worse. Angering the beast only makes it strike out harder.

"What's going on?" Jack's sweet, concerned voice breaks through my gut-wrenching self-loathing and doubt, shaking me back to focus on him.

Jack is all sexiness in his army camouflage pants and too-small T-shirt, a worried pinch in his brow as he assesses my newly wet state. Turning sharp sea foam eyes on me, he searches for the source of my distress.

I can't tell him. I can't admit to him I let Daphne get to me once again. I let her slither her way under my skin and plant that seed of doubt, leaving me questioning what's real.

I cut Peyton off before she can answer.

"Nothing. Just an accident. I'll meet you guys outside."

I don't wait for them to respond. Instead, I leave the remodeled gym to seek solace in the darkness of the late October night, which offers open and accepting arms, swallowing me in its nonjudgmental quiet.

Eventually, they emerge from the gym, and Jack drives me home without asking me again about my wet dress. No doubt Peyton told him after I left.

Whatever. It doesn't matter. I may have won the auction, but I feel like I was the loser tonight.

22 – Jack

She ate it didn't she?

After I dropped off Sally last night, I almost got back in my truck and sought out Daphne to tear her a new one. To put an end to this immature behavior she can't seem to grow out of. After Sally stormed out of the gym with tears brimming in her eyes, all I had to do was look at Peyton, and she told me everything.

I've never hated a person so much in my life. My disgust for Daphne's behavior outweighs even the self-inflicted guilt over Jordan's death that is dwindling with every day I spend with Sally.

Peyton's words of wrathful retribution she's planning on Sally's behalf fuel my own fury. I don't think Sally really knows how much her friend loves her and wishes to make her life better. Even if it is by pulling *Home Alone*-style pranks that would leave Daphne looking like a plucked chicken with a sunburn. A few of her ideas were rather inventive, and I almost agreed to help her. But as I suspect Sally told her, it wouldn't work.

With someone like Daphne, it has to be public, dramatic, and over the top to put her in her place—and not in a way that irritates her skin and gives her a bad haircut for a day. It must be all-encompassing and on a level no one will soon forget. That will stick in the minds of all for years to come. It doesn't have to be a battle but clear enough to not be misinterpreted. That's the only way to solve this problem. And I plan on solving it one way or another, starting with the Pumpkin Festival today.

I've planned a few surprises for Sally I hope she'll like. It's a shot in the dark, but that won't stop me from trying. It's also the first part of my plan to make her more comfortable with and accepted by the community. It pisses me off to no end that a town that prides itself on its Halloween Pumpkin Festival is so disapproving of their most pro-Halloween citizen.

Well, I'll show them how wrong they are. I enact part one to my genius plans for today before returning home and changing to get Sally. I think my little neighbor will be pleased with my new attire I've shopped for this week, with her specifically in mind. I liked the orange-and-black flannel so much I decided I needed more Halloween-esque attire in my wardrobe. Thankfully, I discovered a place called Hot Topic in a mall an hour away in Manchester. It was well worth the drive. I hope Sally approves.

I found a plethora of Halloween-themed T-shirts and sweatshirts, more flannels and patterned pants, but my favorite were the graphic button-up shirts. I even bought a pair of sweatpants with a creepy old tree and bats on it, as well as pajama pants with cartoon pumpkins and ghosts printed on them.

For tonight's festivities, I choose my favorite of my purchases, a black-and-orange button-up that looks similar to a bowling team shirt but with a large spiderweb dangling down one side.

I grab the flannel Sally gave me in case it gets chilly, which it, no doubt, will, and tie it around my waist. The farther into October we get, the lower the temperature becomes.

It's almost four o'clock when I ring Sally's doorbell. I texted her earlier to be ready for me at four because I had plans to spend the whole evening at the festival, which started at noon. But I figured getting there at noon and staying till late evening would be a little too much. Plus, I needed time earlier for . . . things.

Sally opens the door, and I'm so happy I chose the orange-and-black over the red and black skull shirt, because now we match. My little pumpkin is literally dressed like a pumpkin. She's in a soft-looking orange sweater with a large smiling jack-o-lantern face stitched across her chest and matching orange tights with the same print in black right above her knees. Her candy corn brooch looks more like a small lapel pin tacked on her collar. The same tantalizing pleated schoolgirl skirt brushes against her lovely thighs as she twirls to lock her door behind her. Her jack-o-lantern purse swings at her hip, completing the ensemble.

"Well, hello, Pumpkin. I love your outfit."

"Thank—" She freezes, taking in *my* outfit. "Wow, look at you. Someone went shopping."

It's nowhere near as festive as hers, but I tried.

"I did. You like it? I have more."

She raises surprised eyebrows at me as I give her a twirl and smile. "Oh, do you now?"

"What can I say? You inspired me."

She blushes, and even under the orange glitter shimmering on her cheeks, I can see the pink blossoming. Even with the dark eyeliner and orange lipstick, she still looks delectable. A Halloween treat I can't wait to unwrap.

Reaching around her waist, I haul her against me, just because I can, pressing us flush until my lips are a centimeter away from hers. "If I kiss you, will it mess up your lipstick?"

"Oh, um, no. It's the long-lasting kind. Please, kiss away."

Again, because I can, I do.

It starts soft and slow, but soon, I can't control myself, and it becomes heated. Our tongues tangle until Sally breaks us apart, breathing heavily against my chest as we compose ourselves.

"We should really get going before I decide to stay home with you instead," she nearly whispers, running fingers along my collar.

HER FAVORITE JACK-O-LANTERN

I would very much like that, but not tonight. I have a purpose and a goal for tonight. Take Sally out, show her a good time, show the people of this town how amazing she is, show *her* how amazing she is, and have a little fun as well.

"As wonderful as that sounds, I'm rather looking forward to the festival." Grabbing her by the hand and lacing our fingers together, I lead her to my truck.

The festival takes place on the entirety of Main Street. They've blocked each end and set up stalls, booths, tables, displays, carnival games, a few old carnival rides, and even a fun house. The street is lined with orange lights, with bales of hay for sitting and to break up areas. Stands with festive foods and merchandise line the sidewalks and games, surrounded by children and adults alike run the center of the street. The most impressive display are the racks and shelves of carved pumpkins lit from within displaying their carvings. There has to be over a hundred carved pumpkins on display, waiting to be voted on and judged for the competition.

I steer us toward the games and food first. We'll get to the pumpkins and fun house later.

Sally is practically giddy as we walk through the festival. Never once do I let her hand disengage from mine. Not only because I'm afraid I would lose her in her excitement if I were to let go but to show her—and others—we are here together. On a date.

We venture between booths, buying salty and sweet treats, perusing stalls with dipped candles, organic soaps, and hand-knitted scarves and afghans. I buy my Pumpkin fingerless orange-and-black knitted gloves to match her outfit and keep her quickly chilling hands warm. She buys me a black knit cap with green bats stitched on it, reminding me of my less-than-manly response to her "friend," Batty. The cap is slouchy and sits back on my head, which makes her smile when I put it on.

One booth has a plethora of holiday wreaths and little wooden signs that say kitschy things that would fit right in on my mother's front porch.

Sally angles us toward this booth somewhat reluctantly. "Let's stop in here for a minute."

"I didn't take you for the *Keep-Calm-and-Love-Jesus* porch-sign type."

The sign that says just that sits propped up on a spike and shaped like a cross. Definitely wouldn't find that stuck in the grass in front of Sally's house.

"I'm not," she admits with an airy sigh. "This is my sister's booth. If they find out I came to the festival and didn't stop in to say hi, I'll never hear the end of it."

"Oh, so I get to meet your sister?"

This is a good thing, right? When girls want you to meet their family? Although she said she wasn't close with her family. Either way, I'll take it because I plan on sticking around for a while, and they might as well find out now.

We enter the booth filled with not only Halloween décor but Christmas, Easter, St. Patrick's Day, and, of course, Fourth of July. A woman who vaguely resembles Sally stands behind a table, curling ribbon into a giant bow for a wreath.

"Hi, Emily."

The woman looks up and gives Sally a cordial smile but doesn't move from her spot behind the table. She doesn't call out or run around to hug her sister but greets her, almost as if she were a stranger.

"Hi, Sally. Didn't know you would be coming tonight."

"Yeah, um, me neither. Not till yesterday."

Sally doesn't introduce me, and I would be offended if not for the awkwardness emanating between the two sisters who couldn't be more different.

Emily is taller than Sally, slender, with long legs. Because I'm obsessed with Sally's rack, I notice Emily has much smaller breasts, barely creating any feminine curve under the long-sleeved T-shirt with a cliché, tacky embroidered pumpkin on the front. Instead of the sexy skirts Sally wears, Emily is wearing khakis. Like slacks one would see a golfer wearing. Her brown hair is stick-straight. The only similarities between the sisters are the shape of their face and mouth.

Instead of waiting for Sally to introduce me, I take it upon myself. Slipping into the booth and standing directly next to Sally, I slide her hand into mine without hesitation.

"Hi. I'm Jack, Sally's date. I'm the reason she didn't know she was coming until yesterday. I kind of waited to the last minute to ask her."

Reaching out my free hand, I extend it toward Emily,

who stares at me, unmoving, slow blinking in disbelief, her eyebrows nearly reaching her hair line. Her hands still and drop the ribbon bow. To make it painfully clear I'm not going away, I gesture again for her to shake it. This time she does.

"Hi. Sorry, I didn't realize Sally was here with anyone."

I rather like the shocked and dumbfounded look on her sister's face.

"Not a problem. Now you know." Sally elbows me in the ribs, and I can't stop smiling while these two sisters glare at me for two completely different reasons.

Emily finally stops gawking at me and turns back to her sister. "You didn't mention you were dating Jack Campbell when I saw you at Mom and Dads the other day."

"Oh, we're not—"

"It's still new, and she didn't want to say anything yet," I declare.

I very much want to date her, and I want no doubt in hers or their minds.

Sally opens and shuts her mouth.

I just smile down at her and squeeze her hand reassuringly. It's enough to smooth out the wrinkle in her brow and the tension in her mouth.

Before this unusual and stifled exchange can continue, a man carrying the cutest little girl no older than four enters the booth.

"Oh, hi, Sally. Didn't know you were coming," he says in greeting.

HER FAVORITE JACK-O-LANTERN

And the light and joy I would have expected for her sister appears on Sally's face, and for a moment, I think it's toward the man. But it's not. It's toward the giggling little girl in his arms. Her hand breaks free of mine and Sally beelines toward the girl, who is also reaching out to greet her.

"There's the bestest niece in the whole wide world. How is my Elly?" she coo's, scooping up the little girl with the golden curls.

Elly squeals and hugs Sally tight around her neck. The greeting is heartwarming and beautiful.

"Auntie Sawy, weeeeee," Elly giggles.

Sally spins around laughing and smiling, unhindered and open. "I was hoping to see my Elly today. Are you having fun at the festival?"

"Yes. Daddy got me a punkin," Elly exclaims.

The little girl is adorable and seems to love Sally, so she is now one of my favorites.

"He did?" Sally gasps in exaggerated surprise. "Let me see."

From behind Sally's head, Elly produces a tiny pumpkin with a painted face on it that I hadn't noticed she was holding before.

"Wow, this is beautiful."

The two girls have a giggle conversation for a minute before Emily intervenes on their obvious bonding.

"Okay, come on, Elanor. It's getting late, and Daddy is going to take you home now. It's close to bedtime."

Elanor? Must be what Elly is short for. Seems like a rather mature name for such a tiny little thing. Elly, or Elanor, pouts and tries to cling to Sally, who looks just as despondent at being separated from her niece.

"No. I want to stay with Auntie Sawy."

"It's okay, honey. I'll come visit soon, all right? I'll bring over your apron, and we can bake cookies."

"Pwomise?"

"Promise."

Sally hands off Elly to her father, and they say goodbye and leave the booth. Elly waves over her father's shoulder until they're no longer visible.

"I really wish you wouldn't call her Elly," Emily states as soon as they're gone.

"She likes it. And she's not even four years old. Elanor is so . . . old. She much more of an Elly," Sally argues, returning to stand at my side but keeping her hands knotted together in front of her.

Still wanting to support her, I place a soothing hand on her low back, which I feel her melt against. The way she eases and presses into me has my heart doing summersaults.

"Still," her sister persists. Without a response from Sally, Emily turns her gaze back on me. "You're really her date?"

A choked bark of laughter bursts from my mouth, unbidden. I was not expecting that. "Um, yes. I am her date."

"She didn't pay you to be here? Or blackmail you?"

What the actual fuck? Is she serious right now? Her

daughter may be one of my favorite people now, but Emily is one of my least. I can feel Sally tensing against the palm of my hand. I can't help it when my hand slides around her back and settles on her opposite hip, holding her even closer.

"No. She is not paying me, nor did she blackmail me. *I* asked *her*."

"Huh," she grunts, squinting at me like I may be lying.

"Okay, well, just wanted to stop in to say hi. We're going to go now. See ya later." Sally wraps her arm around my waist and pulls me out of the booth.

I don't say goodbye to Emily, but I give her my best dirty look, so she knows I don't appreciate her condescension.

We don't discuss Sally's sister and what happened in the booth. I can tell she doesn't want to talk about it, so I don't, even though I couldn't stop picturing that curly-haired little girl I had pictured before. An imagined daughter that could be hers, could be mine. It's a strange thing when your mind shows you something you never expected to get your breath caught in your chest.

I force my attention to return to making Sally's night the best it can be. Joking around, making her smile, and indulging her every whim.

We pass by a candied apple booth slowly, inspecting their selection.

I haven't had a candied apple in years.

"Would you like to get an apple? My treat."

I tug her up to the glass-covered displays, the man behind the counter smiling and greeting us with a "Happy Halloween."

Sally hums, taking a long look at the choices, nibbling on her still vibrant orange lips. She's tucked under my arm at my side, and I couldn't be happier. Sometimes, when she catches people looking at us, I can feel her tensing and try to pull away from me. I don't let her.

"No." She shakes her head, curls flouncing, her plastic bloody knife hair clip glinting at the movement. Shimmer comes off the matching earrings and makes me smile. I love how weird she is.

"I don't think I could eat an entire apple. There's still so much more to taste. It would fill me up. But if you get one, I'll take a bite." She smiles up at me.

How could I say no?

"Okay, which one should we get?"

She chooses the creepiest one they have, which is dipped in something black and covered with red drips and gummy eyeballs. I'm assured it's only chocolate, caramel, and gummy candies.

I pay and thank the man behind the counter, stepping to the side and letting Sally take the first bite.

HER FAVORITE JACK-O-LANTERN

She holds the paper wrapper to keep the sticky sugary goodness from getting on her new gloves. Her eyes close, and she groans quietly at the taste. She hands it to me, and I take a large bite before handing it back. When I try to take it back again, she shifts her body away so I can't reach it while she continues to eat it.

"Do you like it?"

"Mmhmm." She nods and looks up at me through her eyelashes, licking her lips.

"Would you like to have that one?"

She bites her lips and looks down sheepishly. "Maybe."

"Then, it's yours. I'll get another one."

Returning to the booth, I get a knowing smirk from the man behind the counter. "She ate it didn't she?" he asks.

"Yup. Could I just get the plain black caramel apple?"

"Of course. Enjoy." He hands me the apple, and I pay, returning to Sally, who's halfway through her own apple.

"Come on, let's go check out the pumpkins, and you can explain to me how the voting works."

On our way to the pumpkin displays, we stop to play a game of ring toss and both lose. It doesn't seem to deter Sally's good mood after the candied apple, the unease from the interaction with her sister nonexistent. Hopefully, she'll remain as happy and carefree when she sees my surprise.

"Okay, so explain to me how to vote on the pumpkins."

Disposing of our apple sticks in the trash, we grab a piece of paper and one of those tiny mini golf pencils at the end of a rack of glowing orange faces and shapes. On the paper is a short list, a line next to each. Best traditional, most unique, scariest, best portrait, and best in show. This is some intense voting system.

"Okay, so here's how it works. Each entry has a number next to their name. That's what you write on the line next to the category you're voting in. You have to choose a different entry for each category except best in show. You can vote twice for an entry if you think it's best of a category as well as best in show," Sally explains as we make our way down the line of entries.

"There's also a separate competition for kids under fourteen. We can fill out that one after we finish with the main competition."

They don't seem organized other than numerically. So, it must be in order of entries made. Some are better than others, a few not so great, and a couple are amazing.

"What's the prize this year?" I ask, knowing Sally knows everything about the festival even if she acts nonchalant about the whole thing.

"A spa experience at Cloud Nine Day Spa."

"Have you ever been?"

"No, but I've always wanted to. A day of pampering and relaxation sounds absolutely perfect," she admits wistfully, keeping her eyes trained on the racks to hide her envy.

Perhaps that'll change soon.

Approaching the third rack, I make sure we get a good, long look at these. "Do you see any here worthy of winning?" Raising an eyebrow, I hope she doesn't hear the anticipation in my voice.

"Maybe, a few are—"

"Are what?" I hedge, knowing exactly what's caught her attention.

"They're—is this"—she points to one and leans in to look at the name printed on the card under neath it—"is that my name?"

I can't contain my smile anymore.

This was my main surprise for the evening, entering her into the pumpkin carving competition. Her carvings are the best I've ever seen, and she deserves to be seen and appreciated by all.

I chose the pumpkin I considered the best of the bunch on her porch. Not sure if she had any more inside her house that were better, but I didn't feel like breaking in to find out.

So, I chose this one. A detailed scene of a werewolf stalking through the forest, blood dripping from his bared fangs and long claws. The hair is so realistic you would swear it would leap off the orange skin and eat you. There's no other entry as detailed and perfect as hers.

"Yes, it is. I hope you don't mind. I sort of stole one of your pumpkins and entered it." I watch her intently, unsure if the expression she's making is good or bad.

She could be overjoyed or extremely annoyed.

"I don't mind. I just don't think it was worth your time to enter it. It won't win." Shaking her head as if it's already decided, she looks down at her feet, dejected.

"Nonsense. It's going to win best in show. You just

watch. Look." I pull up my voting paper and write her number in bold on the *Best in Show* line, 283. "See. Now write it on yours, and you'll have at least two votes. I also may have mentioned it to Peyton, so that'll make three and my sisters, who will make Noah vote, too, so that's . . . six."

She worries her lip again, picking at the hem of her sweater, fiddling uncharacteristically.

"If it makes you feel better, I entered one, too." Pointing, I draw her attention to my less than perfect carving.

I did a simple triangle face but slightly snarling, just to give it character. It's no ribbon winner, but I didn't want her to feel alone. So, I entered mine right after hers. Our names sit side by side on the shelf.

Her smile is slow to build, but when it does, she turns it on me, and I melt at the softness in her eyes. Those lavender beauties I marvel at every time she stuns me with their brilliance.

"I guess I should vote for yours as best traditional, then. It only seems fair."

"Of course. It's only fair." I give her my most conspiratorial smile, and she brightens even more.

If I could make her smile like that forever, I would do whatever it took to see the joy spread across her face every moment of every day.

We both enter my number of 284 as best traditional and hers as best in show. I also vote hers for most unique. Since I'm allowed, why wouldn't I?

We make our votes and slip the papers into the plastic

box guarded by a deputy sheriff.

Walking hand in hand back toward the games and booths, Sally presses close to my side, leaning into me. She's calmer, lighter now.

"Have you found anywhere you want to work yet?" she asks, breaking our comfortable silence.

Oh, right. Part of our agreement was she would help me find a job. I'd forgotten about work while helping Sally or thinking about Sally or making out with Sally. I think I might be a little smitten with her.

"No, not yet. I've been a little preoccupied as of late." I give her a wink, and she giggles, actually *giggles*.

The sound, a tinkling of bells against my heart. Jeez, I'm a blubbering idiot for this girl.

"Well, what do you like to do? And I don't mean what kind of job you think you might get. I just mean in general. What do you enjoy? What makes you happy?"

"You make me happy."

The answer is immediate and honest.

She does make me happy. Happier than I've been in a long time, so much so that I've barely given myself time to feel the guilt always riddling me with thoughts of the past and high school and Jordan. I barely feel the effect now. Being around Sally has replaced it with something warm and fuzzy.

Her grip tightens on my hand, and I reciprocate.

"Okay, what else? Besides me."

Her cheeks are a beautiful shade of rosy pink, and

although she's trying to control it, her smile doesn't fade.

"Oh, well, you didn't specify. Um . . ." I take a moment to think of what I like to do. There's not much these days. "Well, something I've always enjoyed is physical fitness, keeping my body healthy and fit, capable of doing whatever I want it to. Hiking mountains, carrying heavy pumpkins, fighting off bad guys, carrying violet-eyed damsels in distress."

"I am not in distress."

"But you could be. And wouldn't you want me to be able to carry you if you were?"

She laughs, and my heart lightens another hundred pounds.

"Would you carry me even if I weren't in distress?" She grins up at me flashing me her teeth.

"I'll carry you to Timbuktu on bare feet if you'll let me."

23 – Sally

My mouth is dryer than a wasteland in hell

I might die from smiling. My anxiety over being seen in public with Jack was through the roof earlier, but as soon as I opened my door, and he kissed me for no reason beyond wanting to, it disappeared. He's kept close, holding my hand, arm wrapped around my shoulder or waist. He even introduced himself to Emily without even a hitch in his voice. He doesn't concern himself with those around us. There's no looking over his shoulder or checking who's watching. It doesn't matter where we are or who's around. All that matters is us. Our happiness.

It's a new concept, not paying attention to what others think of me. I know it sounds weird, since I won't change who I am to appease the masses. You'd think that same defiance would apply elsewhere. If I don't care what they think of how I dress and live my life, why should I care that they stare at me? Why should I care that they gossip? I can't tell you why—I just do. I won't stop being me for anyone ever again. That doesn't mean I wouldn't like it if everyone else accepted me.

Why is it engrained in our brain to need to be accepted by others? My life would be so much easier if I didn't care what the town thought of me. I'm happy with the one person whose opinion of me I value most—Jack. He accepts me, even likes my weirdness. Embraces it and wants more of it. The question is, am I willing to give it?

After little debate with myself . . . yes, yes, I am. I will give him all of me. I have dreamt of this man for *years*. I would be a fool to not accept him and all that he offers. He's my literal dream man. And for some bipolar reason, he wants me, too. This could end in a tire fire that will never go out and burn for eternity in the pit of my heart, but I'm willing to risk it. Without risk, there is no reward—as I'm learning with every hour I spend with Jack.

Therefore, I will try my damnedest to enjoy this time with him, starting with tonight, at this festival.

He's already split my heart in two with his little surprise, entering one of my carvings to the competition. I doubt I'll receive any more votes than ours and those of our friends and his family. Devil knows my family sure as shit won't vote for it. That doesn't matter, the fact that he did it in the first place matters. All so he could vote for me and make me feel special. Well, he succeeded, and when we go back to one of our houses tonight, I will make sure to make him feel just as special.

We haven't done more than make out and feel each other up for the past week, but that's going to change tonight. I will play out every fantasy I've ever had about Jack with Jack. Maybe then I won't care about the others in town, as long as I have Jack.

"Are you ready for the fun house now?" Jack pulls us to a stop in front of the ancient fun house.

Decorated with dark colors, it presents a creepy circus theme, with a spinning hallway, mirror maze, and moving floors.

I've always liked the look of it. I haven't been inside since I was a teenager. I doubt much has changed.

"Absolutely."

We get in line to wait our turn. Unlike the funhouses at the state fair, they don't just feed people through not stop in a stream. Instead, they let each group in together and wait until they leave to let the next group enter. Giving people the opportunity to enjoy the experience without being pushed by those in line behind them or having it ruined by a screaming child or douchey frat bro. After about five minutes, I shift on my feet. My bladder screaming at me after all the apple cider and pumpkin spice hot chocolate.

"I'm going to run to the bathroom really quick."

"You want me to get out of line to wait for you? Or I could go with you," Jack offers, ever the gentleman.

"No, it's fine. I just have to pee. I'll be super quick. You keep our place in line so we don't have to wait another half hour."

Now that I'm paying attention to it, my bladder feels like is not only screaming at me but pleading with its life to be emptied. I feel like a toddler squeezing my legs together and doing the pee-pee dance.

"Okay, well, you better go before you explode." Jack chuckles and pushes me toward Ma's.

Leaving Jack in line for the fun house, I jog to Ma's Diner, hoping my body doesn't decide I'm taking too long and pull an emergency evacuation of my bladder right here in the street.

Thankfully, I make it to Ma's and into the bathroom, where there is only one person in line ahead of me, then make it into a stall quickly enough to not embarrass myself. After relieving myself of what felt like a gallon of liquid, I wash up and make my way back out to Jack.

When I'm outside, returning to the fun house, my path is hindered by none other than the devil's spawn herself, Daphne. I'm forced to stop my progress back to Jack to listen to whatever bile she's planning to spew my way.

"Sally," she sing-songs in a sickeningly sweet tone that makes me want to put a drill in my ears. "What a surprise seeing you here tonight."

"It's the Pumpkin Halloween Festival. Why is such a surprise?"

I don't even have the patience tonight to placate her. I just want to get back to Jack and enjoy the rest of the evening.

"Well, you normally don't attend town social functions, is all. And yet, here you are again, for the second time this month. I must say I was nothing short of shocked to see you at the Halloween Charity Bachelor's Auction. Seeing you again is nearly flabbergasting."

She finishes her little rant, and I take in a long, deep, steadying breath to keep from laying into her the way I know Peyton would be proud of. Instead, I reply, calm and cool, with only a hint of derision.

"Well, Daphne, if you must know, my friends dragged me to the auction, and I'm glad they did. I think I might start attending more town events. I had a lot of fun. As for tonight"—I ponder, wondering whether I should lie and not mention Jack bringing me here on a date but decide against it—"Jack brought me on a date. As a matter of fact, he's waiting for me right now, so if you'll excuse me."

In the past I would have kept my head down and mouth shut, but things are changing now.

I step to the side to get around her, hoping I shocked her enough that she can't say anything else and ruin my mood.

No such luck.

From behind me, she calls out completely calm, "You may have him bewitched for now Silly Sally, but he's not yours. He never will be."

My mood is dampened but not ruined because I have a destination—Jack. When I get back to him, her words will be nothing more than that: words. Worthless, meaningless, desperate words of a pathetic woman who can't seem to move past high school.

When I round the booths to the fun house, Jack has moved up the line but doesn't look very happy. Seeing him without his easy smile and playful sparkling eyes has the sourness from my Daphne encounter curdling in my gut, doubling my fluttering pulse into a pounding in my chest. He's not frowning per se, but he looks displeased, with his hands shoved in his pockets, and his eyes fixed on the back of the guy's head in front of him.

As I approach him, he doesn't even notice me step up next to him.

"Hey." He abruptly turns at the sound of my voice. "Are you okay? Is something wrong?"

Shaking his head, he dislodges the unease and slips a smile on his face. "Nothing's wrong. I was just lonely without you to keep me entertained. Did you know standing in line is incredibly boring if you're alone?" Pulling one hand from his pocket, he slips his arm around my waist and tucks me neatly against his side, right where I belong.

"What? You don't have voices in your head to talk to?" I ask.

We laugh off my weird encounter with Daphne—which I don't mention to him—and his odd demeanor as we slowly move up the line.

We're only in line for another five minutes before it's our turn. Jack pays for our tickets, and we step through the gaping clown's mouth together.

HER FAVORITE JACK-O-LANTERN

It starts with a spinning tunnel hallway, where we both fall on our asses and have to crawl out, laughing hysterically the entire time. We make our way next through a narrow room strung up with bungee cords, then through the moving floor hallway, which slides forward and back and even spins. Next is the mirror maze.

Stepping into the brightly lit space, I see my reflection greet me in four places. Jack's close behind. I promptly walk smack-dab face-first into a clear wall. *Didn't know there were clear walls here, too. Fuck, that hurt.* Reaching up, I dab at my nose to make sure it's not bleeding.

"Careful, Pumpkin. I don't think they have collision insurance, so try not to break anything important." Jack grips my hip and pulls me away from the deceiving invisible wall and directs me to the right, turning into a passage I didn't even see.

He's a lot better at this than I am.

I don't like this maze very much. It's so disorienting I have to keep my hands extended out in front of me, feeling around like an idiot in the dark.

Walking slowly, Jack wraps an arm across my chest against my collarbone and presses a soft kiss to the base of my neck. The corresponding tingle has my feet halting. I want him to do that again.

"How would you like to play a game, Kitten?"

Oh, dear.

The sound of that nickname has more than a faint tingle running through my body. No, now it's a lightning bolt straight to the apex of my thighs. He knows what that does to me. Why is he doing it in the middle of a fun house?

"Uh . . . okay, sure," I whisper in a shaky breath.

"Then, close your eyes," he purrs into my ear, nipping at the lobe when I acquiesce. "Good Kitten. Now, stay still."

Holy shit balls. What is he going to do? His hands and heated mouth disappear from my body, leaving a chill in their wake. After moments of silence, I start to get confused. He's not doing anything.

"Jack?"

No answer. I try again a little more worried this time.

"Jack?"

When he still doesn't answer, I open my eyes and turn to find . . . nothing.

He's not here. What the fuck?

"Jack?!"

Panicking that he left me here and ditched me to have a good laugh at my expense. Thinking I'll probably find Daphne and him at the exit, waiting with a group to point and cackle at me.

A small trickle of paranoia seeps into my chest, my breaths grow shallow and harsh.

"Come and find me!" Jack calls out from somewhere in the depths of the mirror maze.

"What are you doing?"

It's okay. He's just playing a game. He didn't ditch you . . . yet.

I try to calm my nerves, but old habits die hard, and my reaction is all but ingrained in my DNA from years of bullying. *But we're not in high school anymore. We're grown-ass adults, and Jack is* not *like that.*

My reassurances only calm me slightly.

"Hide and seek, Sally. You have to find me, or I win," Jack calls out again from a different direction, a giddy, playful lilt to his words.

He's playing. Exactly like he said, we're playing a game.

"And what is the prize if you win?" I ask, trying to sound nonchalant.

"You have to model every pair of tights you own for me."

"Well, that doesn't sound like much of a prize."

My erratic heartbeat is slowing and smoothing out, my nerves calming. This is just the goofy side of Jack I admire so much.

"Wearing absolutely nothing else," he adds.

I suppose that is a pretty good prize.

"And what do I get if I win?" I ask into the abyss of silver.

I feel my way around toward his voice, moving far too slowly for my liking.

I would very much like to end this game as quickly as possible. The tight corridors of the maze grow closer with every failed attempt to find my way out. I'm so going to lose this game.

"Same thing, except I'll model them for you."

What a goof. His response makes the edges of my lips twitch.

"And what if I don't want that?" I ask, a small laugh carrying my voice.

"Too bad. That's the prize. If you don't want to win, you could just forfeit," he offers.

Not a chance in hell.

"You wish," I take another tentative turn but in the opposite direction of his voice.

This maze is far more complicated and larger than I thought. At this rate, I'll definitely lose. And possibly be lost in a forest of my reflections, which grow more and more agitated at my lack of progress.

I turn another corner and find myself face-to-face with . . . myself.

Dead-end.

I have to turn around, but I have no idea which direction I came from. The walls seem to compress as I hit another dead-end against a clear wall. I see a path on the other side but have no idea how to get to it.

Fucking hell.

I'm liking this fun house less and less. Panic begins to wash over me, one that I haven't felt in years. Trapped, unable to get out, locked in, with no escape. At least this time, there's light. Doesn't make it any better. Neither does the constant creepy circus music. It only adds to my growing anxiety.

What if I can't find Jack?
What if I can't find the exit?
I'm going to be trapped in here, and no one will ever find me, and

HER FAVORITE JACK-O-LANTERN

I'm going to die of starvation.

My mind spirals as more and more horrific what-ifs cloud my rational thinking. Stories from *The X-Files* somehow become reality in my mind. Creatures crawling out from corners with razor teeth and claws, seeking fresh flesh to feed their circus freak family. Mix that craziness with my nearly forgotten claustrophobia, and I'm in full freak-out mode.

Breathing in abruptly, I feel my heart pounding while my head spins. My feet are moving quicker now, but that's not helping me find a way out any faster. It's only making me more aware of how trapped I am. Smacking into wall after wall after wall.

"Jack!"

Jack's name is a croak ripped from my rapidly drying throat. I try to swallow to clear it, but it doesn't work. My mouth is dryer than a wasteland in hell. My hands frantically search the smooth, mirrored walls for purchase in their constant never-ending reflections as I hope to find a way out.

My blood is pumping so hard I hear nothing beyond my own rapid heartbeat. If Jack calls back to me, I don't hear it or the annoying circus music. My hands stay plastered to the mirrored walls as I try to keep moving. My fear rapidly intensifying with every second I don't find a way out.

Don't stop. Stopping will only make it worse.

"Jack! Where are you? I need to get out. I can't get out!"

I'm hyperventilating. Shit. This isn't supposed to happen

on my perfect date with Jack. He will hate me after this. He'll realize what a freak I really am after I break down inside a fucking fun house over a few stupid mirrors, all because of one day in high school, when I had to stay late.

I know I should stop moving, but I can't focus, my vision is blurring, the room is spinning. I feel as if I'm going to pass out as a cold sweat breaks out across my back. Blood drains from my face. My limbs shaking. In a matter of seconds, they'll give out.

Pressing my hands and forehead against a mirror, I close my eyes and try to regulate my breathing. If I can slow my heart rate and control my breaths, maybe I won't die right here in this fucking fun house from hell.

Distantly, I hear muffled, incomprehensible noises, it's like hearing under water. Vaguely, I realize I'm muttering something about Jack and needing help and who knows what the hell else. I think I've lost my mind. My body is shaking harder now, and my vision has narrowed to a pin prick, my head heavy.

"I'm here, Sally." Strong arms wrap around my waist and pull me against a warm body. "I'm here, Pumpkin. Shh. Don't worry. I got you."

Jack mumbles reassurances into my hair and presses kisses to my neck, trying to calm me. I want to calm down, but the panic attack has taken hold of me, racking my body and muddling my brain.

"It's okay. Just breathe. Feel my breath against your back. Match my rhythm," he instructs. I feel nothing. He shushes me soothingly, pressing gentle kisses on whatever exposed skin he can reach. "You have to calm down, baby. I need you to calm down."

I still can't, no matter how hard I try. I no longer feel like passing out, but the fear is still in my veins, setting every nerve on edge, causing my head to feel like a balloon and an anvil all at once.

"I'm going to try and calm you now, Sally, okay? I'm going to touch you to pull your focus," Jack explains. I have no idea what he's talking about because I can't comprehend thought, but I nod all the same. "That's my girl."

One hand slides up under my sweater, pressing his heated flesh to my clammy stomach. I instantly feel a modicum calmer. His fingers deftly move across my stomach, inching up higher.

"That's it. Just relax."

The hand under my shirt reaches my breast, and he cups me over my bra, squeezing lightly, rubbing my nipple with his thumb. *Thank the devil they don't let the next group in until we leave this maze.* A shudder runs through me, relaxing me more. His other hand slides down my thigh, hooks under my skirt, and glides between my legs before running back up the length to my core.

He brushes a finger over my sex, testing my response. A heavy, long breath leaves my chest, and I lean back against his body, resting my head against his shoulder while my hands remain on the mirror. If I remove them, I may crumple into a pile on the floor, even with Jack's strong arms around me.

My panic has receded almost completely as his palm cups me. The clenching of my muscles eases, relaxing against his warm body. My heart beats a rhythm of a different tune. One of lust and desire.

His hands move in tandem, around my nipple and around my clit. His heel pressing in on each circle of his fingers against my entrance through my tights. My focus returns, and the shaking ceases, replaced by a shiver as I grow wet under his touch.

I open my eyes to watch him in the mirror. We're close enough I can see his pupils are blown out as he watches me writhe under him.

"That's it, Kitten. Focus on my touch, my fingers, my lips." He caresses the sensitive skin below my ear with those skilled lips, and I whimper, tilting my head to the side, allowing him more access. He greedily accepts, licking his way down my throat.

Arching back into him, I grind my ass against his crotch, and I feel his cock, hard and long, grind against me. Touching me is turning him on, which only turns me on more. I rock my hips, my aching pussy rubbing into his hand and fingers, my ass into his cock. It feels so fucking delicious and naughty. All thoughts of a panic attack are forgotten. The fun house and its tormenting maze, forgotten. The fear of being trapped, forgotten.

"That's it, Kitten, ride my hand. Later, you can ride my cock. For now, you're going to come for me right here in the middle of a fun house with people waiting outside. You're going to soak through these fucking tights that drive me crazy and know that this pussy is mine. That I can make you come, no matter where we are and what you're wearing."

Jack's words are hot against my ear as we watch each other in the mirror, and I do as he says. My nerves are so sensitive and frayed mixed with the fear and panic still lingering at the edges, with lust and desire that he has me coming against his hand in seconds. My orgasm rockets through me, pulsing and throbbing between my thighs. Jack's hand cups and gyrates to ring out every bit of my pleasure.

"Fuck, that's hot," Jack groans behind me. The hand cupping my breast pinches my nipple, holding tight as he thrusts his hips, rubbing his erection against my ass.

My moans and whimpers are quiet but strangled as the aftershocks of my orgasm fade away, leaving me a satiated puddle of a person in Jack's arms.

"You are so beautiful when you come for me." Jack turns my head with a shift of his shoulders and presses a long melting kiss against my lips.

I realize I'm standing on my own, filled with a warm, soft sensation of after-orgasm bliss.

"How did you know that would work?" I ask, turning in Jack's arms, allowing him to envelop me.

Reaching up, I wrap my arms around his neck. He's much taller than me, and I have to tilt my head back to look him in the eye.

"I didn't. I just figured you needed something else to

focus on. It works when guys panic in the field. Well, not like that. We don't jerk each other off . . . I mean . . . a distraction. Redirecting your attention somewhere else. It helps," he rambles, looking adorable.

"Well, I think you're a genius. I've never heard of a panic attack being thwarted by orgasm."

He smiles, and it makes everything else melt away. I don't care that we're in a freaking fun house, that I almost passed out from a panic attack or that there're probably security cameras in here.

I don't think about any of that as Jack easily leads us out of the maze and fun house and past people who are, no doubt, angry that we took so long. They don't matter for once. They can stare all they want because I'm learning it doesn't matter how they look at me, only how Jack looks at me. And he is smiling at me the whole way home.

24 – Jack

Watch me fulfill your fantasy and mine

I've been half hard the entire trip home. When I first heard Sally's panicked voice in the fun house, I almost broke every mirror in my path to get to her. Whatever was scaring her I would kill it. When I discovered it was her having an anxiety attack, my priorities went from killing the threat to soothing her. Holding her only seemed natural. Keeping her close and shielding her from everything. Nothing mattered but her. When I couldn't get her to calm her breathing, I did the first thing that came to mind.

Now, the fact that rubbing her to orgasm through her tights was my first thought, is something I'll have to dissect later. Perhaps I wanted to touch her to make her feel good. All I could think to do was distract her, pull her focus to something else. That something else being pleasure. I could give her pleasure. I would always give her pleasure. I had no idea if it would work, but I'm thankful as fuck it did.

After that little incident, it didn't seem like she nor I wanted to remain at the festival. So, I directed us to my truck and drove, hence why I'm still aroused after having my hands on her sweet little body, feeling her come on my palm. More than anything, I wanted to slip a finger inside her but was restricted entry, thanks to her tights. That didn't matter, though. A thin layer of nylon can't stop me from pleasuring my girl.

With my house in sight, my need and desire flares to life. Knowing I have a place to take her, I can strip her bare and do everything I was picturing in the fun house to her. I shift a little in my seat, trying to adjust my dick, which is ready to bust out of my jeans.

Sally's been quiet in the passenger seat but not in an awkward weird way but in a contemplative way. No doubt she's embarrassed about the panic attack, no matter how much I tell her it doesn't matter to me. I don't want her to focus on that part of the night. I want her to focus on everything else. The laughing, smiling, and fun we had before and even in the funhouse. I will not let her berate herself over something natural and uncontrollable.

Pulling into my driveway, I turn to Sally before I get out. "Wait right there." I slide out and jog around to her door, where she is patiently waiting for me. Upon me opening her door, she turns to exit, and I step between her legs, forcing her to wrap them around my waist. I scoop her into my arms, and she squeaks in surprise, smiling.

"What are you doing?" She asks wraping her arms tightly around my neck.

"Carrying you inside because I'm an impatient man." Kicking the passenger door shut, and striding to my front door.

Her house is too far, and I can unlock mine in two seconds flat.

"Impatient for what?" She brushes her nose against mine and stretches the tip of her tongue out to flick against my lips.

A pained growl of frustrated arousal rumbles in my chest. She just chuckles. Good. She's not thinking about her panic attack.

"What do you think, Little Kitten?" Griping her ass, I rock her against my hard dick, eliciting the most heart-stopping purr from her throat.

It only makes my cock swell and flex against her core pressed firmly against me.

Finally reaching my porch, I climb the three steps in one long stretch of my legs. My keys already in my hand, I hold Sally with one arm firmly bound around her waist. Before I'm able to open the front door, Sally presses her lips to mine with such reverent desire my knees nearly buckle.

We manage to make it through the front door, and my keys are lost somewhere on the floor. I have to lean against the back of the door to stabilize myself as Sally's tongue finds its way into my mouth. One of us groans, and I can't even tell which.

With one hand, I drag the jack-o-lantern sweater over her head, Sally's legs still wrapped around me securely. It, too, disappears somewhere on the floor, leaving her lace-clad breasts exposed. She fumbles with the buttons on my shirt, and that's when I realize I need to move somewhere more comfortable. Somewhere soft and warm, where I can spread her out and feast on her. I intend to head to the bedroom, but I'm not sure I can make it up the stairs. Instead, I find the nearest stable surface, my boring but sturdy dining table.

It's ironic that the first meal on this table will be Sally. This table just earned its sentimental value.

Setting Sally down gently on the edge of the table, I allow her to strip me of my shirt and hat as I indulge myself in her glorious tits. They are so full and soft, held up with black lace that still shows her dusty pink nipples underneath. Grabbing handfuls of each makes me groan and my dick throb.

I love her fucking tits. I wonder if she'll ever let me fuck them, slide my hard cock between their pale softness. Perhaps she'll even suck on the tip as I do so. Another growl forms in my throat. I need to stop fantasizing and focus on what's happening now.

Sally unties the flannel around my waist. I release her breasts as she unzips my pants and pulls out my dick before my pants even hit the floor. Her small hand wraps around my shaft and squeezes, sliding up and a down, and the feeling is like hot lava being poured over my entire body with how she sets every inch of me on fire.

My brain works enough to start removing the rest of her clothing, clumsily chucking off her shoes, then hooking fingers in her tights and underwear to pull them off. The entire time, Sally casually pumps my cock and spreads the bead of precum around the head.

"You are so fucking beautiful," I mutter right before slamming my mouth to hers again and inhaling her breath, kissing her with an unencumbered impatience I can't control.

I want her so fucking bad it hurts.

Removing her bra, she sits bare before me. Breasts full with peaked nipples, legs spread, and skirt still on riding up around her waist, giving me a glimpse of the holy land beneath. I push it up a little farther, not bothering to remove it. It's fucking hot, and I want it to stay on while I fuck her.

"I'm going to make you scream with the best fucking orgasm of your life, Kitten. Are you ready for me to give you this cock now?"

If she says no, I very well might die. I need to be inside her. I need to feel her tighten around me and her coming on me, knowing I made her feel that way.

She nods and bites her lip. "Yes, sir. I would very much like you to fuck me now." She widens her legs and presents herself like a goddamn present on Christmas morning.

Reaching down, I grab the condom I shoved in my wallet a week ago. After not having one the first time I was blessed with Sally's naked body in my hands, I bought plenty and put one in my wallet, a few in my truck, a couple in my nightstand, and being the horny motherfucker I am, a couple in a kitchen drawer, just in case.

Ripping open the package with my teeth, I kick out of my shoes and pants pooling at my ankles and sheath my painful erection before lining up with her glistening center. Not being a total ass, I run my fingers gently through her wet folds and around her aching little clit, giving it a playful pinch, which earns me a tiny spasm and whimper. I slide a finger inside her to make sure she's ready for me, and holy hell is she. Hot and wet and tight, just waiting for me.

Removing my finger, I place my hand on the table next to her bare ass, steadying myself. Before I can grip my dick and position myself, Sally beats me to it, hooking her heels around my ass, directing me where she wants me, pulling me close to press a soft teasing kiss to my lips.

"I'm going to devour you, Little Kitten. I need to be inside you more than I need to breathe. I need to hear you scream in ecstasy beneath me and writhe in pleasure. It's all I've been able to think about all fucking week."

"Then, make me yours. Take me, claim me, and fill me."

"Fuck," I groan in a husky voice as I slide home inside her. "Mine. All mine."

Filling her, I stretch her in the most delicious way. Her tight heat clamps down around my shaft as I push all the way in to the hilt. Grinding my pelvis into her clit, I memorize the way her eyes roll back in her head and the breathy whimpers and moans as I fill her completely.

"Yes, oh my god, Jack. Fuck, you feel . . ."

"I feel what, Kitten? Say it."

"You feel fucking amazing. God, so thick inside me. I never knew you would feel like this. I fantasized about it, but it doesn't do you justice." Her head rolls back, and her nails dig into my shoulders, where she holds on as I roll my hips and thrust long and slow inside her.

"Are you saying you fantasized about me, Sally?" I ask before pressing a soft kiss to the top of her heaving breast.

"Hell yes. Since I was sixteen, you have been the star of all my sexual fantasies."

We're both panting as I slam into her harder, she can't seem to focus on anything with me inside her. Her lips part on a gasp and my dick pulses inside her at the site.

"You know you're only making me fucking harder telling me that. Knowing you touch yourself thinking of me. That I've been your fantasy for years is a serious ego boost."

"Uh-huh," she mumbles, lost in the throes of passion.

"Look at me, Kitten. I want to see you, and you need to see me. Watch me fulfill your fantasy and mine."

She does as I command, and those gorgeous violet eyes are hazy and half lidded when she pins them on mine.

"Perfect."

Keeping our eyes locked, I lean on the table, and guide Sally to lie back so I can pick up my pace. Thrusting my cock in and out of her heat in an unsteady pace I can't control. Her perfect tits bounce with every upward thrust of my hips. Her breaths become faster and shorter, laced with sounds

I'll never forget. I can feel her pleasure growing. She's going to orgasm soon, and the anticipation only heightens my own pleasure. Balls tightening and pulling close.

"Oh, fuck, Jack I'm going to . . ." She breathes out a loud moan, her nails digging into the meat of my ass, gripping me to her.

"That's it, Kitten. Come for me," I purr into her ear, then suck on the soft flesh of her throat.

Her pussy tightens and clamps down on my cock. Her release has her throbbing as her body shudders around me, her scream throaty and broken in her ecstasy.

"Goddammit, Sally."

"Jack . . . Jack . . . Jack . . ."

Her chants match my thrusts. She's still writhing under me. Her orgasm only elongating with my continued movement.

Pulling her up, I momentarily slide out of her to strip her of her skirt. It was hot fucking her with it still on, but I want nothing between us now. Once it's gone, I slide back inside her and latch my hands to her ass, lifting her off the table.

She kisses me when her face levels with mine, and I groan into her mouth. Standing and holding her, I pump my cock inside her. I need more, though.

I need her to take control. To sink on me and wring my own orgasm from me. Switching our positions, I sit on the table far enough that I can lie back, positioning Sally to straddle me.

She settles on top of me, breaking our kiss. Sitting up and sinking all the way down, her greedy pussy sheathes my entire length. I dig my fingers into her hips and hold her still before pressing into her hips, signaling for her to rock against me. And like a good kitten, she does. Grinding against me and swiveling her hips in a way that has me seeing stars.

"Fucking hell, Sally. I need you to ride me. Bounce on my dick and fuck me how you want. Make me come. Take what's yours."

She replies is a breathy moan, emphasized with one little bounce against my dick, "Yes, sir."

Arching her back, she grips my thighs, presenting me with the best sight on the face of the earth. Sally's tits thrust out and bounce with her movements. Looking down, I discover the second-best sight—watching my dick disappear inside her where we are joined.

Sally is small, but her naked body shows all her glorious curves. The swell of her full, perky breasts, the rounding of her hips as they flare to spread over mine, emphasizing her hourglass figure. The one I knew she had the first time I saw her and wanted to set her on a shelf and stare at for hours. Now I have my wish.

Circling my hands around her narrow waist, I hold on and allow her movements to direct us. Mesmerized by her rhythmic rocking as she lifts up on her knees and drops back down on me.

It doesn't take long before my body is rocking into hers,

lifting to meet hers, seeking the release I can feel building in my spine and balls.

"That's it, Kitten. You're gonna make me come. Fuck yes, don't stop."

My encouragement increases her tempo, demanding I give to her all that she gives to me.

"Yes, Jack. I'm going to come again," she whimpers.

I feel it, her second orgasm rolling through her as her walls tighten down on my dick again. But she doesn't stop. Only keeps riding out her pleasure, forcing mine from me.

"Sally. Fuck yes."

My balls draw up, and I pump out my release inside her. Holding her still over me, pressed flush against her throbbing heat. Each flutter of her orgasm coerces out another spurt of my own. I can feel the condom filling and a trickle rolling down to my balls.

That was the hottest fucking thing I've ever experienced.

Sally falls, limp against my chest, and I wrap shaking arms around her, threading my fingers into her hair as she buries her face in my neck.

Had I known coming home had meant finding Sally, I may have done it sooner. Because now that I have her, I'm never letting her go.

25 – Sally

All man and laundry detergent

My sixteen-year-old self's fantasy just came true. I had sex with Jack Campbell. On his dining room table. *Mother of Mike Meyers fucking shit.* I can't believe that just happened. But the slowly softening dick still inside me and sweaty but perfect man chest beneath me proves otherwise. I don't want to move, don't want to breathe, for fear he might disappear.

But he doesn't. He's here and real and holding me gently but secure against him as if he also believes I might disappear.

Never in my wildest dreams did I ever believe this would actually happen. I mean, I had plenty of fantasies about it, but happening in real life? Never. Which makes it all that more wonderful.

"That was—"

"Fucking amazing," I finish for him.

He chuckles and sighs a deep breath of contentment.

"Yeah, that it was. And perfect. Fucking perfect."

"I'm glad you think so because I think I'm dead. You fucked me to death, and now I'm a ghost, and you'll never be able to have sex with me again. So, it's a good thing you have something to remember on those cold, lonely nights, reminiscing about how you killed me with the best sex ever."

Jack chuckles, and his chest vibrates under my cheek. I didn't plan on saying all that, but it came out all the same, and he doesn't mind as he continues to laugh.

"You are so weird, Sally, and I love it." His arms tighten around me and shifts me.

He finally slides out, and I wince a little at the feeling of losing him. He doesn't care that we're making a mess out of his table and tucks me in at his side, as he's been doing all night at the festival.

Lacing our fingers together on his chest, we lie here naked, sweaty and sticky on his dining table. Not a care in the world.

"Hey, can I ask you something?"

Tilting my head up and resting my chin on Jack's shoulder, I look up at him and grin. "Sure."

"Promise you won't get all weird. I'm just asking this for clarification and don't want you to think I care that it happened."

My grin falls, and I'm suddenly confused and a little

scared he will ask me to leave or something. But the pleading honesty in his worried face forces me to nod and stay silent and still.

"Why did you have a panic attack in the fun house? What caused that? It didn't seem like you had a problem with the tight corridors before we entered the mirror maze. So . . . what changed?"

For a moment, I want to get up and run away. To hide in shame and slink into my little hole of security. His firm hold on me won't let me, though. He doesn't seem upset about or disgusted by it. Just concerned and curious. I suppose he has a right to be. I did kind of flip out on him without warning.

Jack draws calming circles on my back, waiting patiently for me to begin when I'm ready, and I think I fall a little bit more in love with him. Because let's be real, I've been in love with this guy since high school. There's no denying that.

Clearing my throat, I look down at his chest, not able to look him in the eye while I tell my story of high school woe.

"During my junior year in high school, I stayed late one Friday afternoon, working on some Halloween decorations for the Halloween Appreciation Club's display. I hadn't realized how late it was or that there was no one left in the school by the time I left and went to get my books from my locker. At least I thought everyone had left. Turns out, there were still a few people lurking around.

"Daphne, and her crew of cheerleader goonies surprised

me in the hall by my locker. She taunted and teased my outfit and clothes as usual. Normally she would get a good laugh out of making me cry then she would leave me alone to wallow in my self-pity. Only this time, without teachers and adults around to stop her, her taunting turned physical. Shoving me around between all of them, throwing my books on the ground ripping my papers. Classic mean girl bullshit.

"But at the end of it when I was silently crying and not screaming and whaling as much as she wanted, they decided I deserved a worse punishment than ripped homework." Steeling myself with a fortifying breath, I mentally ready myself for the next part. The part that made me panic at the thought of closed, tight spaces.

Jack seems to sense my trepidation and leans down to press a kiss to my hair, then nuzzles his nose against me in the sweetest silent encouragement.

In his arms, I don't feel so raw and beaten, so worn down and used. But warm and full and complete. Whole. Is the only way to explain it. I am whole when I'm with Jack. A strange sensation washes over me and relaxes every tense muscle and worrisome wrinkle. Putting me completely at ease surrounded by his warm skin and calm presence.

He doesn't demand or force it from me, and even in his silence, I feel no judgment or derision, which makes it easier to continue.

"Daphne and her friends shoved me into a locker and locked me inside. I know it doesn't sound like much, but

HER FAVORITE JACK-O-LANTERN

on a Friday afternoon with the school deserted and the foreboding thought of being trapped in there for days, it was terrifying. My panic swelled, and I freaked out. Screaming and crying for them to let me out, to not leave me there. They just laughed and took videos, so they could forever remember the sounds of my tear-filled sobs as I broke down. They left, and I was alone. The lights eventually turned off automatically and the sun outside began to fade. I screamed for hours, but no one came. Not until it was completely dark outside."

Jack's arms reinforce around me, trying to absorb me into his skin. "I'm so sorry, Pumpkin. You should have never had to endure that." I can feel his jaw grinding and clenching as he speaks. He's trying to restrain his anger, and that only makes me relax even more. "How did you get out?"

"The night janitorial crew came in. I heard them and started screaming again for help. They cut the lock off the locker and one of the ladies drove me home." I laugh without humor at the memory. "You wanna know the cherry on the fucking top? When I got home, my parents didn't even realize I was late and should have been home hours earlier. Didn't even ask where I'd been or why my eyes were red from crying and my books and papers were a mess. They're decent people, not abusive in the classic sense, but one could argue being disinterested and not concerned for your child's whereabouts and safety could be considered a form of abuse in its own right. Because it stung as bad as if

I'd been slapped in the face."

The silent, angry tears I'd held through most of my story fall from my cheeks and drip on to Jack's chest. The locker was bad enough, but my parents' utter disregard when I returned home was worse.

Apparently, Jack can't stand it anymore as he sits up, bringing me with him, cradling me to his chest as he stands from the table. Carrying me bridal style, he makes his way to the stairs and up to his bedroom. He disposes the condom from our wild table sex in a trash by the door after gently laying me down in his bed.

It's soft, and the sheets are cool under my naked flesh. His pillow smells of him, fresh and clean and musky. All man and laundry detergent.

Once he has me sufficiently tucked into his bed and back wrapped in his arms against his strong comforting body, he runs his fingers through my hair and settles. "You don't have to think about that anymore because now I'm here. And I will never let anyone hurt you, and I will *always* care. You just call me, and I'll come running."

He punctuates his promise with a heart-melting kiss, brushing his lips softly against mine in a reverence I've never felt before, not even with Myles. His kiss is all-consuming but soft and slow, exploratory in its leisurely conquering of my mouth and soul.

"Can we talk about something else, please?" I ask after he's done worshipping my mouth.

"Of course. What would you like to talk about? How

about the mayor's Halloween party you so graciously purchased me as your date for?"

Remembering the auction and excitement of the party, I breathe out a small laugh and grin at him. "What would you like to know about it?"

Since he hasn't been home since high school, I'm assuming he's never attended the mayor's Halloween party. I myself have only gone a few times in the past. It's a great party, but I usually felt out of place and left early.

"I heard that the person who wins the date gets to pick the costumes. Is that true?"

I give him my most innocent Cheshire grin. "Maybe."

"I'll take that as a yes. So, what have you got planned in that beautifully creepy head of yours?"

He looks down at me, pulling away far enough to give me an inquisitive glare. Not at all worried about what kind of costume I will put him in, he trusts me. And even if it's something ridiculous, he'll wear it with a smile on his face.

"I've got something in mind" is all the hint I give him.

I've been thinking about this since the auction, and I have a specific couple costume I've been wanting to wear for a while but never had a guy to wear it with me.

"It's not condiments or something equally tacky, is it? Because I expect better from you Sally Smithson." He raises an eyebrow in mock sternness.

"No, I would never dress in something so stupid. Don't worry it's a classic, and you'll love it."

"Classic like Sunny and Cher or Morticia and Gomez

Addams?"

"You'll just have to wait and find out."

Keeping it a surprise will be well worth the look on his face when he sees. For once, I'm not concerned about a disgusted rejection. He'll love them.

"Okay, I'm trusting you not to make me look like a fool."

"Oh, you do that just fine all on your own. You don't need my help," I quip.

Jack gasps in mock horror and tickles me until I squirm away, laughing uncontrollably.

It takes a few minutes for my breathing to regulate once he finally stops tickling me and, once again, pulls us close. Curling his large body around mine from behind, he spoons me and presses his face into my hair inhaling deeply.

"You are perfect, my sweet little pumpkin," he murmurs against me. Before I can even blush at the complete sincerity in his words, he lifts off the bed abruptly, scaring the bejesus out of me. "Pumpkins! We forgot to see who won the pumpkin carving contest."

I let out a chuckled sigh of relief after worrying that someone had broken into the house to kill us. "At ease, soldier. They have a whole separate ceremony on Halloween Day naming the winners. We didn't miss anything."

"Oh." Dropping back down, he repositions himself to where he was before his realization. "They really are into all this Halloween stuff, aren't they?"

"More than you can imagine."

"It really makes no sense, then, why they criticize you

for your obsession with it. It's so stupid and hypocritical."

"I agree, but there's nothing we can do about it."

I barely hear it when Jack mutters moments later, when I'm almost asleep, "We'll see about that."

I stay the night at Jack's after the festival on Saturday, but he has a family dinner planned at his parents' Sunday night, so I decide that's a good time for a girl's night. Since both Peyton and Chloe have been hounding me about Jack and what's going on between the two of us, I figure answering their million questions will be good.

Probably super embarrassing for me but good all the same.

After a day spent with Jack baking and watching *Hocus Pocus*—the original—and lots of touching and kissing, the girls arrive around five. Pizza and beer in hand, they scoop me into a group hug, squealing like the sorority sisters we never were.

"Whoa. What's with the long-lost welcome routine? You're acting as if I haven't seen you in years," I manage through the stranglehold my two best friends have on me.

"It feels like it's been years," Chloe grumbles.

"It's been two days."

Chloe steps back, releasing me and making her way to

the living room with the pizza boxes. "It feels like longer. That neighbor of yours has been keeping you pretty busy, huh?" She wiggles her eyebrows at me.

She's not wrong.

Having sex with Jack was like growing wings and flying. Completely unbelievable and thrilling. Almost a dream. Thankfully, it wasn't, as the slight soreness between my legs reminds me.

"He's just been helping me out. You know with the pumpkins and stuff."

"Sure. Just 'helping' you out." Chloe hooks air quotes with her fingers.

"I bet he's helping her out all right," Peyton adds. "Right out of her panties."

We all fall into a fit of giggles. It's only when Chloe notices my face is reddening from more than just the laughter she narrows her eyes on me and points an accusing finger.

"There is definitely something going on there. Something more than just panty removal. I could tell at the charity auction. So, spill it."

Sitting on the opposite end of the couch, I fiddle with a can of soda on the coffee table, avoiding her expectant gaze.

I've prepared for their arrival, laying out plates, napkins, and our favorite sodas. I've also set out a variety of the baked goods I made today with Jack's help.

And by help, I mean manual labor—whipping eggs and

milk, loading the pans into and out of the oven, and, of course, washing dishes. It's nice having a helper around while baking. It takes me twice as long to do by myself and three times as long to eat everything I make.

With Jack around, I don't have to worry about excess. He ate six cookies and two muffins, then took more home with him, leaving me with an acceptable amount for girls' night rather than an entire bakery's worth.

"Yeah, little miss secrets, spill. Tell us every juicy, sweaty, naked muscled detail. Like does he have those adorably sexy but dimples? I bet he does."

I burst out laughing at Peyton's utter certainty that I've already seen Jack's ass. And although we have been naked together, and I felt that glorious ass with my greedy hands, I haven't really seen it yet. I can neither confirm nor deny the presence of butt dimples.

"I have no idea if he has butt dimples, Peyton."

"What? Why not? Haven't you gotten naked with him yet? I would have sworn you had based on how he watched you on Friday."

"And how did he watch me, exactly?" I ask.

My breath stalls in my lungs as I wait for her answer. She can see it, too, my eagerness and interest.

She smiles mischievously. "Like, he could see right through your clothes and knew exactly what was underneath. As if he couldn't wait to see it again. Like he was a man thoroughly turned upside down for you."

"Upside down?" I ask tentativel, unable to voice my real

question.

Did he look like he wanted more than just physical? Was it more than lust?

"Yes. As if his insides were all twisted up. He looked at you with such affection and longing. I wish someone would look at me that way," she admits wistfully.

Her smile softens from sultry seductress to a loving yearning.

It's not sad just wanting, something she very much desires and can't wait to find one day. The fact that she thinks Jack looks at me in a such a way has me feeling all sorts of giddy. To know his sweet words are more than just words. To know there's meaning and feeling behind his gestures gives me hope that I hadn't yet allowed myself to feel. My own tangled feelings become a flutter of wings in my chest. I shake it off, not letting it overpower my sensibility and force me straight into grinning schoolgirl mode.

"If you must know . . . yes. We have gotten naked together."

A chorus of giddy girl screams echoes through my house, scaring one of the nine lives out of Casper and Binx, who were peacefully napping on the chaise in the corner.

Binx, noticing more people in the house, stretches and makes his way over to Chloe, knowing she will give him the most lovin'. Casper just glares at us for disturbing her beauty rest and curls back up. She doesn't come to you. You go to her. This does not mean she doesn't love to cuddle. She just likes to do it on her time. Actually, she's annoyingly persistent when she wants to cuddle. I've woken up in with her sleeping on my side—because I'm a side sleeper—perched like a gargoyle balanced on the side of my ribs. Because, apparently, three in the morning is when she prefers to be affectionate.

"Then, how can you not know about butt dimples? It would have been the first thing I checked."

Of course. Because she would have made him strip for her whiel she ogled and inspected every tantalizing inch of his body. Perhaps I should do that next time we're together. Now I feel like I missed out on something.

"Sorry, I didn't get the opportunity. I'll make sure to check next time and report back to you immediately."

"As you damn well should. It's the only way I'm ever going to know since he's off limits to me. All I have is my imagination."

"Calm down, Peyton," Chloe scolds. "Give her a chance to talk. We're never going to find out why they were naked together and what they did if you keep asking about butt dimples."

Peyton mime's zipping her mouth shut and throwing away the key. We have always been open with one another. Hearing all about the others' sex lives and weird birthmarks and possible rashes. We even know each other's menstrual cycles. Unfortunately, we also know about Sam's nickname for his penis and how he likes to make a funny little voice as if it's talking to Chloe. She thinks it's adorably hilarious—as do I—but it made it hard to look at him without giggling for a good two weeks after she told us about it. I kept imagining the conversations a penis would have with a vagina.

Why, hello, madam. Do you mind if I slide inside? I take up a lot of room but make up for it in orgasms.

Why, of course not. Come right in. Please feel free to stretch out and make yourself at home.

My best friends in the whole wide world sit silent, staring at me expectantly. Legs tucked in curled on the couch with all the time in the world. They know I'll tell them everything if they just give me the time. And I do.

When I'm done they both coo like they just saw a baby deer. I mean, it is adorably cute and sweet that he did all that.

"So, does this mean you guys are dating now? Or is this a hot neighbor with benefits kind of situation?"

Peyton's question is legitimate. I hadn't even thought about asking him if I was his girlfriend. Perhaps we should have discussed that before having sex. I assumed that's where this was going. It doesn't feel like a friends-with-benefits thing. I don't want that—not sure if he does. Doesn't seem like it. Then again, he slept around a lot in high school. But he also had girlfriends, so he can't be completely against the concept.

"Uh, I don't know. We haven't really talked about it out right. I'm pretty sure he wants more than just sex."

"You should really talk with him about that, Sally. Make sure you're both on the same page. The last thing you want is to believe you're in a monogamous relationship and then find out he's sleeping with other women."

The thought of Jack with someone else churns my gut. I never expected to have him, and now that I do, I don't want to let him go. He's mine now, and no one else's.

"You know I love you, Sal, and Jack is a great guy, but... you know how he was in high school. He was a ladies' man, sleeping around with lots of girls. Just make sure everything is clear between you two. Okay?"

I nod, chewing on my bottom lip, worried about where my relationship with Jack is heading. I couldn't handle learning everything Jack did was to get up my skirt and wants nothing more to do with me. Which doesn't make logical sense, since he spent most of today baking with me. Why would he do that if all he wanted was sex?

"I hope you two do date. I mean, can you imagine Jack and Sally? It's too perfect."

I cock my head at Chloe, watching her pet Binx, who is now curled up in her lap, purring happily. "What do you mean?"

She could just mean we would be perfect together, but the way she phrased it has me assuming she means something different.

"Because you're *Jack and Sally*. It's ironic, especially since you love Halloween."

She says our names as if I'm supposed to understand her meaning. Perhaps I should, but my cognitive thinking isn't at one hundred percent at the moment.

"Am I missing something here?"

Chloe stops petting Binx, and slowly blinks at me like I'm the one speaking gibberish. "Jack and Sally," she says again slower this time as if that'll clarify everything, "from *Nightmare Before Christmas*? I would have thought as the reigning queen of Halloween you would have already made the connection."

Holy Halloweentown, she's right. How did I not realize it before? Probably because I was too infatuated with Jack's infectious smile, corny jokes, and magnificent cock. It really is a thing of beauty. Thinking about what he can do with it and his tongue and his fingers . . .

"You're right," I croak out, trying to clear the lust from my brain.

I can still feel the ghost of Jack inside me, and my thighs clench. My core tries to tighten down on the ghostly apparition. Fucking hell. I have sex with him one time, and I'm addicted. Jack is my crack, and I am full and well addicted to him.

"I don't know how I didn't realize it. It kind of would be perfect wouldn't it?" I admit.

"You two could have a Nightmare Before Christmas wedding! It would be perfect. The flower girls and ring bearer could be Lock, Shock, and Barrel. And the officiant could be the mayor. The centerpieces can be pumpkins, and all the guests can dress is costumes. Well, themed attire, costumes are tacky but—"

"Whoa there. Slow your roll. We're not even officially dating yet."

"Okay, but when you two do get married—because you will—this is happening."

I concede to Peyton's demand for a promise to a NBC wedding, which, honestly, sounds amazing. I am not completely opposed to the idea.

26 – Sally

Fuck that's on the internet

We have a movie marathon, rotating between the three of us each choosing a movie. Chloe picks *The Shining*, a classic, I pick *Ginger Snaps*, an underrated werewolf B movie, and Peyton picks *Shaun of the Dead*.

Between *Ginger Snaps* and *Shaun of the Dead* we take a bathroom break. After I empty my bladder and ready it for another round of carbonated caffeine crack, I return to the living room to find Peyton scrolling through Instagram on her phone. Not an unusual sight. She's the most socially active of the three of us. Chloe is a homebody, especially now that she has Sam, and I'm trying my best to stay out of the "social eye."

"Hey, have you seen Daphne's most recent post?"

HER FAVORITE JACK-O-LANTERN

Peyton asks, trepidation in her tone.

She knows I never see Daphne's social media posts. I purposely blocked her.

"You know I haven't."

"Oh, okay. Cool."

Something in her forced casualness has me curious now. Normally, Daphne posts a million selfies and photos of her most recent shopping trip or mimosa. What could she have possibly posted about that would interest either Peyton or me?

"Why?" I ask suspiciously.

"No reason," she answers far too quickly for it to be nothing.

Moving inconspicuously, I meander behind the couch while she's squinting at her phone at this overly interesting post. Positioning myself far enough behind her so she doesn't realize, I look over her shoulder, stop, and wait for her to scroll back up to the photo from all the comments below.

When she finally does, I must make a sound because she starts and yelps, jerking in her seat to look at me over her shoulder. But my attention is focused on the photo. One of Daphne, of course, from the Pumpkin Festival. In front of the fun house, she's next to Jack, nearly fused with his cheek. He's smiling, looking at her like she hung on the freaking moon.

My brain can't keep up with my eyes because my mouth gapes like a fish. I try to form words or a coherent thought, but nothing comes out.

"Shit. I was hoping you wouldn't see that." Peyton hides her phone under the throw blanket as if that'll erase the offending photo from my memory, or the internet.

Fuck, that's on the internet. Everyone in town has probably seen it. The fact that everyone else has seen the photo should be the least of my concerns. What I should worry about is when and why that photo was taken. I was with him the whole night.

Except when I went to the bathroom. Is that when they took it? Did he only stay in line while I left so he could have a secret rendezvous with Daphne? Although, I suppose it isn't very secret if she posted about it on Instagram. Unless that was their plan all along—make me look stupid, make me think I was on a date with Jack, just for them to be all "ha-ha tricked ya" on social media for everyone to see.

Thus, cementing my humiliation.

That doesn't seem right. There's something askew here.

"Why are you two staring at each other and catching flies with your mouths?" Chloe asks when she walks in on us mid-brain glitch.

Peyton turns to her. "Daphne posted a photo on Instagram."

"Nothing new there. She posts like five times a day. The woman has a serious problem with needing validation," Chloe snickers, walking over to the foot of the couch, munching on popcorn.

"It was of her and Jack . . . at the festival last night,"

HER FAVORITE JACK-O-LANTERN

Peyton answers quietly, wincing at the look on Chloe's face, which is frozen, mouth open and popcorn halfway to it.

"I thought he went with Sally?" She points at me, furrowing her brow in confusion, popcorn kernel in hand.

"Yeah, he did. That's why she's just standing there like a glitch in the matrix."

Both women turn to look at me.

I'm not sure how I should react. Angry? Sad? I'm mainly confused. It hurts to see a photo of them together. The picture-perfect couple. Their all-American good looks complementing one another enough to make a stranger stop and go "they would have beautiful children." A small part of my heart shrivels at the thought.

Then the rational part of my brain slowly comes back online. Remembering the things he said, the way he looked at me, his sweet gesture entering my carving into the contest, the way he makes me smile and laugh, how he doesn't judge me or care what others in town think of me, the way he kissed me, the way he fucked me.

Those things don't add up to a guy who's trying to trick me for a good laugh. He most definitely wouldn't have had sex with me if that were his game.

So, the question remains, how did this picture come about?

"Sally?" Peyton hedges gently.

Apparently, I've been staring off into space for far too long. Shaking the fog from my brain, I'm finally capable of speaking.

"Yeah. Yeah. I'm here."

"Thought we lost you for a minute there." Chloe rejoins Peyton on the couch but keeps her eyes on me the whole time. All eyes watching me expectantly.

"No. I just had to process."

"And?"

"And it doesn't make sense." I furrow my brow once again trying to rationalize the photo. There has to be an explanation because what Daphne is trying to infer is definitely *not* the truth.

"Well, that's obvious." Peyton scoffs. "Jack is clearly infatuated with you. So, it makes no sense why he would take a picture like that with Daphne, of all people. I mean, he paid fifteen hundred dollars for you to win him at the auction *specifically* so Daphne couldn't."

True. Just another item on the list in my head of reasons this doesn't make sense.

"Do you think she blackmailed him to do it?" Chloe offers.

Peyton snaps and points her finger at Chloe. "Yes! That's it. She blackmailed him. But with what?" She taps her chin and purses her lips, looking off into the distance, as if she'll find the answer there.

"She didn't blackmail him." I huff out an exasperated breath and move from standing behind the couch like a weirdo and back to my comfortable nest at the end of the couch.

Cuddling under my chunky knit blanket, I pet its

plushiness, the feeling calming my nerves and helping me focus.

"Then, why?" Peyton asks just as confused as me.

"I don't know. But I'm not going to jump to conclusions."

No matter how much I want to. Old habits die hard and all that. But after everything that happened with Myles, I'm no longer going to make assumptions. I will go to the source and discover the truth for myself.

"That makes you a far bigger person than me. If I saw my man that close to Viper Daphne, I would be blowing a gasket," Peyton mumbles to herself, not really helping my new resolve to be calm and levelheaded.

My heart is still racing from the shock, my hands shaking with all the extra adrenaline flooding my system. For the entire third movie, I try to calm my insides to match my feigned demeanor. I have to force joviality at the appropriate times just so they don't suspect the turmoil within me.

By the time we finish the movies and drink all the beer and soda and eat all the pizza and pastries, it's near one o'clock in the morning. Sam picks up Chloe, and Peyton crashes in my guest bedroom, far too buzzed to drive, preferring the comfort of my presence under the same roof than her empty apartment.

I curl up in bed alone, staring out my window, imagining Jack in his bed alone and staring at my window. Well, hopefully alone. I may have claimed to not be jumping to conclusions about the photo, but that doesn't stop my insecurities from spiraling down a dark rabbit hole of doubt. I can only hope deep down that there's a logical explanation for the picture. His curtains are drawn, so I can't see for myself. If I could, it would make falling asleep a hundred times easier. As it is, I take far too long to drift off to sleep.

    Sleep that is fitful and filled with cliché high school nightmares about bullies and mean girls and showing up to class naked. Morning can't come soon enough.

27 - Jack

One does not argue with their mother when she uses your full name

Leaving Sally to have dinner at my parents' house is harder than I expected. I didn't want to abandon her after such an evening, plus the fun I had baking with her for most of today. But she insisted I go. That I made a promise, and I shouldn't cancel on my family last minute like that. I want to invite her and introduce her to the rest of my family. I've met her sister and niece, and she got along so well with my sisters that I don't doubt my parents will love her. However, introducing her to my parents the day after we have sex for the first time might be a little too soon. I'll have to wait till we have sex at least . . . two times. That's not too soon, right?

Am I moving too fast? I want to spend all day and night with Sally. To bake with her and carve pumpkins and help with her interior design work. Hell, I've even contemplated hiring her to decorate my house just so it doesn't feel so impersonal. She told me about a few jobs she's done recently around town, and I may have purposely sought them out to see her work. Most are in private residences, but one was a shop in town. Although I could tell it wasn't her personal style, it was still well done. Great use of space and color, maximizing the potential of the original architecture of the building. She could do well if she could get some publicity about her business. She has a real talent to share with the world. If there's anything I can do to help her with that, I would. I'll have to figure out what that is.

I'm pondering possibilities to help Sally with better marketing and visibility when I pull up to my parents' house. My sisters' cars are already parked on the street in front of their Georgian-style home built originally in the early eighteen hundreds. It's painted a soft yellow and built with slats instead of bricks. The windows are neatly lined in two rows across the first and second floor, a large stately door at its center.

Walking up the driveway, I wonder what someone like Sally would do with such a house. I've seen what she did with her house. I bet she could do wonderful things with my parents'. They haven't remodeled anything inside in decades. Although it's all well maintained, it's out of date. I'm sure I could convince them to let her propose changes, since Sally seems to keep the original architecture and history in mind when designing they're more likely to agree.

HER FAVORITE JACK-O-LANTERN

I'm greeted at the front door by my father, who leads me into the family room.

Autumn is already sipping from a glass tumbler. She gives me a look that has me frowning. I may not have the telekinesis my sisters have with one another, but I understand her expressions. And this one is saying I'm not going to like whatever surprise is apparently waiting for me.

I don't have to wait long—only one whole second, as a matter of fact—as I enter and round the corner.

I spot an addition to our family party I was not expecting.

"Hey there, Jack. It's about time you joined us. We've been waiting forever." Daphne stands, prances over to me, and wraps her arms around me in a brief hug I don't have time to avoid.

Just now, I realize that extra car parked on the street was not Sophie's but Daphne's. A little too late for that to help. Maybe if I'd paid closer attention, I could have avoided this altogether.

Thankfully, she doesn't linger in her embrace. At least she has enough decency to pretend modesty and decorum, showing her "good breeding" in the presence of my family. No doubt to win their favor.

My sisters are privy to her true personality, but my parents are far too out of her social circles to know more than the front she wears out in public.

My father looks accepting of this new outcome but watches me carefully as he sits in his recliner. Autumn is rolling her eyes behind her glass of liquor—no doubt drinking, so she can stand being trapped for the evening with Daphne.

"Uh, hi, Daphne. What are you doing here?"

Apparently, no one is going to tell me, and I'm not too proud to admit confusion. Letting things slide without explanation is not my style. I need to know all the facts of a situation so I can create a battle plan. And after this unseen ambush, I will have to come up with one quickly.

"Your mother invited me."

She doesn't explain further, as if my mother inviting her is all the reason I need, thinking I'll just let it slide and accept her here as an everyday occurrence. It's not, and I won't. Not till I figure this out and put a swift and final end to it.

Daphne hasn't been over to my parents' house for dinner since we dated in high school, and I don't plan on starting that back up again. Why my mother invited her, I have no fucking idea. But I'm about to find out.

"And where would my mother be?"

"Kitchen," Autumn immediately answers.

I thank her with a look that also hopefully transmits my displeasure and also asks that she keep Daphne here while I hunt down our traitorous mother and pry the truth from her lips. Autumn nods and saunters over to Daphne, engaging her in conversation about herself. Daphne would never pass up an opportunity to brag.

I set my sights on the back hall to the kitchen and nearly sprint to find my mother.

"Mom," I call out, lacing all my annoyance and disapproval into my tone.

She turns from the kitchen island, wiping her hands on a towel with a smile on her face that says she ignored my tone and scowl. She's as talented in the kitchen as Sally is, and the smells wafting from the stovetop are a tempting distraction but not enough. Even my love of my mother's cooking won't dissuade me.

"Hi, honey. So glad you finally made it. We were worried you weren't going to show."

My mom's smile is warm and loving, as always. Although since I've returned home, it seems larger than normal. Her eyes, the same bright blue as mine, watch me, and she takes in my rigid posture and frown.

"I said I would, so I'm here. You know who I wasn't expecting to see here, though?" I ask and don't allow her time to answer. "Daphne Brighton. Why is she here, Mother? She said you invited her."

Mom's smile drops. Hooking the towel on the oven handle, she circles the kitchen, trying to read my mood through my eyes.

"I thought you would be pleased she was here."

"And why would you think that?"

"Because of the picture of you two on Instagram. You looked so happy. And when I ran into Daphne at the grocery store earlier today, she implied you two had gone together and were seeing each other again. I figured she might as well come to dinner if you were dating again. You know how I want you to find a girl and settle down here in town."

Cursing under my breath, I let out a deep, frustrated sigh, rubbing one hand over my face. I try to mask the immense rage building beneath my skin, thanks to Daphne's devious lies.

The picture was taken completely by surprise. I was waiting in line at the fun house for Sally to return from the bathroom, when I felt a slender arm sneak around my waist. I thought it was her sneaking up to surprise me. I was surprised all right, when I turned around with a huge shit-eating grin on my face, expecting bright violet eyes and silky black curls but instead finding salon-highlighted brown and Daphne, holding her phone out and snapping a picture.

No doubt the picture looked like we were a happy couple enjoying ourselves at the festival. Pictures can be deceiving, especially when timed just right. I had no idea she posted it on Instagram, nor that she was telling people we are seeing each other. This is utter bullshit, and I'm going to give that girl the verbal smackdown she's been deserving of since high school. Especially after hearing the story of how she locked Sally in a locker. There's not an ounce of civility left in me toward the woman, and she's about to learn that.

"Mom," I start on an exacerbated exhale, "me and Daphne are not seeing each other, and that picture isn't what it looks like. She surprised me, and I thought she was someone else. There's actually a different girl I have been seeing, though. The one I was really with at the festival."

My mother's stricken face morphs from concern to

shame, then to bright, shining hope. I informed my nosy mother that I'm seeing someone in town, and she's already plotting out how to get me to marry her. I can see it in her brightened eyes the longer she watches me. Once again, a smile stretches her face. Her lines deepening at the edges of her lips and corners of her eyes. Ones she's earned through years of laughter and joy in our family. I can't remember a time when there wasn't laughter in our house. Mom and Dad always made sure of it. They're two of the most loving people I've ever met, and their ability to open their home to just about anyone, although commendable, at this moment is infuriating.

"Really? I had no idea. I'm sorry if I assumed, but she insisted you two were rekindling your old flame, and she had the picture. But if you are interested in another girl by all means, please invite her to dinner. I would love to meet her."

Her smile turns mischievous, and I know the moment I bring Sally over for dinner, they'll be picking a date and reserving the reception space.

"Of course you would." I chuckle. I can't stay mad at my mom. "Now can we please tell Daphne to leave? We're not even friends, and I would rather not ruin my night."

"Jack Nathanael Campbell, now I raised you better than that. You may not be dating her, but she's already been invited, and it's polite courtesy to have her stay for supper. Now you go out there and entertain our guest whether you like her or not. And next Sunday I expect this other girl to be present. You hear me young man?"

"Yes, ma'am."

One does not argue with their mother when she uses your full name. Before I can turn to leave and do as she says, she wraps her arms around me and kisses my cheek.

"What's the name of this girl you're seeing anyway? That way I won't make the same mistake twice."

"Sally. Her name is Sally."

In the family room, I pull Daphne aside, interrupting her riveting conversation with my sister about the new paint color in her shop. Autumn looks more than grateful for the reprieve.

"Listen up, Daphne. I don't much appreciate you going around town lying to people about me and us being in a relationship. Get this through your head. I AM NOT INTERESTED. I will never be interested, and my answer will always be no. I want nothing to do with you, and you will stop telling people we're seeing each other. Oh, and you're going to remove that stupid picture you posted on Instagram."

Daphne is still smiling deviously at me, as if she intends on doing none of that. "Oh, Jackey Poo, you know you want me. You always did, and you will again. Stop fighting it and just let it happen. We're meant for each other." She drags her painted sharp nail down my chest, and I swat it away before she gets too far.

"No, we are not, and the sooner you get that through your thick skull the sooner we can both move on with our lives. Now, I told my mother you lied to her and that I wanted you to leave. Unfortunately, she's too polite for that. You're here, so you're having dinner and then you're leaving, and you will not be welcome back here again. *Understood?*"

My angry declaration only makes her smile fall halfway into a polite and, no doubt, permanent fake smile that graces her lying lips. I want to strangle this woman and show her how many ways I learned to kill a man in the army, but I don't. I restrain myself by clenching my jaw almost to the point of breaking a tooth. Daphne still doesn't answer.

"Am I understood, Daphne?"

I use my commanding sergeant voice I would use on my squad. It does the trick enough that she finally concedes.

"Yes, Jack, I understand."

I still don't believe her, but she behaves properly enough for the rest of the evening, engaging in polite conversation with my parents and my brother-in-law Noah.

Autumn and Sophie, on the other hand, ignore her as much as I do. The kids are with a sitter tonight. Apparently, it was planned to be an adult-only dinner after Mom learned about me and Daphne. Thankfully, Daphne behaves appropriately and keeps her hands to herself and doesn't complain when she's seated farthest from me at the dinner table.

This may go down in our family history as the most uncomfortable situation I've ever been in. And I once walked in on Autumn giving a blowjob to her high school boyfriend in the closet in our basement. Talk about awkward.

The night ends, mercifully putting me out of my misery. If I ever see Daphne again, it'll be too soon. Sadly, we live in a small town, and I know it's an inevitability.

Trying not to be too clingy, I wait until nearly noon to walk over to Sally's house. That's enough time, right? I'm sure there's some graph or chart to figuring this shit out, but I'm so far out of practice I have no idea.

I wanted to run over there as soon as I got home last night, but I knew she had invited the girls over and didn't want to interrupt. No matter how great the urge to do just that was. I need to get to her and explain about that stupid Instagram photo before she sees it and gets the wrong idea. She must know by now that I have no interest in Daphne, only her. It's painfully obvious to anyone who takes the two seconds to look.

When I can't stand it any longer, I stride across our lawns and up her front porch.

I nearly crap myself when I'm practically attacked by that damned bat flying overhead in the rafters. Then I almost trip over a white cat with light gray markings along its back. It sits and stares at me expectantly, giving me a lazy meow, which, I guess, means it wants to be pet. This must be the Casper Sally told me about. So, I give her a light scratch on the head. She responds with a quiet purr. Her bright blue eyes squint up at me as I continue petting. Then, when satisfied, she wanders off.

Okay, then. I see now what she meant by ornery.

Ringing the doorbell, I wait impatiently for Sally to answer, trying to decide how I should greet her. Option one, arm propped up on the door frame, leaning in and smirking, hopefully distracting her with my dazzling charm. Option two, hide to the side of the door and jump surprise her when she answers, distracting her with playful laughter. Option three, scoop her into my arms and kiss the living daylights out of her. Although all are good choices, each with their own benefits to distracting her from possibly being mad at me over the photo and making her smile, I think I'll go with option three. It's the most satisfying and immediate. Plus, I desperately want her in my arms again.

My hopes of a steamy greeting are dashed when the door opens, and it's not Sally but Peyton. My wide smile falters to a partial frown as Peyton smirks at me. That's when I notice she's only wearing a sports bra and . . . boxer briefs? I avert my gaze to look up over her head. Not just to avoid staring at her but to also look to see if Sally is behind her.

"Uh, hey, Peyton. Is Sally home?"

"No. She had a consultation appointment."

"Oh, uh, okay."

I'm not sure what else to say to a woman standing there in her underwear, staring at me and grinning.

"She saw it, ya know."

My attention snaps to Peyton. "Saw what?"

"Daphne's Instagram post."

Fuck. I was hoping she rarely checked social media. If Daphne had removed it like I told her to, she wouldn't have seen it.

"How bad is it? Do I need to grovel or buy flowers?" I immediately go into damage control mode. It's been a long time since I had a proper girlfriend, but from what I remember, the green monster of jealousy can lead to righteous wrath. I don't want that with Sally. I never want to make her uncomfortable or jealous or sad. I don't want to hurt her, only make her smile. Feel pleasure. Never pain.

"Depends," she says, arms crossed, tilting her head up to look me in the eye and leaning one hip against the door frame.

"On?"

"The explanation you give for the picture." I groan and rub a hand down my face. "I wagered it was blackmail."

I can't help the humorless chuckle. At least it wasn't something bad. "No, not blackmail, just good old-fashioned trickery."

"Yeah, Daphne's a tricky bitch." One side of her mouth tips up.

I liked Peyton the moment I saw her in front of the coffee house. She was holding tight onto Sally's arm, like a battle buddy standing on the front line, holding their position, no matter the enemies advancing. Everyone deserves a friend as loyal and protective as Peyton.

"I'd really like to explain it to Sally. Is she mad at me?"

I just started this thing with Sally, and I'm already mucking it up. This is not what I had planned.

"No. She's more levelheaded than that. Wants to hear it from you before making any conclusions. She's dealt with the unfortunate results of assumptions before and knows better now."

I can only assume she's referring to Sally's ex-fiancé, who left her two months before their wedding. What an asshole. His loss is my gain. Sally is a catch, and how someone couldn't see that is beyond me.

"Can I make a suggestion?" Peyton asks, watching me with that inquisitive way of hers.

"Please. I can use all the help I can get. I'm a little out of practice."

"Come back later, say around six, with a copy of *The Nightmare Before Christmas* and basically anything from Petra Greek and the biggest bag of candy corn you can find. It'll be a good way to soften her up."

"And why am I bringing over a kid's movie?"

Her grin widens, and she smirks. "You'll see. Just do it. You can thank me later." With a wink, she doesn't wait for me to respond before stepping back inside and shutting the door in my face.

Weird woman. I'm still not sure if she's for or against me dating her best friend. Assuming what she suggested is helpful, I'm going to do as she said and blindly trust she's on my side.

28 – Jack

You spy on me out your window?

While making my way through the supermarket, searching for the candy corn, my phone rings. Dax's name pops up. He's tried to call a few times over the past week, but I was busy with Sally each time and didn't want to be rude to her. Dax just had to wait. I really should have called him back sooner. It probably seems like I ditched him, even though, technically, he was the one to ditch me right in the middle of lunch at Ma's to have some afternoon delight with his wife. Can't blame him. If Sally called me and offered me some afternoon delight, I'd ditch whoever I was with, too.

I answer the phone as I turn down the aisle, hoping to find what I need. This store is so disorganized I don't know how they keep track of anything.

"Hey, Dax."

"Hey yourself. I've been trying to reach you all week. Why have you been ignoring me?" he asks, a mixture of humor and annoyance in his tone.

He won't be mad at me for missing a few phone calls, but he will definitely give me shit over it.

"Sorry. I didn't mean to, just been busy."

"I heard."

"Heard what?"

"That you've been seen around town with Silly Sally."

I growl at him. That stupid nickname needs to die a swift and immediate death. "That's not her name, Dax, and I don't appreciate you—or anyone else in town—calling her that, and I doubt she does, either."

I'm met with harsh silence.

"Wow. I had no idea you, and her had gotten so close."

"Yeah well, we have. Deal with it."

I really shouldn't be so aggressive toward my best friend since high school, but I am getting sick and fucking tired of people talking down about Sally just because she's a little different from them.

"Easy, boy. Calm down. I'm not coming after her. I was just surprised is all. You've only been home a short time and this girl has already got you locked in. I just want to make sure she's not toying with you."

Dax is rightfully concerned. If the situation were reversed, I would ask the same questions, doing my best at being a best friend and protecting him from possible exploitation.

Sucking in a calm, steadying breath, I ease my frustration enough to speak with him evenly. "I know it seems a bit sudden, but I promise you, she's not toying with me." *In any way I don't want her to.* There are many ways I approve of her toying with me, but I'll keep those to myself. "I just really like spending time with her, and she's a lot more than what everyone says she is. If you just spent some time with her, got to know her. I think you'd like her, too."

"Maybe. If after a month she doesn't have you hypnotized or eating your own hair, I'll consider it."

"Really, Dax?" I roll my eyes as I finally locate the freaking candy corn. Who stocks candy corn by the crackers? "Eating my own hair? What do you think she is? She doesn't have magical powers or cast spells on people. She just likes things a little creepier than most."

"Sure. If you say so."

"I do say so."

He just laughs, and the tension in my chest eases. He is a good guy—perhaps a little easily swayed by others but good all the same.

We talk a bit longer and promise that I'll try to not ignore his calls, but if I'm with Sally he will still have to wait. I secure my precious cargo of candy corn and head off to pick up the Greek food I ordered to bring as a peace offering to Sally tonight.

When I entered the little Greek restaurant, I had no idea what to order. The only thing on the menu that I even recognized was French fries and gyros. So, I got one of each for each of us. Along with a Greek salad—in case she was in a salad mood—and something called baklava. The man behind the counter told me it was a staple, and she would love it, so I added it. She has yet to tell me she's allergic to anything, so I figure I'm safe from killing her from anaphylactic shock.

Peyton wasn't lying. When I show up, holding the Halloween movie, fresh hot gyros from Petra Greek, and the giant bag of candy corn, Sally can't hide her smile. Even if she was upset with me, she can't turn me away with the smell of food wafting in through her front door and the promise of a candy corn sugar high.

My choices go over well with Sally. Her beautiful lilac eyes light up at the food and candy I present to her. The movie gets an actual laugh, even if it is short lived. There has to be something more to that I'm not aware of.

I don't get to bring up the photo issue until we're sitting on her couch, halfway through our food. For being so far from Greece, this food is freaking delicious.

"I came by earlier to see you, but you weren't home. Peyton told me you saw Daphne's post," I say tentatively, testing the waters for her reaction.

"Oh, yeah. We saw it last night." Sally averts her eyes, shoving her half-eaten gyro in her mouth.

French fry ends stick out between her lips, and I want nothing more than to lean over and bite them.

"I hope you know that photo was taken completely out of context. I was standing there minding my own business, and she snuck up behind me. I thought it was you." Her eyes drift over to me, still partially hidden beneath her lashes, but she's looking at me again, so that's good. "That's the only reason I look so happy. I was expecting to see you."

Setting down my gyro, I brush the crumbs from my hands and hold hers after taking her gyro from her vise grip and placing it on the coffee table. Forcing her full attention on me. I need to her to hear every word I have to say.

"I want nothing to do with Daphne. I haven't since high school. Hell, I don't think I even wanted her then. *You*, Sally Smithson, are the only one consuming my every thought. *You* are the one I can't stop thinking about and want. In my life, my home, my bed. It's you. No one else."

I have her undivided attention now. Eyes no longer diverted or hidden. She bites her bottom lip, sucking it into her mouth, waiting eagerly for me to continue.

Reaching up I cup her cheek and stroke my thumb across her mouth, causing her to release her lip. It's pink and plump and begging for my kiss.

But not yet. After. I need her to know first. Not wanting to disappoint her and to very much make my intentions *extremely* clear, I continue.

"No matter what people say, or the rumors they gossip about in the market, know this—I am not seeing anyone else. I have no interest in anyone else. I have made that painfully clear to Daphne and if she says anything again, know she's lying out of her ass." Sally giggles and a small smile pulls at the corners of her lips. "Do you understand me, Sally?"

She nods.

"I need you to say it, Kitten."

At the nickname I have now given my little sex kitten, Sally stutters out a breath.

"Yes. I understand," she whispers against the pad of my thumb grazing her lip.

"Good." Leaning in, I give in to my rather obsessive desire for her and slant my lips over hers.

She accepts me eagerly. Melting against me and tangling her fingers in my shirt, nearly climbing into my lap. I don't let her. I didn't come over here and say these things to get in her pants. I also want in her heart, her life. In every part of her.

The overwhelming want that has grown inside me for this woman vibrates down to my very core. A thrumming flutter grows in my chest with every kiss and smile. A seed planted and growing where and when I least expected it.

Coming home, I had imagined my overwhelming guilt would encompass my every waking moment. To claim my life and drag me down. It hasn't, but now I feel guilty for a whole different reason. I am here, alive, and falling for this amazing woman.

I'm planning for the future, which I've never done before. While Jordan is gone. His future and life taken from him before he could make one. He should be here, not me. This is his life I'm living, and the heaviness of it weighs me down.

Breaking the kiss with Sally, I gently sit her back in her seat and turn to face forward. Keeping my face diverted from hers.

"What's wrong?" she asks, settling a soft and gently encouraging hand on my arm.

Her skin, warm against my exposed forearm, sends small goose bumps up my neck.

How can she be concerned for me? She should be mad at me. I'm the one here to apologize, yet she's the one comforting me. What is wrong with me?

"Nothing. I was just thinking . . ."

"About?"

Turning only my eyes, I get a look at Sally, and she's watching me with undisguised concern. Not for what happened with Daphne and the photo or what's happening between us. Somehow, she knows this is something else, and is openly worried about me.

"It's stupid," I admit. "You'll just think I'm being foolish."

"Try me." She gives me an encouraging smile.

How the fuck did I get so lucky to have her as my neighbor? Stumbling upon this perfect woman, simply because I rented the house next door. I can't stop myself from kissing her again. A little more forceful this time. Needing to convey everything I can't put into words.

We pull apart, breathing a little more heavily now, but I don't release her, holding her close in my arms. Anchoring me, she gives me the strength to admit, once again, that the guilt still eats away at me, even all these years later.

"You can't distract me with a panty-melting kiss, Jack. I'm still going to make you tell me."

I chuckle. Of course she's not going to let it slide. I just needed a moment to prepare myself.

"I still feel guilty."

She cocks her head at me in the cutest way, and it makes the ache in my chest ease ever so slightly. "About . . . Daphne?" I shake my head. She furrows her brow at me. "Jordan?" I nod. "I already told you, that wasn't your fault. You can't keep believing it was."

"No, it's not that."

"Then what?"

I sigh. "It's just that I'm still here, and he's not. I feel like I don't deserve this"—I gesture between us with a heavy hand—"any of it. Being with you, laughing, smiling, living. It's like I'm living the life he should've had."

Placing both her hands on my cheeks, she forces my face to line up with hers. I can feel the heat from her breath against my lips, and I just barely stop myself from kissing her again. This time, to distract her from this conversation.

"You, Jack Campbell, are living no one's life but your

own. And I guarantee that if it were Jordan living next door to me, I would not be spying on him out my window every day fantasizing about all the dirty things I want to do to him."

I smirk. "You spy on me out your window?"

"I told you I always had a crush on you. That seems to only have grown since high school," she admits with a barely hidden grin.

"So, what you're saying is that if I were Jordan, you wouldn't have let me touch you in the funhouse?"

"No," she breathes out, inching closer.

"And you wouldn't have let me ravage you on my dining table? If I were Jordan."

"Not the tiniest bit of ravaging." She's practically panting into my mouth now.

My little sex kitten just can't get enough. But her words sooth the guilt. I'm not living his life. I'm living mine.

I ease back, pulling in my lust to calm us both down, trying to remove the gravel from my throat. "Thank you."

Sally blinks away her own lust, hearing my serious tone. Sex can wait till later, after. It can't be the answer to all my problems. She doesn't remove her hands from my chest, though, remaining close but no longer trying to burn through my clothes with her heated gaze.

"You're welcome. How about this? Sometime soon we can go visit his grave. Maybe if you have a little chat with him, it'll make you feel better?"

The thought hadn't even occurred to me to visit his

grave, and, again, I feel like a shit friend. I suppose the guilty fog that blankets my mind every time I even think about Jordan and the accident leaves little room for common sense.

The way Sally suggests it makes it seem like a no-brainer, and I stare at her in awe. This woman has surprised me in more ways than one and, every day, does something new to charm me even more.

"You are . . . well, you're somethin' else, Sally. How did I get so lucky?"

She shrugs one shoulder, a lightness in her movements that has my own body easing. Reaching out, she picks up her discarded gyro to take a giant bite out of it. Man, I love a woman with a hearty appetite.

"Most would say it's the other way around."

"Well, most are idiots. I'm clearly the lucky one here."

"Mmm, I'd say we're both lucky. Because I for one never thought I'd be eating gyros on my couch with high school football super star Jack Campbell, let alone having amazing sex with him." Her cheeks tinge pink with her words, but she doesn't shy away.

No. My kitten is getting bolder, and I like it.

"I suppose I can agree to that."

Returning to my own gyro, I hold up the DVD case for *The Nightmare Before Christmas*, which I learned today is a Claymation Tim Burton film. I've never seen it before and am not sure—beyond that it's a Halloween movie—why Peyton suggested I bring it.

HER FAVORITE JACK-O-LANTERN

"So, what's the story with this movie? Peyton said I should bring it, but I feel like there's more to it than it just being a Halloween movie."

Sally bursts out laughing, almost spitting her food on Casper, who's curled up at her feet. She covers her mouth with her hand to keep her food inside her mouth.

"Um, I'll tell you once we watch it. It'll make more sense."

I learn quickly why Peyton suggested the movie. The main characters are named Jack and Sally.

The patchwork girl has a massive crush on the bone daddy, who is completely oblivious, much like myself. Sally is curled up at my side. Her bouncy black curls press into my chest at just the perfect position for me to bury my nose in them and inhale her tantalizing scent. I'm not sure exactly what it is, but it smells like crisp autumn air and cinnamon. One of her legs is casually tossed over my lap, and I rest my hand on her inner thigh. I rub my thumb lazily across the silky sheer material of her tights, green with little black bats everywhere, which reminds me of our bet in the fun house. Not sure who won. Either way, someone needs to give a fashion show of her tights.

"Is this the only reason we were supposed to watch this movie? Because the main characters are basically us?"

"Something like that. Peyton made a comment that if we get married, we should have a *Nightmare Before Christmas*-themed wedding." Sally abruptly stops talking and stiffens under my arm.

"You're talking to your friends about us getting married? We haven't even met the parents yet. Seems a little presumptuous," I tease.

Honestly, the thought of marrying Sally has crossed my—and my mother's—mind more than once since I started this with her. How could I not think about it? She's kind, thoughtful, funny, resilient, and so strong, more than she knows. Not to mention beautiful and amazing in bed. She has no gag reflex, for fuck's sake. I practically won the lottery with Sally, and I have no plans to squander my good fortune.

Sally squirms and tries to wiggle her way out of my arms and pull her leg off my lap. I grip her thigh, holding her in place, right where she belongs.

"Well, it was just . . . ya know. Girl talk."

"Sally," I say softly, loving her cute stuttering but not wanting her to get the wrong idea. She stops trying to escape me and sits still. "I like you talking about us with your friends. And I especially like you thinking about us having a future together."

Black curls bounce and swing wildly with the force of her head whipping around to look at me. A few bounce off her cheek with the momentum.

"You do?"

Her words are soft and hopeful, and I fucking love it.

"Yeah. I do."

I don't get to see the end of the movie, because my kitten comes out to play and demands my attention. Not allowing me to deny her any longer what she desires.

The first time, we make love slow and languid on her couch her on top straddling me, barely removing her lips from mine. The second time is a little less...soft. I have her bent over the arm of the couch trying to rearrange her furniture with the force of the pounding I give her. And she takes it all. Loving every minute of it as I make her come over and over again, screaming out her pleasure from my touch.

This could be a very good idea or a very bad idea. Ever since Sally took me to the animal shelter the first week I returned to town and introduced me to Sparky, I haven't been able to get the thought of him out of my head. I've never had a pet of my own, but the thought of that poor, energetic, horny dog being adopted and returned again because he's a little overzealous hasn't set right in my chest.

Chloe suggested I adopt him, and I hadn't taken it seriously at first, but now . . . there's a high probability I may be returning home with a dog tonight. After accepting my love for Sally and deciding that it's time to live *my* life, adopting Sparky was the first thing that came to mind.

"Are you sure about this man?" Dax asks from the passenger seat of my truck.

Although I want to spend every moment with Sally

because I'm an obsessed fool, I can't. And after ditching Dax to spend time with her, I'm trying to be a better friend. He called, and I answered. I told him what I wanted to do today, and after laughing at what he thought was a joke for five minutes, he realized I was being serious.

I thought about asking Sally to go with me, but I know she would convince me to adopt him on the spot, and I need someone with an outside opinion to tell it to me straight. If Dax thinks it's a bad idea, he'll tell me. That way, I can make an educated decision, not just fall for Sparky's puppy-dog eyes and floppy ears.

"Yeah, I'm sure. I just need you there to make sure I don't make a snap decision and get all the facts first."

"You know having a pet is like having a child? You can't just put food and water in a bowl and ignore it. You have to train it, take it out, socialize it."

"And that's why I brought you."

He has a child and knows these things. He's probably more of an adult than I am, and I've been in active combat. Yet, I haven't the first clue how to take care of a dog. Because I thought it was mostly that simple. Food and water, let it out to potty, and play with it. What more could a dog need?

"Then there's all the flea and tick prevention, keeping it from eating your socks and shitting on your floor," Dax continues. "Plus, you can't leave it alone for more than six hours, so if you're going to be gone overnight, you have to find a dog sitter."

"Okay, I get it, Dax. It's a big responsibility. I'm not

taking this decision lightly. I just need to know I can handle it before I make a commitment."

Dax looks over at me as I drive down Main Street toward the shelter. The leaves on the trees have all turned and line the street in yellows and oranges, painting a scene straight out of a Thomas Kincade print. Until this moment, I hadn't realized I missed this. The color change of the fall and the cool, crisp autumn air streaming in through my half-open window. It feels like home, something I haven't felt in a long time. And it's not just being back in Laconia that's making me feel this way. One person with a heart as big as my truck comes to mind.

I can see from the corner of my eye that Dax is trying to figure me out. A few weeks ago, I would have been as perplexed as him. I didn't know I was a dog person until I went to the shelter, and, suddenly, I feel like a dog guy. With my newfound desire for home and family, a dog seems like the right addition to start that.

"Does this have something to do with Sally?"

"What?"

How in the hell was he able to see through me so easily? It took me a long time to realize why I wanted this. How was he able to pinpoint it with such certainty?

"Why do you think this has anything to do with Sally?"

"I don't know. You tell me. You've only been home barely a month, and you're already dating her and spending most of your time with her. It seems serious. And you never mentioned wanting a pet before. It just seems out of nowhere."

He has a point. All of what he's said is true. And, honestly, Sally has been influential but more than that I feel like I'm finally finding me. Sure, her generous, kind nature is infectious, but I've always helped others in need. Whether they be human or canine.

Hearing Sparky's story touched something inside me that ignited that part of me that wants to help. If I give Sparky his forever home, where he'll be happy and loved, then I have to at least try.

"It is a little out of nowhere. I didn't think about a pet until we went to the shelter, but it has more to do with Sparky than Sally."

"Who's Sparky?"

"The dog."

"Oh, right."

"It's more about helping him and doing something that I feel I need to do," I say.

Not sure who I'm trying to convince. Dax or me.

The rest of the short drive is spent in silence, and when we enter the shelter, Chloe is behind the front desk.

"Jack. How nice to see you again. What brings you in today?" Chloe looks from me to Dax and gives him a warm smile but waits for me to answer.

I've spent some time with her since our first meeting in this very establishment, and I'm starting to consider her a friend. She's close with Sally, which means we will be close now, too.

"Well, I gave it some thought, and I'm considering what you suggested."

She smiles and looks at me knowingly but plays coy. "What was it that I suggested again? It's been a while, and I don't remember."

"Adopting Sparky."

She knows exactly what I meant.

Chloe shuffles papers on her desk and nods, like she's just now remembering our visit weeks ago. "Oh, right, right. Sparky." She furrows her brow and pinches her lips, like she's about to deliver bad news.

Shit, am I too late? Was he adopted already? I know it's been a few weeks, but I assumed he'd still be here. That wouldn't be a horrible thing. That was the end goal in all this. A small part of me is sad at the idea that he won't be coming home with me. I'd gotten myself so excited at the prospect of having him that I hadn't even considered someone else would adopt him. I'd already started planning all the toys and dog beds I would buy for him. I pictured Sally's face when I bring him over and tell her I adopted him. I can picture her smile now and knowing I may not see it hurts a little.

"You know he's a humper?"

"Yes. That's not a problem. We're both virile young men. I don't mind a little humping."

She laughs and leans against the desk, watching me with inquisitive eyes. "He's got a lot of energy. You'll need to play with him a lot, take him to the dog park to play with other dogs."

I nod. "That's not a problem. I have plenty of time for playing."

"Mmhm. And you're sure you're not going to get tired of him in a week and bring him back? I don't think he can handle losing another family."

Before answering, I think about it for a minute, taking this as seriously as I can. The conclusion I come to is the same one I did before.

"I won't get tired of him. I won't be returning him if I adopt him. I don't give up on people that easily. Once I make a commitment, I stick to it. My word is as good as scripture."

Crossing her arms, her straight blonde hair draped over her shoulder, Chloe watches and listens. No more joking. I have a feeling she's not just asking about the dog anymore.

"Okay. Come on back. Let's see if Sparky still wants you."

Me and Dax spend a good half hour with Sparky, playing and petting, getting to know one another better. Sparky and I get along swimmingly. He humps my leg, and I give him a belly rub. I think that means we're bonded now.

"You can take him home tonight if you like," Chloe offers.

Although I am one hundred percent in on this dog owner business, I need to get set up for him first.

"Can you give me a few days? To get everything set up for him. I need to get his food and bed and leashes. I don't want to just jump in unprepared."

"Well, once he's been adopted, we're not supposed to keep him."

Panicking, I fear she'll say I can't adopt him and that I'll have to leave him, that someone else might adopt him before I return.

"But," she continues, nearly steeling the air from my lungs, "I can take him home for a few days, and you can pick him up once you have everything together."

I could kiss this woman right now.

"You'd do that for me?"

"I'm doing it for Sparky. I think you and him are a good match, and I'd rather he get adopted by you and have his forever home, than keep going through families who get upset when he humps their grandma."

"Thank you." I hug her, and she makes a surprised noise when I lift her up and spin her around. "Thank you, Chloe. I'll get it all taken care of. You won't have to keep him for more than a day or two. Promise."

"I'll hold you to that." She points at me like a scolding sister, a look I know all too well.

No way would I risk her wrath by breaking a promise.

I hold up three fingers in a scout salute. It seems to satisfy her demand for assurance.

We take care of the paperwork, and I pay the adoption fee. Chloe gives me a list of everything I might need and the best brand of food and treats. Before we leave, I turn back to her while Dax waits by the door for me.

"Could you maybe not tell Sally about this? I kind of want to surprise her with him."

Her smile grows even wider. "Sure. I promise I won't say a word." She mimics zipping her mouth shut, grinning the whole time, an approving glint in her eye.

I thank her, and Dax and I take off to the pet supply store.

29 – Sally

I didn't want to look like a loofah

Time moves weirdly for the next week, faster than trotting pumpkin guts in the humid southern sunshine, when I'm spending time with Jack and slower than fresh chocolate chip brownies cooling from the oven when I'm not.

Today, I have to drive into Manchester to pick out tile and wallpaper for a primary bedroom and bathroom project for a nuclear engineer who works in the aerospace industry. I have no idea what she does, but whatever it is allows for an unlimited budget. Every interior designer's dream. I wish I was redesigning her whole house, but she's not sure beyond the primary suite what she wants yet. Once I wow her with her dream bedroom and en suite and closet, I plan on showing her my ideas for the rest of her house. This could be a lucrative job for me, one that can help spread my name to others in her professional and private circles. If only I could lock down multiple unlimited budget jobs, I would be in designer heaven.

Because I have an hour drive into the city, I don't get to catch Jack after his morning workout and shower to tell him the good news.

Last night, I received a call from a friend that I asked about a possible job for Jack. He doesn't seem particularly concerned with finding work, but it was part of our agreement, and I haven't forgotten about it.

When I learned he enjoyed working out and didn't do it because he had to, it gave me the idea to call Zack over at Power Fitness. Zack isn't the owner or manager but he is buddies with the right people there. I may have mentioned to him that Jack was looking for a job, and he was more than excited to talk to his manager about it. The call was to say he arranged an interview for Jack.

Since my car is a hearse and not new, it doesn't have Bluetooth. Instead, I have a phone mount attached to the dash, and I tell Siri to call Jack's mobile. There's nothing I hate more than a person who holds their phone to their ear or six inches away from their mouth on speaker acting like that's the proper way to make "hands-free" calls while driving.

Jack answers on the second ring.

"Good morning, Pumpkin."

I can hear the smile in his voice, and it makes me grin.

"Good morning, Sergeant."

"To what do I owe the pleasure of hearing your beautiful voice so early in the morning?"

I blush at his words. There have been few instances in my life where I have blushed in flattery and not embarrassment.

"I have good news for you."

"Would that good news have anything to do with me coming over to find you sprawled naked on your pumpkin couch?"

His chuckle is deep and rumbly through the phone speaker, and I wish I could feel it against my neck, where it would send shivers down my spine.

It's strange how, in a few short weeks, I've gone from blubbering idiot in his presence to what he fondly calls his sex kitten. It was always there, hidden behind the fear and doubt.

Jack is the only one to fully bring it out of me. Not even Myles learned that part of me. He wanted obedience and quiet. Rarely did I orgasm under his predictable, repetitive motions. That really should have been a warning that we weren't compatible.

"No. I'm not home right now. Work in Manchester today. But I did manage to fulfill the rest of our agreement."

"Our agreement?"

As I predicted, he forgot about finding a job.

"Yes. You help me decorate, I show you the town *and* help you find a job. Remember?"

He grumbles something under his breath, sounding

vaguely like, "You already found me the best job."

I ignore the comment because if we start with the dirty talk, I'll forget why I called.

"Anyway, I got a call last night from Zack over at Power Fitness. He managed to get you an interview with his manager for a position as a trainer. I thought since you liked physical fitness so much you could try out training others."

The other end of the line is quiet. I'm not sure if he appreciates my dedication to fulfilling my end of the agreement. Just the idea that he may not like what I've done douses my good mood with panic that I've overstepped my boundary. Once again, my blind excitement has pushed me across that line of appropriate into intrusive.

"Wow, Sally that's . . . amazing. Thank you. I would love to go in and speak with them. I hadn't even considered something like that. Honestly, I haven't considered much these past weeks beyond spending time with you, but a personal trainer would be perfect."

I let out a giant sigh of relief. "Good. It's at two o'clock. Ask for Zack or Dave. He's the manager you'll be meeting with."

"Thank you, Sally. I really appreciate it. You didn't have to do that, but I like knowing you wanted to help me."

Jack's voice is soft and affectionate, holding more in his tone than I can understand.

"Right, well, don't be late. And perhaps we can celebrate tonight?" I ask suggestively.

If he gets the job, we will definitely celebrate properly.

HER FAVORITE JACK-O-LANTERN

I have been overly excited all week for the mayor's Halloween party. They always have it on the Saturday closest to Halloween. Since Halloween is on a Monday this year, they're holding it the Saturday before. Holding an adult costume party on a weekday in a town filled with families and school days and soccer practices just isn't practical.

The couple's costumes I picked out for Jack and me arrived a few days ago, and I've been dying to see his on him. But I made myself wait until the day of the party to surprise him with it. He's been a good sport about it all, only asking about half a dozen times what it is, hoping I'd slip up and tell him. I don't.

Tonight, however, is the party. Jack comes over to my place to get ready. He seems to prefer my house over his. A few nights we've gone to his place, but he says mine feels more like a home. He's not wrong. The rental house is nice but impersonal and a little empty. Having come from living in the barracks, he had no furniture and only bought the necessary bits.

The party starts at seven, a little early, but there's a lot of parents with kids at home with babysitters who will need to be home before midnight. Jack arrives at two in the afternoon. Impatiently ringing my doorbell and knocking nonstop.

"Okay, where's my costume? You can't hide it any longer, and I'm dying to know what it is," he demands the moment he steps across the thresh hold.

"Right this way, oh impatient one." I gesture grandly to the stairs like Vana White.

Leading him to my bedroom, I've laid out the costumes on my bed, side by side, so he can get the full effect.

"Hell yes!" he exclaims when he sees the striped suit next to my fluffy red dress. Iconic Beetlejuice and Lydia Deetz. Now, I know he didn't wear the striped suit to the "wedding" when Lydia wore the red dress, but I just like it better. It's more recognizable.

And I'm just now realizing I chose a wedding dress as my costume. Shit. I didn't think about that. I just love the iconic red dress and always wanted to wear it but never had my Beetlejuice.

Thankfully, Jack says nothing about it and strides toward the costumes. He wastes no time stripping out of his jeans and T-shirt and slipping into the ensemble. Thankfully, the jacket is only a little tight across his broad shoulders. I think anything that isn't custom made would be.

He looks magnificent in the striped suit. Biting my lip, I can't help but stare as he spins to check out his ass in the full-length mirror. It looks spectacular, by the way. My fingers itch to grip it. I enjoyed doing it so much while he fucked me before. God, he fucks like a rock star. I haven't

HER FAVORITE JACK-O-LANTERN

had sex this good *ever*. Just looking at him gets me all riled up and wet for him.

Clearing my throat and my mind of the dirty thoughts I can't ever seem to smother while in his presence, I make my way over to Jack.

"So, I take it you approve?"

He spins and picks me up by my waist, my legs instinctually wrapping around him. His lips meet mine in a sweet kiss.

"Absolutely. This is awesome. We are going to have the best costumes at the party."

His smile is so wide it nearly takes over his whole face. I don't think I've ever seen anyone smile so widely and definitely not at me. My heart stutters at the pure joy he's directing my way. I want him to look at me like that forever.

"I don't know about that, but they are pretty awesome," I argue weakly.

Knowing this town, we may not be the best costumes, but they are well made and look fantastic. Having someone so excited about wearing a matching costume with me is something I never thought I would find. No one ever seemed to be on my level of hype over Halloween costumes. It appears I may have met my match.

"We are so gonna win the costume contest."

"What is with you and winning contests?"

"I'm an Army man. We like to win." He pinches my ass. "What's with you and not entering contests when you know you're the best?"

Rolling my eyes, I don't answer because we've already been over this. He knows how bias these contests in town are. No one who deserves to win actually wins. It's a trumped-up version of high school favoritism, a popularity contest rigged from the get-go.

He sets me down with a little slap on my ass and kiss on my cheek before turning to admire himself in the mirror. I mean, really, who could blame him?

"Here"—I pick up the green wig to go with the outfit and hold it out to him—"I got this for you, too."

He's over the moon with the addition of the wig. Like a little kid readying to go trick or treating by himself for the first time. It's adorable. Weird how a big guy like Jack with all his muscles and buzz cut—which, honestly, isn't much of a buzz cut anymore—can also be as adorable as a baby fox. Seriously, they're ridiculously cute, look it up.

We spend the next couple hours getting ready at my house—not that Jack takes more than thirty minutes to get his wig in place and paint on a little face makeup. He didn't want to do a whole face of white makeup because—and I quote, "I wouldn't want everyone to know all the places I'm going to be putting my mouth on you tonight."

Needless to say, I had to change my panties.

We show up at the mayor's mansion a few minutes after seven because Jack is eager to show off our costumes. Entering through the enormous double front doors of the mansion, we're greeted by staff members dressed as Victorian Era maid and butler zombies. In the iconic black

HER FAVORITE JACK-O-LANTERN

dress and white apron, not the version everyone wears for sexual kinks. One zombie maid with a dangling eyeball—they really splurged on the special effect makeup—informs us of all the evening's activities.

There is the costume contest, of course, which will be voted on by pictures instead of on a stage in front of everyone. This is basically the only reason I agree to enter. They take our picture in front of a backdrop and props set up in the massive foyer. It's a graveyard scene, which is perfect for us since Beetlejuice lives in the graveyard of the town model. We take our picture, which we are told we get a copy of to take home with us at the end of the night, and they post another on the wall of contestants. People can vote on them throughout the night. Since we're so early, we're fifth on the board.

We discover there is also pumpkin smashing, a three-legged race, cornhole, a photo booth, bobbing for apples, an open bar, dancing, face painting, and ax throwing. Which I think is a particularly bad idea with an open bar, but I'm not in charge here.

Even with all the wholesome activities, I've heard stories of how this party can get rowdy with all the drunken adults away from their kids for the night.

We wander through the rooms and halls hand in hand. The mayor's mansion is huge. Every mayor for the past hundred years has lived here, and the furnishings and décor are fancy and obviously expensive. As an interior designer, I inspect what I can through all the Halloween decorations coating almost every surface. I can see original hardwood floors, crown molding, and plenty of original art on the walls. It's a bit old-fashioned for my taste, but it is a historic building and kept mainly as such with gold fixtures and chandeliers in every room. The one in the ballroom is fitted with real candles, which are lit and flickering in the darkening space.

The decorations aren't tacky as I would have expected but, actually, a bit creepy. Like the mansion was abandoned for years and the creepy crawlies took over and maybe a vampire or two took up residence. It's all very *Interview with a Vampire*, and I love it. We fit right in.

An hour passes of us sipping our smoking drinks and partaking in a few games before Peyton and her date, the doctor, arrive. She told me what their costumes would be, a sexy doctor and sexy nurse. She wanted to role play with this guy, and it looks like they've already started. His scrubs and coat are wrinkled, and her lipstick is a little smeared. No wonder they're late.

"Oh my god! Look at you two. You look fabulous," Peyton practically yells at us over the music that's gaining in volume as the night progresses.

Jack, the apparent showboat, does a spin with his arms outstretched then bows to top it off.

"Why, thank you. But have you seen my lovely bride? Is she not the most ravishing thing you've ever laid eyes on?" Jack grabs my hand and spins me under his arm, causing my red ruffled skirt to twirl in the best way.

HER FAVORITE JACK-O-LANTERN

My dress is almost identical to the movie version except without the giant hoop skirt underneath. It reaches me mid-calf and puffs out with the layered ruffles but not too much. I didn't want to look like a loofah. Luckily, my hair is black and about the length of Lydia's, so putting it up with the short red veil was easy.

Giggling, I give my new audience a curtsey at the end of my spin. The smile has not left my lips since Jack arrived at my house earlier today. This may be the best night of my life. Even my ever present fear of public and social embarrassment for just being me is nowhere to be found.

For once, I'm completely in the moment, ignoring what other people think of me and how they look at me and what they might whisper behind my back. Right now, I don't give a shit. Because I'm here with a man who desires me, who wants to be with me and my best friends, having fun, and no one can take that from me.

Chloe and Sam appear not ten minutes after Peyton dressed as, to all of our surprise, Harley Quinn and the Joker, the new one with Margot Robbie and Jared Leto. Who knew they were so . . . cool.

"Wow, just wow. I did not expect this from you two. Whose idea was it?" I ask Chloe as I give her a quick hug, trying not to ruin her amazing makeup and hair.

She leans in to speak in my ear. "Actually, it was my idea after Sam told me about his childhood crush on Harley Quinn. I kinda wanted to fulfill his fantasy, if you know what I mean." She winks, and I can see the glint in her eye.

Yes, I most definitely know what she means.

I guess everyone has their thing. Apparently, hers is cosplay. While mine is being commanded and doing everything my sir demands.

The party is a huge smash with everyone. Costumes are on point, drinks are flowing, people are dancing, ax throwing is axed after someone aims for the portrait of the first mayor. I knew that was not a good idea.

All six of us try to smash into the photo booth halfway through the night. We manage to get us all in the frame, but I'm pretty sure the hand on my ass was *not* Jack's, but I don't care. Because I haven't laughed this much in years, letting go and enjoying myself. I've always loved Halloween, for many reasons. Now I can add costume parties to that list.

"So, I hear congratulations are in order?" Peyton asks Jack, raising an eyebrow in his direction.

"Wow, news really does spread fast in a small town, doesn't it? It's worse than gossip on base."

"You have no idea," I mumble into the straw of my drink.

Jack ignores my comment, slipping an arm around my waist. No doubt creating more gossip for the rumor mills. I'm sure there's already plenty being created about us since we arrived. I'd wager by the end of the night there will be rumors of a surprise pregnancy and shotgun wedding. Because, of course, that's the only way a man like Jack would be with a woman like me.

"I guess this means I'll be seeing more of you around

HER FAVORITE JACK-O-LANTERN

Power Fitness. I teach a yoga and Zumba class there a few times a week. I'm sure the ladies in my class would love to procure your services." She winks, and I groan.

Because when I got him the interview I assumed, like an idiot, that he would only train men. Silly me, of course women will want a hunk like Jack to be their personal trainer, if only to look at his ass while showing them how to properly squat.

He laughs it off with a good-natured smile. "I guess. I'm going to focus more on strength training and muscle building for athletes. Dave already has a bunch of the high school football players signed up for a group training. Apparently, they need a good stern hand to whip them into shape."

Personally, I don't follow the high school football team, so I have no idea if they suck, but I'm guessing they're not doing too well this season.

"That's awesome. I'm sure after the start they had to their season they'll appreciate it," Sam says, confirming my suspicions.

The guys talk football a little longer, saying words I don't for the life of me understand. When Jack sees me getting bored and sucking on my straw like a hoover trying to inhale a drink I've obviously finished, he redirects the conversation. Suggesting we take to the dance floor, which we all agree to.

Jack and I are on the dance floor late into the evening, his arms tightly locked around my waist, and our lips about half a second away from making out, when we're interrupted. A platinum blonde wig and neon pink dress tries to insert herself between us, but Jack only holds me closer, taking a half step back from the woman dressed as Barbie.

The woman being Daphne.

We've gone the entire evening without seeing her, and now, here she is, ruining our night. Typical.

"Oh my god, I have been looking for you everywhere," she squeals in a high-pitched tone, reaching out and brushing Jack's stripe-clad arm.

He jerks it away without hesitation, and the action has my heart fluttering. He's not placating her anymore or being polite. I think we've both reached our limit with her.

"Why would you be looking for me all night?" he bites out with growing distaste on his face.

"To spend time with you, of course. After dinner at your parents' house the other night, we didn't get a chance to."

My heart does a quick one-two, stalling out a little at her words. Daphne turns her predatory gaze on me. That dig was intended to sting, and she hit her mark.

The hands at my waist only tighten, gripping me closer, the only thing that keeps me from running away, which is what she intended. She's been trying to run me off ever since Jack returned a month ago, and this is the closest she's come. If it weren't for Jack holding me so fervently, I'd already be gone. Confrontation is not my forte.

"Like it told you then, when you weaseled your way into a dinner invite by lying to my mother, I'M NOT

INTERESTED." Jack's voice is growing not only in volume but in anger. His patience with Daphne diminished. "I'm with Sally. We're together. There is not now, nor will there ever be, a time when you and I will have anything going on."

At Jack's loud voice and tone, people stare and listen, acting like they're not while mechanically dancing. But their eyes and ears are trained on our little threesome. It makes me want to recoil. This entire night, I've avoided the looks and glares. Not now. Weirdly, none of the glares are pointed at me, though. They're all watching with bated breath at Daphne as she sputters and stutters and trips over her own words, trying to play it cool.

"I . . . well . . . that's just ridiculous. I mean look at me . . . and look at *her*." She sneers in my direction, as if I were made of vomit chunks and snot.

"Oh, I'm looking all right," Jack begins, not taking his glaring eyes off Daphne, not moving an inch from my side. "And you know what I see?" He doesn't wait for her to answer. "I see a spoiled rotten little brat who was never told no. Who was handed everything to her on a silver platter and never had to work hard for anything in her life. Someone who doesn't know what it means to be a friend, or how to be kind and respectful. I see a woman who is so self-centered and egotistical that she had to resort to pushing others into lockers in high school because she couldn't accept they were different than her. I see a person who acts charitable and boasts of her giving nature when in reality has never given anything to anyone, including respect. *That's* what I see when I look at you, Daphne."

Everyone around us is now still, eyes bugging out of their heads behind face paint and masks. Jack's declarations ring out clearly, even among the music still playing. But he's not done yet, apparently, as he turns to me, and that disgusted scowl turns to soft admiration. One hand reaching up to caress at my cheek.

"And when I look at Sally, you know what I see?" he says, much softer and quieter but still easily heard by all. "I see a woman who even under the constant ridicule of her community still gives back. Donating her time to decorate the animal shelter for free and taking pumpkin seeds to the local bakery. I see a woman who loves with her whole self even if she hides that enormous heart of hers from the outside world. I see life and color and happiness. So much that it can't be contained and bleeds out into her clothing and home."

I'm sure I've stopped breathing. And all I can see is Jack. His charming boy-next-door smile, his hard-earned broad shoulders from years in the army, those dazzling blue eyes that speak of only affection. It doesn't matter that we're in costumes and that he has green hair. What matters are his words and that he's saying them to me.

He leans in close so only I can hear him, as his nose brushes mine, and ours lips come dangerously close to kissing. "I see my beautiful kitten, who knows what she wants and takes it. Demands it even. And I love her all the more for it."

"You . . . you . . . ?"

"That's right Sally. I love you. Didn't see it coming, but I'm not letting you slip through my fingers a second time. I may not have seen you in high school, but I see you now. Now, you're mine."

Like an idiot, I freeze because this cannot be happening. The man of my dreams is professing his love for me in front of everyone. *In front of Daphne.* And it takes a moment to find my voice to respond.

"I love you, too."

"Good because, if not, I was going to have to convince you."

One side of his mouth quirks up as he smirks at me.

"You can still convince me. I am very open to convincing."

Closing the small distance between us, Jack presses his lips to mine in the most devastating kiss of my life. No kiss will ever outdo this one. His lips are soft and sensual against mine. Seeking what he desires and giving me everything I didn't know existed. The kiss is not short nor PG. We kiss like there's no one watching, even though there are at least a dozen people watching. Our tongues reach for one another and tangle together in a way that makes me whimper.

Jack grows hard against my stomach, and all I want in this moment is to hike up my skirt and let him take me right here on the dance floor.

Since I'm not particularly fond of being arrested for indecent exposure or flashing everyone my naughty bits, I break the kiss before I can't control my actions, and end up slipping my hands inside his trousers to stroke at that hard length.

I vaguely hear Daphne saying something and scoffing before stomping off. Nobody cares. Especially me and Jack.

"I think it's about time we got out of here. What do you say?" he asks against the curve of my cheek.

"Yes, please."

We exit quickly, waving at Peyton, who's giving us the double thumbs-up, her doctor date grinning behind her. Chloe and Sam beam from ear to ear and look about two seconds away from ditching the party for somewhere more private.

A lady at the door hands us our picture on the way out, and I only glance at it before we're practically running across the street to find my hearse.

30 – Jack

That's the sexiest sight I've ever seen

Why no one has told off Daphne before is beyond me. I feel fan-fucking-tastic. Letting everything out and telling her what I truly think of her was so freeing, like a boulder was lifted off my shoulders, no longer having to be polite and bite my tongue. That's what made her how she is. People try to be courteous and civil and not offend. When, in reality, they should have been honest the whole time. Maybe then people like Sally wouldn't have been ostracized for being different, and people like Daphne wouldn't be an issue. I mean, really, the whole mean girl thing is so over and done.

I waste no time driving Sally's hearse back to her house. Telling off Daphne and professing my feelings for Sally got me all hot and bothered. When I started talking, I had no idea a declaration of love would slip out. It just snuck up on me. I knew I felt more for her than just lust or friendship. It's been steadily growing, and tonight, it spilled out.

Sally's response was more than I could have hoped for. I know she's had a crush on me in high school, but a schoolyard crush and adult love are two completely different things.

I pull the hearse into Sally's driveway and shut off the engine before stepping out and rounding the hood to open the passenger door for Sally before she can. Pulling her into my arms, I plant a hard and fast kiss on her before she has a chance to take one step. When I pull away, she's breathless and jelly in my arms.

"Come on, let's go for a walk."

I only suggest this because I want to prolong the night and let my over eager cock calm the fuck down. I need to get him under control, or I will embarrass myself.

Sally nods. I'm sure she would agree to anything I suggest in this state. A lesser man would take advantage of such a thing. Who am I kidding? I'm more than willing to make the most of her lustful state. Just maybe after a few deep breaths.

Walking hand in hand at a leisurely pace, I direct us around between our houses and into Sally's backyard. Her pumpkin patch is nestled along the tree line in the back, snug and cozy halfway under long reaching branches. We head in that direction. Pressing past the painted black picket fence, we make our way to a low wooden bench along the back in the darkest part of the fenced in area. Most of the pumpkins are gone, but a few still remain on the leafy vines, sitting peacefully on the ground.

I sit and pull Sally into my lap. Both her legs drape to one side of my thighs as her arm easily slips around my shoulder. Comfortable and relaxed against me. I can't stop touching her, holding her. It's like I can't get close enough. She seems to feel the same, tightening her arms around my neck and settling in against my chest, her ass nestling nicely in my lap.

"So, what now?" she asks.

"What do you mean?" I press a kiss to the crook of her neck, and she sighs a contented sound that goes straight to my heart . . . and my cock.

"Now that we've said the L-word. That usually changes things."

"Oh, it changes things all right. As in now I can introduce you as my girlfriend, and kiss you in public, and beat the shit out of any man who checks out your ass."

"Guys check out my ass?" she jokes, pulling the green wig off my head and dropping it to the bench beside us.

I just grin at her. She has no idea how sexy she is in those little skirts and tights.

"I do. So, I can only imagine others do as well." I slip my hand up her frilly skirt, running my fingers along the outside of her thigh and rounded butt cheek to emphasize my point.

For once, she's not wearing tights. A rarity. I suppose

her costume didn't call for them, so she didn't wear them. Either way, I'm more than pleased about this turn of events. It allows for easy access, and I slip one finger under the edge of her panties.

"Mmm," I growl against her neck. "No tights."

"Not tonight."

"How fortuitous." The skin of her thigh and butt cheek is soft and silky under my fingers. My touch grows exploratory and eager as I spread my hand wide to cup her beautiful ass. "I think I may have to do something about that."

"And what would that be?" Sally leans in and licks the tip of my nose, sending a shiver down my body and settling in my balls.

"How about bending you over right here in your pumpkin patch and taking you from behind?"

My kitten moans and wiggles in my lap, grinding her ass down onto my very solid erection. Gripping her, I hold her down, pressing harder and rocking my hips up against her.

"You like the sound of that, don't you Kitten?"

"Yes, sir," she whispers against my mouth.

Fuck yes.

Pressing her lips to mine softly, the tender touch causes more emotion and reaction in my heart than anything ever has before. The guilt, always hidden but ever present, douses the heat in a cold shiver. Threatening to, once again, create doubt in my heart for my happiness.

Before it can overwhelm me completely, Sally's sweet

voice fills my mind. *That wasn't your fault. You can't keep believing it was. You're living no one's life but your own.* And the guilt melts away. I've dedicated the last eight years of my life to Jordan and fulfilling his dream. Now it's time to fulfill mine.

Looking around, I make sure there's no one out to see us. It's nearly midnight, and there's barely any light from the moon shining through the thick clouds overhead. Our bodies are mostly concealed in the shadows of the forest trees.

Lifting Sally, I carry her to stand at the end of the small wooden bench. Setting her feet down on the soft ground, I pull her face to mine for a kiss that's all tongue and teeth and uninhibited yearning. I've never yearned for another person until I met Sally. Her body calls to me, begging me to touch and taste and feel. I can't deny it, deny her.

She makes a sound of approval into my mouth, and my hands drop to her chest. I squeeze those glorious tits I would love to set free from her dress, but exposing that much of her out in the open like this would be too risky. And I don't want to share all of her like that.

Her hands drop to my chest while her lips remain locked with mine. Her tongue sweeps out and licks the seam until I open, granting her access once again. Deft fingers slip the knot of my tie free and unbutton my shirt. In a matter of moments, my chest is exposed to the night air, and Sally's searching fingers trace the grooves of my abs, dropping lower to my slacks to unzip them.

"Naughty Little Kitten."

"I can't help it." She looks up at me from under dark lashes, all feigned innocence and barely disguised sex appeal.

Her hand goes straight inside my pants and grips the length of me. My body jerks in response, my cock flexing in her grip.

"Turn around, sweet Kitten. Grip the fence."

With a final squeeze and stroke of my dick, Sally does as I command, turning and holding on to the top of the waist-high fence posts. Presenting me with her backside, she glances over her shoulder, watching me. I undo my pants the rest of the way, pushing them and my boxer briefs down just enough to allow my rock-hard cock to spring out. It juts toward Sally, eagerly reaching for what it wants.

I give it a few long strokes, the tip weeping into my palm, and I circle the head and squeeze. Sally's eyes watch every move I make, and her tongue darts out to lick her bottom lip. She started the night off with cherry-red lipstick. It has long since rubbed off with all our kissing and drinking.

"Do you want this, Kitten? Do you want me to pound into you right here in your yard, where anyone could stumble upon us?"

I nearly moan with delight when she nods, her eyes still trained on my dick. Unfortunately, I have to release it to pull her frilly skirt up to her hips, exposing her creamy skin and red lace covered behind. I moan out loud. That's the sexiest sight I've ever seen—after Sally's naked body, that is.

"Prop your foot up on that pumpkin."

She does, and it opens her up, displaying her damp

center. She's wet for me, ready and waiting.

"Good Kitten."

I grip one ass cheek and spread her a little, so I can rub my length up her center, making her groan and shudder against me. Tucking a finger through the damp material, I pull it to the side and reveal the most glorious sight. Her sweet pink pussy glistens in the moonlight peeking between the branches above.

"Perfect. Look at you so ready and wet for me." Sally rolls her hips, causing my fingers to rub against her core, and she whimpers in pleasure.

"Do that again. Touch me, please," she breathes out in a strained whimper. "I need you, Jack."

There's no way I can say no to such a sweetly worded plea for pleasure. I'll give my girl anything she wants, everything she needs and more.

From my back pocket, I pull a condom out of my wallet. Quickly tearing the package with my teeth and rolling the latex down my aching length. Gripping her panties, I hold them to the side, looping the red material through my fingers, twinning it to keep it secure. Her red dress bunches above my arm, keeping her exposed.

Lining up at her entrance, I run the head of my cock through her wet folds, teasing her entrance, testing her readiness. She backs into me, trying to force me inside her, but I hold her still with a strong grip on her hip. My free hand swings, and I smack her bare ass. Leaving a slight red mark, and she squeaks at the sting but doesn't shift away.

No, my kitten backs up again, desiring more.

"Sweet fucking Kitten. You like getting your ass smacked, don't you? Like it when it stings a little before I pleasure you."

She can't form the words, only whimpering and moaning softly, as I tease her. Smoothing a gentle palm over the pinkened ass cheek makes me want to do it again. I like seeing my mark on her far too much. But the ache in my balls wins out.

Lining myself, I pound into her, sheathing my length to the hilt inside her. A gravelly moan escapes my lips at the pure bliss that ricochets through my body. Being inside this woman is every pleasure I've ever experienced times ten. Her hot channel grips me like a vise. I have to still inside her to keep from blowing my load.

"Don't move, Sally," I tell her as she tries to circle her hips against me. Dropping my head to her shoulder, I press a kiss below her ear that makes her quiver.

Wrapping my free arm around her waist, I hold her close. Still and content. There's nowhere else I'd rather be, and I just want to hold her, feel her erratic heartbeat pounding in rhythm against my own. Smell her intoxicating perfume.

When her throbbing pussy clenches down around my shaft, I'm forced to move, to pull back and stand tall, flexing my hips. Pulling out a few inches before thrusting back inside. My pumping steadies in speed and power. My fingers dig into her flesh as her panties tighten their hold around my hand.

HER FAVORITE JACK-O-LANTERN

My eager thrusts force Sally's petite frame forward with each punishing pound against her. But, like a good Kitten, she readjusts and comes right back to her proper position, waiting for my next thrust. Watching her take my cock and then come back each time, wanting more, makes my cock thicken inside her.

Sally's breaths shorten but quicken, her own pleasure building. Her channel pulses around me, her immanent orgasm growing.

"That's it, baby. Take my cock, squeeze your pleasure from me. Play with your clit. Come on my dick right out here in the open. Let everyone know this pussy is mine."

Reaching down, she shoves her hand through her skirt. I can tell the moment she makes contact with the sensitive little nub, not only because of the feral sounds she makes but also the fluttering and pulsing of her pussy increases. My balls pull up, readying themselves for my own explosion of pleasure.

She's close, so fucking close I can't stand it. Sliding all the way home inside her, I stay deep and swivel my hips against her ass. Rubbing my dick deep inside her against that spot that sends her over the edge.

Her cries of pleasure as her orgasm washes over her sends me over the edge. My own release pulsing out of me in great spurts. Breathing heavily, I lean down and press my forehead to the center of her back. Sensations of her spasms around me and my own release spilling from my steel cock, fill every atom of my being.

"Fuck, Sally. You're perfect." She chuckles, and the sensation transfers to my dick still hard inside her.

I would stay here like this forever, but we are outside, and although I think no one has seen us yet, there's still the possibility.

Pressing a kiss to the back of her damp neck, I reluctantly pull out of her and discard the condom over the fence into the bushes. I'll come get it later. I wouldn't leave it there for some nosy kid to find, but I also want my hands free to help Sally right now.

Untangling my fingers from her panties, I slide them back in place over her still pink ass. Just looking at the pink mark and still damp center of her has my cock thickening again. I tuck it back in by slacks and zip up before it can get any bright ideas.

Sally slowly straightens and turns to face me. Slipping her hands through my still-open shirt and wrapping around my waist, she presses soft kisses to my chest.

My heart swells at the tender affection as other things swell at the feel of her lips against my skin.

"Sally," I softly scold, "you keep doing that, and I'm not going to be held responsible for my reaction. And, this time, I can't guarantee your dress will stay on your body."

"Well, then, perhaps we should move this inside? You can do whatever you like to me there. Do whatever you like to my dress." She giggles at the shocked and elated look on my face.

Her happiness makes me happy, and I oblige my little

kitten. Sweeping her up into my arms, I carry her inside to do so many naughty things to her.

There's nothing better than waking up on a lazy Sunday morning curled around your naked girlfriend like a serpent. My face is comfortably nestled between her breasts and my torso is cradled by her legs. Arms wrapped tight around her waist. Somehow my weight isn't crushing her. Just fitting perfectly against her. If I were to detail my perfect day, it would start like this.

Our morning is filled with long lingering kisses and slow, methodical love making. Last night, in the pumpkin patch, was a clashing of eager passions. This morning is a convergence of bodies, an unhurried exploration of softness and caressing.

I don't bring up dinner with my parents until Sally has orgasmed three times, showered, and dressed. I probably should have asked her earlier in the week instead of leaving it till the last minute, but the fear of her saying no and making up some excuse to not go had me holding my tongue.

In the kitchen, I watch her feed Binx and Casper when I finally bring it up. It is, after all, in less than six hours.

"How do you feel about going to dinner at my parents' house tonight?"

She stops spooning food into the cat's dishes and stares at me, lips parted in shock. "Dinner? Tonight?"

"Yes. At my parents. With my sisters as well. My mom has this thing for Sunday dinners. Ever since I moved back, she's made sure I've attended every week, and every week she asks if I've found a girl." I stand and slowly make my way to her from the island stool. She looks like a deer in the headlights, frozen but ready to bolt at any moment. "I told her about you last week when she ambushed me by inviting Daphne to dinner." She flinches. "Daphne lied to her, and Mom invited her, thinking she was doing me a favor. When I explained she was not, I told her about this amazing girl named Sally that I was seeing. She immediately insisted I bring you over for dinner."

"And you thought asking me on the day of was best?"

Her frozen shock finally breaks, and she finishes feeding the cats, who sit at her feet, one patient and one impatient. Placing the matching black-and-white food dishes on the floor, she turns back to me, and the cats turn their attentions to their food.

"I was afraid if I mentioned it earlier, you might say no," I admit. Wrapping one arm around her waist I bring her close, not just because I like the feel of her there but because I'm afraid she might run away.

She gnaws on her bottom lip, worrying it between her teeth, keeping her eyes focused on my chest as she plucks at the material of my shirt. "Do we have to go today?"

"No. But I know it would mean a lot to my mom to

meet you sooner rather than later. She hates learning about people second hand through town gossip. Especially if that person is my girlfriend."

It's probably not right to try and guilt her into meeting my parents if she's not ready. After last night, though, I'm sure there will be far too many rumors and whispered gossip to filter out what's truth and what's lie. I'd like my family to know the truth from our lips.

"I suppose you're right."

"So, you'll come with me, then?"

"Yes," she mutters in an adorable pout, her eyes turned up.

Tightening both arms around her, I pick her up and swing around in a circle. Peals of Sally's high-pitched laughter ring through the kitchen. When I stop and return her to her feet, a smile I plan to put on her lips every day melts away her indecision and fear.

"Don't think this means we'll be going to my parents for a family dinner, though. I'd prefer to keep you from meeting them for as long as possible. Maybe forever if I can swing it." She smacks me on the chest, but I can't stop grinning.

"If they are anything like your sister, I'm okay with never meeting them. If that's what you wish."

Her sister Emily was a snob to the tenth degree, no idea about the husband. He didn't say much. However, if she wants to spend time with her niece Elly, I will more than gladly help make that happen. It seems the only way to keep her from turning into her mother is by spending more time with her aunt.

"I wish I never met them," she chuckles.

And even though one would assume that statement would come with sadness or self-deprecation, it isn't. Sally means what she said. Her parents must be god-awful people to have lost the admiration and love of Sally.

Bending down, I place a soft kiss on her cheek and inhale her scent for a moment, reveling in the fact that I can now call her mine.

"Dinner's at six. They'll expect us a little early to socialize."

Pulling back from me, Sally startles, "Oh my god, what am I going to wear? Are your parents religious? Should I not wear black? Are these tights too juvenile?"

"Sally, Sally. Calm down." I steady her and force her to look at me and relax. "Wear whatever you want to wear. My parents won't judge you like others will. They'll love you, no matter what color your tights are."

"Oh, okay. But should I change?"

Panic lingers in her pinched brow and I smooth it out with my thumb.

"No. You look perfect."

I'd tell her that, no matter what she was wearing, especially were she wearing nothing. My parents won't mind the colorful, patterned tights or skeleton sweater dress. It might take them some time to get used to it once Halloween is over, but I'm sure they'll accept her, tights and all.

"Okay, but you have to feed Batty before we leave."

HER FAVORITE JACK-O-LANTERN

"What?! I most certainly am not feeding that devil bird."

Every encounter I've had with her little "friend" has been him attacking my head and trying to claw out my eyes. Okay, maybe not claw out, but he was definitely reaching for me with those talons of his.

"He's not a devil bird, and if you're going to be my boyfriend, you're going to have to come to terms with Batty being around." With big round eyes she gives me the puppy-dog face—you know ,the one the puppies in the window at the pet store give you every time you walk by.

"Ugh. Okay, fine. Just this once."

Sally claps, and within moments, I have a bowl of fruit in my hands and am being shoved toward the back door. *The things I do for this woman.*

Batty is waiting for me on the back porch, already hooked and hanging from the rafter, eyeing me. Probably looking for the softest exposed skin to attack. His wings flutter open and shut as I approach. Slowly stepping forward, I try not to startle him. There's a thick railing circling the porch with a ledge big enough to set down the bowl on beneath him. Aiming for the banister, I make my way a little closer. When he screeches, I freeze.

"Keep going. That just means he's hungry."

"Yeah, that's what I'm afraid of," I mumble.

He's hungry for my soft, squishy eyeballs and tender ears. I should have worn safety goggles and earmuffs . . . and gloves. *Why the hell didn't I wear gloves? He's going to bite my fingers off when I set the bowl down.*

When I'm three feet away, I stretch to reach the banister. It's still too far away, so I shuffle a few inches closer, leaning back so as not to bring my head any nearer to the bat. The bowl finally touches the banister, but it's not stable, and I lean closer in to push it all the way on. I can hear Sally's muffled laughter behind me, and I don't care. I am not risking it. I like animals—you know, normal ones, cats, dogs, hamsters. I draw the line at flying rats.

Batty decides that moment is the perfect time to swoop down to get the food in the bowl instead of patiently waiting for me to retreat to safety. I scream like a nine-year-old girl when I jump back and run into the house. Again, I don't care that I've seen active warfare and been in battle. I'm man enough to admit that bat scares me.

We arrive at my parents' house at five thirty, and after much begging, Sally has promised not to bring up the whole Batty incident from earlier. They can save the embarrassing stories and baby pictures for, like, the third family dinner.

Instead of my father greeting us at the front door when I swings open, my mother practically tackles Sally in a giant hug before we can even say hello.

"Oh, my goodness. You must be Sally."

"I sure hope so, or you just smothered the wrong

person," I tell my mother as she pulls back from Sally.

Not letting her go, though. Oh no, my mother ignores me and links her arm with Sally's, leading her into the house with a smile so wide I can see every one of her molars.

"It's nice to meet you, Mrs. Campbell."

"Oh, please call me Suzie," my mother preens.

I think I underestimated her excitement at me bringing home a girl. It has been quite a few years, I guess.

"Okay, Suzie."

Sally doesn't look terrified, but she's definitely on edge. Meeting the parents of the man you're seeing can be overwhelming, especially with my overbearing and loud family. At least she already knows Autumn and Sophie.

Speaking of, the two sit in the living room along with Noah. The kids are nowhere to be seen, so I can only assume they're out back.

Dad built a swing set for me and my sisters, along with a clubhouse, when we were kids. They continued the upkeep on them when Sophie had her first kid, so the grandkids would always have a place to play at their house. They're not boring grandparents, they like to say.

"We brought cupcakes." I hold up the container filled with, not one but two dozen frosted cupcakes.

Sally went into a baking frenzy after agreeing to come to dinner tonight.

"They're pumpkin spice cupcakes with maple cream cheese frosting. One of my favorites. I hope you all like pumpkin spice."

Sally is still firmly in my mom's hold but smiles warmly at everyone, doing her best not to panic. She's a trooper, and I know seeing my sisters is calming her anxiety.

"We love pumpkin spice." My dad approaches Sally and extends a hand in greeting. She accepts it tentatively. "Daniel Campbell. Pleasure to meet you, Sally. My girls have been telling me all about you."

"Oh, have they?" I ask, raising an eyebrow in my sister's direction.

They grin at me, and Sophie shrugs.

"Just the normal stuff—you know, when she graduated high school, her profession, and her amazing talent at carving pumpkins." Autumn supplies.

Easing my own anxiety. My sisters aren't gossips, but I still don't want Sally to feel ambushed coming into this.

I give them an appreciative nod and turn my attention back to my mother, who is practically dragging Sally across the room to show her framed photos on the fire mantle, moving past school photos and prom pictures. Thankfully, any with me and my ex have been removed. Only ones with my sisters and close friends remain. The prom photo is of me and Dax in our tuxes, holding flower boutonnieres in the foyer.

"This one is my favorite." Mom pulls down a silver frame with a photo of all of us in the hospital, of when Sophie had Cooper, their first grandchild.

Before the words even come out of her mouth, I know what's coming next.

"Do you like children, Sally?"

"Love them. My sister has a little girl, and she is the cutest thing. I just wish I got to spend more time with her than I do."

"Well, there are four rambunctious kids out back right now. You'll get plenty of interest from them. They're very curious kids. Do you ever plan on having children?"

And there it is. The only reason my mother wants me to marry, to make more grandchildren. I'm sure my happiness is mixed in there somewhere, but I swear as soon as she had one grandkid, it's all she's ever wanted since.

"Oh," Sally starts, obviously taken aback by the significant question. I don't blame her. If I hadn't known it was coming, I would have been more shocked, too. "I suppose so. I haven't thought about it in a while, but yes. I would love to have children."

"Right answer," Autumn mutters just loud enough for us all to hear.

"Hey, Jack." My dad rests a hand on my shoulder, squeezing reassuringly. "Why don't you take those to the kitchen." Shifting his eyes to the container of cupcakes still in my hand, he nods toward the kitchen in the back.

"Oh, right."

"Make sure you're putting them in the right place. You know how your mother likes things set up just so."

I turn to him with a questioning look, and he raises his eyebrows at me, tilting his head in my mother and Sally's direction, indicating I should ask Mom to help me.

"Oh, yes, I wouldn't want to mess up her layout."

Mom has always been a stickler for table settings, so the excuse will be enough to pull her away from Sally.

"Hey, Mom, why don't you show me where to put these cupcakes?" When she doesn't immediately take the bait, I try again. "I don't want to mess up your table setting by putting the desert near the salad."

That gets her attention enough to have her contemplating having to leave Sally to help me. She hates when courses are mixed.

"Well, okay," she agrees reluctantly at my raised eyebrows and insistent look. "We'll be right back. Why don't you make yourself at home Sally. If you need anything, you come find me."

"Will do," Sally agrees.

My mother, everyone, the hostess of the year.

When we're alone in the kitchen, my mother takes the cupcakes and stacks them on a raised display plater.

"Sally seems like a lovely girl, Jack."

"I knew you would like her. But maybe ease back a bit. She's nervous enough as it is, and you've barely let her breathe since we arrived."

"Well, I just wanted her to know she's welcome here. We don't need her running off before we convince her to stay."

I chuckle. "Don't worry, Mom, I've got that part handled."

"You better, young man. We need more grandkids. Your sister can't be the only one having children."

HER FAVORITE JACK-O-LANTERN

"And what about Autumn?" I ask in exacerbation.

She always wiggles her way out of doing anything. It's always me and Sophie.

"Oh, you know how she is. She may never have kids. But you, you'd be a wonderful dad." She finishes placing the cupcakes on the tray and arranges them on the table setting for dinner.

I'd never thought about being a dad until recently, just the uncle, brother, or son. Father wasn't a title I've planned to take, but that image of the little girl who looks just like Sally has me thinking otherwise these days.

I nod but say nothing. Sally and I have just started dating, and I don't want to push the matter. Yet. Maybe in a year or two after we have spent time together getting to know everything about one another. And getting married first because the mother of my children will also be my wife. It's the way I was raised and the way I want to raise my kids. Plenty of people are out there, unmarried with kids, and that's totally fine. Sometimes, life chooses for you. And hell, if we keep going at it like we are she may sport a baby bump down the aisle. But one way or another, I'll get her down that aisle.

"Come on, honey. Let's get back to the others and chat some more. The casserole in the oven will be done shortly, and we'll eat." Mom threads her arm through mine like she did Sally and directs us back to the living room, where Sally has taken a seat on the couch next to Autumn.

The spot on her opposite side is empty, waiting for me. I

give Mom a peck on the cheek and sit next to my girl while Mom sits in her chair across from us.

"So, Sally, Autumn tells me you're an interior designer."

"Yes. I am."

"What around town have you done that I might see?"

Reaching out, I thread my fingers through Sally's to calm her fidgeting. She lets out a deep breath, relaxing at my touch before answering my mom.

"There's a store I did as well as a few homes around town. Most of my work is actually out of town."

"Doing anything interesting lately?" my mom asks, and I can tell Sally isn't used to the attention.

"I'm working on a primary bedroom and en suite for a lady in Manchester right now. Not very busy at the moment." Sally smiles, but it doesn't reach her eyes.

She's trying her hardest to get more jobs but is having a tough time of it. I'm useless in helping, I have no idea how to run a business.

"Oh? Is it the wrong season for it?"

"No. I'm just having a tough time marketing myself and my business. I took classes about it in school but have never been very good at it. I can pick paint colors and arrange furniture and place art, but I can't seem to figure out marketing."

"That's a shame." Mom frowns in concentration. "Sophie, didn't you go to school with a girl who went into the PR and marketing industry?"

Sophie looks at Mom, confused. "Uh . . ."

HER FAVORITE JACK-O-LANTERN

"You know the one from your college sorority, with the short hair and tattoos."

Her description doesn't seem to spark any recognition in Sophie at first, then her face lights up, eyes wide.

"Oh, right. I'd forgotten that's what she majored in. You're talking about Sloane. Yes, she did go into marketing. I think with some firm in Boston, actually. I could totally give her a call." Sophie turns hopeful, bright eyes to Sally, who is stunned silent.

"If you don't mind that is. I'm sure she would love to at least have a consultation to see if she can help you."

Sally's mouth sits agape, staring at Sophie. I squeeze her hand, jolting her from her stupor. "Oh, yeah. Sure. That would be great. I don't know that I can afford a PR consultant, though."

Sophie waves a hand at her dismissing her concerns. "Nonsense. I'm sure she can work something out with you. As a Delta Gamma she'll want to help. She's really cool." Taking in Sally from head to toe she adds, "Actually, you two a have a similar style. She'll probably love working with you."

For the next twenty minutes, they discuss Sally's business, and Sophie texts Sloane about setting up a meeting with Sally.

By dinner, Sally is far more relaxed. The kids join us when Dad calls out dinner's ready. They all are very curious about Sally, especially Melanie, the youngest. She insists on sitting next to Sally, and I'm instantly shoved down a seat to make room. I make sure I can still reach Sally across the back of the chairs to trail a finger through her curls, letting her know I'm still here and not going anywhere.

31 – Sally

Well that's a load of horse shit

IT'S FINALLY HALLOWEEN!

Finally, the day has come. Adults in the town may not appreciate my black house and creepy decorations but kids on Halloween love it. I get hordes of trick-or-treaters wanting to knock on my black door and risk a real trick or treat.

Peyton, Chloe, Sam, and I dress up in the scariest costumes we can think of and hide in my yard in the shadows, jump-scaring kids and giving them a real trick. It's all in good fun. They always run away, laughing. After getting their treat, of course.

This year, Jack will join in on the scaring fun, more than willing to frighten the living shit out of a few teenagers. First, however, there's the Halloween day ceremony in the town square where they will announce the winners of carving contest and costume contest from the mayor's party.

After shower sex with Jack, which I fully support happening every day, we get dressed in our Halloween best. I pick out an orange pencil miniskirt and my oversized black-and-white skeleton cardigan. Pairing those with a top I normally wouldn't wear but was gifted by Peyton years ago. A long-sleeve sheer black top over a solid black scoop neck tank top that shows shadows of cleavage through the mesh material.

Jack's eye snag on it before roaming down to my tights for the day. A type of fishnet with a pattern of snakes slithering up and around my legs, ending in chunky platform black ankle boots. I bought these cute bat wings that lace on to your shoes, and I add those, too. They match the bat ear headband to complete the outfit.

Jack wants to match me, which is the sweetest thing. I never ask him to. He just does it on his own. He pulls on a fitted long-sleeve black shirt with a skeleton body printed on it.

"You're giving me a boner," says Jack as he reaches for my ass.

"Ha-ha. You're so funny."

"Oh, I'm hilarious. You'll learn to love my jokes. Just like you love me." Jack presses a tender kiss to my lips, and I melt against him.

The feeling is so warm and gooey that the fear that I may

be blinded to reality flickers through me. I missed it with Myles, and he said he loved me. What's the difference with Jack? Maybe he thinks he loves me because I'm a diversion from the norm.

With every brush of his lips, my fear slips away, but it will never be completely gone. At least not for the foreseeable future. Myles made sure of that.

"Come on, let's get going before we miss the ceremony."

"It's just going to be a bunch of the 'high society' people giving each other awards they don't deserve," I grumble.

I stopped going when I realized they just give awards to their friends. And since the wealthy families suck up to the mayor and any public officials with any power, by "donating" to their campaigns, they are the ones who tend to win.

"Maybe . . . maybe not. Why don't we just go and find out?" Jack gives me a sultry smile, trying to persuade me.

I already told him I would go, but that doesn't mean I can't complain about it.

I groan, being as overly dramatic as possible.

"Do it for me, Kitten." Jack begs, trailing kisses up my neck, starting at my shoulder and ending below my ear.

"Hmm, fine. But only because you make such a compelling argument."

Most of the town shows up for the Halloween Day Ceremony, mainly consisting of people who entered the contests and their family and friends.

The mayor, sheriff, and for some reason, Daphne,

stand on the raised podium. Behind them, on a table, sits seven trophies. You heard me. *Trophies.* Not just ribbons or plaques but golden trophies. Six with jack-o-lanterns, five for the adult winners of the carving contest and one for the under-fourteen group. Cloth covers items behind each, most likely the winning pumpkins. The final one is a full-bodied skeleton for the costume contest from the mayor's party.

The sheriff introduces the mayor, who gives a little speech. The mayor introduces Daphne as the town's social events coordinator, who will announce the contest winners. Her words are annoying, even though I'm not listening to what she's saying, until she finally gets to announcing the winners.

First, the winner for best portrait, an elderly man who carved a portrait of James Dean. Then scariest, a demon-looking devil done by a man in his thirties. Best traditional is won by a pretty blonde girl who looks to be eighteen or nineteen. I console Jack for losing his category, but he shrugs it off, not caring one bit he didn't win.

You'd think after all the hassle he gave me about entering contests and winning he'd be more disappointed at losing.

"I didn't expect to win. I just wanted to enter so you wouldn't feel alone with yours up there," he whispers into my ear, pulling me close, my back against his chest, his arm wrapped across my collar.

People are staring at us, questions clear on their faces. I ignore them. The looks would normally cause me to shrink

HER FAVORITE JACK-O-LANTERN

in on myself and stand to the back of the crowd but now do nothing. Well, almost nothing.

Daphne moves on to most unique. The category my entry would be most likely to win. With a huge smile, she announces the name . . . not mine.

"Well, that's a load of horse shit."

I agree with Jack. He already knows this. This outcome is exactly what I expected. A soft peck on my cheek makes me smile. I would happily lose every contest if it gets me more kisses.

"It's okay, Jack. I didn't expect to win either."

"Well, there's still best in show."

I squeeze his hand that he slips into mine. Gripping tight, showing his support in the silent gesture. I'm not as optimistic as he is about my prospects for winning, but I love how much he is.

"Next is best in show!" Daphne announces. "And the winner is . . ." She holds her hand over the covered pumpkin, like she did for all the rest. With a flourish, she lifts the fabric. "Jack Campbell."

The audience applauds, and Jack and I stand, watching, neither of us realizing she said his name until people around us start congratulating him.

"No. That's not right. My pumpkin was horrible. There's no way it won best in show."

Nobody seems to hear him as they guide him up to the podium. He tries to drag me along, but I wriggle free of his grip before he can pull me on stage with him.

Daphne greets him as if he didn't humiliate her at the mayor's Halloween party on Saturday. A wide smile grows on her face as she threads her arm through his to lead him to the microphone to hand him his award. Thankfully, she unlatches from him at the glare he points at her hand on his arm. Leaving him a step in front of her at the microphone.

"Um . . . thank you, I guess. I wasn't expecting this since my carving was less than subpar. There were at least a dozen pumpkins far better than mine that I believe deserve this award." He holds up the trophy, the gold glimmering under the light of the dim autumn sun.

The crowd is quiet, only making confused noises at his unexpected speech. It's then I realize they probably did vote for him. Most likely because he's been gone for so long, and they wanted to indoctrinate him back into small-town life.

Although the thought behind the action was nice, best in show really should go to the best, to someone who's spent hours toiling over it to perfection. To the person who plans all year what they'll carve and prides themselves on their work, not to a man who quickly carved something random to make sure his girlfriend didn't feel alone in her entry.

I love Jack, but we both don't believe he should have won best in show.

"As a matter of fact, one of those contestants happens to be my girlfriend." Jack pauses and looks at me for dramatic effect. *Oh, fiddlesticks. Please don't say my name.* "Sally Smithson."

Dammit. He said it.

HER FAVORITE JACK-O-LANTERN

All eyes turn to focus on me. I freeze like a dumb blonde in a horror movie. This is so not good. I like being invisible. It's when people pay attention that things get uneasy.

I'm unable to make my escape before Jack crosses the platform and down the two steps to me. He's got me by the hand and on the stage by the time I snap out of it.

"Sally is one of the most talented pumpkin carvers I've ever seen. Not that I've seen many, but it's hard to argue with her talent. I believe she should be the winner of best in show."

Jack hands me the trophy, and robotically, I take it. Here, I stand. Holding a trophy. On a stage. In front of half the fucking town.

Everyone is silently waiting and staring. I gape like a fish drowning on dry land. Jack realizes I'm freezing, and his sweet smile flickers with concern but quickly recovers. My hero, Sergeant Jack Campbell, comes to my rescue, smooth talking over the awkwardness he created.

"I would like to share this honor with her as a cowinner of best in show. Thank you."

If it weren't for Jack leading me away by the small of my back, I would probably still be a statue on that stage, staring wide-eyed at the crowd of people.

"That was extremely uncomfortable. Why did you do that?" I ask as soon as we're away from the gathered crowd, who's moved on to best costume.

"Because it's what should have happened in the first place. There's no way my carving won fair and square. And if I did it's only because of my name, not my work."

We've left the square and all the townspeople walking back to Jack's truck, slowly, as my limbs are still numb from being frozen in fear. I'm still holding the silly trophy that, for some reason, I feel like I should hug to my chest and protect. I may not have officially won it, but Jack thought me worthy. And, for that, I will hold it dear forever.

"Come on," he says, slipping a warm hand around my hip as we walk. "I think I'm ready to have that talk with Jordan now."

"What? Now?"

My feet freeze, and I pull to a complete halt in the middle of the sidewalk. Jack jerks to a stop beside me. My brain fog only thickening in my confusion. He wants to go to the cemetery? Now? That makes no sense.

"Yes. I think it's time to clear everything out. After telling off Daphne—and, in a way, the town—I feel like I'm on a roll. With every word out of my mouth another weight is lifted from my chest. I want to start my life here with a clean slate and a light heart. I'm tired of the guilt and pain. With you by my side"—he pauses, tracing the tip of his finger along my jaw, delicate and adoringly—"I think I'm ready to move on, leave all that behind. Start living *my* life. With you."

My heart swells to near bursting in my chest. Looking up at Jack, I can see his truth. Feel it in the weight of his words. The need to complete this evident in his pleading eyes. If now is when he needs to go, then now is when we go.

Readjusting the trophy to one hand, I twine my fingers with his. I will go anywhere this man wishes to lead me. I will walk by his side as he walks by mine. Giving him strength when he needs it and leaning on him when I'm weak.

Jack leans in and presses a soft kiss to my lips, both of us taking a steadying breath. Those sparkling sky-blue eyes of his nearly drown me as he looks at me with a reverence I hope is reflected back at him.

"I also have a surprise for you when we get home."

There's so much joy and happiness in Jack that has always been beneath the guilt and uncertainty of life back in Laconia, that is now shining through with little obstruction. He no longer seems adrift trying to figure out his life but sure and determined in his path ahead. A path that includes me. Us. And I will gladly travel this path with him.

"Is that so?" I ask, squeezing his hand, which he reciprocates without hesitation.

"Yes. I think you're going to love it."

"I'm sure I will. Okay, then, let's go."

Epilogue – Jack

One year later

There are no words to describe being with Sally. When I returned to my hometown from the army, I had low expectations for my future. Being a single, depressed janitor at my old high school was more how I expected things to turn out. Thankfully, I was way off base.

Day one in my rental house, I met the woman who would, in a matter of weeks, turn my life down a path I hadn't even known to be an option, pulling me in with her uniquely violet eyes and petite curves and keeping me with her silly humor, charitable nature, and sweet thoughtfulness—let's not forget the lack of gag reflex. That's not exactly a deal-breaker, but it sure is a mark in the "pro" column. My kitten is insatiable, and that hasn't changed over the past year.

I kept my house next door until my lease was up, which

HER FAVORITE JACK-O-LANTERN

was a few weeks ago, at the beginning of October. As soon as it ended, we moved my few personal possessions across the lawn to Sally's house. Not that I spent much time there anyway, but Sally insisted I keep my own place through the lease. Even though I wanted to jump in heart first, Sally was still cautious after the whole ex-fiancé dumping her right before the wedding.

I like to rub our awesome relationship in his face whenever I see him around town. His wife, Sally's replacement, is as boring as plain toast. Once, I even thanked him because if he hadn't left Sally, I never would have met her. He stuttered and gaped, not knowing how to respond. It was hilarious.

Now it's my toothbrush that sits right next to hers on the bathroom counter and my clothing that hangs in the closet. I still have my army clothes and fatigues, but my civi's have blended my basic solid color T-shirts and jeans with the spooky Halloween designs I've been drawn to since meeting Sally. Ever since she gifted me that first orange plaid flannel my infatuation with her and her style has only grown.

Sparky loves his new home. He basically claimed it as his the first day I brought him over. To him, this has been his home all along, not the empty rental next door. Casper and Binx don't appreciate a dog in their space, but they've gotten over it. I've even caught them all cuddling together on the plushy dog bed in the living room.

People still look at us a little funny sometimes, but over all, they've mainly accepted that we're a couple. It took a few months and lots of questions and side glares, but they got the hint.

Daphne leaves us be ever since the mayor's party when I publicly told her how little I thought of her or respected her. I don't like telling anyone off like that in public let alone a female, but it had to be done. Someone needed to say something, and as it seemed, Peyton and I were the only ones willing to, so I had to get it all out.

Now the only stares we get are when we get a little matchy-matchy with our outfits—okay, fine. When I get matchy-matchy with our outfits. I love matching her. Don't know why. Just do. Kind of like I'm publicly stating my claim on Sally and making it clear where I stand in this town, which is right next to my girl.

As I learned the first day I met Sally, Halloween is my girl's favorite day of all the days in the year. Last year, we celebrated it together for the first time, but this year, we planned it all together. I got to help pick out our couples' costumes for the mayor's Halloween party this time. Jack and Sally from *The Nightmare Before Christmas*.

Ironically, I am, once again, wearing a striped suit, this time black with jagged skinny white lines, though. This year, I did go all in with the face paint, full black-and-white grinning bone daddy face. I also convinced Sally to go full blue face for her costume. It took a week to figure out the proper paint and setting technique so the paint won't spear and rub off. That way, I can kiss her to my heart's content wherever I like, as much as I like.

It takes us hours to perfect our face paint, but we

HER FAVORITE JACK-O-LANTERN

were smiling and laughing and kissing and getting a little frisky—which messed up our non set makeup, and we had to start over, but who cares?—before heading out to the mayor's Halloween party. I am determined to win this year's costume contest. We were robbed last year. Our Beetlejuice and Lydia were amazing, although losing to Chloe and Sam for their Harley Quinn and Joker was acceptable. At least it wasn't Daphne, and her bimbo Barbie costume.

We meet our friends at the party. Because, yes, they are now *our* friends. My sisters also show up this year, and our group has grown from just us two to a whole clan.

Dax and his pregnant wife are here as well, despite her being ready to pop. It took a few months of trying, but they finally got their number two baby in the oven.

Peyton and Autumn bought dates from the bachelor auction. I'm pretty sure Peyton's is the same guy from last year, but as far as I know, they aren't dating. Maybe she had so much fun last time she wanted a round two.

Autumn snagged herself a rugged-looking fireman, which means we're all paired off tonight. No third or fifth wheels to make things awkward.

"Nice start to the season," Sam, Chloe's now-husband, says when we all settle with our drinks around a standing table. "I see those boys have bulked up a bit and are flying down the field. You must be making them run ten miles a day to get that kind of speed."

We dive into the football talk, it is the fall, after all. And, not to toot my own horn, but I've been instrumental in whipping the boys on the high school team into shape. It's nice to see others can see that, too.

"Not quite ten miles, but I definitely make sure they get their cardio in. How else are those boys going to be able to get the ball in the end zone?"

I'm still working at the gym but have been contracted by the high school to train the football team a few times a week since they don't have a weight trainer at the school. It gives the coach a break. Lately, I've been considering applying for an assistant coach position at the school or move my training to the school. I also lead a weekend workout bootcamp with a group that wants to know what it's like to train like a soldier. I had a lot of dropouts the first weekend I offered it, many not physically able to fulfill the demands of my regime. There were also a lot of women that first weekend, that I can only assume showed up to stare at my ass and abs and were very disappointed when they actually had to work out. Now I've assembled a group that is more dedicated to sweating and building stamina and strength rather than ogling me.

Sally interrupts our conversation on current stats of the players with an open-mouthed kiss on my jaw that ends with the slight nip of her teeth. With the amount of time I put in to researching this body paint, I know her love bite won't affect it in the least. She can kiss and bite to her heart's content.

Ever since I started calling her Kitten and exploring her very rambunctious sexual side, she's been far flirtier and hands-on in public. In the first months of our relationship, she would barely let me touch her around people. Kissing took a couple months to work up to. Now? She is all over me when she gets randy. Doesn't care who's watching. I think she's discovered a new kink we'll have to explore. Voyeurism. Could be fun.

"Are you done talking boring sports ball yet?" she pouts.

Her lips plump delectably as she bats those large fake eyelashes at me. I love my pint-sized kitten. And she knows very well it's called football and even understands most of it. She just likes to mess with me. It's a little game we play, and it usually gets me all horned up for her and ends with us naked and me inside her.

"Yeah. Can we talk about something more interesting, please?" Chloe snarks, inserting herself against her husband. "You know like how Sloane just helped Sally become the new hottest interior designer on the east coast."

If Chloe wants to boast about my girl, I am more than happy to oblige. She's done well with the help of Sloane, Sophie's college sorority sister and marketing guru extraordinaire, who's gotten her seen through social media and even regular media by the right people. She's been so busy she even hired an assistant.

Even my mother has enlisted her services to update my childhood home. It's almost even modern now. But before I can agree and compliment Sally on her achievements Chloe continues, talking animatedly.

"Didn't you just get hired to decorate the governor's

daughter's house?"

If her face weren't covered in blue body paint, I'm sure Sally would blush something fierce right now. But her smile is wide and appreciative. "Yes. I'm heading over there next week to do my initial walk through and go over design aesthetic options."

Slipping my arm around her hips, I pull Sally closer, proud beyond words about how she's opened up socially over the past year. I'd like to think I had something to do with that, but she had it inside her all along. She just needed someone to show her that. To point out her ability to make strangers feel welcome and how when she smiles, it's infectious.

Every time I see it, I want to smile like a fool. Seeing her happy makes me happy, not to mention my family—specifically my mother—because Sally making me happy keeps me in Laconia, which makes them all happy. So, like I said, Sally's happiness is infectious, affecting everyone who comes in contact with her.

"How many high-profile clients does that make now? Three?"

"Four."

"Right. I forgot you consider the girl from Tik Tok who plays dress up for likes as high-profile." Chloe chuckles and rolls her eyes good-naturedly.

"Queen Astrea has over two million followers and gets to wear ballgowns and crowns to work," Sally protests. "And she gets paid for it. To me that's high profile. Not to mention she was one of my favorite jobs, designing a gothic and mythical set for her videos. I literally got to make a castle. How many interior designers get to say that?"

Chloe concedes with a shrug. "You have a point."

Sally grins in triumph before turning back to face me. Her grin turning mischievous but affectionate. Open and comfortable, relaxed in a way so far from how she was last Halloween when we attended this very party.

Luckily, this year, Daphne has turned her attentions toward another man, a lawyer I believe. Much better suited for her. He seems to want the same superficial things she does.

Looking down at the woman I love, I caress her cheek with the backs of my fingers. "What is it that I can give you? What is it my Pumpkin wants most?" Pulling Sally into my chest, I hold her petite, curvy body against mine, tilting my head down to look directly into her eyes. My growing erection is obvious between us, pressing against her soft stomach. Even with her blue skin, I can't deny that I still want her. To hold her, kiss her, give her anything she asks of me. She's carved out a place in my heart and made a home there inside me.

"Just you," she says.

A sweet smile spreads across her red lips. That place in my heart where she resides expands and fills even more.

"Is that all?" I ask, matching her smile.

"Yeah."

Her admission is a breath upon my lips.

"Well, then, me you shall have. How would you like me?" She scrunches up her nose in concentration.

When she puckers her lips, I give in to temptation and steal a kiss. Her laugh could make angels weep.

"I will take you just as you are, Jack Campbell, because you're perfect."

Reaching up on her tiptoes, she presses a soft, loving kiss to my lips. My fingers dig into her backside, holding her close. The kiss is deep and sensual, loving caresses. A hint of tongue. The kind of kiss that is slow and seeps into your bones. It stirs within me more than just lust but love. A tornado of swirling particles that spread and settle over every inch of me, making my body burn for her in a way that could never be mimicked.

"I love you, Sally Smithson. I don't think I've told you that enough today."

"You have, but I always love hearing it."

"Because you love me, too?" I ask jokingly.

I know she loves me. That kiss proved it, but I too love hearing her say it.

"Yes, because I love you, too."

"Good because, if you didn't, I'd have to convince you right here in front of everyone." She raises one blue eyebrow, and a shine glimmers in her eyes.

She likes that idea.

"Would you, now?" she practically purrs against the soft skin of my neck. "And would that entail lifting up my skirt?"

I nod.

"And running your fingers between my thighs, finding out how wet I am for you?"

Her words are whisper soft near my ear, and I groan as the mental picture.

"Yes," I grind out between clenched teeth.

"And perhaps slipping inside? You know, to show everyone who I belong to? And who *you* belong to?"

If I grip her ass any harder, I fear I might rip right through her patchwork dress.

"Sally," I warn.

She knows what taunting does to me. She still has a nice pink handprint on her ass from last night, when she taunted me in a set of sheer lingerie.

"Yes, Jack?" she says all innocently, like she didn't just cause the massive situation in my pants.

"You are a naughty Kitten. And you know what happens to naughty Kittens."

"They get pet?"

Fuck yes, they get pet. But no matter how much we talk and tease about fucking in front of everyone, we won't actually do it. It just gets us worked up, and we like to play the game. I just cock my head down at her ever with a look I know she understands.

"Would you like me to take you to the hidden bathroom under the stairs I saw earlier and show you?"

Sally sucks in a sharp breath when I not so discreetly roll my hips against her, so she can feel every inch of me. Her eyelids drop, and her lips part, and damn if there isn't a part of me that wants to see my dick slide between those pretty red lips. I've seen it with her orange, purple, black, blue and red before. And it never grows old.

"Yes, please," she pants.

"Good Kitten." Turning to our group of friends, I wipe the sex eyes from my face and put on a casual smile. "We're going to find the restroom. We'll be right back."

Most don't question us, but Peyton and Autumn, who've become fast friends, give us knowing looks.

Peyton mumbles, "Uh-huh," and Autumn winks.

Me and my girl find our way to that hidden bathroom, and I get to see those red lips around my cock, and I get to flip up her skirt and fuck her against the small vanity, nearly breaking something in the process. And when we return to the party twenty minutes later, not a smudge of body paint out of place, no one is none the wiser.

Just as Sally is none the wiser about the black onyx ring in my pocket I plan on giving to her tonight behind our house, in the pumpkin patch under a full moon. I couldn't think of a more perfect night to propose to the woman who stole my heart.

The End.

Acknowledgements

Once again to Nat aka Speckled Plum for making my cover idea a reality, she always somehow makes them perfectly adorable! I can't wait to see all the covers side by side in the end.

To my Editor Samantha at Miss Eloquent Edits, you are my savior and I'm so glad I found you. You helped to elevate my writing by making my vision clear to the reader. It makes so much difference having a wonderful editor.

To my BETA's for asking for more. Because of you this story is at least five thousand words longer.

And to all my book influencers especially on Tik Tok & Instagram, thank you for loving my book and spreading the word. This series wouldn't be what it is without you.

For more information on Rebecca's books please visit her website at
www.rebeccarennickauthor.com

Books in the Gummy Bear Orgy Series
Pinky Promise
Her Favorite Jack-O-Lantern

Note from the Author

I've always loved Halloween and been a little bit Goth on the inside. This book was all about creepy, spooky, Kawaii Goth, Halloween fun. If I had the ability to commit to one style I would totally live like Sally. Goth lovers have long been looked down upon for their love of black and creepy. But really they're just as soft a squishy on the inside as the rest. I knew from the start Orange would be a Halloween book and I love Jack and Sally's story and I hope you did too. The Gummy Bear Orgy Series is just starting and I hope you'll continue on this journey with me. This collection is a series of stand alone's that can be read out of order. They will not interconnect in any way. If you don't want to read one of the colors, you don't have to. Please use these stories to have fun, laugh and smile, and maybe even blush.

Printed in the USA
CPSIA information can be obtained
at www.ICGtesting.com
LVHW092304211023
761656LV00051B/705